"Between the heroine's gripping mystery and Frelick's silken prose, *Unchained Memory* was a book I could not put down. And did I mention heat? A sci-fi romance must-read!"
--Sharon Lynn Fisher, author of *Ghost Planet*

"Part political thriller, part sci-fi, part romance, *Unchained Memory* is an exciting read full of unexpected twists and turns highlighted by Donna Frelick's excellent prose."
--Linnea Sinclair, author of *The Dock Five* series

UNCHAINED MEMORY

by

Donna S. Frelick

INK'd
PRESS

PRESS

First INK'd Press edition February 2015.

ISBN- 13: 978-0692366455
ISBN-10: 0692366458

For Olene, who never found the one she was looking for, though she never stopped trying. For Graeme, who was mine from the beginning. For Michelle and Jessie, Gavin and Lana, who must define the concept anew for themselves and their generations.

And for heroes everywhere.

PROLOGUE

For years I couldn't remember what had happened to me that night. All I knew was that three hours of my life were gone, unaccounted for in any way that made sense. The search for those lost hours changed me. Finding them nearly killed me. Even now, there are times when I lie awake in the dark heart of night and wish to hell I'd left it all alone.

Except for Ethan. I could never regret anything about him.

I remember well enough how the night began. If I'd stayed home where I belonged I wouldn't be telling this story now.

The crowd in the Holiday Inn lounge was just getting loose. The band had finally found a tune even the broken-hearted could move to, and the dancers were taking on the glow of too much alcohol.

I was out of place in that happy community of the drunk and the unattached. "I gotta get back to the kids, Sherry. It's going on midnight."

"The kids are fine." Sherry pushed the over-processed hair out of her eyes. "You've hardly been out of the house for weeks. Ronnie don't never take you nowhere. Every once in a while even the Mom of the Year deserves some down time, don't you think?"

With three little kids, I didn't have much choice but to stay home full-time, not if the family was going to stay relatively sane. Sherry thought I was the crazy one for sticking it out with a man whose idea of excitement was a beer so cold it made him shiver. She was a free bird and thought I should be one, too. But, then, she'd been married three times. Her only child was an overfed Cocker spaniel.

I ignored the invitation to discuss my home life and dug my keys out of my purse. "The mall closed hours ago, Sherry. Our alibi's shot."

She wasn't listening. Her attention had been snagged by a tall specimen at the bar with the gone-to-fat look of a former high school football star. Sherry and I had run together since we were both new to the course, so I recognized the signs: she and Mister Right Now were headed for a tumble in the sheets a few drinks down the line.

I shook my head and reached for my jacket. "I'm outta here, girl. If I stay I'm just gonna cramp your style."

Sherry sighed, returning her focus to me. "Tell me what Ronnie did to deserve a wife that looks like Shania Twain and acts like an angel to boot."

I snorted. *Guess he won the lottery the night the condom broke and he "did the right thing."* "Yeah, well. I'm running home right now to polish the old halo. I'll call you tomorrow."

Outside, the chill of late October had laid a damp hint of frosts to come on the pickups in the hotel lot. I could see my breath in the still air as I shrugged into my jacket. Despite the drinks, I didn't stagger as I looked up to admire the spray of stars across the black of night. My head was clear when I got in my old Ford pickup and turned out onto the highway. I didn't as much as wobble in my lane on the way home.

That's why, even months later, I couldn't explain what happened next—not to my husband, not to Sherry, not to the police or the counselors or the doctors. Oh, I could blame myself, all right. But I couldn't find any reason in this world why one minute I could be driving along Deerhorn Road, not a mile from my house, and three hours later be waking up in my pickup on the side of the road.

I opened my eyes, and for a long baffling minute I couldn't see anything at all. In the moonless midnight dark, all I could see was the dusty shadow of the truck's dash hanging above my face. The view through the windshield revealed only a starlit sky and the ragged outline of a stand of pine framing the road.

I lifted my head from the sticky vinyl seat and sat up. Razor-sharp pain ripped from my forehead to the back of my skull and tore the air out of my lungs. The inside of the Ford spun like a carnival ride, and I fought not to blow the contents of my stomach all over the front seat.

When the steering wheel and glove compartment settled back into their usual places, my first thought was that I'd had one Lemon Drop too many. But no amount of vodka could justify the pounding inside my head. In fact, I wasn't sure there was that much of the stuff available outside Moscow. And the little I'd drunk wasn't enough to make me pass out in the middle of the road, practically within sight of home.

I listened for a clue as to what might have left me sitting on the shoulder, the keys dangling from an ignition turned to OFF, but the road was as quiet as it was dark. In the woods, a mockingbird protested being awakened out of a sound sleep with a run through his repertoire. In the weed-choked ditch, a few late-season crickets still trilled. In my chest, my heart thumped with something close to panic, though the source of my fear was nowhere to be found.

"Now, think, girl, think." My hands gripped the steering wheel like it was the last railing on the *Titanic*. "There must be an explanation."

I remembered slowing down to take the curve just before the Dry Run Bridge. I'd been listening to the radio—Stevie Ray or somebody—then . . . I'd lost the signal. It was as if my mind had switched off with the radio. I couldn't remember anything else, and thinking about it made my head want to twist off my neck.

All right. Shit. I sat up straight, clicked the seat belt and turned the ignition key. The truck started right up. No warning lights, gas tank almost full. I shook my head—a mistake that cost me a wave of dizzying pain—then I put the truck in gear and got back on the road.

I had almost convinced myself my little nap could

be shrugged off when I thought to check the clock on the dash. The numbers made no sense.

"That can't be right." My throat tried to close up on the words.

The clock read 3:22. Impossible numbers. Unbelievable numbers. Because if the damn clock was right, I'd been passed out for three hours on Deerhorn Road, and Ronnie had been home for at least ten minutes.

Oh, God. I'm dead. My breath, short and ragged, tore in and out of my lungs. *It's fucking three-thirty in the morning, and I'm dead.*

I stomped on the gas, pushing the aging vehicle up to a reckless 65 on the unbanked road, but I knew it wouldn't do much good now. I was going to walk in with no possible explanation for where I'd been, and Ronnie and I would be yelling about it for hours. First it would be about the fact that I'd been out at all, then it would be about my crazy friends, then it would be about the money I'd spent and how much I'd drunk and how many guys I'd slept with and *shit!*

I came up on the bend before the house, and I was within a cat's hair of turning the truck around to head for the Kentucky line. I even slowed down, but I didn't stop. Ronnie would have been easy to leave. It had been a mistake of my wild and wicked youth to marry him in the first place. The kids, though—my sweet, funny, bright, loving children—they were another story. I would never have left them behind, no matter how big an idiot their father was.

But, you see, I'd already done it. I'd left my kids sleeping peacefully in their beds, the babysitter in the next room, Benjamin surrounded by Spiderman and little Micah cuddled up with Samantha in her room full of pink frou-frou. I believed they would be there, safe and sound and wrapped in their sweet dreams, when I got back. I'd left the bar at midnight for a trip that should have taken fifteen minutes. How could I have known it would take me three hours to get home?

I turned that last bend and, sweet Jesus, even now I want to scream. I can still see the house in flames, black smoke rising through the leaping red and orange, the trees, the road, the cars, the fire trucks reflecting the fire back like the surface of a burning lake. My mind wouldn't accept what I was seeing, couldn't hold the concept of my home on fire, my babies inside. I've had years to accept it, a thousand nights soaked with sweat and tears to put out those flames. And still, a part of me believes I can come around that curve and see my house and my life as it had been, as it should have been. Safe and quiet. Unremarkable. Whole.

The truck careened up into the yard by itself; I know I wasn't driving it anymore. I threw myself out of the driver's seat and stumbled toward the burning house, though what was left of my rational mind was shrieking at me that it was too late, too damn late. Someone tackled me and trapped me in a bear hug. To this day I don't know who it was, and I thought I knew all the boys on the volunteer squad.

"You can't go in there, Asia," he kept repeating. "There's nothing you can do."

I fought him. I struggled like I would kill him if he

didn't let me go. "My kids are in there!" I screamed, my heart shattering, my soul shredding. "They're in there!"

"They're gone, Asia. They're all gone—even the girl who was watching them." He held on until I finally slumped to the ground in shock, no fight left in me, no hope left in me, nothing left in me but horror and guilt and wrenching pain. He went down with me and we stayed like that on the cold, unforgiving ground, the heat from the flames washing over our heads, until Ronnie came over and pulled me to my feet.

His face was marked with soot and tears and a kind of furious misery I never want to see on a human face again. "Where were you, Asia?" His hands twisted and tightened on my arms. "They're . . . Jesus! Where the hell were you?"

I know Ronnie would have hit me if the sheriff hadn't pulled him off me. He might even have killed me in that moment. And who could blame him? I know I didn't. For once, he had a right to be out of control. He had gone to work, leaving me to care for the only thing that meant anything to either of us. Now they were gone, and I had no explanation. I had no excuse. What happened was my fault; even I believed it.

It was three years before I stopped wishing Ronnie had done what he wanted to do that night. It was a long time after that before I found any reason beyond sheer apathy to keep from putting a .45 to my head and leaving this world behind.

Lucky for me, apathy is a bigger survival mechanism than most people think.

CHAPTER ONE

Nashville. Three years later.

I spent more than five sleepless hours prowling my apartment before arriving at my job at Music Rowe that morning, and it showed in the shadows under my eyes. The nightmares again.

My supervisor took one look at me and went for the coffee pot. "What bridge did you sleep under last night?" Rita asked, shoving a mug into my hand.

I couldn't meet her eyes. "Good morning to you, too, Miss Sunshine."

"I'm not the girl who looks like she's been hit by a semi. And from what I see, it wasn't one of them six-foot-four, good-looking kind neither."

"I wish." Unless a naked man dropped into my living room out of the clear blue sky, there wasn't much likelihood of that happening. I worked. I tried to forget. I passed out. The nightmares came. Then I got up and did it all over again. Not much time for romance. I'd tried half a dozen jobs in Nashville before settling into a receptionist position at this three-person talent agency with its second-rate client list. Rita liked to say our boss, JW, broke hearts for a living, and my job description read like a bouncer's. I was the gatekeeper, the troll under the bridge for any musician seeking fame and fortune behind the inner office door.

Still, it wasn't such a bad job, once JW and I reached an understanding about what constitutes sexual harassment. I liked the office, a converted bungalow with a window that looked out on dogwood and crape myrtle. I liked the clients, who worked hard to make me like them. And the best part of the job was Rita Davidson, who ruled the inner office and whose true job title should have been vice president (or maybe queen), rather than executive secretary.

Rita perched on my desk and gave me the evil eye. "Asia, darlin', you make out like you're just a little ole country gal come to the big city, but I ain't buyin' it. There's something different about you. I just haven't figured out what it is yet."

I swallowed coffee that was too hot for my throat. "Damn. Now everyone will know I'm really a Harvard Ph.D. doing research on the life of a lowly worker bee in the hive of Nashville's signature industry."

Rita waved her mug in my direction. "See, that's just what I'm talking about. My smart-mouth, college-graduate kids would know why that's funny. My Aunt Patsy from Donaldson wouldn't have a clue."

"You know why it's funny, and you didn't go to college." Rita wasn't the only one in Music City who wore her country accent like she wore her hair—big and brassy. And like the others, she was a lot smarter than she let on.

"I didn't need to go to college. I had three Brainiacs at home to do it for me."

"Well, they must have gotten their smarts from somewhere." I slipped around her to get to my chair.

"Yeah, and it sure as hell wasn't their father," she agreed. "But we're not talking about me. We're talking about you."

I looked her in the eye. "No, we're not."

"Asia, I'm not trying to pry into your business, but I know a little bit about people." She refused to look away. "And I know there's more to you than you're willing to tell."

"There's more to most people than they're willing to tell."

"All right. You don't have to confess your deep, dark secrets." She shrugged and shuffled papers on my desk. "I just hope that psychiatrist you're seeing— what's his name, Claussen?—does you some good. If he don't, you're going to explode one of these days— most likely all over my desk."

I scowled. In fact, my pompous ass of a psychiatrist was only making things worse. I had another appointment with him that afternoon, and I wasn't looking forward to it.

She sighed. "Okay, I'm sorry. Maybe I'm out of line. The old mama hen in me is just worried about you, that's all."

Suddenly, all I wanted to do was lay my head on Rita's soft, round shoulder and cry. Instead, I found the quickest lie I could.

"Rita, there's no big mystery in my past. Just a short childhood, a bad marriage, and an ugly divorce.

Nothing you haven't seen a hundred times before." I tested out a smile. "Hell, if it weren't for people like me, this town would be left with nothing to sing about but huntin' dogs and moonshine."

"Oh, sh . . . oot!" Rita stared out at the street, shaking her head. A line of potential clients was headed in our direction, carrying guitars and backpacks full of demos, promo shots and hope. "I just hate it when I have to look them in their moony cow eyes and tell them they can't carry a tune in a wheelbarrow."

"Better you than the kind folks on *American Idol*." I braced myself for the onslaught. "Looks like a busy morning. Let's hope the boss is in a friendly mood."

"Oh, hell, no. JW looks even worse than you do."

Rita caught me in that raptor-like stare of hers as she turned to go back in her office. I could see it in her eyes: I hadn't fooled old Rita. Not by a long shot.

Ethan Roberts was late. And, as usual, the elevator was stuck on the second floor. He took the stairs, cursing the pain that shot through his right leg with every other step. By the time he got to the Psychogenesis Institute offices on the third floor, he was sweating, his hair clinging to the back of his neck, his thigh burning with effort.

As he checked in with the receptionist, a door banged shut in the corridor leading to the inner offices. He looked up to see a woman charge into the waiting room, her high cheekbones flaming with color, her amber eyes snapping with fire. She was so furious she seemed on the verge of tears. She was so beautiful he forgot to breathe.

Her long, angry strides carried her to within paces of him, close enough for him to see her full, sensual mouth and the jump of the pulse in her graceful neck. She stopped and glanced down at something in her hand—a business card? She started to crumple and toss it, but seemed to change her mind, and stuffed the card in her purse. Then, without a word or a look for anyone in the office, she jerked open the outer door and swept through it.

Ethan watched her go, a smile lifting his lips. The Institute was usually such a model of quiet and efficiency. For a brief moment, her emotions had transformed the lackluster room. Now that she was gone, the place seemed lifeless and gray.

Dr. Robert Claussen appeared in the inner doorway and gestured at him to follow. "Ethan, how are you? Have you been waiting long?"

Ethan held on to his answer until he was inside the older psychiatrist's office. "Long enough to see the show. Little anger management session?"

Claussen laughed and shook his head. "Yes. The patient I called you about."

Ethan turned back toward the door, a smile on his lips. "*That* was Asia Burdette?"

"In all her glory." Claussen lowered himself into the deep leather of the chair behind his desk. He waved Ethan into the smaller seat across from him. "You read the file I sent you?"

Ethan placed a manila folder on the desk. The file had been short on details, but full of emotional impact. His amusement vanished. "That's a lot of pain to carry. This was, what—three years ago?"

"You must have read about it in the papers."

Ethan shook his head. He avoided the news whenever possible, and he'd had his own problems to deal with three years ago.

"Your intake interview mentioned an investigation." He thought back over the file. "Faulty wiring caused the fire; the deaths were all due to smoke inhalation. It was an accident."

"Yes, well. Asia blames herself, nonetheless. Her husband's since divorced her. She joined my loss group last January."

"I take it that hasn't gone so well."

Claussen winced. "It's been a spectacular failure. Asia doesn't have much patience, and she's not afraid to speak her mind. Not that I can blame her—some of those patients are, shall we say, extremely difficult? She finally lost her temper in last night's session. Probably set therapy for some of the others back a year."

Ethan arched an eyebrow. "And she's still angry this afternoon?"

"I told her I can't keep her in the group. Though I'm not sure what she's upset about. It's not doing her any good anyway." He blew out a breath. "That's why I thought of you."

"Is she even open to therapy at this point? What does she hope to get out of it?"

Claussen's hands spread before him on the desk. "A good night's sleep? She's a borderline alcoholic. She's obsessed with three hours of 'lost time' from the night of the fire. She's perfect for you."

"She believes she was Taken?"

"No, she doesn't seem to have any theories about what happened. Still, I suspect she's hiding something. And I thought it would be interesting to see if our methods worked on a patient who has no preconceived notions."

Ethan studied the man who had been his mentor for more than ten years, noted the heavier jowls, the shock of gray hair now turning white. The steel-gray eyes were as sharp as ever, though, and it would be a mistake to think the old man had lost a step. He was used to taking on Claussen's odd cases, the "alien abductees" in particular. Now, for the first time in their long association, the old man struck him as more than just professionally interested in a case. He found the hint of calculation in the doctor's expression disturbing. Or was he just allowing the glimpse he'd had of Asia Burdette to affect him more than was appropriate?

He got to his feet and paced to the window. Below, the Institute's parking lot was framed in spring-leafed trees and washed in Tennessee sunlight, but all he could see was a house—a life—consumed by orange flame.

"So what do you think, my boy?" Claussen rose from his chair to clap a hand on Ethan's shoulder. "Can you help her?"

He nodded, not at all sure. "I'll give it a shot."

"Good." Claussen smiled and showed him to the office door. "I gave her your card, but it may take her a while to make the call."

Ethan remembered the way she'd looked at something in her hand and started to throw it away. *His* card. His lips ticked upward. "Whenever she's ready."

An endless rocky plain under a roiling purple sky. A choking haze of yellow smoke. What kind of place is this?

A shuffling, jostling fight to stay upright in a sea of bodies. Who are these others?

A room of cold stainless steel. Freezing metal against bare skin. No! Get away from me!

Hunger. Dark. And pain. Limitless, unrelieved pain.

The scream woke me. My voice, echoing in my ears. I sat up and hugged my knees to my chest, gasping for breath. I fought the fear, as I fought it every night. Still, it reached down and squeezed my heart until the blood running through my veins was ice cold.

I was on the floor. The phone was ringing. It took me a minute to realize what the sound was, another three rings to find the phone.

"Hello?" The sound of my voice was like gravel poured in a plastic cup.

"Jesus, Asia, are you all right? You sound like death warmed over."

"Rita. Yeah, I'm . . . I'm okay, I guess. Why are you calling me?" I couldn't find the clock. It wouldn't have done any good anyway; my eyes refused to focus. The significant amount of alcohol in my system wasn't helping.

"Because it's 9:30 on Wednesday morning, and you're not at work. That's why I'm calling you. Are you sick?"

"Shit. Yeah." My stomach lurched as my heart responded to the adrenaline surge, giving me a plausible excuse. "Been up all night with a stomach virus. Sorry. I meant to call in. Guess I didn't hear the alarm."

"Oh, I'm sorry, darlin'. You go on back to bed. There's nothing going on here that we can't handle. Take tomorrow off, too, if you need to. Lord knows you got enough sick days saved up. You want me to bring you some soup or something?"

Feeling like an asshole of the lowest order, I stuck with the lie. "No, thanks, Rita. Wouldn't want you to catch this thing. I'm sure it's just a 24-hour bug. I'll be back in tomorrow. See you then."

"Okay, hon. Hope you feel better."

I hung up the phone and curled into a miserable ball there on the living room floor, surrounded by the evidence of my attempts to keep the nightmares at bay—the glass and an almost-empty bottle of Stoli, the last of my tiny stash of killer weed. No matter what I did—no matter how late I stayed up, no matter how much I drank or smoked—I couldn't drive the images from my mind. And I couldn't keep them from coming back, night after night.

I had long ago stopped reliving the true nightmare of my life in my sleep. A dream of consuming fire and the faces of my lost children would have been understandable, even expected. God knows I'd had enough of them in the years just after the fire—tortured, guilt-ridden, *explainable* creations of my psyche. But this nightmare of unseen terror had no rational explanation, yet it left me witless with fear every night.

My life was becoming a sinkhole with ever-steeper sides. I was no longer sure I could even maintain a grip on the edge, much less find a way to scramble to higher ground. The loneliness, the guilt, and now the dreams were sucking me down.

The tears I'd been holding back for weeks burst through in a flood. I was lost beyond any hope of finding my own way out. And I was so tired of wandering, alone in that wilderness of pain.

It took a while, but I cried myself out, sobbing until there was nothing left but the question of what the hell I was going to do. I got up and staggered into the kitchen to find my purse. I dumped the bag out on the counter and stood staring dully at the choices the universe had given me.

I had to think for a moment to remember just why my gun—a next-to-new Glock 27, carefully tended and fully loaded—came tumbling out of my purse. I shouldn't have had to work that hard, really. The reason was still circulating in my bloodstream, slowing my thought processes. My preferred liquor store was in a bad part of town; I'd needed a refill late. I'd been packing when I went shopping.

Now, the Glock was a matter of choice. Use it and end all this shit. Or put it away and live with the pain.

I stood frozen, trembling like a rabbit in an open field, the hawk circling lazily above. Death was close, as close as the brush of wings, the rush of air, and no more under my control than that rabbit's. I waited, wondering what Death would do, what I would do. An impulse, a twitch of nerves, traveled down my arm and into my hands. I picked up the gun.

But I didn't use it. Instead, I pressed the release to let the magazine drop into my open palm. Then I ejected the cartridge from the chamber and, hands shaking, put the gun down again. I sank onto the closest stool at the counter, struggling to suck in air around the horror that was still clutching my throat. First the dreams. Now this. God help me. God, *help* me.

On the counter was the other choice I'd been given this bright, dangerous morning: a business card, crumpled and torn, the card that Claussen had given me. I wiped a sleeve across my face, took a deep breath, and made the call.

CHAPTER TWO

A week later I was pulling up in front of Dr. Ethan Roberts' dark brick two-story on a narrow street overlooking Belmont Avenue. I got past the broad front porch and inside the hallway. Then I froze, not sure whether I was going to bolt. Why should this therapist be any different from the others?

The doors to the doctor's office, in the former living room of the house, stood open, though there was no immediate sign of him. The big windows in the room let in the morning sunshine and a view of the overgrown garden lining the front sidewalk. He'd hung cut glass in the windows, filched from old chandeliers, to scatter the light into rainbows across the far wall. But that was the extent of his decorating talents. The heavy desk and lumbering, lumpy couch that served as furnishings for Roberts' professional environment were obvious deserters from the Salvation Army.

A cramped office on the other side of the broad entryway belonged to Cindy, the doctor's round, rosy-cheeked receptionist. I'd made my appointment with her. She waved at me, busy on the phone. I hesitated, wondering if I should take one of the chairs in front of Cindy's desk.

Dr. Roberts himself emerged from a door at the back of the hallway—the rest of the house was apparently his home—to rescue me from my indecision. So, okay, the setting wasn't overly impressive. The good doctor was a different matter entirely.

Ethan Roberts was the deluxe edition—his dark blond hair a little too long to be fashionable, his deep-set gray-blue eyes examining me with what seemed like X-ray vision, his strong jaw skimmed by the barest shading of beard, highlighting the cleft in his chin. He was a gypsy, a pirate, a swashbuckling hero in a loose sweater and tight-fitting jeans. Ethan Roberts was the one Mama warned you about. And he was supposed to be my therapist?

"You must be Ms. Burdette." He held out a bear-paw of a hand; the handshake it offered was warm and enfolding, protective, comforting. Somewhere between my shoulder blades, muscles relaxed in response. The feeling was vaguely alarming, as if I'd already started spilling my secrets without opening my mouth. "Call me Ethan."

"Asia," I allowed in return.

"Welcome." He smiled, revealing tiny laugh lines at the corners of his eyes. "I see Cindy's still tied up." Cindy was murmuring with patient understanding to the phone, but her face showed exasperation. "We can deal with the paperwork later."

He turned to lead the way into his office. I followed him, trying hard not to notice how those worn jeans seemed molded by long practice to his narrow hips, how that silky sweater clung to his broad shoulders. Oh, hell yeah. I was in trouble.

He waved me toward the couch and claimed the threadbare armchair beside it for himself. The couch was more comfortable than it looked, and was angled so he and I both had a view out the windows. The arrangement made me want to curl up with a book and a long afternoon. Or maybe with Ethan Roberts and a long afternoon.

"So, how long were you with Dr. Claussen?"

Small talk. He probably knew all the ugly details of my breakup with Claussen, but I figured I'd play along.

"Weekly sessions for about four months, plus the group. He was all right, I guess, but the group was a waste."

Ethan laughed, a deep, intimate sound that made it seem as if we'd been friends for years. "Arthur indicated you didn't have a lot in common with the other members of the group."

"There was more to it than that."

"Oh?"

I felt a flush of red creep up my neck. He was going to make me admit it.

"I said some things that weren't very nice at the last group session. I guess I'd lost patience with the process." I put little air quotes around the last two words.

Ethan tried unsuccessfully to hide a smile. "It's possible your needs didn't mesh well with those of others in the group. It happens."

"Uh-huh." I hoped we were finished with that subject. "What else did Dr. Claussen tell you about me?"

Ethan met the challenge without a flinch. "He said you'd had some significant trauma in your life and had built up quite a shell around it. That's not so unusual. It's not even particularly unhealthy. If that had been all there was to your case, Arthur would probably have kept at it for a while longer."

"I doubt it." I offered up a rueful smile. "I think my grand performance in group was the last straw. We weren't getting anywhere."

"Where is it you want to go?" All trace of smartass banter was gone from Ethan's voice. The train of our conversation had suddenly switched tracks.

"Go?"

"Yes. Where do you want therapy to take you?" He waited, his gaze holding mine, finding a way in deep where I would have sworn he could see everything.

My mouth closed on the answer I was about to toss off, something along the lines of how I needed someone to talk to, blah, blah, blah. The real answer fluttered in my chest, but I refused to let it out. Ethan's deep-sea eyes were warm and caring; his smile and his humor were disarming. But it was too early for me to trust him with everything. I didn't know yet whether I could trust him with anything.

"I know about the fire, Asia," he said after a moment. "I know about your children, and I'm so sorry."

He moved closer, and I began to shake. "You suffered a horrible loss. You wouldn't be human if you didn't still feel the pain of it. But you don't strike me as the kind of woman who would lean too long on others—especially not on strangers. I think you would have taken this hit and found a way to keep going, with or without professional help. There's something more to it, something that's keeping you from moving on. Tell me why you're really here."

Unexpected tears started in my eyes, and my chest tightened around my breath. I studied the stirring of the breeze in the greenery outside the window. What was it I wanted to tell him? What was it that was eating away at the new shoots of my life now, three years after the forest fire that had burned it to the ground in the first place?

I didn't know how to tell him everything. So, in the end, I simply told him the first thing.

"I was only going to be gone a little while." My voice was husky with unshed tears. "I hadn't been out—"

"You feel guilty for taking a night out for yourself?" He looked as if he wanted to lecture me about that. No—as if he wanted to *defend* me.

I hesitated. "Yes. No. I mean, that's not it."

"Take your time, Asia." God, that voice was like a warm blanket for my naked nerves.

I shook my head, started over. "That Holiday Inn is 15 minutes from my house. I know because it's next to the grocery store where I used to do my shopping. I'd made that trip a hundred times, and it only took 15 minutes. But this time . . ." I stopped again, shivering so hard I thought my bones might break. "This time something happened. And I've tried over and over to explain it, and I just can't."

I looked up and found him watching me, his face open, accepting. His patience gave me courage. I took a breath and went on.

"I lost three hours of my life that night. I can't account for them. They're just gone. And in those three hours I lost everything. My children, my home, my whole life." I met his eyes, hope struggling to emerge through the weight of my doubt. "I want to know where those hours went, Ethan. I'll never be able to move on until I know what happened to those three hours."

I expected skepticism in response. Or pity, which was the most I had ever gotten from the others I had asked for help. Instead I saw something in Ethan's face I hadn't seen in anyone since the accident. I saw understanding.

"I think I can help you," he said.

For no reason I can think of, I believed him.

I went in to work the next day feeling better than I'd felt in weeks. The dreams had left me alone that night—and I had something new to think about.

Rita noticed the change, of course. "Well, aren't we chipper this morning? What happened, you get lucky last night?"

"Not hardly." I laughed. "I did get a new psychiatrist, though. Maybe he's doing me some good."

Now, don't ask me why I said that. I should've known Rita would jump on it like the information was a fat mouse and she was a hungry housecat.

"A psychiatrist? You're drooling over some old professor with a goatee? Girl, you're more desperate than I thought."

"There's no law that says your therapist has to *look* like Sigmund Freud."

Rita's eyebrows reached for her hairline. "Oh? So what does he look like?"

I shrugged. "Tall, blue eyes, good-looking in a scruffy kinda way." *Looks real good in faded jeans and a sweater.*

"Uh-huh." Rita studied me closely. "Isn't it against the rules to be so interested in your doctor?"

"What do you mean, interested?"

"You know what I mean. And if he's interested back, you're either going to have to get a new doctor or he's going to have to find a new job."

"Jeez, Rita, it's not like we're making out in his office." I got busy refilling the office coffee pot. "He's very professional. I just think he's easy on the eyes, that's all."

"Right." Rita stood, considering me, her arms folded over her ample chest. "Is there any other reason you're seeing this new guy? What was wrong with the old one?"

"You could say I'd worn out my welcome at Dr. Claussen's therapy group." My face flushed. "He recommended Dr. Roberts. Said he specializes in these kinds of cases."

"And what kind of cases would those be?"

I sighed, realizing I'd said way too much. "Selective amnesia. Lost memory. Blackouts. That kind of thing."

Rita took a breath and broke it down: "Selective amnesia is where your kids suddenly can't remember that you told them to be home by midnight. Drunks have blackouts. And I reckon everyone has a few hundred lost memories. So which is it for you?"

"That's what Ethan is supposed to tell me." I turned and took my cup of coffee back in the direction of the outer office. Rita's window of opportunity had just shut tight. I was no longer in a sharing mood.

"Nine o'clock," I tossed over my shoulder. "Time to thrust JW's spear of indifference into the trusting hearts of the hopeful."

"Smartass," Rita threw after me. "*Ethan*, huh? Maybe I'll just hold the paperwork on your insurance claims for a while. I hate resubmitting all those damn forms."

Rita had a funny way of making it, but, as usual, she did have a point. I'd suffered a major emotional trauma. I'd been through a divorce and left behind all the friends and family I'd grown up with. I'd gone a little crazy in the first few months after I moved to Nashville, but the novelty of one-night stands had soon worn off, and I hadn't been with a guy in months. Emotionally vulnerable and horny wasn't a good combination. Maybe seeing a psychiatrist as attractive as Ethan Roberts was asking for trouble. And *damn,* but those blue eyes could look right through you.

Maybe we could skip the therapy and go directly to the social interaction/dating/sex. No rules against that.

But he'd said he could help me. He'd made me feel safe and warm and strong enough to wrestle my demons to the ground for good. Whether that was Ethan Roberts the man, or Ethan Roberts the psychiatrist at work, I wasn't sure. I only knew I wanted more of it. And to hell with the rules.

Jab-jab-cross. Hook-hook-uppercut.
Jab-cross.
Again. And again.

Ethan attacked the heavy bag until the chains sang and the sand inside hissed, punished his target until his arms ached and his sweat flew. Still the battle raged, the victory undecided.

"The problem's in your stance, you know." Dan Parker had coached inner city Golden Gloves teams for years; he would know. As Chief Psychologist for Nashville city schools and Ethan's closest friend, he would know what the real problem was, too.

Dan waved a hand. "The leg still bothering you?"

The stark neon lights of the old boxing gym and the smell of stale sweat and rubber mats crowded into Ethan's awareness now that his concentration had been broken. His hands dropped from their guard and reached for the support of the bag chains.

"Damn it, I shouldn't be so stiff. I've been out of physical therapy for months."

"From a second surgery."

"Do you see a limp?"

"Not unless I squint. Are you still taking pain

pills?"

Ethan avoided Dan's unwavering stare, but he confessed. "Occasionally. To sleep. I know I sound like somebody's ancient uncle, but the thing aches like a sonofabitch when it's gonna rain." Dan didn't need to hear that the pain disturbing his sleep was more often psychological than physical. He didn't need to know about the dreams, either.

Ethan tugged off his gloves and started unwinding the damp wraps from his hands as he moved toward the weight machines. "I've only got one refill left. I don't intend to get another script."

"Glad to hear it." Dan propped a burly shoulder against the cement wall behind the quad machine while Ethan set up. "Maybe you're just too damn old for all this. I hear they revoke our memberships when we hit forty, and we have to go to the Y."

Ethan gritted his teeth through the first few lifts, his thigh muscles screaming in protest. "I still have two years, but you're way over the limit, old man."

"Damn. Busted."

In the rest between sets, Ethan looked up at his friend. "Are you going to work out, or are you just here to give me a hard time?"

"I was done an hour ago." Dan made no move to leave. "You haven't been out to the house in ages. The kids miss you. What's new in your life? Got a girlfriend yet?"

Ethan paused halfway into the next lift. "What?"

A younger gym-rat at the next machine dropped his weights with a clank and barked out a laugh. "Are you kidding, Dan? You didn't know Ethan's nickname around here is The Monk?"

"Yeah, dude." The guy beside him grinned. "You have no idea how many girls have hit on the man when we go for a beer, and *nothin'*, zip, nada."

"Thus, The Monk." The first man clapped Ethan on the shoulder as he moved to a different machine. "Our sparring partner is serious about his celibacy."

Ethan just smiled and let the comments wash over him. It wasn't the first time he'd been teased about his lack of female companionship. The young men he worked out with didn't know about Elizabeth, about the accident that had ended her life and nearly ended his. Only Dan Parker knew about any of that and he, thankfully, wasn't sharing it.

"Maybe Ethan isn't interested in robbing the cradle, ever thought of that, gentlemen?" Dan made an inept attempt to save him. "It's not like y'all hang out with a lot of ladies who might have some experience in life."

The guys howled at this, and the conversation barreled on to what kind of experience Parker might be getting at. Ethan let the banter roll on without him as he pushed his aching leg through his reps, and thought suddenly of the only woman who had caught his interest in . . . God, since he didn't know when. He knew it was dangerous to be thinking of her in that way, but he couldn't seem to help it. From the first time he'd seen her, before he'd even known who she was, she'd been on his mind. Surely it was better to acknowledge the attraction and deal with it rather than to try and repress it?

When he thought of her now—her dark hair falling

in loose curls around a graceful neck, her brown eyes so light and full of fire they seemed to be filled with gold, her smile that was like sunlight breaking through heavy clouds—his chest tightened around his breath and his heart slowed to a labored pounding against his ribs that had nothing to do with exercise.

Her story was compelling enough in itself. The mystery of her "lost time" would probably prove to be a simple matter of trauma-related guilt, but, Jesus, who wouldn't want to help the woman? He didn't think he'd acted inappropriately with her that afternoon in his office. He'd listened. He'd responded sympathetically. He knew he could help her, and he would.

And yet he couldn't stop imagining what it would be like to feel the silky skin of her neck under his fingertips, to let his tongue follow the path his fingers had made and end with a kiss in the warm, pulsing hollow of her throat.

He forced himself to switch his attention to the inane conversation taking place around him. Because despite the physical exertion of his workout, despite the stark setting and the curious eyes everywhere, and especially despite the inappropriateness of the situation itself, thinking about Asia Burdette was making him so hard it was going to be impossible to stand up from this machine any time soon.

CHAPTER THREE

The good feeling I'd enjoyed after my first session with Dr. Roberts didn't last long. Before the week was out, the dreams had returned, as vague and haunting as ever. What was it about that landscape that was so familiar? It was like no place I'd ever seen, and yet I knew it as if I'd spent months there. But when I reached for the details, they slipped my grasp like so much smoke through my fingers.

By the time I showed up for my second visit with Ethan Roberts, I could feel the lack of sleep pulling at the skin of my face, slowing my movements. Even my reaction to him was muted. I could recognize the impact his smile should have on me, but I just didn't have it in me to respond fully. *Not now. Maybe later.*

On the couch in his office I fought an impulse to lie down and close my eyes.

"You haven't been sleeping," Ethan noted.

I stopped mid-yawn. "Now, what makes you think that?"

"I don't mean just last night or this week." He watched me as he spoke, alert to my reactions. "You haven't been sleeping for a long time. Do you still dream about the fire?"

"No."

"What then?"

I shook my head. "I don't know. Crazy stuff. It makes no sense." I wished he'd drop it. I didn't want to talk about the dreams; they already consumed far too much of my time. "Too much vodka and tonic, I guess."

"That's probably not the case." God, those eyes. Who had eyes that color? "But if you don't want to talk about it, we can leave it for another time."

I flashed him a warning glance. "That's not the reason I'm here."

"Really?" He looked at me as if he suspected I was lying, as if he knew just how big a lie it was. When I refused to take the bait, he went on. "Okay, why don't you tell me what you think happened the night of the fire?"

"I don't know what happened. That's the whole point."

"I didn't ask you what happened." He made certain I was looking at him. "I asked you what you *think* happened. Do you think you got drunk and passed out?"

"I wasn't drunk."

"Do you think you had a stroke, an epileptic fit, early Alzheimer's?"

"What the hell are you talking about?" Anger flared in my chest. Did he think this was a joke? If so, his face didn't show it. He looked deadly serious.

"Asia, something happened that night. You lost three hours. Could you have lost track of time at the bar?"

"No!" I shouted at him. "I left the bar before midnight. I was sober. I headed home. The next thing I know I'm waking up on Deerhorn Road, and it's three hours later. I can't explain it. Can you?"

"Yeah, I can explain it." His gaze was level, his voice even. "You were tired. It had been a long day, and you weren't used to being out drinking. You caught yourself nodding at the wheel and pulled over."

"No, damn it, I was wide awake!" *Aren't you listening? I need you to believe me.*

"You're human, Asia. You were tired. You'd had a little too much to drink. And though your brain was not acknowledging these facts, your body did what it is programmed by evolution to do. It saved your ass by pulling over to the side of the road."

NO!

"You may even have been effectively unconscious by the time that car came to a stop." He went on, relentless. "Your body knew from long experience what to do. It's no surprise you don't remember it."

"That's not the way it happened!" I jumped up and started to pace in front of the window. "Do you think this is the first time I've heard this? Every goddamn doctor I've been to has said the same thing. I've tried to convince myself that's what happened. Hell, it's the only logical explanation, right? But I can't believe it. Something in the back of my mind won't let me believe it. I want to know *why.*"

"That's just it, Asia." His gaze followed me around the room, but his voice was as calm and still as deep water. "You already know why. There is an explanation, but your guilt won't let you believe it. The answer is not in your mind. It's in your heart."

I stopped pacing to glare at him. "You're saying I'm obsessing over this because I feel guilty?"

"The process is much more complex than that."

"The process," I repeated, furious. "*The process.* Let me tell you something, Doc. The process is like having your guts ripped out. It's like being tortured in some South American prison month after month. Only there's no end to it because you can't tell your torturer what he wants to know. Do I feel guilty? Yeah, you bet your ass I feel guilty. I should have been there, and I wasn't. And because I wasn't there, my babies are dead. You don't ever forgive yourself for something like that. *Ever.*"

I pulled up short and forced myself to sit across from him on the couch. I stared into his eyes, as if I could will him to understand.

"I'm telling you: I wasn't drunk. I wasn't tired. I didn't pull over and pass out less than a mile from my house. *Something happened.* Something happened, and I lost everything."

Ethan didn't look away. "I know. I know, Asia. And you can never replace what you lost that night. Still, you've survived. You've begun a new life. That's a hell of a lot. It shows incredible strength. Admirable strength. With a little help, you'll escape that torturer. In time the scars will heal."

I studied him, trembling, unwilling to give up what had been with me for so long. The rage. The guilt. He gave no sign that my anger was inappropriate or disturbing, or that the tears that washed in a stream down my cheeks were anything but necessary. In the space he had created, warmed by his understanding, I suddenly felt safe, comforted. I almost felt that the future he saw was possible. The fists I held clenched in my lap relaxed a tiny fraction.

Ethan reached across his desk and took up a prescription pad. "I'm going to give you something to help you sleep. You need to be rested before we can start work."

"Work?" I rubbed at my face.

He smiled. "You didn't think I was going to let you off that easy, did you?"

"Well, no. But I didn't expect to be digging ditches either."

"Emotional work can be every bit as hard and dirty." He handed me the prescription.

I took this as a signal the session was over. I rose to go, grateful that my shaky legs were strong enough to hold me. I managed a tentative grin.

"Guess I'd better wear my overalls next time."

Ethan saw me to the door. "Guess you'd better."

It didn't sound like he was joking.

Arthur Claussen settled onto the battered couch in Ethan's office as if he was afraid the furniture would give way under him. "You know, you really should get yourself a nicer office." His gaze slid from the curtainless window to the smudged walls and back to the scratched desk before rising to meet Ethan's questioning expression. "You can afford it."

Ethan regarded him with amusement. "Can I?"

"I send you plenty of patients." Claussen waved a hand at him. "You're a bachelor, with no family to support."

"No, Arthur." That familiar band tightened around his chest. "I'm technically not a bachelor, though it's true I don't have family to support."

"Yes, you're right, my boy." The old man dipped his head. "I'm sorry. Still, why do you hide away here in your hobbit hole like some college professor from the nineteen-sixties? Why not live a little?"

Ethan lifted his chin with dramatic flair. "I refuse to take on the trappings of a corrupt bourgeois society." Then he shrugged, dismissing the subject. His mentor had been pushing this point a bit too much lately. Ethan was comfortable in this room, in this house. He liked having some money squirreled away for the future. He had no need of a fancy car or office, though he had to admit he could use the family. That had been something he'd wanted and hadn't been likely to get, even when he'd had the wife.

Claussen frowned as if he could see he was getting nowhere. "I have a couple of interesting cases I thought I'd send your way. One swears she's pregnant with an alien baby."

"I'm a psychiatrist, not a reporter for the *Enquirer*." Ethan smiled and rearranged the files on his desk. "Besides, I don't think I want any new patients just now."

"Oh?" Claussen's eyes narrowed a fraction. "And why not?"

"I'm still trying to resolve the last batch you sent me."

"The engineer with the scars? That should have been an easy case. And the schoolteacher should have resolved within a few weeks."

Ethan shifted in his seat. In fact, he had been able to convince the engineer his unusual scars were a previously unnoticed byproduct of an active lifestyle. And the schoolteacher had never really wanted to believe she had been part of a science fiction cliché. Both cases had been relegated to the follow-up file.

"There's something else, isn't there, Ethan?" Claussen studied him with an air of self-satisfaction. "Don't tell me you've been out scaring up cases on your own."

"If I had, don't you think it would have been about time?" He was trying for a light tone, but aggravation gave the sentence a bitter edge.

Maddeningly, Claussen agreed with him. "Perhaps you're right. What, then?"

Ethan left his seat for a post by the window. Outside, a cold spring rain dripped from the overhanging trees and pooled in the low spots of the patchy lawn. He watched it for a while before he answered, wondering why he was reluctant to speak.

"It's the last one you sent me," he admitted. "Asia Burdette."

"Oh, yes." The older man spoke as if he'd been expecting Ethan's response. "I'm not surprised you're finding that one a challenge."

"She's different, Arthur."

"Are we talking about the woman or the case?"

The woman. Well, the woman was different enough to have been on his mind a lot lately. But he knew better than to admit that to Claussen.

"The case, of course."

"Of course." The corners of the doctor's mouth revealed a knowing smile.

"Arthur, the cases you send me all have one thing in common. The procedure we've developed is designed to address that problem. But Asia doesn't fit the profile. She hasn't mentioned the 'a' word once—and I've given her plenty of opportunity. Why did you send her to me?"

"I told you why. I couldn't help her. I thought maybe you could. Besides, there's no reason our methodology shouldn't work on any case of hysterical amnesia."

Ethan shook his head. "I'm not so sure."

"Well, there's no harm in trying, is there? You can always fall back on standard talk therapy if the approach fails."

"I'm afraid we may not have enough time. She seems . . . fragile."

"Asia Burdette? Surely you aren't suggesting she's suicidal? That woman's a survivor if I've ever seen one."

Ethan turned to look at him. "No, not suicidal. Just . . . stretched thin. To the point where something has to give."

"Stretched thin—I'll have to review my medical journals for that new clinical term."

"It may not be precise, but I imagine you know what I mean."

"And if she is at the point where something has to give, isn't that the best time to intervene with therapy?"

He said nothing. His friend was right, of course. Why did he feel so strongly that there was something else at work in Asia's case?

After a moment, Claussen exhaled a paternal "humpf." "Have you had any luck getting her to open up about herself? What she does with her free time, for example? Boyfriends, sex, that kind of thing?"

Ethan immediately flushed hot with a reaction that was both primal and totally inappropriate. Hell, no, he hadn't asked her about any boyfriends. His muscles clenched to think of her with someone . . . else. *Jesus Christ!* Was he actually feeling possessive? He resented the fact that Claussen had even asked the question.

Horrified, he stumbled over an answer. "We've, uh, the sessions so far have been focused on the night of the fire."

Claussen pushed himself up from his position on the couch. He laid a hand on Ethan's shoulder. "You know what I think? I think you're a lonely young man who is letting an attractive woman with a compelling problem interfere with his professional detachment. Perhaps this was a mistake. Maybe I should take her case back and try to resolve it myself."

Ethan struggled to recover his composure. He responded with a grin he hoped didn't look too forced.

"Not on your life, old man. This is the most interesting case you've sent me in months. And I'm just starting to establish a rapport."

The hand on his shoulder tightened slightly. "All right. But be careful, Doctor. Avoiding emotional attachment—"

"—is the most imperative rule of psychotherapy," Ethan finished for him, his anger subsiding into mere irritation. "Didn't I read that on a wall plaque somewhere?"

The mentor seemed unaware of the depth of his protégé's turmoil. "You were the best research assistant I ever had at the Institute, Ethan. I would give a lot to have you back, even now. Despite your mule-headed obstinacy." He patted Ethan's shoulder in dismissal and moved toward the front door.

Ethan ignored Claussen's clumsy enticement to take up his old position at the Psychogenesis Institute. Any response usually led to the same long, fruitless discussion they'd had many times before. He simply walked the doctor to the door and followed him out onto the porch. The rain dripped rhythmically off the eaves and onto the boxwood under the windows. He shivered in the chilly air.

"A pleasure to see you as always, Dr. Claussen." He smiled. "Despite the insults."

"No, it is my pleasure, Dr. Roberts." The old man smirked. "Insults included."

Claussen clumped down the steps and got behind the wheel of his late-model Cadillac. *No skimping on luxuries there*, Ethan thought. The man who actually had been a college professor in the 1960s now showed little sign of it. Instead, he looked more like the successful doctor in private practice that he had been for thirty years. Ethan saw quite clearly the path the doctor had tried to lay out for his protégé.

The only question was why he couldn't bring himself to walk it.

It was a slow day at the Music Rowe office.

JW Rowe himself was in L.A., trying to wrangle a crossover deal for one of his better performers. The wannabe country stars that normally haunted the office had been made aware of the great man's absence and were away pacing the floors of their apartments or practicing their guitar pickin', awaiting his return. Rita and I had the place to ourselves.

"Now here's a story for you." Rita grinned at the newspaper she'd spread across the desk. "'Taken for a Ride? Locals Claim Alien Abduction.'"

I laughed. "You've got to be kidding."

"'Brentwood resident Myrna Hofstetter woke up one night last year to see a half-dozen small, gray beings with enormous black eyes standing around her bed,'" Rita read. "'She tried to scream, but found she was unable to move or make a sound. "I knew they were aliens," Hofstetter said. "It was real. It wasn't a dream. I was desperate to get away, but I couldn't do a thing." The beings took her to their ship, Hofstetter claims, where they conducted experiments on her.'"

"Oh, for chrissake." I made no secret of my opinion. "Where do they find these nuts?"

"Oh, but wait—there's more! 'Austin Green—sounds like one of our clients, doesn't he?—a carpenter from Bowling Green, Kentucky, says the aliens took him right up out of his truck on a lonely country road last summer.'" Rita affected a heavy country accent. "'My radio got all screwed up. Then my truck just stalled out. Next thing I know I'm riding this big beam of light up to their ship,' Green said.'"

Rita kept reading, but I was no longer listening. The blood had drained from my head into my feet, leaving me cold and shaking. A truck. A lonely country road. Then something unexplainable. Austin Green might have been crazy, but I knew that feeling. Deep in my gut I could feel his disorientation, his terror, his disbelief. What was happening to him— what *had* happened to him—made no rational sense. I suspected that even now, months later, Austin Green didn't understand what had happened that night. His explanation was aliens. It could just as well have been pixie dust or time travel or a rift in the space-time continuum. Nothing could explain it, really. Austin Green's life had been changed forever, just as mine had, and there *was* no explanation.

"Hey! What was the name of that doctor you're seeing?" Rita said. "Isn't it Roberts?"

"What?" I had to force myself back into the present.

"Your shrink—the new guy you've been seeing." Rita looked up and demanded my attention. "His name is Roberts, right?"

"Yeah. Ethan Roberts. Why?"

Rita studied the newspaper. "Says here, 'Nashville psychiatrist Dr. Ethan Roberts specializes in treating the victims of these so-called abductions. He is neutral on the subject of whether the abductions are real. "The people I see are unhappy. Their lives have been disrupted, sometimes profoundly. Whether or not the experience they believe they've had is real, their suffering certainly is. It's my job to help them through that."'" Rita looked up again from the desk. "Sounds like a sensible approach."

I was well aware there was a question behind Rita's comment, but I wasn't inclined to answer it. I shrugged.

"I suppose."

"Don't guess you've been seeing any little gray men lately?"

I laughed shortly. "Girl, I haven't been seeing men of any description lately. And just because Dr. Roberts has some wacko patients doesn't mean he can't help me. He is a psychiatrist, after all. If his patients were normal we wouldn't need to be seeing him."

"All right, all right." Rita tried to placate me. "But it does say here that Roberts's colleagues think he's a little eccentric himself. Guess it's not the best thing to be seen as an expert in treating alien abductees. What do you think of him?"

I didn't have to think long. "I trust him. I don't know yet whether he can help me, but I think I'm ready to let him try. I don't think I care that other folks consider him odd."

"Um-hmm." Rita smiled before returning to her newspaper.

The warmth that had kindled in my chest in

response to Ethan's name rose to inflame my cheeks. There was no use denying what Rita obviously assumed. As inappropriate as it was, I was attracted to Ethan Roberts. That could be a positive thing—it might keep me going back to him long enough for him to do me some good. After all, if he could help the Myrna Hofstetters and Austin Greens of the world, he ought to be able to help me. I wasn't anywhere near that crazy.

"What the hell is that?"

I stopped short as I entered Ethan's office. An element of cold, hard technology had been introduced into the cozy room. The machine on his desk was no bigger than a desktop computer and looked harmless enough. But for reasons I could not identify, it filled me with foreboding.

The doctor laid an affectionate hand on the top of the machine. "It's an alpha wave synchronizer, but I just call it AL."

I dredged up a smile, but I stayed where I was. "Is that for me?"

"Yes. It's part of the therapeutic regimen. Does it bother you?"

I knew he could see that it did. Still, I couldn't explain my reaction, even to myself. I made an effort to lighten up.

"What are you going to do—scan me for alien implants?"

Ethan flashed me an embarrassed grin. My stomach fluttered in response.

"Oh, you heard about that, did you? My not-so-secret life as an alien buster." He came from behind his desk to steer me to the couch with a gentle touch at my elbow. More fluttering. I sat, trying to control my breath; he took the armchair beside me.

"I try to avoid talking to reporters, but every time they do one of these stories they come looking for me." He rubbed at the back of his neck. "They make it seem like I'm the only psychiatrist in the world who has delusional patients."

"So you don't believe these people have really been abducted by aliens?" I wasn't sure whether I was teasing him or testing him. Maybe it was a little of both.

He lifted his shoulders. "Who am I to say? They're certainly convinced of it when they come in here. But ninety-nine percent of them no longer believe it when they leave."

I grinned. "What about the other one percent?"

"Oh, they really have been abducted by aliens." He laughed. "No doubt about it."

"And this machine"—I examined it with renewed distaste—"I suppose it's been reverse-engineered from a UFO?"

The doctor seemed relieved to be back on therapeutic ground. "Actually, it started life as a fairly common psychiatric tool. You've heard of biofeedback?"

"They use it to teach people how to control headaches."

He nodded. "Or anxiety or anger. Lots of things. Dr. Claussen and some of his colleagues took a simple biofeedback machine and made some modifications. The machine identifies and amplifies alpha waves—it essentially puts you in an enhanced alpha state. You feel good, you're calm and relaxed, but you're also alert and highly aware of what's going on in your mind. What we're looking for is a kind of conscious hypnosis in which it will be easier to gain access to any thoughts or feelings you've been repressing."

My heart began to thud dully in my chest. "What if I haven't been repressing anything?"

"Then we'll have to think of another approach. In any case, you'll still get the benefits of the relaxation." He was responding to my discomfort with a big dose of matter-of-fact calm, his entire demeanor communicating, *Relax. This is no big deal.*

It wasn't working, but I had to give him credit for the effort. "I think I saw this once on a *Star Trek* episode. It didn't end well."

He laughed again. "Don't worry. I can't wipe your mind clean or reproduce your personality in an android or mindmeld with you—it's nothing like that." He leaned forward, his forearms resting on his knees, his hands open and expressive. "Your mind seals off painful memories and emotions as a way of giving you time to deal with them. In a crisis it's a useful mechanism—otherwise these things might overwhelm and paralyze you. But over time those sealed packages can cause trouble. We have to open them back up and examine their contents. The synchronizer just convinces the mind that it's safe to do that."

"You're assuming I'm hiding something about that

night." My anxiety was honing itself to an angry edge.

"Not consciously."

"Unconsciously, then."

"That's what the procedure will tell us."

"And what if there's nothing to find?" Suddenly I was trembling like that rabbit again, trying desperately to decide whether to freeze into invisibility or run like hell for the safety of the warren. I wanted to walk out and never come back. I wanted to take the damn machine and throw it through the window. Only the barest scrap of rational thought kept me in my seat.

"Like I said—then we take another approach." He looked at me closely. "That's the problem, isn't it? You're afraid we won't find an explanation."

I met his eyes briefly—he'd hit on it, all right—then I exhaled a tight laugh. "You know, when I read about your other clients, I almost envied them. At least they have an explanation for what happened to them. It may be crazy, but it's an explanation." I looked at him again and this time did not look away. "How do they feel when you take that away from them?"

"Relieved." He said it as though he believed it, but there was something in his eyes. Could it be the doctor had his own doubts? "Asia, explaining what happened is not the same as understanding it. Explanation is intellectual. Understanding is emotional. An understanding that encompasses acceptance is much more satisfying in the long run."

Acceptance. How can I accept it? Three hours are gone and my kids are dead. How is that acceptable?

"Look, why don't we just give AL a try? Maybe

you'll see what I mean."

I thought about it a moment longer, then I lifted my chin. "All right. Let's get on with it."

"Good." He got up to retrieve a pillow from the foot of the couch. "You'll be more comfortable if you lie down. Is that okay?"

"I guess." The thought of lying down on his couch had my mind moving in entirely the wrong direction. I squelched that line of thinking and stretched out as he placed the pillow under my head. The act was strangely comforting; it touched me that he was trying so hard to put me at ease.

I stared at the ceiling—the plaster was veined with tiny cracks—while he puttered around in the room behind me. I heard the soft *snick* of electronic equipment being turned on, then the room filled with the sound of wind chimes and curtains blowing in a gentle breeze. I felt him moving behind and above me, and a warm, moist cloth appeared to cover my eyes. It smelled deliciously of something I could not identify.

"My grandmother was Cree, from upstate New York." His voice was quiet, soothing. "She had an herbal answer for anything that ailed you. Do you like the smell?"

I murmured assent, too relaxed for words.

"One of her mixtures. I could tell you the scientific names for what's in it, but the Indian names are much more colorful." There was gentle amusement, even fondness, in his voice. I thought I'd have to ask him about his grandmother someday. Right now I didn't seem to have the energy.

"In a minute I'll have to attach some electrodes to your temples and the back of your head. I'm just going to massage those areas a little first, okay?"

The mention of electrodes sent a spike of apprehension through my chest, but I nodded anyway. I'd agreed to do this; I was determined to see it through.

At the touch of his fingers at my temples, my fear receded into the back of my mind. His hands were warm with something more than the warmth of circulating blood. It was as if there was a mild current flowing through them, an energy that worked to erase the lines of tension between my eyes and around my mouth. I felt that energy at my temples even after his hands moved behind my head to stimulate twin spots at the base of my skull. Something let go in the muscles of my neck, releasing a long-held tightness.

Forget the damn machine, I thought, drifting. *This is all the therapy I need.*

Just as I was about to suggest to Ethan that he'd missed his true calling, his fingers withdrew, leaving behind only a residual tingling. Then a drop of something cool and gelatinous hit my skin, just before an electrode was pressed to each spot.

"We're all set. Are you ready?"

I murmured agreement.

"I'm switching the machine on now. You shouldn't feel any discomfort."

I could barely perceive a low hum as he turned on the machine. I felt no pain, no physical effect at all. I lay and listened to the wind chimes turn in the breeze. I let the sound and the smell of

Grandmother's herbs loosen the knots in my shoulders. I waited without anticipation for the next step.

After a moment, Ethan spoke. His question wasn't what I'd expected, but it made perfect sense. His lips close to my ear, his voice intimate and compelling, he asked, and I knew I'd answer without hesitation: "Tell me about your dreams, Asia."

CHAPTER FOUR

A cold sun rose through a sooty yellow haze, bringing unwelcome dawn. Its reluctant light advanced across the hunched shoulders of the jagged hills, and slowly the naked flanks of rock lifted out of the murky shadows below. In the camp at the base of the ridge, darkness lingered, untouched by the promise of day.

As she stood in line to receive food, 1408 stamped her feet in the gray dust and shivered. The single layer of the jumpsuit she wore was not enough to keep out the cold, even in the shelter of the barracks. Here on the open ground of the quadrangle, the rough cloth was like a tattered rag fluttering on the stick of her body. She folded in on herself and endured, shuffling forward with the rest toward the warm bowl of sticky, colorless gruel, and the chance to huddle in the lee of the cook shack.

Fourteen-oh-eight spoke to no one in the line. She had no energy for talk. Food was what she wanted, only that. Until she had it, nothing else interested her. She followed the broad back of the woman in front of her, a woman from her barracks she knew only as the number on the back of her jumpsuit, 6320. Behind her, 4216 kicked dust on her heels with every step, but 1408 did not turn to glare at her. She put her head down and moved on.

At the cook shack, the wet-dog smell of the boiling grain rode a wave of warmth out of the serving window. If it had not been for the aching emptiness in her stomach, this would have been 1408's favorite section of the line. She craned her neck to feel the brief heat on her face while she waited to receive the bowl in her reaching hands.

She hesitated half a step as 6320 received her portion, then was shoved forward as soon as her own bowl touched her fingers. She would have snarled at 4216, the pushy bitch, but the food took all her attention now. She carried it close to her face, protecting it against loss until she found a spot between two other women at the corner of the shack. She hunkered down and shoveled the lumpy stuff into her mouth, hardly waiting to chew one bite before taking the next. Her growling stomach relaxed as it received the gift of food; for one moment she forgot the cold and spared no thought for the work waiting at the end of this brief pleasure.

Fourteen-oh-eight had nearly come to the end of her portion of the morning meal when she felt the women on either side of her stiffen and move away. She looked up, but saw only a hulking shadow outlined against the sky. Then the shadow's heavy boot crashed into her ribs, and the bowl, with its last precious mouthfuls, was snatched from her hands. "No!" she shouted, scrambling after it. The boot caught her at the shoulder this time, rolling her into two others not quick enough to move.

She heard a laugh from overhead, then a dusty scrape of boots carried the sound away, and she was left alone. She spit grit and blood out of her mouth and lifted her head cautiously. Her tormentor had melted into the huddle of bodies in the quad. Only one woman was looking in her direction, and she was far too small to have been the owner of that boot to the ribs. The look of sympathy on the woman's face transformed 1408's useful rage into helpless self-pity.

Fighting back tears, 1408 picked herself up off the ground before the guards could investigate. When the work whistle blew, she brushed at the dust on her jumpsuit and joined the line forming to snake through the gate to the mine entrance.

"Work with me today." The whisper came from just behind her in the line. "I saw who took your grub."

She moved a half-turn with her next step to see the tiny, dark-skinned woman who had been watching in the quad. She faced front again, careful to keep her face blank for the guards who were stalking the line, electric prods at the ready.

They said nothing more as the line filed out the gate, up the rocky path and into the tipple that housed the elevator over Shaft 16, but 1408 positioned herself to ensure that she stayed near her witness. The pair entered the same elevator car with more than twenty others and waited out the long, creaking descent into darkness in silence.

At the bottom, they exited the car quickly, shoving along with the others to get clear of the cage before it started back up the shaft. Fourteen-oh-eight had seen the consequences of moving too slowly—women with arms or legs torn off as the car shot back up the shaft without warning.

Her companion remained at her elbow as they picked up their headlamps and cutting lasers. They started to follow the others into the railcars that would carry them through the tunnels to the working face, but a burly guard stopped the smaller woman.

"You. 1012. They need you out on G tunnel. Blazer duty."

Fourteen-oh-eight stopped breathing, her heart battering at her ribs. She didn't know what "blazer duty" was, but it never paid to attract the attention of the guards for any reason.

The other shrugged. "I'll need a rigger."

The guard scowled, creasing his heavy brow ridges. "Fourteen-oh-eight, go with her. Azlac, take them in the hand cart."

A second guard put a gnarled hand on her shoulder and pushed them both in the direction of the hand cart. "Move." They took up their places on the platform, the two women on opposite handles of the push bar, the guard on the rear seat, his weapon resting loosely in his hands. Fourteen-oh-eight tried to ignore the squeeze of fear around her heart and focused on moving the cart—*push down to start the cart rolling, lean back as the handle comes up. Push down, lean back.*

They continued until, up ahead in the gloom, she could hear the whine of laser against rock. Diggers chipped away at the tunnel surfaces, planting roof and wall supports, opening up new seams for the miners. She and her partner eased back on the push bar, allowing the cart to coast to a stop in front of a barricade that marked the end of the cart rails.

"Off." The guard gestured with his weapon. The two prisoners jumped off the cart and followed their wavering headlamps toward the noise and leaping shadows that marked the work site.

"Vong'Ta! I've got your blazer and rigger."

The crew boss turned to glare at them. "About time! I've lost a segment already." The boss was big enough to block a third of the newly started tunnel, and distinguished by a drooping rectangular face and elongated ears. There were many who looked like him among the bosses, and none among the prisoners. That much 1408 could have said of him. She'd never speculated as to his origins. The mystery of his people, like her own identity, was as dark and unexplored as the cracks they followed in the rock.

The boss dismissed the guard with a curt, "You can go."

"What am I supposed to do—push myself back?"

"Either that or sit on your ass in the dark until the end of the shift and draw a punishment tour for jerking off." Vong'Ta scowled at his new workers. "Come on. The hole's down here."

They squeezed past the diggers working in the narrow passage, then down a twisting worm of empty burrow extending into the smothering darkness. The earth closing in around her made 1408 want to scream, but she knew if she began, she would never stop. She would become one of the screeching wild things they dragged out to be shot and tossed into the debris carts with the rest of the slag. She was afraid to die. So she shut out the panic and focused on the boss's broad, sweat-stained back bobbing ahead of her in the circle of light from her lamp.

They were still within earshot of the digging crew when they reached a cramped bay in the passageway, as wide as her outstretched arms and high enough for them to stand upright. At the base of one wall was a ragged triangular hole.

"Sonics show a crack at least as big as that hole running for twenty meters." The boss stood aside to let them look. "Then it opens up—maybe a cavern, we can't tell. One thing's for sure, though. Just beyond the open space, the whore's full of crystals. Find me a way in."

The tiny woman nodded. "Sure thing, boss." She pointed at a pile of shiny debris beside the hole. "What's the matter, crawler let you down?"

"*Shalssiti* robots are worthless in this pit." He kicked at what was left of the digging probe. "It took two men three segments just to pull that fucking thing back out of the hole. So you're up."

Ten-twelve's grin only widened. "No problem. Got the gear?"

The boss let a load of rope and rigging tools drop off his shoulder. He squinted at 1408.

"You ever rigged before?"

She started to shake her head, but her companion spoke up. "She's new at it, but she's got the touch. We'll be okay."

The boss frowned, deepening the ridges on his forehead. "I don't want any screw-ups. You get stuck or fall off a ledge in there and I'll lose my finder's bonus. And I got plans for that finder's bonus. You get it?"

"Sure, sure, got it, boss." The woman cocked her head at him. "And the sooner we get to work, the sooner you'll be spending that bonus, right?"

Vong'Ta took a step, as if he meant to strike the blazer. He loomed over her much smaller form, forcing her to look up, but she didn't back down. Fourteen-oh-eight waited, her heart racing.

"You know, if you weren't so useful, 1012, I'd *vardzo shalshitti idzta purzin.* Get to work." He turned and trudged back through the passage toward the digging crew.

"Yeah, but I am useful, you bastard, so you won't be kicking my ass anytime soon." The woman threaded her arms through a webbed harness, then suddenly smiled up at 1408. "It's not like *he* could crawl through this hole!"

In the light of this woman's fiery spirit, 1408 stood mute and awkward. The only smile she'd seen in this hellish place had been the grin of a gloating guard. The only laughter had been a brief bark of ridicule at some poor sufferer's expense. She'd never seen anyone like this woman.

"Call me Dozen. It's short for Ten Dozen— 1012, get it?" She peered up at 1408 with ebony eyes as if searching her face for something.

Fourteen-oh-eight caught a brief answering flicker in her mind. *Dozen.* The word was familiar, part of something distant and forgotten. She couldn't remember where she'd heard the word before. *A dozen. Twelve.* The lines around her mouth softened a fraction.

Dozen nodded. "I knew there was a little left in there. I can always spot it. Do you have a name?"

"I'm 1408."

"So the answer is no. Give me some time; I'll think of something." She held up another harness. "Here, get into this. No, like this. Buckle up here and here. Make sure they're secure." She stooped to shine her headlamp into the tunnel they would be navigating. Then she glanced up at 1408. "Well, you'll make it, but just barely. Maybe it's a good thing you lost half your breakfast."

A joke. Fourteen-oh-eight rummaged in the wreckage of her mind for a response, but couldn't find one.

"Okay, so I go first." Dozen knocked a piton into the floor of the bay and secured one end of a cable to it. "It's my job to blaze the trail—you know, find a way through and mark it so we can find it again. You have two jobs: Make sure I come back out, and haul the hazard rigging."

"Hazard rigging?"

"Ah, the Sphinx speaks! I was beginning to wonder if you had the power of independent thought." She was smiling again. Fourteen-oh-eight perceived this as another joke, but she had no idea what "Sphinx" meant. "We have to rig cables around the dangerous spots so others won't drop off into a bottomless hole somewhere. Hazard rigging. You'll help me do that."

Fourteen-oh-eight stared at the hole, transfixed with terror at the thought of the airless tunnel behind it. *Twenty meters*, he'd said. Her mouth went as dry and bristly as the rope in her hands.

Dozen looked up at her, assessing her degree of paralysis. "Scared, huh? Don't like tight spaces?" She stood and put a hand on 1408's arm. "Look, this crack has been here for millions of years. It's not going to close up now. Nobody's digging here, disturbing the structure of the rock. This is probably the safest place in the mines."

It was mostly a lie, 1408 knew, but something warmed in her anyway.

"Just look at my feet—unless, of course, you prefer to look at my ass." Dozen grinned at her. "Don't think about anything else. We'll be through and into the cavern in ten minutes. You can stand anything for ten minutes."

Fourteen-oh-eight offered a tentative nod. "Okay."

"Okay. And trust me. It's my job to get you out of this hellhole. Here we go."

Dozen ducked and scrambled through the opening. Fourteen-oh-eight paid out a few feet of rope, then passed through behind her. The rough sides of the passage clawed at her hips and shoulders; the rock tore at her palms and knees as she crawled. The passage twisted and turned, at times so tightly that it seemed her bottom half could not follow her top half around the bends. Her headlamp showed her nothing but her hands, the rope ahead of her and the rock.

The blazer issued a steady stream of instructions and encouragement, punctuated by grunts of effort as she maneuvered through the torturous passageway. Abruptly, the drone of observation ended with an emphatic "Shit!"

"What is it?" Fourteen-oh-eight came to a halt, panting in apprehension.

"Can't see where this goes."

Hysteria rose into her throat, choking the breath out of her. What was left in her lungs came out in a thin, pitiful whine.

Dozen apparently recognized the signs of panic and spoke quickly to reassure her. "Hey, Sphinx, it's okay. There's air in this passage—can't you feel it? It's moving down the tunnel from that cavern the boss told us about, remember? There's an opening. We aren't stuck. Just relax, okay?"

Fourteen-oh-eight willed herself to lift her face and feel the movement of the air. She imagined she could feel it. She thought if she could just believe in it, the draft would become perceptible. She clung to that idea with desperate strength and tried to breathe.

"That air is coming in somewhere." A methodical tapping of pick and hammer against rock started up ahead of her. "I'll find it in a minute. Just hold on."

The metallic tapping continued until one strike sounded a duller note. There was the sound of crumbling rock, of pebbles tumbling. A lifting of dust.

Then a triumphant grunt from Dozen: "Gotcha, you sonofabitch!"

From her prison of stone, 1408 listened as the blazer attacked the hole she'd discovered. She could hear the rock falling away in larger chunks. Then she heard a single word. "Man!" Wonder and admiration filled Dozen's voice.

It had been so long since 1408 had heard those emotions expressed that she almost didn't recognize them. She could not connect the sound of Dozen's voice with any feeling that made sense. Confusion and frustration were her only response. She just wanted to be free of this damn tunnel.

"What do you see?"

"This sucker's huge!" Dozen laughed. "Baby, we are set for days! No scratching away at a fucking rock face for us—we've got exploring to do!"

Dozen contorted her body to turn and look at 1408. She was grinning. "Only problem is, this tunnel comes out close to the top of the cavern wall. It's a long way down to the bottom."

Terror returned to grab 1408 by the throat. "Now what are we supposed to do?"

"No big deal. We rig a rope and rappel down."

"*What*?"

"Don't worry," Dozen tossed off. "It's easy. You'll be fine."

The blazer busied herself with enlarging the exit hole to person-size and hammering in the pitons that would hold the lines. Meanwhile, 1408 lay sprawled in the darkness of the tunnel, sweating with barely controlled panic. She had more than enough time to trace back over her morning, searching for the moment her miserable life had gone off track, until Dozen scrunched around to give her a handful of line strung with weighty clips.

"Hook those up here and here." She indicated rings on her own harness at chest and hips.

Fourteen-oh-eight did as she was told, her hands shaking.

"I'll go first. Don't worry. If I run into trouble, I can haul my ass back up easy enough. Once I'm down, I'll belay you. You won't fall. I'll have hold of the lines from below." Dozen paused to get a look at her rigger's face. "Sphinx, are you listening to me? Nothing can happen. All you have to do is work your way out of the hole feet first and let go. Just try not to move a whole lot and keep yourself away from the wall with your feet. Safe as houses, okay?"

"Okay." Her voice was nothing but a dry rasp.

Fourteen-oh-eight watched in the circle of light from her headlamp as Dozen twisted and rotated again to bring her feet to the tunnel mouth. The tiny woman pushed back with her elbows and rocked her hips to work her way out of the hole. Then she dropped from sight.

Fourteen-oh-eight drew in a terrified breath and held it, anticipating a horrible *crump!* as Dozen fell to the cavern floor. Instead, some seconds later, she heard the blazer call up from below. "Hey, Sphinx! Come on down!"

She worked her way to the tunnel mouth, sensed rather than saw the vast open space beyond. The wisp of air from the cavern was like a howling wind, feeding her fear. She froze, unable to move.

"Sphinx! Come on. You can do this!"

"No! I can't—I can't move."

"Just take it one move at a time. Turn around first. Then you won't even have to look."

Sobbing, she contorted her body to turn around in the tight space. The effort took several minutes and left her panting and sweating. Dozen was right; not having to see the emptiness beyond that opening helped. Still, she felt the panic rising again as she wriggled backwards to send her lower half through the hole. She froze again, numb with terror.

A beam of weak light played around the mouth of the tunnel. "Hey, Sphinx, I see you mooning me. Come on out."

She shook her head, hands scrabbling in the loose rock on the passage floor. "No," she moaned.

"Trust me. You can't fall. Just push out and let yourself hang on the ropes. Keep your feet on the wall."

She knew she could not stay as she was, but the knowledge did her no good. Her arms and legs would not obey the conflicting orders of her panicked mind. The tug of gravity on her lower half was terrifying.

"Okay, you're forcing me to ruin the surprise I had for you." Dozen's voice seemed so far away. "If you don't come down, I won't be able to give it to you."

"What the hell are you talking about?"

"Food, baby. I've got some here for you. But you have to come down."

"You lying bitch!"

"Oh, you think I'm lying? Okay, fuck you. I'll eat this bread myself."

She couldn't help it; she was salivating at the mere mention of food. What if the other woman really had some?

"You don't have any bread."

"Yes, I do. But if you want any, you'll have to come down. And I'd hurry if I were you. Once I unwrap it, I may not be able to stop myself from eating it all."

"Why would you share?"

"Oh, for chrissake! Stay the fuck up there if you want. I'm done talking."

There was a faint jingle of equipment as Dozen made herself comfortable below. Then there was nothing. No sound. No light except the small circle thrown by her own headlamp. Fourteen-oh-eight imagined she could hear Dozen unwrapping the precious food, imagined she could hear her chewing. The remembered smell of bread filled her nostrils, and her mind. Soon even the thought of dropping into the silent darkness was nothing compared to her desire for the promised morsel.

"I'm coming down."

"About fucking time." There was another faint noise from below as the blazer got into position. "Okay. Come on out. Nice and slow."

Sweating, shaking, 1408 inched out of the tunnel mouth, her feet, then her legs bumping the rock face below the opening. Her chest and shoulders cleared the hole, and she felt the harness take the full weight of her body.

"I'm out!"

"I can see you." The reply was calm, matter-of-fact. "I'm going to start lowering. Just hold on and use your feet to keep from swinging into the rock."

Once it began, the trip down was easy. Breathless, her heart pounding, 1408 watched the rock face slip steadily past her. She refused to look down. Instead, she did as she'd been told and worked to hold herself off the wall. In seconds, she was on her feet again on the floor of the cavern.

Dozen grinned and slapped her on the back. "See? You made it!"

Weak-kneed with relief, 1408 could only nod. She let Dozen unhook the lines from her harness. Then she stood, waiting.

Dozen looked up at her. "What?"

She took a step toward the blazer, hands clenched into fists.

Dozen grinned even wider. She pulled something from inside her jumpsuit.

"Oh, you looking for this?" She held out a twist of rag.

Fourteen-oh-eight fell on it and unwrapped it with trembling fingers. Inside the stained cloth was a hunk of dark bread half the size of her fist. She smelled it, nibbled it, then devoured it to the last dry crumb. It was gone in seconds, so quickly she wanted to cry.

"I have a friend on the night guard. He gets me stuff sometimes." Dozen pointed to the metal bottle hanging from 1408's harness. "Have a drink. We've had a thirsty morning."

Fourteen-oh-eight tipped the container back to let the water slide down her throat—and paused in mid-swallow. The light of her headlamp had caught a hint of color and sparkle in a jagged spike hanging from the cavern's distant ceiling.

"Yeah." Dozen nodded. "This place is spectacular. Let's take a look." She pulled something from her pack and aimed it at the far side of the cavern. There was a heavy *thunk* from the tube she held, then a sizzling splash as the projectile hit high up on the wall. Whatever had been in the projectile splattered across the wall and began to glow white against the rock. In seconds the material was giving off enough light to illuminate an area of the cavern four meters square. Dozen reloaded and repeated the process methodically until the full dimension of the space they were in was revealed.

Fourteen-oh-eight stared in awe. The huge dome was washed in color—salmon and coral and pale blue-green—and sparkled with light refracted by trace crystals in the rock. Graceful, tapered columns fell from the roof of the cavern and rose up from its floor; here and there they met to form a fragile latticework of stone, as delicate as glass. The living rock formed flowing curtains and swirling spirals of fanciful color.

The beauty of the place created a hollow ache in 1408's thin chest. She had no words to describe what she saw, no emotions with which to respond to it. She put a hand to her face and was surprised to find it wet with tears. She realized with a start that she had cried more in this one day than she had in—how long? She couldn't remember the last time she had felt anything—anger, longing, desperation, even fear. She had felt them all today. And now there was . . . this.

"The PhosGlow will last 24 hours or so— enough time for us to get back here with some light packs." Dozen threw her bag against a relatively smooth outcropping of rock and stretched out. "We can waste a few days scouting around in here before they expect us to find a way through to the crystal vein."

She waved at the floor beside her. "Relax. We got all day now."

Fourteen-oh-eight lowered herself uncertainly to the floor. The concept of idleness was foreign to her; there had always been a guard at her back to make sure she was working. Days on the cutting face were a blur of unrelenting labor; nights in the barracks were a fog of exhaustion, cold and hunger. She couldn't remember another life, a time that might have included rest and warmth and the opportunity to—what was the word?—*relax*.

Dozen pointed at a sinuous river of blood-red crystal running across one quarter of the far wall. "See there? That's what the fuss is all about. The Grays can't live without the focusing effects of those crystals—most of their technology depends on them. But, *oh, hell!* There's some kind of psychotropic fungus inside that drives the little bastards crazy until it's refined out. So us dumbass humans have to do the scut work for them and dig the shit out of this godforsaken planet."

When 1408 said nothing, Dozen went on, her voice bitter. "That's what started all this mess, anyhow, generations back. Then they discovered we were useful in so many other ways. I mean, why expose yourself to toxic chemicals or harsh working conditions or, hell, just plain old hard work when you can get big, strong humans to do it for you?"

Fourteen-oh-eight looked at her companion in utter confusion. She had no idea what the woman was talking about. She sat hugging her knees, her mind full of unformed questions.

One question coalesced at last. "Why did you bring me here?"

"Here?" Dozen repeated. "You mean here on this job?"

When she said nothing more, Dozen shrugged. "Because I had a feeling about you. And it looked like you could use a friend."

"I don't even know what that word means." She scowled, annoyed by a conversation—no, a relationship—that increasingly made no sense.

"Maybe it's time you learned."

Suddenly 1408 was angry, a charge of unaccustomed emotion exploding up through her consciousness to erupt in blinding fury. "What the hell do you want from me? You come to me, you bring me here. What the hell do you want?"

Dozen shook her head. "Nothing."

"Bullshit! Everyone wants something!" She jumped to her feet and paced with short, stiff steps, remembering how her day had started with pain and humiliation. She whirled on Dozen, thrusting an accusing finger in her direction. "You saw who did it! This morning. You saw. Who was it?"

"Yeah, I saw. So what?"

"Who?"

The smaller woman got up and came in close. "What difference does it make, Sphinx? What are you going to do, jump her?"

"My business. And don't call me that!"

It was Dozen's turn to get angry. "You prefer a number? Fourteen-oh-eight—the number *they* gave you when they stole everything else from you. Or maybe you remember your real name—the one everyone's forgotten, the one you had before."

"Before?" Her hands fisted. "There is no before. I don't remember anything but this . . . this hell."

Dozen watched her, saying nothing.

Fourteen-oh-eight clutched her head as a wave of pain crashed through it. She moaned and sank to the floor under the weight of the pain and the confusion.

"I don't understand."

"You will." Dozen placed a warm hand on her shoulder. "Give it time. And meanwhile, as your friend, I have one piece of advice for you: stay away from Marge."

She raised her head. "Who?"

Dozen smiled tightly. "That's just what I call her. Number's 1540. She's the one who took your grub this morning. She's big, she's mean, and she has a gang of little helpers. I don't think you were a deliberate target—you were just an opportunity. Don't let her get in the habit of finding you. Stay out of her sight."

It was good advice—1408 could see the wisdom in it. Her anger was impotent, useless, even dangerous. Still, it sustained her in a way despair never could. She fed it to the engine of her survival, and waited, Sphinx-like.

CHAPTER FIVE

"All right, Asia. We're done for today. Open your eyes."

I blinked and squinted into a room filled with late afternoon light—as bright as the caves had been dark. The contrast stunned me.

"Do you recognize where you are?"

His voice, coming from somewhere just above my head, was deep and soothing. My mind would not supply a name for the voice. I waited, hoping he would say something else.

He must have read the question in my face. "It's Ethan Roberts. You're in my office. Do you remember now?"

I struggled to sit up, felt his hand slip behind my back to help me. The room—and his face—began to come into focus. "Yes, I remember. I must have really been out."

Ethan nodded, a puzzled smile on his lips. "It was a remarkable session. Do you remember what you told me?"

The images were clear in my mind. It was as if I had been transported instantly from that universe to this one.

"It felt so real."

He didn't try to hide the excitement in his voice. "Have your dreams always been so vivid?"

"No. This didn't feel like a dream."

"Part of that is the effect of the machine. But part of it . . ." He stopped and shook his head. "How often do you have this dream?"

I rubbed my face. "Every night, if I don't take those pills you gave me."

"And how do you feel afterwards?"

"I wake up screaming. But . . ." I looked at him, a frown creasing my forehead. "I could never remember any of it before today. Doesn't seem so scary now that I can remember it."

Ethan studied my face. "There's more to the dream than what you remembered today. I had to bring you out of it; we've been working for hours."

That explained the light. It had been morning when we'd started. I hadn't fully believed him when he'd said to set aside most of my Saturday.

"The people in this . . . prison . . . with you—the guards and so on—did they seem like everyday people you'd meet on the street? Or was there something different about them?"

I met his gaze. He was watching, waiting. What was it he expected me to say?

Then I realized. "No. Dozen could have been my neighbor. She was just like you or me. But the others . . ." I shook my head. I refused to say the word, though it was there in my head. *Alien.*

"Sit still for a while." He left his chair. "Let me get

you some tea, something to eat. Can't have you passing out on your way home." He spoke to Cindy across the hall. I heard her footsteps retreat to someplace in the back of the house.

I liked the idea of letting him fuss over me a little. It was sweet, in a way. Homey. And I had to admit I was worn out, as if I really had been working all day instead of lying on a couch in his office.

Cindy came back in a few minutes with a hot mug of fragrant tea and a sandwich neatly presented on a plate with a napkin. He took it from her at the door and set it on the table in front of the couch.

"Thanks. Another of Grandma's brews?"

He shook his head with a little smile. "Plain old green tea and honey. Didn't want to scare you off with the exotic stuff."

"Mmm." The tea was light on the green and heavy on the honey, just the way I liked it. How did he know? I made short work of the sandwich, hardly pausing to take a breath.

All the while he watched me with those eyes as blue and unfathomable as Northern seas. When I had recovered enough to notice, the attention began to warm me in places that hadn't been warm in a long, long time.

I searched a little frantically around the room for a source of small talk. My eyes lit on a framed medical degree from Cornell. I put that together with his Cree grandmother and took a shot.

"So, what's a Yankee boy like you doing down here in Nashville?"

The smile widened. "Let me guess—my accent's a

dead giveaway."

"Well, there is that. But you mentioned upstate New York and . . ." I pointed at the degree behind his head.

"Ah."

I waited, and when the answer wasn't forthcoming, I pressed. "Nashville's a long way from where? Albany? Buffalo?"

"I grew up in Syracuse; got here by way of Baltimore. Arthur Claussen recruited me from Johns Hopkins."

Something in the way he said it made me think there was more to the story, but there was a warning in the set of his jaw. "You no longer work for him?"

"No. I'm on my own now."

"I see." I retreated into my mug of tea.

Since this line of questioning was leading nowhere, I decided to try another. "So what about family, Ethan? Everybody back in New York?" I didn't see a ring on his finger and there was no evidence of a significant other in the house, but you never knew. The real question was, what business was it of mine?

His lips lifted as if he knew what I was up to, but the smile didn't make it to his eyes. Those eyes caught mine and held them, his gaze somber and wary except for one fleeting second when they flashed hot with something that seemed so much like desire my heart stopped. I watched him, fascinated, waiting to hear what he would say.

"I have a brother and a sister in New York," he said at last. "I was married to a Nashville girl. She died in a car accident two years ago."

Ethan fought to hide a cold tremor in every muscle, appalled at his lack of control. Why the hell had he told her that? He could have stopped at "brother and sister"; she would have been satisfied with that. This was only small talk, after all, wasn't it?

But there was something in those golden-brown eyes that watched him so intently, something that even now made him want to tell her everything, though he could see she was already overwhelmed with the little he'd shared. Her hand moved a fraction, as if she wanted to reach out to him. He ached for the comfort that small movement offered.

"Oh, God, Ethan. I'm sorry. I had no idea."

He shook his head and found a smile. "How could you? It was a long time ago."

She frowned. "Not so long ago." She looked around. "You don't keep pictures of her."

It wasn't a question, but he answered it anyway. "Not in my office, no."

Her expression changed, as if she understood. He doubted she did. He didn't display pictures of Elizabeth anywhere in his house, for reasons he was not about to share. At any rate, this conversation had gone way beyond the bounds of appropriate doctor-patient interaction. It was past time for him to end it.

He made himself look down at his watch. "How are you feeling?"

She got the hint and stood. "I'm good to go now." She was pale, though, and subdued. His fault. "Thanks for the snack."

"My pleasure." He walked her to the door. "I think we need another session with AL as soon as possible. Can you make it on a weekday afternoon?"

She looked up at him and grinned. His breath caught in his throat. It was as if the sun had just emerged from behind a thundercloud.

"Is dinner included next time?"

"I'll order pizza." He was barely able to keep his voice level, his demeanor professional. "How about Tuesday at 4:00?"

"Works for me. See you then."

He closed the door behind her. He made himself breathe. He sent Cindy home as if it were any other day. Then he ran a hand through his hair and paced into his office to face the shambles of his world.

What Asia had shown him today shook the very foundations of his sense of reality. If he didn't get a tighter grip on what he knew to be the truth, it just might slip away from him in a rush of wonder. The vivid, horrifying details of the world in Asia's dreams—the hunger and fear; the black confines of the mines; the way Dozen's reckless energy had brought Asia's flat persona to life—were as clear to him as if he had been there himself. He could see that world because Asia had described it precisely under the influence of the alpha wave generator.

AL had the opposite effect on most of his patients. Their "memories" of midnight abductions and ghastly experiments and little gray men with big black eyes gradually eroded under the influence of the machine and his own gentle suggestions. The details dropped from the narratives, the colors muted and faded, until the patients could hardly imagine what had disturbed them so profoundly just a few weeks before.

Asia's dreams included no spaceships or aliens of the kind Ethan was used to hearing about. What she described was day after day of servitude, not a few hours of probing and pain. The setting of her dream, at once familiar and foreign, was consistent, even logical. The narrative was sequential, not sporadic or leapfrogging from moment to illuminated moment. In fact, it was not like a dream at all. Her description had emerged more like a genuine traumatic memory being relived under standard hypnosis.

He blew out a breath in frustration. How could she have a memory of a place that couldn't exist? Other than the undeniable effects of sleeplessness, Asia herself didn't believe the elements of her dream were capable of affecting her in waking life. She didn't collect "alien" toys or watch science fiction movies for "clues" or read the *National Enquirer* for the "real" news.

She wasn't like his other patients. And his reaction to her was unlike his reaction to any of his other patients.

Ethan had been trained to stand outside himself and be objective. From where he stood he could see he was under assault, both body and soul. His professional objectivity was in serious jeopardy. He was attracted to his patient—God, was he attracted to her. His body's response to the thought of her was intense and immediate. He rationalized that he could hardly be blamed for the purely biological reaction of a healthy male to an attractive young female, but he knew it wasn't appropriate for a psychiatrist to be carrying a permanent aching hard-on for his patient, either.

And that wasn't the worst of it. The real danger was that Asia had slipped through all the barriers he'd so carefully erected to protect himself. She'd made him want things from her he had no right to ask. By merely beginning an innocent conversation, she had opened a floodgate of emotion that should have remained firmly closed. The realization drew a frustrated groan from deep in his chest and sent him striding across the worn oak of his office floor in agitation.

Ethan took a deep breath and struggled to set his feelings aside. Asia was his patient; he needed a way to help her. Unlike conventional psychotherapy, the AL protocol called for him to find a weakness in the patient's delusion as the entry point for his counterbalancing suggestions. He hadn't found one yet in Asia's story. He would have to hear the whole fantasy before he found a toehold for reality. With a thrill of emotion somewhere between anticipation and dread, Ethan acknowledged that task was likely to take some time.

He felt a familiar tightening in his groin as his body showed it was clearly pleased at the prospect. He released a breath that was almost a growl. "Oh, God, Asia. You're killing me."

By the time I got home I'd already called myself an idiot for my behavior with Ethan; enough that I was tired of it. The Outlaw Jesse James took up the challenge, though, offended that I hadn't been there to top up his Meow Mix or entertain him sufficiently, this being a Saturday and all. I gave JJ some love, poured myself a big glass of cabernet, and went to run water for a long, hot bath.

While the tub filled, I paced the living room, trying to make sense of the story that had played out in my mind, under the influence of Ethan's machine. That place—it was like no place on Earth, but it was as recognizable as the skyline outside my window. And the woman who'd helped me—Dozen—I knew her better than I knew Rita or Sherry or anyone else in this world. How could that be? A dream couldn't be that real, could it? But if it wasn't a dream—

I shook my head and set the thought aside. I was too tired to think about it anymore. Besides, everything else that had happened that afternoon needed consideration. I stripped off my clothes and settled into the tub, letting the bubbles and the warmth leach the tension from my muscles. Then I let my mind wander over what had passed between me and Ethan.

I wasn't sure, but it seemed like the kind of exchange we'd had went way beyond what was supposed to happen between doctor and patient.

That was your fault.

Damn it. What did I think I was trying to do, anyway?

You know.

Yeah, I knew. I'd wanted to know what his status was. Was there someone else who had a claim on him? Turns out there was—and she held the most heartbreaking, most unassailable claim of all. A claim I had no business challenging, even if I wasn't Ethan's patient. My heart twisted in my chest, thinking of the way his eyes had burned with cobalt fire when he'd told me. Grief and guilt nearly as flammable as my own fed that fire. He'd be a long time extinguishing the flames, and any woman who got too near him in the meantime was likely to get burned.

So how could I have glimpsed something else in his eyes? Had I imagined fire of another kind sparking in the space between us, smoldering under the surface of his skin—and mine?

He's a man. Past or no past, he's gonna act like one.

Yes, Lord, he was. And the thought of treating him like a man was driving me to absolute distraction. The suspicion that he might respond to being treated that way—that he might need it as much as I did— was tempting to the point of intoxication.

I longed to step inside that circle of professional distance he'd created to keep us apart, to be close enough to dissolve his pain and mine in the steamy heat we could create between us. I wanted to slip my hands under that soft, loose shirt, to slide them over the smooth skin of his chest, his back, his belly. I wanted to lift the fabric over his head so I could have the pleasure of looking at him half-naked, the hard muscles under the pale skin, the breath rising and falling in his chest.

In my fantasy now I'm naked, completely so, and I

wrap my arms around his neck so I can press my aching breasts to his chest. His arms enfold me and hold me close. The denim of his jeans is rough against my skin, but I don't mind; I can feel the hot ridge of his erection behind it, and that's what I crave. His hands slide down to my ass to press me against him. I moan, encouraging him. He bends to kiss me, his unshaven cheek scratching my face. His tongue carries his taste into my mouth—sweet, hot, demanding.

His hands, warm and strong, sweep up my sides to cup my breasts, his thumbs coaxing the nipples to taut attention beneath his touch. Blood pulses between my legs in response, flooding me with need. I'm desperate for the feel of his hands, his tongue, his—

"God *damn* it!" My fantasy shattered as JJ leaped onto the edge of the tub and skittered across the wet surface. Water geysered out of the tub as I bolted upright, sputtering and cursing, and pushed the cat back off onto the bathroom floor. He took a moment to glare at me and shake himself in disgust before sauntering out of the room, his intrusive work done.

"Stupid freaking animal!" I took a breath, trying to calm my heart, pounding now for more than one reason. But it was no good. My pulse was still reverberating deep inside with an ache of desire for a man I knew I could never have. I groaned with frustration.

"Oh, God, Ethan. You're killing me."

I had to admit I had a hard time looking Ethan in the eye when I arrived for Tuesday's session. Some evil part of my personality insisted on directing my gaze below his belt, and my fevered imagination supplied a larger than usual bulge in his weathered jeans when that gaze happened to land in the right spot. Ethan himself seemed a little nervous that day. I could only think I'd made him uncomfortable with my questions the last time. I put a leash on my bad girl and made an effort to behave.

He started in once I'd settled in on the couch. "Have you been sleeping any better?"

"Those pills are like falling into a black hole." I wasn't complaining. "But if I stopped taking them, the dreams would come back, wouldn't they?"

"I suspect so. Until we figure out what's causing the dreams."

"What kind of weird symbolism can it be anyway? Slave labor? Mines? Crystals? I mean, I know sometimes a cigar is just a cigar, but this?" I'd been trying to puzzle it out all weekend and my frustration was showing. Something so richly detailed, yet it made no sense.

Ethan shook his head, and I could see he was choosing his words very carefully. Either he had no idea, or he was afraid to say what he thought.

"The human mind is a wonderful thing, Asia. Creative. Imaginative. Devious. Playful. Protective of its owner in the extreme. Any or all of those things may be at work here."

"But nothing about what I remembered Saturday was particularly frightening. Unpleasant, yes, but . . .

why do I wake up screaming?"

He met my eyes. "I don't know, Asia. We have to keep looking. Are you ready?"

I took a breath and swung my legs up onto the couch. "Hook me up, Doc."

Fourteen-oh-eight huddled in a shivering mass under the thin blanket. The cold seeped into her bones, contracting her muscles as they tried in vain to hold onto her body heat. In the unquiet dark of the barracks, the others snuffled and rasped in sleep or cried out in dreams. Yet, despite the depth of her fatigue, 1408 could not find her own way to oblivion.

If it had not been so cold, she wouldn't have minded. Her day in the cavern with Dozen had given her so many new things—extraordinary things—to think about. The play of light off the crystalline walls, the arch of stone high overhead, the colors splashed over the rock at her feet—these alone were enough to lift her mind above the squalor of the camp.

But Dozen—there was a puzzle to challenge her stupor and awaken her dulled senses. Dozen was like no one else she had encountered here. (Here? As opposed to where? She could not remember any other place.) The tiny woman was alive with an energy no one else seemed to possess. She saw, she felt, she knew things in a way 1408 was now aware she herself could not. Comparing herself to the blazer made her feel stupid and slow. She should have resented it, but instead she felt the stirring of something that had lain dormant so long she hardly recognized it. She was curious, intrigued. For the first time she could remember, 1408 actually looked forward to living another day.

She turned over in her bunk, willing herself to sleep. She had nearly drifted off when the door at the end of the barracks hall banged open. She jumped, but struggled to stay still, lifeless, hidden. Even with her eyes tightly closed she knew that the light in the doorway revealed the silhouette of one or more of the guards. She could hear his progress down the row of bunks—heavy-footed, clumsy with drink, cursing as he stumbled into bunk frames along the way.

Was it one like her? She prayed it was one of the others—she was too thin and pale for them. There were only a few guards that had the small nose and ears, the smooth, light skin of her kind. Most nights it was one of the others. They blundered into the bunks around hers and grabbed the women sleeping there. The bigger women—2217 or 1530—went with them without complaint. The guards usually chuckled and staggered out with their prizes, leaving the barracks quiet again, and relieved.

But tonight was different. Tonight the guard was one named Tomar—tall and angular, his skin the color of the gruel that served as food. He was of her kind, and he had chosen others of her kind from the barracks before. But not her, never her. She cowered under the blanket and did not dare to breathe.

It did no good. It was as if he had chosen her before he even came to the barracks, as if he'd come looking just for her. He loomed over her bunk.

"Fourteen-oh-eight. Come with me."

There was no use resisting. She would only be beaten and then taken. She had seen it happen to others. The barracks might be full of women, but the guards were all male. There would be no sympathy—and no help—from them. Quivering, she slipped out from under the blanket and pulled on her boots.

"Hurry up. I don't have all night." He waited another ten seconds, then turned and stalked back toward the barracks door, expecting her to follow him. She did, her heart thundering. In the light from the corridor she saw faces turned in her direction, saw apathy, fear, even envy. Envy? For the crumb of food she would be given in exchange for the brutality she would endure?

She followed the man across the quad to another building, not the guards' quarters, as she expected, but a storage shed behind it. He opened the door and pushed her inside, into a dark as profound as that of the mines. The door slammed behind them, then his body pressed hard up against hers.

"You're nothing but bones." His breath was sour in her face. "Still, I guess you'll have to do."

His fingers entwined in her hair and yanked her head back, exposing her neck. He licked at her skin, causing a shiver of revulsion to bleed from the agony of her scalp down her spine. She stumbled, nearly losing her footing as he pulled her back against him. His hips slammed against hers, grinding his erection into her backside.

His cruel laughter was in her ear. "Don't worry. You'll be on your knees soon enough."

He ripped at the fastening of her jumpsuit, stuck a cold hand inside to grope her breast. His panting breath became a grunt, and after a moment he released her hair. He backed away slightly, fumbling in the dark. With his clothes? She didn't know. She didn't want to guess. She stood blindly, shaking, and waited for the assault.

It never came.

She heard a rustle of movement, a crack of bones twisted beyond human tolerance and a stifled scream. Then she heard a snarl, deep and low.

"This one is mine, Tomar. I told you that. I paid the camp director for the privilege."

"Bullshit!" Tomar hissed and spat, his voice distorted with pain. "That much . . . ah, *shalssit*! . . . for a mine cunt?"

"You believe what you want to believe, but if I see you near her again, I'll cut your dick off. And no one will give a shit if I do."

"And once I report you for breaking my

fucking arm?"

"You're right. Maybe I should just kill you now and throw you down the mine shaft. Save myself a lot of trouble later."

More movement. Another muffled whine. "Okay, okay, I get it. *Baraz!* What is it about this bitch anyway? She's as thin as a stick."

"That's my business. Get your ass out of here."

She heard the door to the shed open and frigid air brushed her as Tomar stumbled past. Then it closed and there was nothing but the dark—and the stranger who now owned her. She drew her prison rags together over her breasts, fighting nausea at the memory of Tomar's hands on her.

She heard a *scritch* in the darkness, and a small pool of light flared—a tiny light cell in the hands of the man who had saved her. He held it up so she could see his face. She recognized one of the other guards, another that looked like her, except for eyes the color of a cat's, with no whites around the outside.

"My name is Mose. I'm a friend of Dozen's."

She watched him, waiting.

He nodded as if he understood. "Are you all right? Did he hurt you?"

She shook her head. "I'm okay."

He took a step forward, but she backed up and he stopped. "I have some food for you." He took a small package out of his jacket pocket and held it out to her.

Her mouth watered, but she stayed where she was.

"No strings attached."

Somewhere in the deep recesses of her mind, that phrase made sense. The meaning flitted back and forth there like the shadow of a lamp on a cavern wall.

"No strings," she repeated.

He exhaled slowly. "Sphinx. That's what Dozen calls you, right?"

She nodded.

He smiled. "I can see why. I'm here to help you. Dozen asked me to look after you. When Tomar went down to the barracks tonight I followed him."

"You didn't pay for me?"

"Well, yes. I did."

"What?" Her question indicated only confusion, not outrage. The limits of her life left no room for that kind of emotion.

"The people we work with are looking out for you," he explained. "We can't do it for everyone, but we do it for a few."

"Why?"

His eyes glowed. "Because you resist them, Sphinx, though you don't know it."

None of what he was saying made sense. Her mind simply would not process it.

She moved toward the door. "I have to go back."

He offered the package again. "Aren't you going to take this?"

Her stomach gurgled. She reached out and took the package from him, tore it open.

"Oh, my God." The grateful words tumbled from her lips when she saw what it was. She smelled the small cube of cheese, put the delicious morsel in her mouth, chewed and swallowed around the tears that threatened to choke her.

He smiled, his cat eyes bright. "I can bring you some more in a few shifts. Next time I'll come for you myself—keep up the pretense that you're my, uh, lover. That okay with you?"

She nodded, savoring the taste of the cheese in her mouth. Later, curled in her bunk in the freezing barracks, she could still taste the tangy, nutty flavor of that cheese on her tongue as she drifted off to sleep.

"Asia?" The voice was familiar, but I couldn't quite place it. "Asia, wake up. Tell me where you are."

I looked up, saw Ethan hovering over me with concern swirling like a dark storm in his eyes. "Ethan? What's wrong?"

The frown between his eyebrows relaxed. It took him a moment to say anything. "Are you all right?"

I attempted to sit up, but he put a hand firmly on my shoulder. "Stay put a minute."

"How am I supposed to tell you if I'm okay if I can't even sit up?" I frowned, annoyed.

"This was a rough session. Do you remember any of it?"

I thought back and began to shake. "I remember everything." The taste of the cheese was still in my mouth. "Do you think I could get some of that tea?"

Ethan looked at me closely. "Sure. I'll be right back."

When Ethan brought the tea back, I sat up and wrapped my cold hands around the mug. I blew my breath across the surface, watching the rising steam scatter and reform. I couldn't get warm enough, and the shivering was sloshing the tea over my fingers. Ethan gave me a napkin to wrap around the mug and draped a blanket around my shoulders.

"I didn't fight him." My face reddened with shame. "It never even occurred to me to fight him."

"You were afraid of being beaten. You had seen others beaten and raped. You had no hope that fighting would save you. There's no shame in wanting to avoid a brutal beating, Asia. What you were ready to do took courage enough."

"But that's . . . that's not like me. I was so different there." I shook my head. "Everything was so different."

"Is it really so surprising to find things are different in a dream? Even certain aspects of your personality?"

Anger flared. "No! *They* had altered my personality."

He stared at me, unformed questions drawing his brows together.

"And this can't be a dream."

He took a breath. "Why not, Asia?"

I met his eyes. "Because if this was a dream, I

wouldn't be able to remember all the times Mose helped me. How kind he was." Grief blew through me like a bitter wind.

Ethan caught my shudder. "He became . . . important to you. A lover?"

I shook my head. "He was my friend, my protector. Until word came one night that he'd been killed in a tunnel collapse. An accident, they said."

Ethan watched my every move as I talked—my eyes, my hands, the way I held my body. There was an intensity about him, as if just below his skin he was vibrating wildly, though he was as calm and deliberate as always.

When I stopped talking he simply asked me, "You *remember* these things?"

"As if they happened yesterday." I leaned forward. "How can that be, Ethan?"

He opened his mouth to speak, but no words came out. He shook his head. "There is no logical explanation for it."

"So you're saying I'm crazy." For some reason, I wasn't angry. I was almost relieved.

"Delusional would be the correct term," he said absently, his gaze directed out the window. "But these are like no delusions I've ever encountered. Except once."

He seemed fascinated by the puzzle I presented, but at a loss for what to do about me. I wasn't sure whether to feel sorrier for him or for me.

"What do we do now?"

He exhaled and met my gaze again. "Try again in a few days? Every session gives us new information to work with. We can only hope sometime soon there'll be a clue to all of this."

I nodded. Suddenly I was exhausted, my body and my mind feeling bruised and battered as if I'd been only recently liberated from that labor camp. And my heart—my heart felt newly broken for the friend I'd met and lost in the space of an afternoon. What I wanted more than anything else in the world was for someone—anyone—to hold me, just for a minute. It seemed like forever since I'd felt the warmth of human touch.

I looked at Ethan. "You know, this is probably completely out of line, but I really need a hug right now. Would you mind?"

His face softened in sympathy as he slid next to me on the couch. He gathered me in and held me close, his chest warm against my cheek, his heartbeat steady under my ear. He smelled wonderful, like citrus and spice and something uniquely his own. He didn't seem to mind that my tears soaked his soft knit tee-shirt through to the skin below. He held me until I had given up all my grief for a life neither he nor I could explain.

When I was done he handed me tissues and offered me the bathroom to freshen up. Then he sent me home with plenty of questions, but no answers.

CHAPTER SIX

Ethan closed the door behind Asia and went to find a glass and the bottle of Maker's Mark that he kept in a cabinet over the dishwasher. The hand pouring the drink shook, and he knew it wasn't because he was tired. No, not tired, beat to shit. Or because his leg hurt. Hurt? It was fucking killing him. Or even because he hadn't eaten anything since breakfast—he'd had back-to-back clients since 10:00 a.m. and it was now 8:15 p.m.

He knocked back the bourbon, hissing against the fiery trail it burned into his stomach, and poured another three fingers' worth. Then he made himself a sandwich and carried it into the den. He eased himself into the recliner and hit the remote, surfed idly for a few minutes before settling on a soccer match between two Caribbean teams, and sat staring at the screen, not watching at all while his mind reeled from the events of the day.

That bastard had almost raped her. That fucking bastard had put his filthy hands on her and . . . *Jesus Christ!* Ethan couldn't stand the thought of what she'd been through in that place. And then . . . God, he wanted to scream in frustration. He wanted to go back in time. He wanted to kill that asshole Tomar for touching her. God help him, he even wanted to challenge Mose for the right to be the one to save her. For chrissake, he shouldn't even believe her, and yet his emotional response was out of control. He felt like a freaking Neanderthal.

And the way she'd felt as he'd held her, soft and yielding against his body. He'd gone hard the second he touched her, and he was sure that no amount of delicate maneuvering could have hidden that fact from her. She'd smelled so good—sweet and exotic, a scent that intoxicated him as he breathed it in and made him want to bury his face between her breasts. It had been all he could do to keep from running his hands through her hair, tipping her face to his, kissing her full lips.

Ethan shook his head, trying to free himself of the images that threatened to drown him in a sensuality he knew was forbidden. He took a mental step back, reaching for an objectivity that was slipping from his grasp, and tried to determine how Asia had been reacting to *him*. If she was beginning to transfer her emotions onto him . . . but, no, he didn't see any evidence of it. The experience she'd relived today had been traumatic, devastating. The emotional exhaustion, the grief, the need for comfort had been legitimate and most likely temporary.

"Jesus, she even recognized that it crossed a boundary and asked permission," he muttered. "How well-adjusted is that? I'm the one with the transference problem." One that he needed to get under control.

He forced himself to consider a less volatile aspect of the case. Only to find yet another trap. *I can't help her*, he thought, and the thought wouldn't let him go any more than his earlier one. She still wanted to know where those three hours had gone, and he had no more idea than she did. Probably never would.

All this time, all this work, and it'll end up just like Ida Mickens.

Though he was well aware he shouldn't think of them in this way, Ethan had accumulated several "failures" in his five years of private practice. People he'd been unable to help. People who had given up before they'd broken through to healing. But he'd had only one other patient he could compare to Asia.

Ida Mickens had been nearly 80 years old when she'd made the 300-mile trip from West Virginia to see him. Mrs. Mickens had said her home was "so far back up in the hills you have to pass the middle of nowhere to get there." How she'd found him was still a mystery. She merely said she'd prayed on it, and one of those articles mentioning his name had found its way into her hands.

Mrs. Mickens had been plagued with "visions" since she was a little girl. She made it known this wasn't "the sight," which would have been a tolerable gift of God of some use to her family and neighbors. Her visions had nothing to do with life in her tiny mountain community. Instead they showed her a world of suffering and pain far from West Virginia: vast stretches of stinking yellow mud under a green sky. Fields of head-high plants with thick, oozing stems and leaves so sharp they gashed the skin. Tribes of children with hands lacerated by the work of harvesting sticky globes from the plants and adults with backs and limbs distorted by years of the same work and worse.

She had come to Ethan to be rid of the visions. They worked with AL for days without results. The money the old woman had brought for living expenses didn't last long. Ethan asked his friend Dan and his family to put her up. She baked them biscuits every morning, and every afternoon they tried again. The work only served to bring out more details of the horrible place she imagined. After weeks of failure, they gave up.

"Don't fret over it, son," she told him when he put her on the bus for home. "Reckon I was meant to remember for a reason. I just hope I live long enough to learn what it is."

Of course, Ethan had worried about it. For months he questioned whether he had the power to help anyone. Dozens of successes gradually rebuilt his confidence, but he still thought of Ida Mickens on his bad days. Days like today.

He exhaled and stared at the ceiling in frustration. There was still another thought circling his brain demanding recognition, one that was even crazier. One that began *What if* . . .

What if Asia was telling the truth? What if she really had experienced all the things she described? What if the world she described was real?

He shook his head. "No," he said aloud.

What he was thinking was not possible by the laws

of nature as he understood them. *Where was this so-called world?* he asked himself. *How could she have gotten there and back? And when? The narrative of her life is complete except for three hours. Are we saying that she experienced all these things in the space of three hours of "real time" here on Earth?*

"That's ridiculous."

Okay, how about a past life? he proposed. *People claim to have them all the time.* There was even less evidence to support that theory. And it didn't help explain the missing hours. Shirley MacLaine was going to be no help on this one.

So, we're back to the theory of another world in this life. His mind skidded away from the obvious explanation, the one many of his clients would offer without hesitation. Still it kept intruding, and he was forced to consider it. The weird thing was that Asia herself hadn't mentioned it—not once in all of their sessions, except as a joke when she'd teased him about that article she'd read.

He slammed the recliner down and stalked into the kitchen. "So I'm supposed to tell this beautiful, bright, *incredibly sexy* woman that my explanation for what happened to her is that she was abducted by aliens." He stared at his reflection in the kitchen window. "Sure. That'll go over great."

Better than telling her you have no clue how to help her, his reflection answered.

God, he was miserable. His leg ached, despite the bourbon. He picked up the bottle of Vicodin from beside the sink and contemplated it for a long moment. No refills, it said. He had meant it when he'd told Dan Parker he didn't intend to get a new script, but there were only five pills left. He felt the deprivation already, the need to hoard, to "save up" for those times when he wouldn't be able to do without. Was this one of those times?

No, he decided. He would try to do without tonight. Maybe the bourbon—and the exhaustion—would be enough.

Elizabeth's voice on the other end of the line was jittery and shrill, the effect, Ethan suspected, of too much caffeine ingested to compensate for too little sleep. She'd screamed herself awake again last night and refused to let him comfort her. It had become a pattern for them.

"What is it, Liz? I'm just about to go in with a patient."

"So what else is new? In fact, that's what I'm calling about. You haven't scheduled anything after four today have you?"

He sighed. "Elizabeth, you know I have a standing appointment every Friday at four. I'll be done by five."

"Damn it, Ethan, this is important. Cancel the fucking appointment. I want you home in time to change. We need to be there *on time* for once."

He started to cave, then found he had a backbone after all. "No. Pick me up at the office. I'll change here. I was going to get the tux on the way home, but I'll send Cindy out for it at lunch instead. We'll make it in plenty of time."

There was a moment of silence on the other end of the line. "Fine. I'll see you at five. But if you're one minute late coming out that door, I'm leaving your ass. You can take a taxi." The line went dead.

Ethan woke with a gasp, his heart racing in his chest. He raised his head to look at the clock. Just past two in the morning. *Fuck*. He shifted to ease the ache in his thigh and tried not to think about the day his mind had dredged up as the subject of his dreams. He concentrated on his breath, consciously relaxing his muscles. He thought of the lake house where he'd spent summers as a kid. And gradually his eyes closed, his mind let go.

His 4:00 appointment sat across from him on the worn leather couch and told him, "This can't be a dream."

"Why not, Asia?" Even as he said her name he knew there was something wrong about it. The time was off, or the place, or she wasn't the person he should be talking to. But it didn't seem to matter at the moment. All that mattered were those golden-brown eyes of hers. The way she used them to look right into him, to see him the way no one else seemed to see him.

"Because it's too real." Her smoky Southern blues voice was barely above a whisper. "I can feel everything as if it's really happening."

He realized with a shock that it was the same for him—that the warm breeze coming in the open window was like a caress on his skin, that it carried the light, sweet scent of her for him to breathe in, that her scent and her nearness were sending the blood to his groin in a searing rush. His mouth was suddenly dry and wordless.

The spell was shattered by the blaring of a car horn from the driveway. Elizabeth.

Asia started and turned to look out the window. "Guess my time's up, huh?"

He glanced at the clock with a frown. "You've got five more minutes."

She stood. "That's okay. Looks like you've got somewhere to be."

But Elizabeth was impatient. She turned the car around with a spray of gravel and peeled out of the drive without a second look.

Again, Ethan knew in the way of dreams that things had happened differently two years ago. And again, he didn't care. This was a dream. No matter how real it felt.

"Looks like now I don't have anywhere to be but here." His heartbeat accelerated at the thought.

Asia knelt in front of his chair, placed her hands on top of his knees. He could feel her warmth through his jeans. Her eyes were full of—was that sympathy?—as she looked up at him. "You're not happy. You haven't been for a long time."

He swallowed back the emotion that rose to close off his throat. "No," was all he said.

She began to move her hands, sliding up and down the tops of his quads, her thumbs squeezing gently on the sensitive muscles of the inside of his thighs. He inhaled a shaky breath.

Her head tilted. "Why do you stay?"

"She needs my help." Though he knew it had done no good.

"It wasn't your fault." Her right palm skimmed the hardening flesh of his erection.

"That's what they say." The words ended in a gasp as she rolled his aching cock against his thigh. "Jesus, Asia."

"Shh. Let me take care of you."

He watched, the muscles of his stomach clenching, as she unbuckled and unzipped him, freed him from his jeans and welcomed him into the cradle of her hands. He bucked at her touch, his hips arching with need as she stroked him.

"Asia," he whispered. A plea. A prayer.

"Ethan." Her voice was thick with desire. "We both want this. Don't hold back." Then she rose over his hips and took him into her mouth, sending an arrow of intense sensation from his balls straight up his spine. He came within seconds . . .

. . . and woke still pulsing, the evidence of his pleasure wet on the skin of his belly. Groaning, he curled in on himself, his cock still aching. He didn't know whether to laugh or cry. He hadn't had a wet dream since college. And this—God, *this* had to be the most inappropriate wet dream of all time. She was his *patient*, for chrissake!

The blood pounded in his groin, his erection refusing to flag despite his orgasm. His mind might acknowledge the rules that set clear and inviolate boundaries between him and Asia Burdette. His body clearly did not give a fuck.

Parking was at a premium outside Ethan's bungalow the afternoon of my next appointment. I was early; his three o'clock appointment—a beat-up Camry I recognized—was still parked in the driveway next to a late-model Cadillac. I found a spot for my Civic on the street and took my time coming up the walk to the front door, knowing I had some extra time. I was quiet when I came in, too, trying not to disturb Ethan with his patient.

The man sitting at Cindy's desk had his broad back to the door; he didn't look up or turn around when I came in. But I knew instantly who he was. What gave me an uncomfortable chill was that Dr. Claussen was staring at Cindy's computer like it held the secrets of the universe. Surely a man like Claussen would carry his own tablet or phone and wouldn't have to borrow a desktop to check his email?

I cleared my throat.

To give the man credit, he didn't panic. He hit a key, and whatever he'd been doing vanished from the screen. Then he turned with a smile his face. Either he hadn't been doing anything wrong or he was really good at hiding it.

"Asia! I was hoping I'd run into you today. You look well."

"Thanks, Doc. I'm feeling much better." I realized this was the first time I'd opened my mouth and said the words. To anyone.

But Claussen looked as if he didn't believe me. "I'm glad to hear it. Dr. Roberts has been able to help you, then?"

"Yes." My chin lifted. He was the last one I wanted to talk to about it, but I felt I had to defend Ethan. "The AL sessions have been . . . useful. I'm sleeping a lot better now."

A swift, predatory gleam lit his eyes. "Indeed? Well, that's wonderful. I'm so glad my recommendation worked out."

I smiled and nodded, but I didn't want to give him any credit for what Ethan had done. It hardly seemed possible that these two men, so different from each other, could be associates.

"Um, were you waiting for Ethan?"

Claussen shrugged. "My office takes care of some administrative work for him—billing and such. I had something for him, and I couldn't just drop it off since Cindy wasn't here."

I'd nearly worked up enough courage to ask him about his unauthorized computer access when Ethan ushered his patient out of his office and came in to greet us.

He seemed surprised to see Claussen. "Doctor." He held out his hand for a shake. "To what do I owe the honor?"

Claussen waved a hand at a large manila envelope on the desk. "Jerry in Billing asked me to bring that over. Says to sign and return ASAP."

Ethan grinned at me in apology as he unclasped the envelope. "Insurance stuff. Sorry. Just take a sec."

Claussen just smiled that oily smile while Ethan read and signed the documents. All I could think was he must be short on patients to have the time to play messenger.

Ethan put everything in order and handed the package back to the old man. I could see there were the same questions in his mind that were swirling around in mine.

But Claussen forestalled him. "I was hoping I could entice you to leave your little office for an early drink at the club this evening, my boy, but I see you are engaged." He clapped Ethan on the shoulder. "I'll leave you to it." With a nod at me, he trundled out of the office.

Ethan stared after him for a moment, then turned to me. "I'm, uh, I'm sorry about taking up your time."

"No problem. I'm in no hurry today." I wondered if I should mention Claussen's familiarity with his office equipment, but decided that was overstepping my bounds. Who knew what kind of arrangements they had?

Ethan seemed to have something else on his mind. He hesitated, shuffling some papers on the desk.

"I tried to call you, in case you wanted to reschedule today's appointment."

I looked at him, not understanding. "Why would I

want to do that?"

"Cindy's out today. It'll be just the two of us in the office." He rubbed at the back of his neck. "The way you've been reacting to the AL sessions—they tend to go on a long time. Are you okay with that?"

He stole a quick glance at me. Our eyes met and held, exchanging emotion neither of us meant to share. I couldn't keep myself from wanting him. And what was it Rita had said about the consequences of *him* wanting *me*? Jesus, we were in deep trouble.

Ethan looked away, shutting down that bright beam of connection between us. I struggled to find my voice.

"No, that's fine. We can go ahead with the appointment."

"Okay, good." He motioned me into his office. Did I hear him take a deep breath?

I lay down on the couch, my heart thumping in my chest. The room was cool, but I was sweating, and not because of the September afternoon heat outside. I tried hard to gain control while he puttered around with the machine, but it was no use. I was trembling by the time he came out of the kitchen with the herbal mixture and sat beside me to put the warm, scented cloth over my eyes.

"You seem a little tense today."

Speak for yourself, buster. "Do I?"

"Hmm."

"Guess after last time I'm a little nervous about what we'll discover." That wasn't far from the truth. I'd spent most of the week with my memories and the edges of my hurt were only now beginning to blur.

"I don't blame you. Last session was difficult."

I blew out a frustrated breath. "I still don't understand what all this has to do with those three hours I lost. Why doesn't AL help me remember that?"

Ethan was silent a moment. "I could try to direct the session a little more to answer that question specifically."

Well, hallelujah! Why didn't we do that to begin with?

"But, understand, Asia, we might not get the answer we want. The subconscious mind doesn't work like the conscious mind; it likes symbolism, substitution of one thing for another. We may get some insights; we may just get confusion."

"Okay, I get it. This is like asking a Ouija Board for the answer. Let's try anyway."

He chuckled, a low, sexy rumble I could only imagine would sound incredible in my ear as we—I turned my mind from that beguiling image as soft music started to play in the room and his voice began: "Think back to that night, Asia. You were driving in your truck on Deerhorn Road . . ."

. . . I had the radio cranked up, the sweet, high wail of Stevie Ray Vaughn's guitar lamenting that the floods down in Texas wouldn't let him talk to his baby on the phone. It was just past midnight, but I was wide awake. I was a night owl by nature; even three kids hadn't changed that. So I hadn't copped my first yawn yet that night; I figured I had a few pages of the book I was reading still in me before bed.

As I slowed down to take the curve before Dry Run Bridge, the radio started acting up. Static rose up out of nowhere to drown the signal and got so loud I had to turn the radio off. Strange. Usually I got a clear signal for that station, any time of day.

I glanced down at the radio. "Wake up, boys. Your transmitter's on the blink."

Then the truck started to cough, the engine sputtering like it was running out of gas. "What the hell?"

I checked the gauge and confirmed what I already knew—the needle was resting close to FULL. I slipped the truck into neutral and gunned it and got nothing but a dying wheeze as the vehicle began to coast, powerless. I hauled on the dead weight of the steering wheel to get the truck off to the side of the road and slammed my palms down on the rim as she finally died.

"Son of a bitch!" The only thing I knew that could kill a vehicle that quickly was a busted timing chain—and that was nothing that could be fixed in a hurry or on the cheap, either. I cursed again, louder and bluer.

Suddenly the truck, the road, even the inside of my eyelids though I'd shut my eyes tight, were set aflame with a searing white light. My brain erupted with blinding, agonizing pain. I couldn't move. I screamed . . .

. . . and woke screaming in another place and

time, one I couldn't recognize at first. My eyes were open, but I saw nothing. My muscles were locked, frozen into immobility. The only sound I could hear was my own voice, distorted in a high-pitched, keening cry, wordless, terrorized.

I felt warm hands on my face. I heard a voice calling me back. I blinked and saw Ethan, his face inches from mine, his eyes full of concern. I stopped screaming and took a breath. And I started to shake, tremors racking my body until I could do nothing but curl inward and try to hold on.

"Asia, look at me. You're okay. Do you hear me? You're safe. Tell me you know where you are."

"Okay." My throat spasmed. I swallowed. "Okay. I'm good."

He backed off a little, letting his hands drop from my face. I grabbed them in my own, unwilling to let him go. There was the tiniest shadow of movement in his body, as if he would have pulled me into his arms, then the slightest tensing of his jaw as he controlled the impulse. Or maybe there was nothing but a natural sympathy and professional interest as he watched me. God knows I was no longer in any shape to sort it out. I clung to his hands, which was all he would give me.

"What do you remember, Asia?"

I struggled to capture the details. "Not much more than I did before. Only the truck conking out. And the light. And my head—it still hurts like a sonofabitch."

He stared at me for a long, silent moment. Then he shook his head, defeated.

"We can't keep doing this."

I looked at him. "What do you mean?"

"Asia, I think we've gone as far as we can with AL. I doubt further sessions are likely to give us any new information. And they're hurting you. We've hit a wall."

"So what do we do?"

His gaze slid to the floor. "I'm still thinking about that." He got up from his chair and headed for the kitchen. "How about some tea?"

I turned to stare after him. "Is that all you have to say?"

Aware I was crossing some kind of boundary, I got up to find him in the kitchen.

His head snapped around to gape at me when I came in the door.

"Well, is it?" I repeated.

"What is it you want to hear?"

"Do you have a theory?"

He met my angry gaze. "Frankly, no."

"Really? Not alien abduction? That's why I'm here, isn't it? It's why Claussen sent me to you. You're the specialist on the subject."

"You think you were abducted by aliens?"

"God *damn* it, Ethan!" I shouted at him. "You're the fucking shrink here! You tell me. Am I crazy or not? Because from where I'm at it sure as hell *feels* like I'm crazy!"

He stopped what he was doing at the kitchen counter and came to pull me into his arms. His breath was warm in my ear.

"Shh. It's all right. We'll figure it out. Just take a minute and breathe."

Of their own accord, my arms snaked around his waist and held on to the strength he offered. It was a strength I needed, because in that moment I had begun to glimpse the true nature of the fear I'd been holding at bay with all my denial. I was scared to my soul, more frightened than any child in the dark of midnight. Because no explanation could avoid the truth of what I had seen and felt and knew in my heart to be so.

"Come on," Ethan said after a while. "Let's go sit down and we'll talk."

He led me to the couch and sat down close beside me. "Asia, you ask me if you're crazy, and what you really want me to tell you is whether you've lost touch with reality." His gaze was locked on my face, his voice as gentle as his embrace had been earlier. "Believe it or not, that's not such an easy thing to do. Reality's pretty subjective in the best of circumstances. And crazy's not so easy to define. But it seems to me we have two paths we could take here."

He paused, and the struggle he was waging in his own mind was clear on his face. I waited, watching to see which side of him would emerge the victor.

He took a breath and raised his eyes to mine. "There would be some doctors who would . . . suggest . . . that what you've told me is pure delusion—an elaborate paranoid fantasy or even schizophrenic hallucination. They would prescribe medication and intense therapy, maybe even a brief period of hospitalization to reorient you to reality."

It was his turn to wait as he looked for my reaction

to his words. My heart thudding in my chest, I could only nod, though my mind was shrieking *NO!*

"I understand. Is that what you think?"

He hung his head, shoulders slumping, his hands between his knees. For a long moment, he didn't speak.

"Ethan?"

When he lifted his head again, his blue eyes were dark with determination. "No, Asia, that's not what I think. By every criterion I know you are as sane and well-adjusted as anyone. You've overcome an incredible tragedy and moved on to lead a relatively productive and sociable life. You're dealing openly with your remaining issues from that trauma. Damn it, there's just no indication you've invented any of this out of a desire for attention or to mask other traumas or for any of the other reasons we usually look for."

He stopped and shook his head. "I can't justify doping you up with powerful drugs to rid you of your delusions. And yet I can't explain what you've told me."

He stumbled to a halt, at a complete loss for words, and gave me the faintest of smiles. "I guess that means we're both crazy."

I'm not sure, but I think that's the moment I fell in love with Ethan Roberts.

CHAPTER SEVEN

"Okay, you've been working like a freaking demon all day. Not that I don't appreciate it, but what the hell's wrong with you?"

Dan Parker threw the log he was carrying into the back of his battered pickup truck and paused to wipe the sweat streaming off his face with the sleeve of his tee-shirt.

Before he answered, Ethan tossed his own slab of wood into the truck and trudged back to where the fallen pine lay in pieces in the yard to grab another one. "What makes you think anything's wrong?"

Dan watched him with one elbow propped up on the side of the truck. "We've been working pretty steadily since noon, and I bet I've heard three words out of you."

"You've been running the chain saw." Ethan dumped another piece of wood in the truck. "We're supposed to chat about the latest journal articles over that noise?"

Dan started moving again and picked up more of the downed pine, one of several casualties of the last big thunderstorms of summer littering his suburban

Nashville yard. "Okay, so I'm done with the chain saw. What's bothering you?"

Ethan scowled, squatting to pull a particularly heavy chunk of the tree into his arms. "Nothing." He grunted as he stood and wrestled the piece to the truck, where he released it with a bang into the metal bed.

"Uh-huh." Dan tossed in a lighter piece. "It's the nightmares again, isn't it? Can't sleep?"

Ethan stopped, sweat running down his chest and back despite the thin breeze that had kicked up to relieve the afternoon heat. He stared up at the vibrant robin's egg blue of the sky through the trees of Dan's front yard, and wished for the cool of New York at this time of year.

"No," he said at last. "I haven't dreamt about the accident in a long time."

Dan was suddenly standing right next to him. "If I didn't know you better I'd say there was a woman getting under your skin."

He couldn't control the split-second of shocked reaction that crossed his face. "What the hell are you talking about?"

"Come on. You're showing all the signs of a man on testosterone overload. Who's the lucky girl?"

Ethan growled and threw another log in the truck. "Fuck off, Dan."

His friend's eyes grew wide. "Jesus, man, don't tell me I'm right. You've found a girlfriend at last?"

Ethan forced a huge grin, as if Dan had fallen for it big time. "Yeah. Twins. They're stewardesses on Swedish Air Lines."

"Fuck you, too, Roberts. So what is it, really?"

Ethan shook his head. "Work. It's nothing."

"Work?" His friend tilted his head to squint at him. "One of your Trekkies has you stumped?"

"Hey, not funny!" He went back to work, hoping Dan would let it go at that. "They may be eccentric, but they're all mine."

"And welcome to them." Dan looked like he would have said more, but a cranberry-colored minivan pulling in the driveway caught his attention.

The van pulled even with them and stopped. Dan's wife Lisa leaned out the window to flirt with her husband.

"All this sweaty work got you feeling pretty manly there, hon?"

Dan grinned, his face lighting up when he saw her. Ethan swallowed a smile. Dan had been a confirmed bachelor for years until he'd fallen hard for Lisa. Now he was just as confirmed as a family man and swore he'd never been anything else.

Close up to the van, Dan said something to Lisa that made her laugh out loud. Ethan heard the kids—three-year-old Kayla and six-year-old Michael—telling Dad all about their afternoon. Ethan rubbed at his chest, that hollow feeling somewhere between loneliness and envy creating an ache he wished he could massage away.

The van drove on to the rear of the house, and Dan turned back to him. "Come on. Let's get this truckload around back, then we'll call it a day. I'm ready for a beer and something to eat."

They made short work of the wood in the truck,

stacking it behind the more seasoned oak in the woodpile in the backyard. They washed up and were out on the deck with their feet up and a cold longneck in hand in less than half an hour.

"Okay, so you've got a patient giving you fits." Dan studied him. "Can you talk about it?"

Ethan finished the debate he'd been having with himself since Dan had broached the subject of his silence. If he'd been honest, he'd have just admitted he'd wanted to talk to Dan about Asia from the beginning. It was one reason he'd been so ready to give up his Sunday to help Dan with his yard work.

"Do you remember the woman Arthur Claussen referred to me last spring, who'd lost her kids in a fire?"

"Yeah. Jesus." He shifted in his lawn chair. "Her?"

Ethan nodded.

"For God's sake, E. I can't imagine what it must be like for her. Of course it's a tough case."

"Yes, but that's not the problem. She's come out of that trauma in good shape emotionally." Ethan's lips softened into a brief smile. "She's incredibly strong. She doesn't need me for that."

A frown drew Dan's brows together. "What, then?"

He thought for a second, careful not to divulge too many details of Asia's case. "She's missing time from that night—three hours that she can't account for. It's why Claussen referred her to me."

"You're using Claussen's protocol to help people deal with blackouts, hysterical amnesia, that kind of thing, I know." Dan nodded. "So, it's not working on this woman?"

"That's the thing. It's working too well. It's revealed a story that can't possibly be true, but that can't possibly be a lie, either. We've been at this for weeks now and . . ." He stopped, ran a hand through his hair. "I don't know how to help her, Dan."

"All right, hold on." Dan used one hand and the beer bottle to frame the question. "You say she's apparently moved on from her trauma, but she's still having trouble dealing with this blackout."

Ethan started to explain that it was probably something more than a blackout, but thought better of it. He simply nodded.

"None of the standard explanations apply?"

"Explanations? For the lost time, you mean?" Ethan shook his head. "No."

"Just her word on that?"

"Testimony at the inquiry into the fire. Fire and rescue and sheriff's deputies at the scene swore she was sober. No underlying physical or mental conditions, unless you want to call the anemia and possible anorexia I saw in one doctor's file contributory."

"Huh. No wonder she's a little obsessed." Dan took a drink from his beer, thinking. "So, okay, you run the AL thing on her and what? Something weird comes up?"

Ethan let his gaze rest on his friend's open face, wondering how much to tell him, wondering how much he would believe, how quick he would be to pick up the phone to order the ambulance to Happy Acres for a sadly distraught Dr. Ethan Roberts.

"Dan, I can't tell you what she's told me," he said

after a while. "I can only tell you that if it came from anyone else it would be a lot easier to label complete fantasy. But this story—it's like an intact memory. It has narrative form and cohesion far beyond what we usually see in these cases. It makes sense, in its own way—much more sense than the typical paranoid delusion. And coming from this woman, who in every other way is very practical, down-to-earth, intelligent and not the least bit delusional, I just don't know what to make of it."

Dan took another long pull on his beer, swallowed hard and narrowed his eyes at Ethan. "What exactly is it about her story that is so easy to believe? I mean, without going into the details—you don't have to tell me the details. You know, a lot of paranoid schizophrenics can sound really convincing until you start picking their stories apart. Or worse, if someone's just trying to manipulate you, they can have you believing just about anything. It's a real problem for us working with teenagers, trust me."

Ethan shot him a glare and started to respond that he wasn't a complete idiot, but he clamped down on the impulse and gave a more considered answer instead. "First of all, the story is emerging under the equivalent of hypnosis. It's virtually impossible for someone to lie or embellish the truth under the influence of AL."

"Really? You've never had an instance of that happening?"

"Never," Ethan said firmly. "You're accessing levels of consciousness that are without filters of any kind. It can be a little voyeuristic sometimes, frankly."

"Weird. Okay. What else?"

"Secondly, the level of detail is downright scary. It's full of sensory input. I can practically *see, feel* and *smell* this place as she's describing it."

"Place? There's a place involved?"

Shit. Knowing he'd already said too much, Ethan stonewalled.

Dan sighed. "Okay, okay. Can't blame a guy for trying. All I get to hear every day is how much the kids hate their parents and vice versa. What does Claussen say about it?"

Ethan shifted uncomfortably in his seat and said nothing.

"You haven't discussed this with the guy who a) invented the protocol and b) sent you the patient?" Dan gave him a look. "What's wrong with this picture?"

"Come on, Dan. What does it look like if I go whining to Daddy that I can't solve the puzzle he gave me?"

"Oh, I see. Little Ethan has father issues. Okay, we'll leave that for another session. So, to recap, she's telling you this wild-ass tale and the problem is you think you actually *believe* her? And that would be what? Unprofessional? Unwise? Unhelpful?"

"Yes. Not to mention crazy."

"Shit."

"Exactly."

The late afternoon sun was lowering toward

evening, throwing long shadows across the curving, multicolored flowerbeds and the parking lots, the replica of the Parthenon and the band shell of Centennial Park. September heat still hung in the air, but the cool promise of fall sighed occasionally on the breeze. Not a bad time for a run, if you had to run. And I did have to run. It was either run in the park or run completely amuck, and the police tend to frown on the latter, I've learned from hard experience.

The park would be closing in a half-hour or so. Most of the crowds had already moved on to cocktails or whatever they did at home before supper. It was quiet and just this side of forlorn under the tall oaks on either side of the main entrance road. Running was easier this time of day. It was my favorite time in the park.

Three times I ran the loop around the duck pond and garden behind the Parthenon before the endorphins kicked in. Once that happened, it was possible to relax and simply exist for a while outside the pain and the effort. I lived for that moment—I guess all runners do. The rest of the process I could definitely do without.

Of course the danger, once your body hits that groove, is that your mind is free to drift along with whatever currents may be streaming through your consciousness. And on this particular evening, like most evenings lately, all my rivers were flowing straight into the Sea of Ethan.

The way I wanted him had gone far beyond fantasy now. I wanted him with an ache that was deep and constant and rooted in some primal part of my being that had very little to do with my higher brain functions. I had seen women act like cats in heat before, but I'd never felt like one myself. It was humbling to be that enthralled, that disarmed, that *vulnerable* to what was basically a chemical reaction.

It *couldn't* be anything more than that. Ethan Roberts was a kind and sympathetic man, but he cared for me in a professional way, not a personal one. He was smart and used a wry sense of humor to make me feel comfortable, but he wasn't interested in getting close or being friends or having a relationship beyond the doctor/patient one. I was clear on all of that.

So why could I still feel the warm imprint of his arms holding me? Why did the thought of hooking my hands around the back of his neck and pulling his head down to press my lips against his drive me crazy? Why did the thought of him at odd times of the day and night leave me wet and throbbing with need? *Damn it!*

I picked up the pace as I came around the shuttered kiosk that stood beside the duck pond, trying to bleed my frustration out onto the pavement. There was a car sitting in the little triangle of gravel at the side of the building, a man sitting in the car. It struck me as odd, for some reason. There were plenty of other parking spots. What was he doing there? I glanced back at him. The man seemed to be engrossed in his phone, minding his own business, but the hairs rose on my neck. I ran a little faster.

Then there was the question of how much longer Ethan and I were going to bang our heads against the wall of my particular form of insanity before either he or I or both of us gave up. I remembered a place and a time that couldn't possibly be real, yet I knew in my heart that it was. I had memories of that place that lasted months, yet I was gone from my real life for only three hours. Ethan admitted *that* was crazy, but refused to say *I* was. None of it made sense. And now even he seemed at a loss for how to proceed. It was beginning to look like I no longer had a legitimate excuse to keep seeing him. He wasn't going to be able to help me much longer.

Shit. I slowed and nearly stopped, tears starting in my eyes from out of nowhere. *Oh, God, that is SO inappropriate.* I didn't want to stop seeing him, whether he was helping me or not. Which probably meant I should *Stop right away; Do not pass GO; Do not collect my bill for $200.*

I took up my jog again, but not before I noticed the car that had been parked by the duck pond kiosk was now behind me on the road. He was driving much too slowly, though not too close, as if he was keeping pace with me. *What the hell?*

My heart rate kicked up beyond what was necessary to keep me moving. It was getting late, and I knew better than to take any chances. I pretended not to see him and kept on to the right side of the garden, watching to see if my paranoia was founded in reality.

He followed behind me. When I could see he would have no choice but to continue on the one-way drive, I cut back and sprinted for the other side of the Parthenon, where my car was parked.

I didn't look back, but I heard him gun the engine, trying to get around the loop in time to see where I was headed. I was faster. I got to my Civic, popped the door, dropped into the seat and started her up. I was out of that lot, down the drive and burning rubber onto West End before the guy in the white sedan got to the front of the faux Greek temple.

I checked my rear view mirror all the way home, but there was no sign of him. I was still shaking when I pulled into my driveway. I decided a drink was definitely in order, maybe two. And I wondered if I had any of that weed still hidden away somewhere.

"Can Uncle Ethan read us a story?"

Michael turned on the charm for his mom, but it was Ethan who felt the lump in his throat, seeing the youngster dressed for bed in SpongeBob pj's, holding a well-read copy of Dr. Seuss in one hand and his sister's tiny fingers in the other.

Lisa had been catching up with Ethan after dinner. She grinned at him.

"I swear I didn't put them up to it."

"No. I did." Ethan stood up and looked at the kids. "And it's *Cat in the Hat*! My favorite! Let's go!"

The three of them raced down the hall to Michael's room, threw pillows on the floor and sat. Ethan settled in the middle with the book on his lap and a child curled under each arm. He opened the book and cleared his throat, looking to each side to catch a glimpse of the anticipation on the faces of his young audience.

"Ready?"

"Yeah!"

"Really? Should I read now?"

Kayla sighed. "Uncle Ethan, you do this every time." She laid her hand on his thigh and tilted her head up at him. "Just read it."

"Okay," he conceded. And began. The laughter started almost immediately, and didn't end until Lisa and Dan came in to call a halt to the proceedings after the third time through.

The kids hugged him and left him with sloppy kisses on each cheek. He got up stiffly, a smile clinging to his lips, and went back down the hall to the kitchen. He helped himself to another beer and stepped out on the deck, thinking he would wait for Dan and Lisa, then say good night. It had been a long day, a good one overall, though questions still nagged him like the pain that was creeping into his leg.

"Hey, you know we usually set a limit of two readings of *Cat in the Hat*." Dan flopped into a lounge chair beside him on the deck. "You can, too."

"What? And lose my status as cool uncle? No way."

"Pushover." Dan stretched out his legs and switched gears. "You know, I was thinking about your problem all the way through dinner—you know, the non-delusional patient with the crazy story?"

"Oh?"

"She's not the only one you've had with this problem. What about Ida? Where was she from again? Kentucky?"

"West Virginia. There are a lot of similarities in their cases."

"But that doesn't make you feel better."

"I wasn't able to help her, either."

"Have you ever followed up on her case?"

Ethan turned to look at his friend. "It hadn't occurred to me."

Dan shrugged. "Might be worthwhile now. Maybe things resolved on their own or maybe she came up with her own explanation. Either way, you'd have some insights you can use here."

"That's a good idea, Dan, thanks."

"Ida wasn't the only one, either." Dan waved his beer bottle in Ethan's direction. "There was that Air Force colonel you saw for about a month a few years ago, remember him? He didn't last long, but he threw you for a loop."

"God, I haven't thought about him in years."

"He was before the accident." His friend made a careful study of the label on his beer. "You've had some things on your mind."

Before the accident. There had been a few in those first years on his own after leaving the Institute. He'd have to look through the files.

"Speaking of which," Dan went on, "something tells me there's more to this particular patient than you're letting on."

Ethan's eyebrows shot up. "What do you mean?"

"You know damn well what I mean, E. If I bet you twenty bucks she was smart and good-looking, would you take my bet?"

Not if I wanted to keep my money, Ethan thought. He let his head fall to the back of the chair and stared at the sky full of stars.

"That's what I thought. So we've got two healthy, young, good-looking, heterosexual people in a room together for hours at a time over almost five months. Do I detect a little trans/counter/trans going on here?"

"Come on, Dan. I'm aware of the pitfalls. I've been extremely careful to keep everything strictly professional."

"No doubt you have. In fact, you've always been very good at fending off the inappropriate advances of your female patients before, even the lookers." He laughed. "Remember that model with the OCD that Elizabeth was so jealous of? Lord, I thought your lovely wife was going to kill you over that one."

"Liz almost did kill me over that one," Ethan reminded him. "And it was pretty easy to reign in the old libido in that case, given the details of her life the model insisted on sharing."

"Not so in this case, I gather."

Ethan sighed. Should he lie or just keep his mouth shut?

"Oh, boy. That bad, huh?"

"Bad enough I should probably send her to someone else." The admission shocked him. His body clenched with unhappiness.

Dan was staring at him, eyes wide with what Ethan prayed was only surprise and not horror. "Wait a minute, you have *feelings* for this woman? Feelings that, need I remind you, might possibly be mixed up with unresolved issues from a failed relationship with your late wife?"

The effect of what Dan was asking him hit Ethan

like a punch in the gut. That couldn't possibly be true, *could it?* Because if he answered yes to that question, continuing to treat Asia would be totally out of line.

"No," he said, not at all sure if he was lying.

"Well, that wasn't exactly a resounding negative." Dan was still watching him closely. "But I believe you. Maybe more than you believe yourself. You're a good doc, E. You wouldn't put your patient or yourself in a compromising position. Still, if you even suspect you should send her to someone else, why haven't you done it?"

He shook his head. "I don't know. It's like I don't want to give up. She's been through every other doc in town. Even Claussen says he can't help her. Where is she going to go? What am I supposed to say—just get over it?"

"Eventually, whether you say that or not, she may just have to." He leaned forward and caught Ethan's gaze. "It's the dirty little secret of our profession, and we all know it. Especially with the strong ones. Sometimes we just don't know what the hell else to tell them."

Ethan was silent in the face of his friend's insight. Not long afterward, he put down his unfinished beer and bid Dan and Lisa goodnight. But he didn't go home. Instead, he spent an hour following the dark, twisting turns of Old Hickory Boulevard around the city, wondering whether he was attracted to Asia Burdette because he loved the way her smile lit up her eyes or because he admired the strength that had carried her through so much trauma in her life or because, God help him, his lonely soul craved the warmth and sympathy he sensed in her heart.

In the end, he knew, it didn't matter. Whatever their source, his feelings were inappropriate. And there wasn't a damn thing he could do about them.

Except vow never to act on them.

CHAPTER EIGHT

"Hey, wake up, girl! The next Kenny Chesney just walked in the room!"

I jumped six inches off the worn cloth seat of my office chair when the cowboy banged open the door and rolled in, a wide grin spread across his square jaw. Couldn't blame him for trying to make an impression, but I wasn't in any mood for it that day.

"Is that so?" My tone was as dry as the wide place in a Texas road he'd come from. "Let me guess, you got Mister Rowe's name from a friend of a friend and you're here all the way from Podunk to see him without an appointment. Don't suppose you have a tape? A portfolio? Photo? Something?"

The cowboy, who wasn't bad looking once you got around the dusty Stetson, grinned even wider. "Honey, I got all three and anything else you need. I even got an appointment, believe it or not. Look there in your little book. Dillon Marks."

I glanced down and, sure enough, the boy had it right. "Well, aren't you special?" I gave him a syrupy smile. "Have a seat, Mister Marks, and I'll tell Mister

Rowe you're here."

"You do that, sweet thing." He winked at me and sat.

I left the roomful of wannabes who'd been waiting all morning to see JW gaping at the newcomer and went in to Rita's office.

"Got a live one out in reception."

She laughed. "Yeah, that'd be Dillon. JW's been trying to hook him for a month now. Guess maybe he's coming around."

"Well, this is the first I've heard of him."

She got up and moved toward Rowe's office. "Uh-huh. That's because you got somebody else on your mind. You haven't been paying attention to much of anything. Send him on in."

I scowled at her and went to give Dillon the keys to the kingdom. I sent all the other kids home, knowing it would be a waste of their time to wait on Rowe any more that day. Part of the wooing of Dillon Marks would involve lunch and a tour of the studio and drinks and dinner and more drinks with important people until the poor boy's head would be spinning. He winked at me again, though, as he and JW left the office, so I would say he was one who could handle it, at least for a while.

Once the office was quiet, Rita came out and perched on my desk. "You might as well go home."

"Think I'll stay for a while." I started sorting idly through a stack of filing. "I need the cash."

"I hear that. Fine, then, we'll do the crosswords after lunch. You done the wild thing with that doc of yours yet?"

"Hey, come on, Rita, you know I can't do that!"

She just grinned. "No, but you want to awful bad."

My face turned as red as my three-hundred-pound uncle's at a Fourth of July picnic. "Actually, I haven't even seen Ethan in over a week."

"Oh? And why is that?"

"We've kind of hit a snag in the therapy." I frowned. "He's asked for some time to do a little research."

"What kind of research?"

"Damned if I know. Something about similar past cases. We've got another appointment next week."

"Um-hmm."

"Oh, hush." I started to laugh, but what I saw when I glanced out the window stopped me cold. A white Impala, a middle-aged, dark-haired goon behind the wheel.

Rita's gaze bounced from me to the window and back in gathering confusion. "What's wrong?"

"You see that white car on the other side of the street? Call me crazy, but I think that guy is stalking me."

Rita's jaw dropped. "What the hell are you talking about?" She sounded like she didn't believe me, but she stood up and went to the window to get a good look at him. She must have been visible from the street, because the Impala started up and moved off in a hurry. "Damn! I didn't get the license."

"No, me neither. It's a temp tag. Can't read the numbers."

She turned to consider me, arms folded across her chest. "What the hell is going on, Asia?"

"I saw this guy at Centennial Park Sunday a week ago. Seemed like he was following me in his car, you know? Then I see the same car—or it seemed like it anyway—a few days later in the park again when I'm running. Then last night, I see the *same* car, *same* guy down the street in my neighborhood. I'm really starting to freak out."

Rita strode behind my desk and picked up the phone. "All right, girl, we are calling the police *this minute.*"

I shot her a glare that asked if I looked like an idiot. "Rita, have you ever actually dealt with the police? They won't do a damn thing unless he lays a hand on me."

"I don't give a shit." Her foot tapped as she waited for the call to go through. "They're gonna hear about it anyway—Hello? Yes, I need to report an incident."

Several transfers and repetitions of the problem later we were connected with someone who agreed to send an officer out to take a report. While we waited for the assigned unit to show up, we speculated. Or rather, Rita did.

"Do you have any idea who this guy is? He's not one of ours, is he?"

I shook my head. "I don't know. I don't think so. He doesn't look the type." None of the broken-hearted songsters who haunted Music Rowe had it in them to do anything like this, and, besides, I didn't recognize the guy from the office. "He looks more like a serious thug, or a PI or something."

"A private investigator? You pissed off anybody in a bar lately? Maybe taken home somebody's husband?"

I sighed. "Rita, you know good and well I haven't taken *anybody* home with me in a hell of a long time. As for pissing somebody off, who knows? Not that I can remember, anyway."

When Officers Harkin and Monroe of the Metro Nashville Police Department arrived, they asked for a description of the car and its driver, and started in on a long list of the same kind of questions Rita had just asked.

Harkin led off. "Can you think of any reason someone might be stalking you, Miz Burdette?"

Monroe followed. "Are you in the middle of a divorce or child custody case? Are you a principal or a witness in any court proceeding or litigation?"

"No."

"Wait a minute!" Rita injected. "What about your ex?"

I rolled my eyes. "I think I would know my own ex-husband, Rita. That guy's got about seventy pounds and maybe ten years on Ronnie."

The police officers waited while I sorted it out in my mind. Then Harkin made sure.

"Are you certain your husband has no reason to have someone following you, Miz Burdette?"

"*Ex*-husband, and no, I can't imagine he would. We've been done for three years and I haven't heard a peep from him. He lives in Knoxville now, at least that's what I heard."

The officers exchanged a look and one of them wrote something down. The questions continued.

"Have you met any new people recently?"

"Is there anyone in your work environment that might harbor a grudge?" (Rita and I started to laugh about that one until the look on the officers' faces silenced us.)

And on and on. The more I answered in the negative the more I could see the skepticism growing in the officers' eyes.

After about fifteen minutes of this, Officer Harkin asked the $64,000 question. "And you say this man has not approached you or spoken to you or threatened you in any way?"

I glanced at Rita, thinking *I told you so*. "No, sir."

He closed up his little notebook. "Ma'am, you understand there's not a whole lot we can do right now. The man has technically not broken the law."

I nodded.

Rita protested. "Wait a minute! You're not going to try and find him? Give him a warning or something?"

"No, ma'am," Officer Monroe declined politely. "Even if we could find him, I'm afraid he's well within his rights to share the public streets with Miz Burdette. He hasn't done anything wrong in the eyes of the law."

Rita sat shaking her head in disbelief.

"Make sure the locks on your apartment are secure, don't go anywhere alone late at night, and follow sensible safety precautions," Harkin advised. "Don't hesitate to call us if he does escalate this situation in any way."

I showed them to the office door. "I'll be sure to do that."

"And you ladies have a nice day."

Ethan ended his phone call and paced his office like a dog whose owner has just reached for the leash. What the hell had he been thinking? He'd started out his call with Ida Mickens wanting only to ask her a few questions, find out if she'd found some sort of resolution to the visions that were so like Asia's. She hadn't. She had only resigned herself to them. She was intrigued that someone else might share her situation, however, and, in her practical way, Ida had suggested the two women meet. Ethan had been unable to refuse her invitation.

But how could he ask Asia to go to West Virginia with him? It was a five-hour drive to the Virginia state line and God knew how much further to Ida's little town. That was an overnight at least—maybe two. And on the flimsiest of therapeutic foundations.

Maybe that was at least a partial solution to his ethical dilemma. None of what he was doing now really qualified as therapy. Detective work, maybe. Research. Information gathering. Networking, even. But not therapy. He should sever his therapeutic relationship with Asia immediately. There was nothing more he could do to help her on that level anyway.

Then he could present the meeting with Ida completely outside the context of therapy. Still dicey, but it felt more legitimate. And Asia should feel less pressure to say yes.

God, he hoped she said yes.

He stopped pacing and picked up the list of names

he'd culled from his "failed" files. Not many—fewer than ten over the years since he'd left Claussen's Psychogenesis Institute. Seven people with stories he couldn't explain, whose delusions had only grown stronger under the AL protocol. He needed to talk with them, maybe bring them back in for further sessions with AL if they were willing. Somewhere in their stories could be a clue to Asia's.

He'd tried without success to track down his former patients using computer and paper files. The contact information he had was incomplete or out of date for all seven of them. The next step was to ask the administrative staff at the Institute to help him out. They'd all been referred from Claussen, and the admin staff had done the billing for him.

Ethan pushed his arms into the sleeves of a blazer and paused to check his appearance in the mirror before he headed out the door. Dr. Claussen hated for his doctors to show up looking like his "crazies" at the Institute. Even if he was only going to be in the back offices, Ethan had to look the part of one of the staff today. Thank God it was only for the afternoon.

Twenty minutes later he had sweated his way through the heavy traffic out West End to the Psychogenesis offices and pulled his ancient BMW into the parking lot. He swiped his ID at the back entrance and breezed through the door, headed directly for the administration offices on the second floor.

His hand was on the door to the stairs when he heard Claussen's voice behind him. "Ethan! Where are you going in such a hurry?"

He turned with a smile he didn't quite feel. "Hello, Arthur. Just back from lunch?" He broadened his smile to include the two men who stood behind Claussen in the hallway.

"Why, yes, as it happens. With my newest partners. Allow me to introduce Colonel Donald Gordon and Dr. Seung Park. We're working on a very interesting research project together. Gentlemen, this is Dr. Ethan Roberts, once my most promising research assistant."

Colonel Gordon wore his military bearing like his U.S. Army uniform, crisp and straight, despite the approach of retirement age. He, at least, offered an engaging smile and a handshake. The younger Dr. Park, on the other hand, appeared to consider the formalities of human interaction a waste of valuable research time. He allowed a curt nod and no more.

Ethan knew better than to pry, but he couldn't resist just a little poking. "It must be an interesting project if it involves the U.S. military," he said to Gordon.

"I'm afraid it's not exactly cutting edge, but it may mean a great deal to our fighting men and women, Doctor." Gordon inclined his head to make sure he had Ethan's attention. "We're studying the use of Dr. Claussen's protocols in the treatment of post-traumatic stress disorder."

Of course. AL would be tremendously useful in that application, reducing the power of the traumatic memories that took over the veterans' lives. Ethan felt both envious and embarrassed.

Claussen chuckled. "You see, Ethan? Should have

taken me up on that offer to come back aboard." He turned to Park and Gordon. "Will you excuse me a moment, gentlemen?" He pulled Ethan aside. "And the research is even more interesting once you get into it. Better than scraping up cases out there on your own, wouldn't you say, son?"

Ethan felt his temper rise. "Arthur, you know how I feel about that."

The old man's expression went flat. "Yes. I suppose I do. Well. And how is your latest case progressing—the patient I saw in your office the other day?"

"Asia Burdette." Ethan knew full well Claussen hadn't forgotten her name. He kept his voice neutral. "Unusual case, I'll give you that. It's taking some time to sort out."

Claussen smiled as if he knew Ethan was hiding something. "Why don't you come by the house for a drink sometime this week? We'll talk about it. Maybe I can help since I'm already familiar with the details."

"Sounds like a plan." *For disaster.* The old man was taking an unusual amount of interest in Asia's case. He'd be going by for that drink when hell froze over.

Ethan pushed through the door and up the stairs to the second floor, his heart pounding. He took a minute to get himself together before he opened the door to the admin office. Amanda in Accounts Receivable looked up at him with adoration in her green eyes. Lucky for him, the girl was just out of college and viewed him as unattainable or he'd have a serious problem on his hands.

"Anything I can do for you, Doc?"

He pressed his advantage, leaning in and lowering his voice. "Well, yes, Amanda, there is. I have these former patients that I can't seem to track down." He passed her a sheet of paper with the list of names. "I was wondering if you could locate them for me. Get a phone number or something?"

"Sure," she whispered. "What did you need them for?"

"Research project," he whispered back. "I'm doing a paper."

"Ooh! Gonna be published?"

He shrugged. "Who knows? Maybe."

"Give me a day or two. I'll get back to you."

"You're terrific, Amanda. Thanks."

"My pleasure, Doc."

He felt a little guilty when he left the office. He decided flowers were in order—for the extra work, if not for the outright exploitation.

I sat in my Honda, hands on the steering wheel, and stared through the rain at the bungalow where I knew Ethan was waiting in his office. He didn't know it yet, but this would be our last appointment, and the weather suited my mood.

The therapy had done its job. It was time to end things with Ethan. I told myself I should be glad to be rid of the constant prodding, the revelations from the world of my nightmares, the questions for which neither he nor I had any answers. It did no good. All I could think was that I wouldn't be seeing Ethan

Roberts again, that I would miss his slow smile and his calm strength and the sympathy in his warm voice and . . . *damn it.*

I made myself get out of the car. I ran through the driving rain and onto the porch, ducking into the entryway where I shook myself like a wet dog.

Cindy was at her desk off the hallway as always. "Hey, Asia, nasty weather out there!"

I suddenly realized I was going to miss her, too. I took off my jacket and hung it by the door. "Supposed to last all night."

"Yuck." Cindy summed it up. "He's ready for you. You can go on in."

Ethan stood when I entered the room and came around from behind his desk. He smiled, and my steely resolve dissolved into something resembling Jell-O.

"Hi, Asia." He gestured at the couch. "Missed you last week. How have you been?"

Make that unset Jell-O, quivering in a little bowl. "Fine. You?"

"Uh, fine, thanks."

I sat on the couch. He sat in his chair. We looked at each other, then both started to speak at once.

He laughed. "You first. It's your dime."

I looked at my hands, twisting in my lap. "Well, actually, that's what I wanted to talk about today." I looked up at him. "I think we may be done here."

The corners of his mouth ticked upwards. "What makes you think so?"

I could have said I was feeling better than I had in a long time—almost whole again, almost comfortable in my own skin. I wasn't happy, not by a long stretch. I was still lonely as hell and . . . drifting. But I could think of my children without trembling. I could live now.

I tried to sum all that up in a few words. "I don't have the nightmares anymore. I'm not drinking or smoking like I used to. I don't . . . hurt . . . like I used to. You did your job, Ethan. I don't see where there's anything left for us to do."

He nodded. "That's great, Asia, but I didn't do anything. All of that was a result of the work you did. I just showed you what needed to be done. What about the lost time?"

I shook my head. "I still don't understand it. It still bothers me, but I don't think coming here every week will answer that question for me. No offense."

"None taken. And your . . . visions . . . of the labor camp?"

"Visions? That's an interesting way to put it." I pinned him with a stare. He shifted in his seat, but he met my gaze evenly enough. I sighed. "Again, nothing you can do will provide an explanation for what I saw. I've thought a lot about it in the last week or so, though, and one thing I'm sure of. I'm not crazy. Whatever they are—dreams, visions, memories— they're linked to something real. One day maybe I'll figure out what."

I no longer expected him to solve my problem. I had questions, hundreds of them, and very little possibility of ever having them answered. But I no longer questioned my own sense of reality, as strange as it was.

Ethan was quiet for a long moment. I almost started to get up and say goodbye, but he spoke before I moved.

"We're thinking along the same lines here, Asia. I was going to suggest the same thing today. I don't think there's anything more I can do for you as your therapist. As far as that goes, I think we are done here."

My gaze shot to his face, detecting something behind the words that made my heart race. He was watching me, vulnerability a current in the blue sea of his eyes. I waited, breathless, knowing my reaction to what he said next would make all the difference.

"If you're interested in pursuing the mystery of what you remember, I'd like to help. Not as your doctor, but as a co-investigator, of sorts."

I just looked at him, not sure what to say—or think. "What do you mean?"

He leaned forward, elbows on his knees, his hands doing a lot of the talking for him. "You're not the only patient I've had with a story like this. There have been several, but the one whose case is most like yours is Ida Mickens, an older lady who lives in West Virginia. I spoke with her this week. She wants to meet with you."

"You told her about me?" I sat back, not sure how I felt about that.

He held out a hand in my direction. "I didn't share any of the details of your story. That would be for you to do, only if you wanted to. I just told her I was working with a woman whose case was similar. Ida's been living with what she calls her 'visions' for most of her life."

I thought about what it would be like to be saddled for a lifetime with the kind of memories I'd been dragging around for mere months. And I thought about what a relief it might be to speak to someone else who had seen what I had seen.

But what if this woman was really crazy? "What kind of visions does she have?"

His gaze caught mine. "Slave labor in fields of yellow mud under a green sky. They started when she was a child. She's in her eighties now."

"My God." I couldn't breathe. "She told you that under AL?"

"Just like you did."

"And she wants to talk to me."

He nodded. "There's only one hitch."

"What's that?"

"We'll have to make a weekend trip to see her." The color rose slightly in his cheeks. "Are you free the first weekend in October?"

I grinned, my stomach doing flips. "That can be arranged." *Oh, hell, yes, it can.*

CHAPTER NINE

The BMW prowled the street, slipping between tightly parked cars with a stuttering growl to climb the steep curves overlooking the city. Behind the wheel, Ethan cursed and began to sweat. Asia had described the converted 1920s-era Tudor that housed her tiny apartment, but he hadn't found it yet, and now he would be late picking her up.

Damn it! It should be right . . . there. He saw the building at last, but his frustration only grew. Cars lined both sides of the street, leaving him no place to park in front of the house. There was even some asshole just sitting in a white Impala, smoking a cigarette, like he had nothing better to do than take up a perfectly good parking space. Ethan blew out an exasperated breath and moved on, squeezing into a truncated spot two blocks up.

He got out of the Beemer and tried to stretch some of the tension out of his back, fully recognizing that the state he was in had little to do with finding parking and a lot more to do with spending the weekend alone with Asia Burdette. He had tried to talk himself out of it more than once, for her sake as much as his. In the end, he hadn't been able to resist the pull he felt from her. He knew it was wrong, but he couldn't stay away from her. So here he was. He would just have to do his best to keep things . . . professional.

Ethan inhaled a lungful of the crisp October air and started down the hill toward Asia's house. The neighborhood wasn't so great, but the view was spectacular from up here. It was a wonder the real estate sharks who had savaged so many of Nashville's older neighborhoods hadn't yet discovered this one, replacing the original houses that lent it character with mini-mansions shoehorned into tiny infill lots.

Ethan was at the edge of the yard in front of Asia's rambling Tudor when he passed the white Impala, idling at the curb. The man inside glanced at him, flicked a cigarette ash out his window, returned his attention to his phone. He appeared to be perfectly innocent, but something about the guy's bulky build and short, military haircut flashed a warning.

He was just some guy, but Ethan couldn't help wondering, *Who the fuck is he? The bastard might be watching Asia's house!* Maybe it was her ex-husband, hanging around to harass her. No, Asia hadn't mentioned him. And come to think of it, this guy seemed a little old to be Asia's ex. Ethan shook his head. *What the hell has gotten into me?*

Before Ethan reached Asia's door, the man gunned the Impala's engine. Then he nosed the car into the street and laid a strip of rubber a yard long to disappear down and around the winding street. No one had come out of the building to get in the car. He'd been loitering in that parking spot for some other reason.

Ethan glanced up at the house, then back at the street. He paced a little, trying to get himself under control. It was going to be a long weekend; he didn't want to blow it by dumping his own paranoid fantasies on Asia before they even set out. Someone watching her house? Unlikely in the extreme. There had to be another explanation. A *logical* explanation. The high boil of Ethan's outrage subsided to a low simmer of wariness. Whether the man in the white Impala was something to worry about would reveal itself over time, and it could remain his problem for now. After all, Asia wasn't alone and vulnerable; he was there to look out for her. It might break every rule in the freaking book, but he was clear: Asia was his to protect.

I had hardly slept the night before the trip to West Virginia. I'd been restless, anticipating the answers to so many of my questions. And it wasn't just my mind that was antsy, ready for the night to be over and the day to begin, the morning to be over and the afternoon to begin, two o'clock to be over and three o'clock to be here. My body was vibrating like a dynamo, humming with charged energy so tangible it was as if one touch could kick off a visible spark.

I knew nothing had really changed between Ethan and me. On paper, he was no longer listed as my doctor. I was no longer officially his patient. But I knew Ethan wouldn't see that as a green light to change our relationship. Even if there wasn't any regulation that insisted we had to wait a certain length of time before we fell into each other's arms, Ethan struck me as the kind of man who would have his own set of rules demanding distance.

And yet . . . I just couldn't help thinking about what it would be like to close that distance. To end up falling—me into his arms, him into mine. Naked. In a hotel room. All night long.

Like I said, I hadn't slept that night.

Fortunately Ethan didn't keep me waiting long, imagining more possibilities. He arrived just a little past 3:00 p.m. I forgave him his tardiness, though I'd been ready for fifteen minutes before he knocked on the door. I was too nervous to be judgmental.

His eyes widened a little, and he smiled when he saw me. "Hi. Sorry I'm late. Had a little trouble finding parking."

"Well, thanks." I missed a beat, dazzled by that smile, I guess. "What? Oh, yeah, I should have warned you. Come on in. I'll just get my stuff."

He took a few steps into the living room and stood awkwardly while I bustled around.

"You want a Coke or some water for the road?"

"No, thanks, I've got something in the car." He walked over to the couch. JJ, who hated everybody, surprised me by standing for a nice stretch-and-pet from the new guy. "Hey, fella, what's goin' on?" Ethan scratched the cat between the ears. JJ purred.

My jaw dropped. "Well, how about that! He never does that for strangers. Meet Jesse James."

"Oh, an outlaw, huh? I know the type."

"Yeah, he's a bad one, all right." I tilted my head at the little mercenary, wondering.

Ethan looked up at me. "Ready?"

"Let's go." I took a look around, grabbed my stuff, and followed him out the door.

At the outer door at the foot of the stairs, he paused and turned with a little shrug. "I had to park up the street. Wait while I bring the car around?"

"That's okay. I can walk."

"No," he said quickly, scanning the street. Then he forced a smile. "What kind of limo driver would I be if I didn't pick you up at your door?"

"Lord, if my mama could see me now," I drawled in response. "All right, then. Hurry back."

I watched him move up the street with that long-legged wolf-lope of his, his head swiveling to take in both sides of the street as if something might be lurking between the vehicles on either side. If I hadn't known him, I might have thought he was a cop or a soldier or one of those heroes in a crime novel with a bad past and one shot at redemption. He sure didn't look like your everyday psychiatrist walking down the street.

Of course, I had my own reasons to be wary. I'd heard a squeal of tires on the street earlier and nearly jumped out of my skin. I still expected to see that white Impala around every corner, but a glance out my window had only shown me Ethan walking up my sidewalk. The street was free of thugs now, too, I noted. I relaxed another fraction.

When he drove up to the house in what had to be

the oldest functional BMW I'd ever seen, I wasn't sure whether my street impression of him had just been confirmed or destroyed forever. The boxy sedan was at least twenty years old and sported a faded yellow paint color I don't think they even make anymore. Someone, and I was fervently hoping it was Ethan, had driven this car into the ground.

Ethan got out to put my single bag in the back seat and opened the passenger side door for me to get in. The worn leather upholstery seemed to fit me like my favorite pair of old shoes. The car's interior was roomier than it looked from the outside. It was clean, and it smelled like Ethan.

"Boy, this one is a classic, huh?" I smiled as Ethan situated himself behind the wheel. "How long have you been driving it?"

Ethan's lips edged upward, and he glanced at me for a second before he put her in gear. "This car was ten years old when I bought it fifteen years ago."

"Wow." I stared at him. "That's what you call a long-term commitment."

He laughed. "You could say so."

"Bet she has a name, too, huh?"

He actually blushed. "I call her Baby. Couldn't tell you how many miles I've put on her. The odometer turned over twice before it gave out. Suppose I'd have to have that fixed if I ever planned to sell her."

"Yeah. Like that's going to happen."

We headed out of town on I-40, Baby purring smoothly under us, Ethan handling the early weekend traffic with patience and skill. Once we got away from the city's craziness, I said what had been on my mind.

"Tell me about Mrs. Mickens."

"She's one of a kind." He smiled with true affection. "One minute you think she's just the stereotypical Appalachian granny rocking on her front porch, the next minute she's confiding her favorite author is Dashiell Hammett and talking about a collection of paperback murder mysteries that would fetch a small fortune on eBay."

I was delighted. "Likes her detectives hard-boiled, huh?"

"Ida stayed with my friend Dan while she was my patient. He couldn't keep her in books." He grinned. "And the Tommy guns were always blasting on her TV."

"Who knows? Maybe she has a still out back and reads the books for pointers."

"Good thing she likes me then. Don't mess things up."

I raised my hands to show I had no ulterior motives. "You're the boss, boss."

He shook his head, still smiling. "She's unusual in so many ways. I only wish I'd been able to help her."

My chest warmed in sympathy. "I'm sure she felt you did."

He glanced in my direction, a world of emotions on his face. What he said next reflected little of it.

"Anyway, I'm hoping maybe the two of you . . . you know, the opportunity for you to compare notes may yield something of help to both of you."

"Yeah, me too."

He switched conversational gears abruptly. "So,

tell me about your background, Asia. Are you a Tennessee girl, born and bred?"

I gave him a sidelong glance, eyebrows raised. "You don't think I came by this accent by anything other than natural means, do you?"

"I like your accent. It's sort of . . . I don't know . . . slow-cooked and sweet."

I sputtered, laughing at the image. "You make it sound like barbecue sauce."

"I was thinking more like apple butter. It's best when it's got a little tang to it." He laughed too, his eyes bright with more than amusement.

"Hmm." Was he flirting, or was that just wishful thinking on my part? "But, yes, I grew up not too far from Cookeville. Working-class parents, just off the farm, thought I'd hung the moon, especially since I was their only baby. Grew up in the country with lots of relatives around. Liked school, so Mom and Dad sent me to college. I might even have made it through, too, if it hadn't been for Ronnie."

"Your husband."

"Yeah. He came along right about the time my mom died. I sort of lost focus there." I sighed. "Guess you could say he took advantage."

"Have you heard from him since the divorce?"

I looked up, surprised. Ethan's eyes were fixed on the road.

I shook my head. "We didn't have much of a marriage to start with. The fire took what was left of it. We'd never have been together at all if it hadn't been for Benjamin."

"He was your oldest?"

My smile quavered. "Yeah. He was seven. An old soul."

"You never told me about your children, Asia."

I couldn't find the words to speak. Hot tears pooled in my eyes, poised to fall, but I refused to let them. I took a deep breath and waited out the pain.

"It can be really hard to talk about the people you've lost, but it gets easier the more you try." Ethan's voice was soft, deep, matter-of-fact. "When you're ready, I'd like to hear about your kids."

The tears did fall then, and I was in serious danger of letting everything go. That wasn't how I had planned for this trip to proceed at all. I clamped down hard on the emotion that was expanding like a black hole in my chest.

Ethan put a hand on my shoulder and squeezed, then went back to his driving.

After a while he steered the conversation onward. "What were you studying in school?"

I gave up a shaky grin. "Psychology."

He grinned back. "Really. Why?"

"I was always the one people came to with their problems. Figured I should look into making a living at it."

He laughed. "So it was either psychologist or talk show host as a career choice, huh? I hate to tell you, but Oprah gets paid better."

"Oprah gets paid better than God."

"Have you ever thought about going back to school, picking up psychology again?"

"People stopped coming to me with their problems a long time ago." I stared at the hands in my lap.

"Even if they hadn't, I don't feel like I have the answers anymore."

"None of us have the answers, Asia. That shouldn't keep you from trying."

I let a moment go by before I confessed an old dream, nearly forgotten. "Maybe someday."

"You should." His glance this time was sharp, full of intent. "All those smarts need an outlet."

My face reddened under the compliment. I wanted to make some kind of smartass response, but found I couldn't. In the end, I just looked back at him and murmured, "Thanks."

There was another little stretch of silence before I recovered enough to pick up my end of the conversation. "So, what about you? Why did you choose to become a psychiatrist?"

He smiled, but it seemed tinged with irony. "The standard answer is because I wanted to help people."

I raised an eyebrow. "And the real answer?"

He shook his head. "I'm not sure anymore. Helping's still part of it, but I have to admit curiosity is a big part of it, too. I like to figure out what makes people tick."

I didn't think he saw his patients as just a puzzle to be solved. He was selling himself way too short.

"For what it's worth, it's the caring part of you that comes across to your patients," I told him. "You don't have to worry that you're losing that."

He looked at me, quick emotion sweeping like a cloud across his face. "Thanks." The single word was barely audible above the sound of the car engine.

I smiled and turned my head to look out the

window at the rolling hills of central Tennessee. Awash in the golden light of the westering sun, the green fields and red-orange and yellow woods slid past in a constant stream of healing color. They caught the soul, as well as the eye.

That wasn't the reason I kept staring out the window, my face averted, as afternoon dropped into evening. Sometime during our conversation, my heart had begun to ache for Ethan Roberts. I had begun to want something from him I couldn't describe, something so much more than a just a look or a touch or even the stirring of affection I could sense in him already. Even more, I yearned to fill a need in him so deep I doubted he would ever express it.

I couldn't understand this sudden longing; I couldn't explain it, either, but I knew my eyes showed it. And I couldn't let him see. Not yet. So I watched as the sun went down and held my breath.

Ethan slid into the vinyl-covered booth with a ragged sigh and shifted so he could lever his right leg up onto the bench beside him. He gave the perky young thing who came to take his order his best smile to distract her from his sprawl.

"Jack and water. Please. I can really use it tonight."

She pursed her lips at him. "Ooh, poor baby. I'll be right back."

He reached into his pocket for the bottle of pills, popped the top and shook one out into his palm. Four left and he hoped to God they'd be enough to get him through the weekend. He hadn't calculated the effects of five hours of driving to their stop for the night in Bristol, his first long trip since the last surgery. It hadn't even occurred to him to think the leg might be a problem. Until now.

"Thought I might find you here." Asia slipped into the booth across from him. She nodded at the pill bottle in his hand. "Headache?"

His hand went to his thigh, almost against his will. "Old war wound."

The waitress arrived with his drink, set it down and looked at Asia. "What can I get you?"

"Vodka tonic, thanks."

Ethan threw the pill back in his throat and swallowed it with a slug of the whiskey and water. The pain in his leg screamed defiance at him. *Just a few more minutes.*

Asia watched him, his pain reflected in her brown eyes. "All that driving aggravated it, huh? Leg injury?"

He nodded, a wry smile tugging at his lips.

She stood up and moved to his side of the booth. "Move," she ordered.

"What?"

"Sit up a minute." She waved a hand at the leg he had stretched across the bench.

He scowled. "What's wrong—the view not so good from your side?" He swung the leg down with a grunt and watched as she sat down beside him. What the hell was she up to?

"The view's fine." She patted her thighs. "Leg."

He looked at her, heart thumping in his chest. *Boundaries,* his mind screamed at him. *Boundaries!* "I'm not sure that's a great idea."

She raised an eyebrow at him, a gesture he was really beginning to like. "Would you rather do this in your room? Or mine? I admit you'd get a better massage, but as far as being appropriate . . ."

"Okay, I get the point." He swallowed. "It's just that I'm not sure a massage in any venue is appropriate."

She tilted her head, a corner of her mouth quirking upwards. "Come on, Ethan. I can tell that son of a bitch hurts. I can help."

The temptation was too much. And she was right—it had nothing to do with being close to her, having her hands on him. Well, it did. But it was mostly about the fact that his leg hurt *so damn much* and a massage would feel *so damn good* right about now.

He hoisted his leg onto her lap—there was just enough room behind the table and it was just dark enough in the bar to get away with it—and tried to stay calm when she started in kneading the aching muscles of his thigh. Maintaining that pretense was a losing battle. Her touch—gentle at first, then much firmer as she tested his tolerance—was like healing fire. A groan, as soft as a sigh, escaped his lips as she followed his quadriceps from the knee to the top of his thigh and back again.

"Can you tell me what happened?" She began to work the outside of his thigh. The flesh there was scored with scars—he tensed even though he knew she couldn't feel them through the jeans he wore—

but she didn't hurt him. He relaxed again.

"I was injured in the accident that killed my wife." He found the words cost him more than he would have thought. "Smashed up the femur and the right knee pretty badly." He didn't mention the right elbow or the ribs or the internal injuries. It had been only because the impact flipped the car that he'd survived at all. Elizabeth had been on the bottom of the pile of crushed metal when the rescue squad cut them out; he'd been somewhere in the middle of a pincer of steel.

Her hands stopped moving. "God, I'm sorry. That sounds terrible." When she started up again, her hands dug into the muscles near his hip, and he pulled in a sharp breath against the pain. She looked up in alarm. "Am I hurting you?"

"Yes, but don't stop." His breath caught in his throat until he forced himself to breathe. His overtaxed muscles burned as she worked them, freeing them from the tension and toxic stiffness of hours of driving. He closed his eyes and endured, until the pain in his muscles subsided into the warmth of healing and the deeper ache in his bones that was always with him was tolerable.

"You still with me?" Asia's voice seemed to come from a long way off.

He opened his eyes and looked at her. God, she was beautiful. The urge to reach over and pull her to him, to slip his tongue past those full lips into her mouth and taste her, was overwhelming.

He found his voice. "You have great hands. That felt incredible. Thank you."

She smiled. "You looked like you needed it."

He made an effort to sit up and lowered his leg to the floor. "I should have thought . . . I'll take more breaks on the way back home."

She studied him. "Let me guess. You were probably pretty active before the accident—you're not used to this."

Anger—raw and unexpected—flared in his chest. "To what? Playing the invalid? No—should I be?"

She seemed momentarily flustered, and he instantly regretted his burst of temper. Even as he watched, her jaw tightened and her embarrassment was hidden behind a shield of cool reserve.

"I only meant you might be pushing yourself a little hard. You don't strike me as a couch potato."

"Yeah, actually, you're right. And I'm sorry. I didn't mean to snap."

"Forget it." She downed the rest of her drink. "It's late, and it's been a long day. I think I'll call it a night."

He nodded, disappointment hanging on him like a weight. He called for the tab and signed for it when the server came over, waving off Asia's offer to pay for her half. Then he followed Asia out of the booth.

"I'll walk you back."

She looked up at him and smiled, her own apology in her eyes. "You don't have to do that."

"Waal, little missy," he drawled in a bad approximation of John Wayne. "That there's a mighty dark parking lot, and it's a long way home by yourself."

Asia laughed. "Never let it be said that a man can't

be a Yankee and a gentleman at the same time. Lead on, sir."

Ethan gave her a little bow and held open the door. "My pleasure, ma'am. After you."

The air still held the last of summer's warmth and only an occasional breath of wind hinted at the chill of fall still to come. Ethan watched Asia as they walked the short distance to their rooms, watched the smooth glide of her hips and the stretch of her legs as she walked, the play of her shoulders under the sweater she wore. She walked like she owned the world, like she feared nothing. After all she'd been through, that simple demonstration of her courage made his heart swell with tenderness.

He shook his head. What the hell was wrong with him? Just because he'd formally ended their therapeutic relationship didn't mean he could allow himself any other kind. Beyond a strictly platonic, friendly kind of thing. *Right,* his id answered slyly, and gave his cock a twitch, just to make the point.

They arrived at her room, and it was all he could do to keep from touching her. He couldn't read her expression; the light was too uncertain. But it seemed as if her smile was tentative. Or sad.

He found himself without anything to say. He wanted only to kiss her.

She looked up at him. "Thanks for the drink."

"Thanks for the massage." His voice was a dry, breathless rasp.

Her breath caught; he heard it. "What time tomorrow?"

"We should probably get an early start. Say,

breakfast at eight?" Not what he wanted to say.

"That works." A pause. "See you then. Good night."

"Good night."

She turned and let herself into her room. He waited until the door was closed and locked before he walked away, so hard he hurt, and so lonely his beating heart echoed in his empty chest.

CHAPTER TEN

We were on the road by nine the next morning, Ethan's battered BMW climbing gamely into the mountains, following the mist rising from the valleys. The hillsides were splashed with color—red and yellow and lingering green leaping to life as the sun rose higher to hit the trees on the slopes. It was beautiful. It was home.

We didn't say much on the two-hour ride up to the little town where Ida Mickens lived. Ethan put some bluegrass on and we let Lester and Earl, Doc and the Carters do the talking. What they had to say seemed more profound anyway.

The mountains always made me feel this way—quiet, introspective, *settled*. Any apprehension I'd been feeling about my meeting with Ida melted into that sense of calm, and I just went with it for a while.

Ethan seemed to have his own preoccupations this morning. Whatever they were, he wasn't inclined to share with me. At least he wasn't favoring his leg. When I asked him about it, he said it felt fine. After the way he'd bristled last night, I wasn't going to push him on it.

Around 11 o'clock we pulled into the tiny town of Clay Fork, a mountain metropolis boasting a post office, a Piggly Wiggly, a Dollar Store and a few houses. At the single intersection in town we took a left, crossed a shallow creek on a new concrete bridge and followed the narrowing road up the mountainside toward the Mickens home place.

"You sure we don't need four-wheel drive up here?" Baby was struggling around the hairpin curves leading up the mountain.

Ethan grinned. "Welcome to West Virginia. How much further?"

I glanced down at the sheet he'd handed me at the start of the day's outing. "Another half-mile? Past the Seventh-Day Adventist Church there's a private road."

Around the next bend we saw the church, and the road appeared through a gap in a barbed-wire fence enclosing pastures on either side. The car bounced and slid along the dirt road, Ethan wrestling the steering wheel to avoid potholes that would have swallowed the Beemer without a trace. The track rose through the open pastures to a little knoll, where a sturdy farmhouse sat surveying the folded mountains for miles around.

On the porch in a rocker sat Ida Mickens, waiting with a big smile on her face for us to rattle to a stop in her yard. Once we had, she got up and came down off the porch to greet us.

Ethan opened the window and hollered, "Hey, Ida," before the car even stopped moving.

She was already teasing as Ethan opened the

driver's side door and got out. "Lord have mercy, son, you still driving that old car? I even got me a new Jeep last year." She laughed at his shrug and wrapped her arms around him. "You look good, honey. Almost grown, I declare." She pulled back from admiring him and turned to me. "This must be the girl you were telling me about."

I had come around the car by then and stepped up with a smile to say hello. "Yes, ma'am. I'm Asia Burdette."

She reached out to hook my arm with one of hers and took Ethan's with the other. "Well, Asia, hit's a pleasure to meet you. Just call me Ida. Y'all come on in and make yourselves to home."

The sun was well up in the sky by this time and had warmed the air to comfortable sweater temperature, so we sat on the porch with some hot coffee and admired the view. The mountains rolled as far as vision could carry you. Behind, the shoulder of the mountain rose up to deflect the worst of wind and weather.

I exhaled. "It's gorgeous here."

"Mmm," Ida agreed. "This land has been in my family since the 1700s, they reckon. Got records in the church going back to 1806. Used to be an old log cabin back in the woods there. Reckon the termites ate it all up by now, though."

"Guess there wasn't any coal under it, huh?" Ethan said.

Ida laughed. "Lucky for us. I still own this old farmhouse and the two pastures down there. My nieces and nephews still farm around here, too. Lot of folks sold out and went in the mines in my granddaddy's time. Too late to turn back now."

I was curious. "So you grew up in this house, Ida?"

"Born in the back bedroom in the middle of a snowstorm." She grinned. "Went to school down the road with five grades in a room until it came time to ride the bus to the high school across the mountain. Married Billy Mickens the spring we graduated, and he went off to join the Army a week later. That was 1942."

I thought about all she had seen and done in this world, right from this front porch, and fell silent with awe. We hadn't even begun to talk about the "visions" she lived with, and I already admired this woman.

Ida looked at me, an awareness in her gray-green eyes that saw right through me. "What part of Tennessee you from, Asia?"

"I grew up near Cookeville." Wondering how much Ethan had told her, I glanced in his direction.

"Oh, don't worry, honey, he didn't tell me a thing about you," she said. "I'm just guessing from the way you talk you don't come from up north like he does."

"Well, we know he's a Yankee, but we don't hold that against him."

Ethan just smiled and rocked.

Ida brought an end to light-heartedness with her next question. "Are you married, Asia? Got kids?"

The band of steel that I had almost forgotten existed tightened at once around my chest. Ethan straightened in his chair but said nothing. I took a breath. If I expected to get anything out of today, I had to be brave enough to open up.

"I was married." I was surprised at how even my voice was. "I'm divorced now. My three kids died in a fire three years ago."

Ida's eyes widened in horror, and her hand went to her mouth. "Oh, my Lord Jesus, child. I'm so sorry." She threw a look in Ethan's direction. "I had no idea."

I shook my head. "Of course you didn't. I don't tell many people. Ethan knows that."

She nodded. "That's an awful heavy thing for a soul to carry, Lord knows it is. My boy Charlie's been gone thirty-eight years this June, and I still miss him. He was in Vietnam."

Tears welled in my eyes, threatening to spill over onto my cheeks. I struggled for control and just barely managed to find enough manners to say, "I'm sorry."

Ida saw that I needed a minute and rose from her rocker. "Well, children, I suspect dinner's close to being done. I'll just go and put the biscuits in the oven. If you need to use the outhouse, it's around back."

Ethan tilted his head back to grin at her. "Now, Ida, even I know you've had indoor plumbing for fifty years."

She laughed. "Can't fool you, huh, city boy? All right, throne room's just inside."

From the way Ida had cooked that day, you'd have thought Ethan was a long-lost son returned home to kith and kin. The tiny table in her sunny kitchen was laden with fried chicken, mashed potatoes, green beans, pinto beans, tomatoes, corn, squash, biscuits, gravy and three different kinds of homemade jam. Plus the apple butter, which Ethan made an absolute pig of himself over. Really made me wonder about that comment he'd made in the car the day before.

We ate and talked about things that didn't matter so much until I couldn't hold one more mouthful of food. I could barely move to help clear the table.

"Ida, I haven't eaten like that since my grandmama passed on. And it's a good thing, too, or I'd weigh three hundred pounds."

"Well, you could stand to gain a little weight, darlin', if you don't mind me sayin'." She gave me a look. "A man likes something he can hold on to."

I snorted. "I always thought there was plenty of me to go around."

Ethan smiled and ducked his head, fleeing for the safety the porch. I glanced after him, feeling a little warm inside.

"Um-hm, that's what I thought." Ida nodded, up to her elbows in dishwater at the sink.

I picked up a towel and started to dry the glasses she placed in the drainer. "What?"

"You and Dr. Ethan."

"Oh, no. It's not like that," I said, maybe a little too quickly. "He wouldn't. I mean, he was my psychiatrist until a couple of weeks ago."

She looked at me like I'd just grown another head. "You don't seem crazy to me."

"Are you sure?"

She went back to washing dishes. "Reckon that's what you're here to find out, isn't it?"

Ida, like Rita, didn't miss much. "Guess you're right about that."

"Well, let me tell you something, little girl." She stopped washing and pinned me with a hard stare. "Doctor or no doctor, that boy's got it bad for you. He hadn't hardly taken his eyes off you since y'all got here."

"Oh, I don't know about that." But a shiver ran down my spine.

"You don't, huh?" She smiled as she returned to her dishes. "Maybe you're thinking he's still carrying a torch for that dead wife of his."

My jaw dropped. I scooped it up as fast as I could, but she caught me, all right, and grinned. "I started in with Ethan not long after the accident, and I can tell you that woman left him a mess. But it wasn't because she was any good for him. She was one them kind of women that rhymes with witch. He didn't want to tell me much about it, but I found out anyway. I don't read them detective books for nothin'."

My heart was slamming against my ribcage. Why the hell was she telling me all this? And, God, why did I find the information so welcome?

Ida was reading my mind. "I'm telling you this for one reason, Asia Burdette. If you break Ethan's heart, I'm gonna drive down off this mountain and come looking for you. Because there ain't no sweeter man in this world than him. You understand me?"

Shaking, I took the next glass from the drainer and dried it, afraid to meet her eyes lest she see the hope in mine. "Yes, ma'am."

The shadows had already started to lengthen across the grass in front of the farmhouse when Ethan opened his eyes. He stretched and sat up in the porch swing, turning an embarrassed smile in Ida's direction.

"I'm sorry. I guess I fell asleep. What time is it?"

"Oh, I reckon around three." She glanced up at the sun from the book in her lap—Elmore Leonard's last novel in hardcover. "Don't fret. I had me a nap, too. Big meal like that usually needs one."

"Where's Asia?"

Ida smiled. "Inside in the guest room. Once she saw you were out like a light, she took my suggestion."

Ethan ran a hand through his hair and settled back into the swing, letting his gaze roam over the russet hills. He sighed, suddenly in no hurry to go anywhere, do anything.

"She's a good girl, Ethan. Got a good heart."

"Yes, she does." He looked at the old woman, wondering what was on her mind.

"And she likes you. More than you know."

"What?" He had the idea he was going to lose control of this conversation very quickly.

"Why haven't you told her how you feel?"

"Ida . . ."

"Now, son, don't go gettin' on your high horse." She laid her hand on his arm to forestall the leap to his feet he was considering. "I'm old enough to be your granny so I can say what I want to. Y'all are both way yonder too old and too hurt to be a-wasting time. She wants you. You want her. What are you waiting for? You better be asking her to marry you before she slips away. Believe me, son, chances like this don't come along too often of a lifetime."

Ethan stared at her, speechless. What in God's name had led her to conclude there could be that kind of relationship between him and Asia? *Married?* They barely knew each other—and what they did know had come from a professional, not a personal, relationship.

"Ida, you have this all wrong." He hardly knew where to begin to explain.

"Hey, y'all," Asia said from the doorway. "What did I miss?"

Ida turned to her with an innocent smile. "Not a thing, honey. Come on out here and set a spell. I'll make us some coffee."

She went inside and Asia sat down next to Ethan on the swing. She smiled up at him, kicking his already accelerated heartbeat into overdrive.

"Hey, sleepyhead. Did you have a nice nap?"

He smiled. "Yeah. You?"

"I did. Seemed like the thing to do."

His arm was draped over the back of the swing. He wanted to drop his hand down onto her neck, curl his fingers in her hair. He resisted the impulse.

"You ladies talk about anything special while I was out?"

Asia seemed to lose her composure for a second, but recovered quickly. "Not really. I wasn't sure how to ask her about the visions. Guess that's next on the agenda, huh?"

He nodded, then jumped up to hold the screen door open for Ida. She put the coffeepot and cups on a table in the corner of the porch, went back to the kitchen and brought out sugar, cream and sliced applesauce cake.

Asia laughed. "Lord, Ida, you act like we're going to starve once we leave here."

"Well, you ain't leaving here hungry, that's for certain." She served them each a huge piece of cake. "If I didn't have a big day at church tomorrow, I'd ask you to stay over tonight and I could really fatten you up."

Ethan shook his head. "You've already done enough for us, Ida. We've got a long trip back in the morning, too."

"Well, then, I reckon you come here to hear this story, so I might as well tell it," Ida said, settling into her seat with a cup of coffee. "Ethan says you have one a lot like it, Asia, so maybe you'll understand me when I say this is the Lord's honest truth. Ain't nothing of a lie about any of it. I been beat often enough for telling it, so if it was a lie I would have given it up before now.

"The first time I remember telling the tale I was ten years old, and I woke the house up screaming in the night. Mama and Daddy said it was a dream, but it was so real, I just knew I'd been somewhere else. I got a beating for talking back that morning. And the next day. And the next. Until I stopped talking about it. But the visions didn't stop. They kept up every night for a while. Then it was just ever once in a while. Then not so often, but often enough that I was sure to remember.

"It got bad after Charlie died and again after Bill died. That's when I went to see Dr. Ethan. The machine just seemed to bring back all the details. And that's when I knew for sure."

Asia touched her hand. "Knew what, Ida?"

"That what I'd seen was real."

Asia met Ethan's eyes, sending a cold ripple of apprehension down his back, before she looked back at Ida. "What had you seen?"

Ida shook her head. "A place like nothing on this earth. The sky was as green as that grass yonder and the sun was never yellow like ours is. It was white, like a neon light, so white it was nearly blue, and it burned like a diamond in that green sky.

"It was hot all the time there, like I reckon it must be in Africa, and the plants grew tall and thick, like some kind of jungle. But they wasn't no plants like you'd ever seen before. I could swear they looked like giant ferns. Yes, ma'am, ferns as big as that oak tree there, and the colors—well, I can't even describe the colors. Seems like we don't even have colors like that in this world."

Ida stopped talking and looked at Asia, waiting for her reaction. Ethan waited, too, wondering what Asia would say. Asia looked at him, and her feelings were there in her face for anyone to read—astonishment, relief, kinship.

Asia turned back to the old woman. "Go on, Ida. There's more, isn't there?"

"Well, I suspect you know the rest, child. They

brought us there to work the fields, to weed and harvest the fruits off the plants that grew in that heavy, yellow mud. The plants grew high, over my head, and their leaves were as sharp as knives. They cut you when you reached in to pull out the big, round fruits. And they were sticky, too. You were covered in sap as thick as pine tar as soon as you started, and the bugs just loved the stuff. Drove you plumb crazy. Saw many a young'un run off to get shot on account of them bugs."

"They needed your smaller hands."

Ida nodded. "The adults couldn't reach in. They carried the loaded baskets to the hoppers. How did you know?"

"It was the same in the mines. Some jobs were reserved for the children, or the ones with smaller bodies, like my friend Dozen."

Ida laughed. "Mines! Lord 'a' mercy, if they was looking for miners, they could have found aplenty around here!"

"Shoot, Ida, these guys gotta be the worst temp agency in the universe! From what I could see, not a one of the folks I was working with knew a damn thing about mining!"

The two of them cracked up, and Ethan had to join them, if only in admiration of the black humor that would let them laugh after all they'd been through.

Asia giggled and dabbed at a tear that rolled down her cheek from the laughter. "Yeah, the only question is, who the heck were these guys anyway? That's assuming you and I didn't both just dream all this up in a fit of imagination."

Ida shook her head. "That's the one thing I been trying all these years to remember, and the one thing I've never been able to see. We had guards, but they looked just like you and me. And as far as being taken somewhere—well, I reckon Mister Sandman musta done it, 'cause I don't remember a thing about it. I went to sleep just like always one night and woke up the next morning with all of this in my mind."

"Mister Sandman," Asia repeated with a little smile. "Have to admit it beats my explanation."

"What's your explanation, child?"

Asia sighed, and Ethan's stomach clenched in sympathy. "I don't have one."

CHAPTER ELEVEN

We spent the two hours driving back to Bristol from Ida's trying to talk around the big, otherworldly elephant taking up space in the rear seat of Ethan's Beemer. We approached the subject from every side, except head-on. We couldn't pretend the damn thing wasn't there, but we were still too afraid to call it what it was. Ida and I both knew what we had seen was not of this world. And we knew the worlds we had seen were as real as this one. What Ethan and I didn't know and didn't want to talk about was where that left us.

We were still skirting that problem when we hit Bristol. It was late, and we were still full from Ida's cooking, so we decided to skip dinner and head over to the motel bar for a nightcap. Once we'd settled into the booth, I took up the discussion again.

"Have you ever heard of these kinds of visions before, Ethan? I mean, does this kind of thing happen to other people?"

He looked up at the waitress with a distracted smile, waiting until the drinks were set down and we were alone again before he answered. "There's very little in the literature that parallels what you and Ida seem to have experienced." He studied the swirl of ice in his glass. "I've only had a handful of other patients who had anything similar. I pulled their records, tried to get in touch with them. So far, I haven't been able to find them."

A subtle little chill washed down my spine. "What do you mean you haven't been able to find them?"

He rubbed at his forehead. "They've moved, changed phone numbers. I've got somebody working on it, but so far she's having no luck."

"What do you think they can tell us that we don't already know?"

"I don't know." He sighed. "I just want to talk to them, see if anything has changed."

His shoulders sagged in defeat. He was taking this way too personally, as if he had failed to find the right clue to solve the puzzle and was blaming himself for it.

I nudged the conversation in another direction, determined to undermine the seriousness with which Ethan watched me over his drink. "Thank you for today."

He almost matched my smile. "What do you mean?"

"For Ida," I clarified. "She's wonderful. And she makes me feel like I'm not so alone in this . . . whatever it is."

"I think she feels the same way about you."

"Well, I hope so. We seemed to get along, anyway. Too bad it's such a long drive back to Nashville. I would have enjoyed some more time with her." I pushed on, wanting him to feel good about bringing us together. "I really enjoyed myself today. It meant a lot to me. Thank you."

"Me, too." He fell quiet again, watching.

I began to get a little self-conscious, the color rising in my cheeks. I couldn't think of another word to say.

"Asia . . ." Something about the way he said my name struck sparks in the vicinity of my heart. I waited, barely breathing. He cleared his throat. "You want another drink?"

I took a moment to recover. "No, thanks. That first one went right to my head." God knows why my inner Scarlett O'Hara had suddenly decided to make an appearance, but if she was there to save me from showing my ass, she was welcome.

I gave Ethan a speculative glance, deciding to take the offensive. "How about a dance instead?"

The expression on his face could only be read as sheer panic. "Uh . . ."

"Oh, come on." *Lady in Red* was just starting up. "This is a nice, slow one. You won't have to pull out any major moves. We'll just stretch our legs a little from the drive, what d'you say?"

A slow, shy smile spread across his handsome face as he made up his mind, a smile so charming and sweet it stole my breath. He stood and held out his hand, and it was all I could do to keep from tripping over myself in my rush to take it and follow him to the dance floor.

We found a corner away from the lights and the jostling elbows of the other dancers, and came together. Despite his protest he knew what he was doing. He took my right hand in his left and tucked it in close to his chest, slipped his other arm around behind my shoulders to hold me just tight enough that I could follow him. I smiled, encouraging him, letting him know how much I was enjoying this, and relaxed into his embrace, sliding my free arm around his waist to complete the fit.

He moved—nothing fancy, just a simple sway and step to the rhythm of the music—and I moved with him. I let him take me, step for step, breath for breath, his body moving against mine. I could feel the heat coming off his chest, the strength in his hands where he held me. I was achingly aware of the light brush of his hips against mine as we moved, contact we couldn't have avoided even if we'd wanted to.

I couldn't help it; the music, the dark, his warm hand on my back—all of it made me drop my head to his chest and hold him closer than I know I should have. He didn't object. I felt his cheek brush my hair, his arm tighten around me. I inhaled his clean, citrusy scent, spread my hand to feel the muscles move in his back, shut out everything and everyone except him. That he allowed me this closeness felt like a miracle. I didn't stop to ask why; I just let it happen and thanked God for it.

Because I needed this. I needed *him*—his touch, his warmth, his arms around me. I suddenly needed it more than I needed to breathe. And when the music came to an end, I sighed and stood away from him, opening my eyes like I'd awakened from some kind of dream.

"That was nice." I smiled. "Thank you."

His eyes met mine. "It's been a long time since I did that. I'd almost forgotten . . ."

I waited, but he didn't finish. The tempo of the music picked up, and he steered me back to our table. The waitress had cleared our empty glasses, thinking we'd left, so we just kept going, threading our way through the crowded bar to the outside.

I could smell the rain as we came out of the lobby, hovering in the heavy air and ready to drop. Thunder rolled through the clouds not a mile away.

Ethan peered up at the sky. "We'll be lucky if we make it to our rooms before this breaks."

"Well, I'm not running." I stepped out ahead of him. "I'm feeling way too mellow to let a few raindrops dampen the mood. Guess I'll just have to get wet."

He laughed as he caught up with me, his boots crunching on the gravel of the parking lot. "We'll see how mellow you feel once you start looking like a drowned cat."

"This cat has claws, baby." I took a swat at him to prove it. He responded with more laughter, opening a way for a warm rush of feeling through my chest, a gentle assault that took me by surprise and left me breathless.

We rounded the corner that led to our section of the motel as the first fat raindrops began to spatter the windshields of the cars in the lot. Within seconds, the rain was washing down in sheets, blowing through the breezeway enough to lick any exposed skin, leaving goose bumps behind.

The breezeways protected us most of the way back to the room, but the last hundred feet or so required a dash across the open parking lot to the other building. The sluicing rain had set up a stream of water three inches deep and twelve feet wide sliding down through the center of the lot, and the rain was pelting down harder than ever. I took off my jacket and held it over my head, but by the time we'd splashed and slogged through to the other side I was soaked to the skin from top to bottom.

My room was closest. I pulled out my keycard and swiped it in a hurry. Dripping, we tumbled inside and slammed the door behind us. Ethan's hand hit the light switch just as a *boom!* and a flash took all light from the room. I jumped and grabbed for him in the sudden darkness. He caught me with a laugh, and we stood together shivering while thunder shook the walls and I slowly realized lightning had just taken out the power.

"Shit." I was more than a little embarrassed that I'd reacted so dramatically. "Not only a drowned cat, but a scaredy one, too." But I couldn't control the trembling that had started up in my arms and legs and was quickly progressing to every muscle in my body.

Ethan pulled me into his chest and wrapped his arms around me. "You're just cold." And I admit the warmth of his body had an immediate effect on me. The tremors slowed, replaced by the slow thud of my heart recognizing suddenly how close we were, how easy it would be to touch and be touched, to take the next step and the next until we lay naked and satisfied in each other's arms.

But if Ethan was thinking that way, he gave no sign of it. Smiling, he pulled back a little and brushed the wet hair out of my face. "Better?" I could have nodded brightly and turned away to end the moment, but I didn't. I left my hands lying lightly on his damp chest, feeling his heartbeat and his heat through my fingertips. I brought our hips together, grazing the thick ridge of his erection down the left leg of his jeans. I sent a challenge deep into his eyes, eyes that even in the dark watched me with growing understanding. And I waited.

We stood in that tortured limbo for a long moment until at last he moved, bending to brush his lips across mine. When I arched against him in response, he covered my mouth with his and kissed me hard. There was hunger in that kiss and a deep, searching need that ignited a kindred fire in me. I let the taste of him and the smooth, slippery slide of his tongue feed that flame inside me until it began to run like molten metal in my veins. Our bodies melded together, his hands slipping behind my back to press me close, and I felt every inch of him, hard and insistent, in the hollow of my hip. In seconds I was softening, opening to make room for him, already wet and ready to receive him without so much as a touch.

So I was stunned when he drew back and broke the connection. I couldn't read his expression in the dark, but I could still hear his labored breathing. I could still feel his heart pounding in his chest. And I knew without looking or reaching to measure it, that his hard-on was still just as evident.

I managed to find just enough wits to ask him, "What's wrong?"

"I have to go." He backed up half a step, trying to re-create a distance between us that now no longer existed.

I closed the space again. "What the hell are you talking about?"

"Asia, we can't do this." His voice was barely audible. "You were my patient."

"I'm a grown woman, Ethan," I shot back. "I can make my own choices. Unless you still think I'm crazy."

"You were never crazy. That doesn't mean this isn't wrong."

His actions had already spoken loud and clear. His words scarcely penetrated the haze of sexual energy we'd generated. This darkened hotel room full of mutually consenting pheromones was a long way from my idea of exploitation. I was mad now. His rejection hurt, and the throb in my groin was like a hand squeezing me. I wanted him so much I couldn't think straight, so much I did something then I would never have done in a more rational moment. I ripped at the snap on his jeans, pulled down the zipper and reached inside for him.

We gasped together, groaning as my fingers closed around him. My God, he was built! Velvet and steel, length and thickness, an eager leap of response met my grip as I maneuvered my prize between us. I captured him beneath my T-shirt, between my palm and my bare belly, and I held him there, skin to skin.

"Hell, yes, it's wrong." I tried, and failed, to keep

my voice from shaking. "I shouldn't want you, but tell me you don't want it as bad as I do, Ethan. Tell me you don't want me, and you can walk out that door, and we'll forget this ever happened."

For an endless time he said nothing, did nothing. Nothing moved except for his breath and mine lifting and falling raggedly in our chests, my hand sliding slowly up and down between us. In that timeless moment my heightened senses flooded me with awareness—the hot spike of his cock pressing into my belly, my frantic heartbeat and his pulse beating into my palm, the clean, masculine scent of his skin, the sound of the rain and the thunder outside.

Then, at last, just when I was sure he would leave me desolate and alone, he surrendered. With a growl of desperate need he clamped a hand on either side of my ribcage and lifted me up and back until he had me pinned against the wall. "*Damn* it, Asia." He pulled my sweater and both my arms above my head and held them there, leaving my mouth turned up to his bruising kiss and my body open to the press of his chest and hips. His tongue slipped in and out of my mouth, carrying his taste across my lips, and I alternately pursued and invited him, soft moans escaping me with every breath.

He broke off and rocked into me. My core responded with a rush of pulsing need.

"How can you think I don't want you?" His lips were warm at my ear. "You're the most beautiful, most *amazing* woman I've ever known. Every rule says I can't have you and yet . . . oh, *fuck*." He dropped his head to nip at my earlobe and the sensitive skin where my neck met my shoulder. The contrast between his lips, so soft and warm, and the rough abrasion of his beard against my skin made me shiver.

There was something incredibly sexy about the fact that he was still completely clothed except for one heart-stopping detail—his denim shirt still buttoned except for the front shirttail that split over his emerging shaft, his jeans still clinging to his hips and thighs, covering everything except that delicious package—and I was almost completely naked for him. And now that I could no longer touch him, I wanted only to feel him in my hand again. I wanted to stroke him, to tease him, to squeeze and fondle him. To have my hands held prisoner, unable to experience him at all, was exquisitely frustrating. I whimpered, wriggling in his hold.

Ethan pulled back to look at me, and I heard him suck in a breath. I was no longer cold from the soaking I'd taken in the rain, but my skin was still wet and my nipples were tight with desire. In his devouring gaze I saw the woman I was, and I felt a kind of power I'd never felt before, a power I wanted to use only to give him pleasure.

He was still looking at me, watching me, as he dropped one hand to my breast, warming the skin with his palm, teasing the nipple between his thumb and finger. I moaned as he bent to lift me to his mouth, and his tongue flickered across the sensitive peak, sending a sizzle of liquid fire deep into my belly. But he was only giving me a taste of what he could do to me; he shifted and teased the other breast lightly in the same way, leaving me hungry for more.

He moved to one side and drew my hands up higher above my head. Then, just as I had done, *God, yes!* he yanked open the snaps of my jeans and slipped his hand inside. He groaned as he discovered how wet I was for him.

"Jesus, Asia. I could take you here against the wall right now."

"Do it." It sounded like an order, but I would have begged him. I was mindless with need.

"No." His hand gently squeezed and released, massaging my swollen flesh until it melted under his touch. "I want to make this last." His fingers slid into the slick groove between my thighs, circling, circling and finally—*God!*—penetrating.

"Ethan!" I moaned, sliding down the wall as I lost nearly all control. I was hot and aching, so close to coming I couldn't stand up.

He picked me up, then, and carried me to the bed. He stretched me out and freed me from the rest of my clothes, then quickly stripped off his own and came back to me. I reached for him, free at last and eager to touch him, and he placed one knee on the bed near my shoulder and gave himself over to me with a smile.

Lord, he was beautiful—long and thick and lusciously erect, rising straight out of his taut, heavy sac. I wanted to taste every inch, every contour and pulsing vein, but I knew we were both too tightly wound to stand it. Instead, I took just the juicy plum of his tip into my mouth. I wrapped my hand around the rigid shaft and savored Ethan's sharp intake of breath and deep groan as I slowly slid my grip down to the root and back up. I could feel the rising tension in his body as I gently explored him with my tongue; he endured it only briefly before his hand closed tightly over mine.

He bent over me and tilted my head up to receive his kiss, a gentle touch of the lips. "When I come, it's going to be deep inside you. And not until you say you've had enough."

Jesus, the man could talk me right into an orgasm. I wasn't sure I could ever say I'd had enough of him now that I'd started. I pulled him down on top of me, thrilling to the slide of his skin on mine, the movement of his muscled body against my breasts and my belly and my thighs. His tongue ravished my mouth while he rocked gently back and forth, his shaft heavy and hard against my wet core. My hips rose to meet his every pulse, my thighs opened to take him in, and I flooded us both with my body's response.

He slid down my body to nip and suckle at first one breast and then the other. He used his tongue and his hands to alternately tease and soothe the sensitive skin, until I felt every electric flicker all the way down to the heart of my building climax. I was suddenly alive in a wholly new way; every nerve was responding to his touch, every cell awakening under his attention. I began to believe that before he was through with me he would be able to stroke my arm or brush his lips across my eyebrow and I would come for him.

He continued down my body, leaving a wet,

tingling trail of rough-edged kisses along my belly, into the crease between my hip and my thigh and across the pubic bone to the other side. Then, as I quivered with anticipation, every part of me on fire for him, he spread me with his thumbs and invaded the tender folds of flesh between my thighs with his sweet tongue. He worked me slowly, confidently, as if he knew exactly what would drive me crazy. The muscles of my abdomen and pelvis clenched, empty and craving. My shoulders lifted off the bed as I curled inward with longing. He didn't stop, but changed the movement of his tongue to a torturous flutter.

That sent me over the top. I was coming, Jesus God, like a freight train, and I only wanted one thing. "Ethan, please, I want you inside me." I breathed, trying not to scream. "Now, Ethan."

He moved to help me at last and oh, God! the feeling of coming with him pushing inside me, opening me up, filling me. Once he'd made a way for himself, he began to thrust into me with long, powerful strokes and I did scream then, calling his name over and over as wave after orgasmic wave washed through me, each one deeper and stronger and more devastating than the last.

I had only begun to breathe again when he seated himself in deep and ground into me in slow, pounding circles that brought me immediately to another annihilating climax. I clung to him, tore at him, writhing in an ecstasy I had never experienced before and couldn't control. There was something almost frightening about its intensity, had I been lying under a lesser man, my fear would have overruled my pleasure. But it was Ethan's body moving with mine and Ethan's heart beating with mine and Ethan's soft words of encouragement in my ear as he brought me up each feverish crest and rode with me down the slope of each contracting wave. I gave him everything; I held back nothing, trusting him to keep me safe.

The last spasms wrung grateful tears from my eyes, and I let them fall, unembarrassed, as he kissed the salt from my lips, my cheeks, my eyes. He whispered to me, "My sweet, beautiful Asia." He touched his warm lips to my throat, to my neck at the shoulder, to my ear. Then he brought them to my own and parted them to let his tongue slip inside my mouth, starting again as we had started earlier, with a kiss. And after all he had given me, I responded to that kiss as if it was the first time—my heart hammering, my breath rising, the blood rushing to swell the flesh that had only minutes before been rolling in orgasm.

Ethan had almost stopped moving, but I could still feel him inside me, still iron-hard, still stretching me, then expanding in the next second to fill me. I contracted in on him, signaling my readiness. It was what he'd been waiting for. He broke off his kiss and put his lips to my ear. "Tell me what you want."

"Come with me, Ethan. I want to feel you come with me."

His voice fell so low it was almost a growl. "Once more, slow and easy." I felt him breathe deep into his belly. "One last time, then I'll have to let go."

He began to slide in and out of me, letting me feel every inch of him with every stroke. I could feel the pressure building toward the climax he had promised me, and I knew it wouldn't take long. I was tuned to him now and he to me. This final climax for me was effortless, natural, as beautiful and fulfilling as a sunrise. As I arched into him, orgasm taking me again, Ethan's strokes came harder and faster until at last with a groan he exploded deep inside me. I felt every muscle in his body contract violently, then gradually relax as his pleasure ebbed.

I took a long, shuddering breath and exhaled a lifetime of unhappy, desperate, disappointing, angry and just plain bad sex. When I breathed again, I breathed free and clear for the first time in years.

"God, that was good." I was barely able to form the words. In that state of post-coital bliss, I just wasn't capable of telling him how I felt. The words were wrong and were coming out slurred, like a drunk's, but I had to say something. "That was so damn good. Thank you, baby."

He smiled and kissed me lazily on the lips. "So much more than good. Thank you for insisting."

I'm not sure it's possible for a naked woman to blush, but I felt my cheeks redden anyhow. "Just so you know, I've never done anything like that before—grabbed anyone, I mean."

"And I've never been propositioned quite that directly before either." He laughed softly. "God, it turned me on. There was no way in hell I could have refused."

The power kicked back on and threw an

unwelcome light in our eyes from the bedside lamp. Ethan reached across me to turn it off, but I put a hand on his arm to stop him. I needed to see the answer to my next question clearly in his face. He let his arm drop as he settled back onto his other elbow, one leg still draped across my thigh. He watched me with those eyes the color of deep rolling waves and waited.

"I didn't give you much choice. Are you sorry we did this?"

"Sorry? Never." He gave me that slow smile of his. "Why would I be sorry? This was the best thing to happen to me in a long time."

It would have been so easy to leave it at that. I wanted so badly to believe him. I searched his eyes, and at first all I could see was warmth and openness. But behind what could have been interpreted as bland and comforting (and just as quickly gone in the morning) was something truer, needier, a banked fire that was suddenly causing my heart to leap up and slam against my ribs like a deer flushed from hiding in a tangle of briars.

Abruptly his eyes widened. "Oh, God! I didn't use a condom. Is that it? I mean, you don't have to worry, I can't even remember the last time I—"

I put a finger to his lips to stop the rush of words, wanting to laugh, knowing I shouldn't. We hadn't been smart, after all.

"No, that's not it. I'm on the pill. I haven't had sex in months. I wasn't worried. I trust you."

Ethan let it go and lifted a hand to brush a strand of hair from my forehead. "So what's bothering you?"

I no longer wanted to, but I asked the question anyway. "Do you still think it was wrong to have sex with a former patient?"

His eyes darkened, like the surface of a lake when a cloud passes over. "With a former patient or with *you*, Asia?"

When I didn't say anything, he put a hand under my chin and turned my face to his. "Doctors have it beaten into them from the first day in med school that there are boundaries we can never cross." He was suddenly serious. "The rules are there for good reason, and the sanctions are severe for those who break them, also for good reason. They're not to be taken lightly."

My heart sank. "But there must be exceptions. Or a statute of limitations or something? What if we'd met on the street instead of in your office?"

His expression softened. "Then life would've been a lot easier. We'd have been here a lot sooner and poor, old Dr. Claussen would've had to struggle along with you in his therapy group quite a while longer."

"Oh, God, not that!" The thought of another session with Claussen's group was enough to make me glad it had happened the way it had. "Let me put it a different way, then." I had to know. "How much do you mind that we're breaking the rules?"

Ethan took my face in both his hands and kissed me long and slow and deep enough that my body was primed for yet another go-round. "Asia, even if hell was the price, you'd be worth every bit of it."

What was it about this man that made me want to settle into his arms and let him wrap me in that soft voice forever? The power of those words warmed my heart, calmed my spirit in some way I was only just beginning to understand. For the first time in a very long time, I felt something open up inside me. And I knew it wouldn't be long before all the things I'd been missing for so many years—gratitude, joy, hope, even love—would start flooding in.

Ethan lay awake long past midnight and watched Asia sleep, her hair falling in tousled curls around her face, her body outlined in the curve of her shoulder and hip, her breasts and the sweet triangle where her belly met her thighs hidden in shadow.

There was no question in his mind what was happening between them would be viewed as a breach of ethics. No matter that Asia was no longer his patient. No matter that she was perfectly capable of clear thinking and showed no signs of emotional transference. No matter that he had been careful not to exploit her emotions in any way. He could guess what Claussen would have to say once he found out. Ethan could only hope the old man didn't drag him in front of a review board. Extenuating circumstances or not, he'd likely lose his license.

But that wasn't what was keeping him awake with unresolved questions, despite his need for sleep. He'd meant it when he'd told Asia she'd been worth it. Not just physically, though God knows the days and weeks of wanting her had built up such a charge in him, he'd been like a machine. Even now, his cock was sending signals the rest of his exhausted body was trying to ignore.

He was responding to something in Asia, something on a deeper level that he could scarcely name. From the beginning, she had seen him for what he was, rather than what he could do for her. And when she said she wanted him, it touched him someplace deep inside. A place he showed no one. A place he barely acknowledged even to himself.

He had laid the first bricks in the wall that protected his heart long ago, when Elizabeth had begun to use his love for her to slice him casually in passing. By the time she had perfected the art of torturing him with a surgeon's precision, he'd sealed a tiny portion of himself off where she couldn't reach him—so effectively even he couldn't get in.

Now, suddenly, it was as if he'd stumbled upon a locked room in his own house, a room he'd forgotten was there. He gazed at the woman in his bed and wondered if maybe she had the key. The thought of that made his heart expand and bump against the inside of his chest with a restless, rising rhythm.

Asia sighed softly in her sleep, making him smile, and he reached out to caress the skin of her shoulder. He trailed his hand down her upper arm and back up, then across her upper back and down the curve of her spine to the swell of her buttocks, savoring the sensation of her smooth skin under his fingertips, admiring the symmetry of sinuous muscle and luscious, tempting curve.

As his hand came back up toward her shoulder, his fingertips skimmed an uneven ridge in the skin over her right shoulder blade. Curious that such perfection could contain even a tiny flaw, he moved so that the light slipping through a gap in the room curtain could fall across her back and show him the mark. He drew in a breath when he saw it—jagged and ugly, raised and dark, following the line of the scapula as if the bone itself had been pushed through the skin. She'd never mentioned an injury on that scale—she'd never mentioned an injury at all. Even the sessions with AL hadn't revealed it. Here was another mystery to add to all the others about this woman who had fascinated him from the start.

He pressed his lips to her poor, abused shoulder, wishing he could take the pain of it as easily. Then he brushed the hair aside to bare the nape of her neck and kissed her there, inhaling her spicy/sweet scent as his lips lingered at the spot. He loved the way she smelled, like nectar from some exotic desert flower. He had loved immersing himself in that scent as they made love, rolling in it, covering himself in it. Breathing her in now brought it all back, and he couldn't restrain a low growl of remembered pleasure deep in his throat. He was hard again, too, as if he had not had enough opportunity to taste her tonight.

"Mmm, again?" she murmured, awakened by his touch. She stretched, catlike, her back arching against him. "Don't you ever sleep?"

He molded himself to her and reached around to cup one firm, round breast in his hand. "You could tell me to behave myself. If I were you, I'd start to set some limits now, rather than later."

She captured his shaft between her thighs. Then she grasped him where he emerged from between her legs and pressed him against her. Her flesh was hot and wet and melting everywhere except for the engorged pearl of her clitoris where she was using it to tease his sensitive tip. It was all he could do to keep from coming like a schoolboy in the heat of that delicious flame.

She spoke, her voice a whispery purr that resonated against his chest. "When I was first married I would try to wake Ronnie up in the middle of the night to make love." Ethan tried hard to focus on what she was saying, but what she was doing to him made it all but impossible. "He would always tell me to go back to sleep. I remember how that made me feel. I would never do that to you."

He pulled her closer to him and caught her earlobe gently in his teeth, grateful that the raging hard-on he was carrying would find relief in bringing her to climax—the way it was meant to be. "My sweet Asia. I can't believe he could have had this any night. He could have had *you*— your silky skin,"—he kissed her neck—"your beautiful brown eyes,"—he kissed her shoulder—"your long legs,"—his hand traveled down the length of her thigh and back up across her hip— "your perfect breasts,"—he cupped her breast once again and gently plucked the nipple between thumb and forefinger—"your round, tight ass,"—he rolled into her, offering her another inch of his swollen shaft—"and, oh, God, that juicy . . ." His words devolved into an animalistic groan as she took what he had offered, stroked it, squeezed it, crushed it against the slick, intimate folds between her thighs. A shiver of white-hot anticipation racked his body. He waited it out, knowing that in seconds he would be inside her and the waiting would be over.

"I love the way you talk to me." She moaned sweetly. "I love the way you make love to me."

She shifted again so that he lay poised to enter her. With a single, easy movement he thrust deep inside, sheathing himself in searing heat. He withdrew and pushed in again. She opened for him, her hips wide, and he knew he was reaching places inside her that were his alone. The knowledge of that intimacy brought him close to orgasm, and he struggled to find the control he needed.

He slid a hand down her belly to her mound, found her pulsing nub with his fingers, matched the rhythm of his thrusts to the press of his hand. "Oh, yeah, I like that," she told him. He smiled, his shaft swelling in response.

Her hand closed over his, her body ground into his, begging for more. He pushed into her, harder, deeper, feeling her need, feeding it, until at last she shuddered under him, crying his name into the pillow. Seconds later he found his own release, ecstasy issuing like fire from the base of his spine to engulf his body and leave him spent, his heart thrashing in his chest.

Later, much later, he withdrew from the warmth of her body, and she turned to look into his eyes. The hand she raised to touch his cheek trembled. "I—I can't stop shaking."

"It's all right, Asia. I'm here." He thought about reaching for the sheets, but that much movement seemed beyond his capabilities. Instead, he pulled her tight against his chest and kissed the back of her neck, wrapped her in the warmth he felt for her until her trembling—and his—subsided. There were words that described how he felt in that moment, but he didn't say them. Too much had already happened in one night for the two of them to think about. There would be plenty of time for the rest of it to unfold.

For now, it was enough just to hold her, and dream.

CHAPTER TWELVE

Ethan had no way of telling what time it was when he next opened his eyes. Thanks to the power failure, the motel's bedside clock flashed a meaningless 12:00. He lay quietly and listened. He could hear the muffled sounds of a busy motel outside—cars starting up, voices approaching and receding along the outside breezeway. So, morning. Not too early, he suspected, but not too late, either.

He disengaged from Asia's embrace and slipped out of bed, not wanting to wake her. They hadn't had much sleep, and there was no particular reason to hurry. They could take their time getting back to Nashville. He knew lots of little places to stop, maybe spend an extra night. He smiled and forced himself to think of something else quick so he could at least hit the bathroom before he got hard again.

He glanced through the gap in the room curtain on his way around the bed—the day was overcast, the remnants of last night's storm clouds still scudding across a glowering sky. Rain pooled in wide sheets across the uneven parking lot; the cars coming and going splashed sullenly through the puddles to get to the exits. Two doors up, a van sat with its lights on, the wipers on intermittent to catch the drizzle that still spit from the sky. Ethan dismissed one idea he'd been toying with for the day—hiking would be muddy and miserable, no matter how romantic the view.

A few minutes later he was rinsing shampoo from his hair and running through a variety of alternatives to hiking, any number of which were pleasant enough to send the blood rushing to his groin, when Asia grinned at him from around the shower curtain.

"Hey, good lookin'. You want some company in there?" Her amber eyes sparkled. She was irresistible. And thank God he no longer had to try.

He held out a hand to her and pulled her in under the hot shower, laughing as she giggled and sputtered under the spray. He gathered her to him and took the force of the water on his back so he could tip her face back and kiss her. Her lips parted to receive him, and his tongue slipped inside to caress and explore and tease her sweet mouth. He could have gone on kissing her forever, while the water pounded down and his heart pumped blood into his growing erection. But he retreated at last, with a lingering pull at her lower lip.

"Good morning, beautiful."

"Oh, my God," she murmured. "You are like some kind of drug." She pushed back from him just enough for the water to hit her body. Then she reached for the soap. She began at his chest, rubbing the slippery square of cheap motel soap across his skin, working up the lather with her hands, licking and nibbling at his taut nipples once the water had rinsed him clean.

Then she turned him around and repeated the process on his back, down his legs—he held his breath as she skimmed the scars on his ravaged right leg, but she didn't pause and he relaxed again—and his buttocks.

She turned him back to face her and began on his belly, his thighs and—*Jesus Christ!*—he was so fucking hard he was *this close* to coming! Her hands were between his legs and they were warm and slick and wet and slippery and squeezing him tight just like she did when he was inside and it was all he could do to keep from letting go, but she whispered, "Not yet," and he held on.

Asia handed him the soap and smiled. Then, because the shower was running into her face, she turned her back to him. With a shock, he saw again the jagged scar ripping across her shoulder blade, saw clearly in the glaring light of the bathroom how cruelly the skin had been torn, how deeply the muscle had been gouged, in how many places the bone had been broken. And he saw something else.

Higher up, on the nape her neck, was another, smaller, rectangular scar, one similar in shape to a scar he'd seen on a patient years before. One of his first patients, and another of those he'd failed to help. He stopped breathing, and the soap slipped from his hands.

Asia laughed and stooped to fish it out of the bottom of the tub. "Hey, I'm not falling for that old trick." She handed the tiny square back to Ethan. "I want the full sensual treatment, mister, just like you got."

He laughed softly and put his questions on hold. She was beautiful, she wanted him, and he was still hard enough to hammer nails. Everything else could wait. He began with her back, took special pleasure in working the lather over her perfect, heart-shaped ass. Then he leaned her body back against his and slathered the creamy foam down from her luscious breasts to her thighs and worked it between her legs with both hands until she whimpered with the same need she had created in him.

He wanted her *now* and the hot water continued to flow, so he gave no thought to moving to the bed. When the soap had been rinsed away, he turned her toward him and in one smooth movement, joined them. The position was awkward, perhaps even precarious, but it didn't matter. Her core was liquid fire, already closing on him in orgasm. He gripped her buttocks, pulled her into him and drove hard and deep into her yielding center. Asia arched up into him, lost and crying out in desperate pleasure. He rode it out with her, giving her the sweet-hot friction and satisfying penetration she needed, until it all became too much for him and he came, shuddering, spilling what was left of his seed after a long night of love deep inside her.

He stood motionless for a few shaky breaths, his heartbeat slowing, the tension of need falling from his muscles like the water. He looked down into Asia's upturned face, still caught in the transcendently beautiful moment of orgasm, lips parted and eyes closed, her skin wet and glowing. He bent to kiss her, just touching the tip of his tongue to hers. He felt her breath as she sighed.

"You know, I have never been loved the way you've loved me." Her eyes were still closed, as if she was savoring something sweet. "Never in all my life." She took a deep breath, then she smiled and looked up at him. "But I have to say this is enough for a while. Any more and I won't be able to walk."

Ethan laughed and moved at last, slipping from her warm body and releasing her. "I'm not sure, but I think that was more sex in one night than I've had in three years."

Asia giggled. "Aw, now, that's just a damn shame. All that gorgeous manhood gone to waste." She pulled him in and gave him a quick, teasing kiss. "Now, go on. A girl needs *some* privacy, after all. And would you grab my overnight bag out of the other room for me? God, this feels terrific. I can't believe there's still some hot water."

Grinning, he rinsed efficiently and stepped out of the shower into the steamy bathroom. He dried off with one of the coarse, too-small motel towels from the stack over the toilet, pleased that despite the shower the slight trace of Asia's scent still lingered on his skin. He snagged another towel to wrap around his hips and went to retrieve her bag from the next room.

"What the hell are you hauling in here, girl?" He hefted the bag, curious. "Thing weighs a ton."

She answered him from behind the shower curtain. "Oh, you know, the usual—breaking and entering tools, gold bullion, spare refrigerator."

"Good thing you left the jet engine at home."

"It was just a weekend trip."

Ethan couldn't remember the last time he'd felt this lighthearted, this—he almost couldn't recognize the feeling—playful. He hadn't always been grim and serious, had he? No. But once Elizabeth became part of his life, playtime was over. She'd sneered at his so-called immaturity until he stopped bothering to tease or joke and eventually rarely smiled. She'd liked him better that way—"brooding and dark."

He shook his head to clear it of painful memories as he padded back into the bedroom and reached for his clothes. He got dressed and had just finished tying his boots when someone knocked at the door.

The hair rose on the back of Ethan's neck. There was no reason for it—the knock was probably just housekeeping. *Still* . . . He heard the shower stop, so he stepped to the bathroom door and warned Asia in a low voice, "Hey, there's someone at the door. I'm going to get it."

"Sure."

The knock came again, louder this time. Ethan was even less inclined to answer it, but the logical part of his mind refused to let his fear win the argument. He looked out the peephole. Nothing. He took a breath and unlocked the door.

Two men slammed in through the entry. "What the fuck?" he shouted as the charge knocked him backward. Somehow he kept his feet, but then they were on him in a maelstrom of fists and elbows and knees. He lashed out and clipped one of his attackers on the chin. Blinding pain exploded as rough knuckles connected with his cheek, his temple, his ribs. He tasted blood.

Someone tried to pin his arms, and he grappled with him, twisting first right, then left. He caught the bastard in the nose with an elbow and heard a grunt. It wasn't just his blood flying now. The man's partner barreled into him, and all three catapulted into the bedside table. Ethan's hand closed on the lamp, and he smashed it into the side of the little guy's face. The man collapsed, moaning, but his friend kept coming, driving Ethan to the floor with a punishing knee to the ribs. He heard a snarled "motherfucker," before the bastard punched him twice across the face and ended it.

Stunned and sick, Ethan had no defense as the man swung toward him with something sharp and shiny. It jabbed into the top of Ethan's shoulder, sending a hot burn up his neck. He fought for consciousness in the time he had left.

His blood roared in his ears. A fall of heavy snow descended over his vision. Still Ethan struggled, twisting under the big man's weight until the man pushed off him without a word and stood up. He dropped the injector and backed away, his hands held out away from his body, his face full of angry surprise.

Ethan stared blearily up at him. *What the hell?*

"I said get away from him, you sonofabitch." I held the gun as steady as I could, given all the adrenaline that was running through my system.

Everything had happened so fast, I'd barely had

time to pull a tee-shirt over my head, put a mag in the gun and get my ass out of the bathroom in time to be of any use.

"Back against the wall." My voice shook. I tried hard to put some steel in it. "Now."

The asshole grinned at me. "Now, honey, you ain't gonna shoot me, are you?"

"Wanna find out?" I slipped off the safety and made sure a bullet was in the chamber. He lost his grin and settled back against the wall. I spared a glance at his companion, still napping under a blanket of broken glass from the lamp Ethan had shattered over his head.

Ethan rolled to his hands and knees and grinned lopsidedly up at me. "Guess I know what's in that bag now." He started to collapse back down on his face and caught himself with one arm. "Close the door."

I did what he said, instinct telling me my next question wouldn't be the right one. "Shouldn't we be calling the cops?"

"No." With considerable effort, Ethan grasped at some device on the floor. The man against the wall squirmed. "This-s-s no robbery." He stared muzzily at the thing in his hand. "Fucker drugged me. Lasts four-five hours." He blinked, wavered. "Use . . . use it. Drive. She's not safe." And he was out. Just like that, leaving me alone with two guys who looked like they might have stepped out of one of Ida Mickens's paperbacks.

Asshole Number One grinned again. "Well, well, little lady. Looks like it's just me and you." He started to move.

"Don't." I lifted the gun to point to his right eye. I was steadier now, despite the breath heaving in my chest. "I grew up in the country. My daddy taught me how to shoot when I was just a little bitty thing, and I've been around guns all my life. Still, it wouldn't take much for this thing to just go off in my hand, you know."

He glared, but it seemed like he believed me. He sank back again.

"Your boyfriend's crazy, you know. You should call the cops."

Why did I have the feeling I was talking to Br'er Rabbit, wanting me to throw him in the briar patch? I glanced at the phone.

The thug kept talking. "Yeah. Go ahead. We should get all this sorted out. I mean, he barely gave us a chance to explain before he started swinging."

"Uh-huh. And this?" I took the device from Ethan's slack hand and scanned it. There were three ampules left in the grip of what was apparently an injector.

"Just a little insurance. We needed you to come with us."

"Why?"

"Sorry. That's classified."

"Right. You got a badge or anything?" The bastard wouldn't meet my eyes, and I made up my mind. Badge or no badge, I wasn't inclined to let the police sort out this mystery. There was a reason Ethan didn't want the police involved, though I was damned if I could figure it out at the moment, and I was going with what he'd told me.

With a little investigation, I could probably have figured out how to load the injector and use it, but I saved myself the trouble. I slid it across the floor to my captive.

"Load 'er up, doc."

He glanced up at me, running the scenarios.

I shook my head. "Ah-ah, easy does it. I don't think you can cross the room before I can pull this trigger, do you? Just show me how it's done."

When he was done loading one of the ampules, I praised him. "Good. Now inject yourself."

"What? You think I'm nuts?"

I raised the gun again. "No, I think you'd rather go to sleep and wake up embarrassed than get your ass shot and not wake up at all. But first, I don't guess you'd like to tell me who hired you?"

"Fuck you."

It figured that my lame tough-guy routine wouldn't work on this tough guy. He seemed like the real deal. I gave it up with a shrug.

"Okay, I'm waiting."

He didn't move.

Recognizing a showdown when I saw one, I took a step and pointed the gun at his left eye. "Officer, these two men broke into our room, they attacked me, my boyfriend tried to defend me. I only shot the man in self-defense—"

"Okay, okay, shut the fuck up." He glared at me, then raised the injector to his neck and squeezed the trigger. He was out within seconds.

After I made sure he was truly unconscious, I took the injector from his hand, reloaded it and used it on his partner. I had to roll the man over to reach the right spot on his neck and as I did, a set of handcuffs fell out of his pocket. I looked from one slumbering body to another and weighed my options. It would require a lot of heavy lifting, but it would be worth it for the sheer evil fun of it, not to mention the head start it would give us to leave the two thugs handcuffed to the plumbing. I set to work.

An hour later, the boys were stashed under the sink, there was a "Do Not Disturb" sign on the door, and I had informed the Front Desk that we'd be using one room an extra night, just charge it to the same credit card, please. Frank at the Front Desk was happy to oblige.

I stretched poor Ethan out in the passenger seat of the BMW with a pillow, a blanket, and a couple of ice packs for his bruises and drove to the outskirts of town before I pulled off the road to get breakfast. It had been a rigorous night and an eventful morning, and I was ravenous. I parked where I could watch the car, went inside, and ordered the Farmhouse Breakfast with black coffee, *stat*.

"Drive," he'd said. "She's not safe." What was that supposed to mean? Who the hell were these goons anyway? What did they want? Ethan sure didn't look like the kind of guy who owed the wrong people money. I tried really considering that and found myself smiling. No, not a chance.

So, if they weren't after him, they had to be after me. *Shit*. Ice slid down my spinal column and froze it in place. That guy in the white Impala—I'd never been close enough to really get a look at him, but it hardly mattered anyway. This was all part of the same puzzle.

And, oh, my God! "She's not safe." *Oh, my God, Ida's not safe!* We had something in common, though it made no sense to any of us. Her visions hadn't been anything like my dreams. Except . . . whatever we saw was not of this Earth. And Ethan was convinced we weren't crazy. Maybe these guys worked for someone who thought the same thing. They'd been dressed alike in identical cheap suits, so I'd already started thinking of them as the Men in Black. Now it didn't seem very damn funny.

My breakfast arrived, and I made quick work of it—eggs, grits, bacon, biscuits, and all. I swallowed the last of my third cup of coffee and called for the waitress.

"Hey, could you wrap up a couple of ham biscuits to go, please? And I'll take the check."

"Well, somebody's hungry this morning." She grinned. "Are we eatin' for two, honey?"

A fist squeezed my suddenly tender heart. I swallowed hard and tried for a sigh of resignation.

"My boyfriend's sleeping one off in the car. He'll be hungry when he wakes up."

"Oh, okay." She winked at me and whisked off to get what I'd asked for.

One thing I knew for sure. If we were going up to Clay Fork today, we wouldn't be getting back to Nashville tonight. That meant I wouldn't be at work Monday morning. I dug out my phone to call Rita.

I put on my best girlfriend voice when I heard her pick up. "Hey, girl, what you doin'?"

"Well, that ain't hardly the question, is it?" There was laughter in her familiar voice. "If you're calling me on a Sunday morning when you're supposed to be on a hot weekend out of town, either things are going real good with you and Dr. Dreamy or they're going real bad. Which is it?"

"I'm just calling to say I won't be in to work tomorrow. I'm, uh—cough, cough—not feeling well."

"I knew it!" Rita screamed with laughter. "Yeah, you're sick all right and that hot doc has got the cure for what ails ya, hasn't he?"

"You better believe it." That much of the story was true, at least. "It's not going to put you out too much if I take an extra day, is it?"

"Hell, no. I'll cover for you with JW. You should be good until Wednesday, anyway, when those guys come in from L.A. Take your time. Have some fun. You sure do deserve it, honey."

"Thanks, Rita, I appreciate it. I hate to ask, but could you stop by the apartment on your way to work and check on JJ? He should have plenty of food, but he likes the attention."

"Oh, he's my boy. I'll be glad to do it."

"And, hey, by the way, if anybody comes by the office looking for me, could you maybe put them off and give me a call?"

"Anybody like who?" I could practically hear Rita's hackles rise. "Don't tell me this guy turned out to be married."

"Oh, hell, no, nothing like that." My life was never *that* simple. "I'm just a little late on my car payment is all. You know how those guys can be."

"Oh, I getcha." She sounded relieved now. "I'll take care of 'em."

"Rita, you are the best."

"I know. Say hi to Handsome for me—and don't hurt yourself!"

"Oh, believe me, it don't hurt a bit. Bye, sweetie."

Rita was still laughing when the phone clicked off. I brushed off the guilt I felt at lying to her—much better for her to know I was knocking boots with Ethan than to worry about me being knocked in the head by some goon, at least for now.

The waitress came back with my biscuits to go and the check. I paid for the food and went back out into the gray drizzle of late morning. I checked on Ethan, still motionless and pale in the side seat of the BMW. Then I slipped behind the wheel of the car and drove like hell back up into the mountains.

Two hours later I was closing in on Clay Fork and I *really* had to take a bathroom break. I was getting worried about Ethan. He hadn't moved from the position I'd put him in three hours before, despite the curves in the road and the approach of the supposed four-hour limit on the sedative he'd gotten. And there was the matter of the little red needle pushing "E" on the gas gauge.

A crossroads up ahead sported a convenience store—not one like you find in the suburbs, but one offering bait and country ham and hunting and fishing licenses along with the only fuel for miles. I pulled in with a grateful sigh.

Ethan still hadn't stirred by the time I finished getting the gas and taking care of my business, so I bought a roll of paper towels, soaked a couple in cold water and took them out to the car. I didn't want to scare Ida by pulling up at the house with him unconscious in the passenger seat.

I lowered the driver's seat and worked awkwardly from beside him to take stock. The skin covering the bone under his left eye was red and swollen, but the eye itself wasn't puffy. He'd be spared an ugly shiner. His lip, though, would be sore and thick. No more sweet kisses for a few days.

I touched the wet paper towels to his forehead and his throat and spoke to him.

"Hey, baby. Time to wake up. Come on. Naptime's over." He groaned and turned his head slowly, but he still didn't open his eyes. I tried the towels against his temple, where there was another ugly bruise. "Come on, Ethan. Open those baby blues. Can you hear me, Ethan? Wake up, hon."

He moved—an arm, a leg, his chest as he dragged in a big, uneven breath—and at last he opened his eyes and looked at me. "Asia?"

"Yeah, baby."

He started to sit up, then winced and fell back. "Shit."

His voice was so weak it scared me. "Take it easy, babe. Just lay there a minute." Maybe this wasn't such a good idea. Maybe he needed to go to a hospital. I lifted his head and put a couple of the cool towels on the back of his neck. I put another one on his forehead and kept it there.

He opened his eyes again. They were a little clearer this time.

"Thirsty. Got anything to drink?"

I reached for a bottle of water, popped the cap, and held it to his lips. He grimaced again as he tried to function around the injury to his mouth, but he was thirsty enough that he kept at it. In a couple of minutes he was able to sit up, though it was obvious to me he was still pretty woozy.

"Where are we?" He peered through the window.

"About five miles from Clay Fork, close as I can figure."

He smiled, a wispy shadow of his usual transforming grin. "Should I even ask what happened after I passed out?"

"Is your head still hurting?"

"Like a sonofabitch."

"Then I'll save the story for later when you can enjoy it." I looked him over. He was pale and shaky, and I figured Ida was still in for a shock, but we needed to be on the road. After all, if he was awake, so were the Beastie boys back in Bristol.

"Do you want something to eat? A Coke or something?"

He blanched. "Maybe a Coke in a minute. Help me out of here."

I climbed out of the car, circled around to his side and held out a hand for him. He unfolded in slow motion and stood up, leaning heavily on the car door and my arm.

I wasn't sure he was going to stay vertical. "Christ, what was in that stuff?"

"More than I accounted for, apparently." He took a few stiff steps. "I'll tell you one thing, though. I'll never sedate a patient using that shit again without a damn good reason." He stretched his back and rubbed at his neck, then glanced toward the store. "Give me a minute."

"You sure you don't need help?"

He shook his head and mustered the effort to lift himself the four inches from the pavement to the sidewalk in front of the building. I watched as he shuffled inside and waited anxiously for him to reappear.

A few minutes later Ethan came back, blinking like an owl as he emerged into the daylight. He made his torturous way to the car, opened the front passenger door, and dropped into the seat with a sigh. He reached into the glove compartment and pulled out a pair of sunglasses, though the sun had yet to break through the blowing clouds. The glasses completed his new sexy gangster look. Poor Ida.

"Let's go," he ordered.

Who was I to argue with Scarface?

The old Beemer toiled around the mountain curves that took us to Clay Fork, and with every swing and sway of the vehicle I imagined the pull of gravity on Ethan's battered body. He tried to hide it, but I caught him with a hand on his ribs a few times. I slowed down as much as I could without making it obvious I was doing it for him.

His sunglasses tilted in my direction. "Did you find any identification on those guys at the motel?"

"No, nothing. No badges, no driver's licenses. No

room keys, either. Or cell phones. Guess they were real pros at whatever it is they do."

Ethan's brows came together. Apparently his thinking process was still slower than usual. "Pros, but probably not government officers. If they were FBI or Homeland Security or someone like that they would have flashed badges first. They wouldn't have found it necessary to drug us and kidnap us."

"If you ask me, they would have saved themselves a lot of trouble by pretending to be FBI. It's not like we would have fought them if they had flashed a badge at us, even if the badge was fake."

"Okay. So professionals of a certain, let's say, criminal type. That is, not very smart." Ethan's smile tipped up the corners of his mouth. "They expected us to run. Why?"

"Why any of this, Ethan? None of this makes sense." I took a breath, my heart in my throat. I didn't want to tell him what I knew I had to say. I felt guilty, like I should have known this was coming. "There was a guy, back in Nashville. For a few days a couple of weeks ago I felt like I was being . . . I don't know . . . stalked. I think this may be connected."

Ethan's head snapped around, and I could see it hurt him to move so suddenly. "What?"

"Yeah, uh, I'm not sure if the goons that attacked us were connected or anything, but there was this guy in a white Impala—"

"Shit! How long had you known about him, Asia?"

He was furious, his hands catching the dash in a white-knuckled death grip. Where the hell had that come from?

"I don't know. A few weeks."

"And you didn't think to tell me about it?"

I found myself getting heated in response to an anger that seemed to make no sense. "So you could reconsider whether I might be crazy after all? No, I didn't think to tell you." I held up a hand. "And before you even ask—yes, I called the cops, but they told me it was nothing. I saw the guy a few times. It was creepy. I was extra careful. Nothing happened. End of story." *Until now.*

He let his head fall back against the headrest, closed his eyes and let out a breath that was almost a groan. "I saw the man in the white Impala outside your apartment yesterday. I thought it might be your ex-husband."

I gaped at him. *Now who was keeping secrets?*

"I haven't seen Ronnie for years. It's not him."

"Anyway, it doesn't matter." His jaw clenched. "You could have been hurt."

I swallowed, unwilling to think about what might have happened. "But it doesn't make sense. If they wanted me, why did they wait?"

He turned his head and met my gaze, but had no answer for me.

We pulled into Clay Fork for the second time in two days and took the left turn that led up the mountain toward Ida Mickens's place. Ethan fell silent as we climbed that last mountainside, whether lost in thought, or struggling to pay the toll in pain each hairpin turn exacted from his badly bruised ribcage, I couldn't tell.

The last part of the drive was bumpy and slow as I

maneuvered around the potholes in the long dirt drive up to the house. I risked a glance over at Ethan; he was the color of an oyster and holding grimly to the door safety handle. I rounded the last bend, fully expecting to breathe a sigh of relief, and found instead that I suddenly couldn't breathe at all, that my heart was stopped in my chest, the blood motionless in my veins.

Something was wrong at Ida's little farmhouse.

CHAPTER THIRTEEN

Several cars were pulled up in Ida's yard, including a long, black Cadillac with a discreet sign on its side advertising its sole purpose. People were standing on the porch; some of them were crying, or looked like they wanted to. They turned to look at us, the strangers coming up the drive, the ones who hadn't heard the news yet.

"Ah, Jesus," Ethan whispered. It was the most broken-hearted sound I'd ever heard.

I found a place to park that wouldn't block anyone. Then we took a moment to collect ourselves before we got out of the car. Ethan took off his glasses, and the pain in his eyes when he looked back at me now was much more than physical. It was all I could do to keep from bursting into tears at the sight of him. I squeezed his hand instead, took a deep breath, and opened the door.

We made our way up onto the porch and nodded to a few of the folks in the outer ranks as we shuffled toward the doorway. Ethan seemed to know someone to ask for, and we were ushered into the tiny living room. In a few seconds, a short, round woman in a pink sweatshirt and gray knit pants came bustling out of the bedroom to greet us. Her eyes were red with tears—she held a wad of tissue in her hand against any fresh onslaughts of grief—but the lines in her face showed she was usually of the inclination to smile.

She stuffed the tissue in a pocket and held out a hand to Ethan. "I'm Helen Lazeby, Ida's niece. You're Dr. Roberts, aren't you? Aunt Ida said you were coming up this weekend."

Ethan took her hand. "That's right. Ethan. And this is Asia Burdette. We were just here yesterday to see Mrs. Mickens. What happened?"

"Nice to meet you, Asia. Lord, I hate to be the one to tell y'all this." She stopped, the tears threatening once more. "Mrs. Connors over there"—she nodded across the room at a frail woman being comforted by several others—"came by to check on Aunt Ida since she wasn't at church this morning. She found her in bed. She'd died in her sleep, I reckon." This last was delivered in a soft sort of wail, a tale no easier to get through for the number of times it had been told already that afternoon.

I knew what was expected of me, though I'd just met the woman. I put an arm around her round shoulders in sympathy.

"I'm so sorry, Helen. She seemed just fine yesterday."

Ethan put a hand under her other elbow. "This must be so hard for you." He led her to the nearest chair. "Come on and sit down for a minute. Asia would you get Helen a glass of water?"

"Sure." I went off to the kitchen, glad to be of help.

By the time I got back, Ethan was kneeling at Helen's side, and she was confiding in him like he'd grown up in Clay Fork with everyone else in the room. In fact, no one there seemed to notice the fresh bruises on his face or the turn of phrase that marked him as a city boy. They all just seemed to be standing a little bit closer to him, like he was a fire on a cold night.

"It's just that it was so sudden," Helen was saying. "She hadn't been sick or anything. It had been years since she'd been so bad off with them headaches that she came to see you for, Doctor." Helen smiled at Ethan. "Oh, she set great store in you. Said you just about saved her life."

Ethan's gaze dropped to the floor, and I thought he might lose the control he'd so flawlessly maintained. I put a hand on his shoulder, and after a time I felt him breathe again. The softest tremor shook his voice when he spoke. "She was more than a patient. She was a very good friend."

"She was a special lady." Helen started sniffling again. "Anyway, the doctor said there weren't nothing for it. It was just natural causes."

Ethan nodded, but the lines between his eyes told me he didn't quite believe it. I admit the timing seemed much more than coincidental, but where was the evidence that anyone had been here to do Ida harm? And why would they kill her? The thugs who'd broken into our hotel room had meant to kidnap us, not murder us. Had this one gone wrong? Or were our imaginations just working overtime trying to fit an old woman's natural death into our private paranoid delusion?

The questions wouldn't leave me alone as we sat in that living room and minutes turned into an hour, then two. The hearse left for the funeral home with Ida's body. People pressed food and coffee into our hands; neighbors came and went, offering condolences; relatives introduced themselves. Helen asked for Ethan's help in making the choices one has to make at those times, and he was steady, thoughtful, kind. I looked around and wondered whose shoulder poor Helen would have leaned on if he hadn't been there.

At the end of that long afternoon Helen asked us to follow her into the kitchen.

"I think Aunt Ida musta had something she wanted to give y'all." She reached under the table and hauled out a big basket filled with heavy glass jars of canned fruit and jam. Colorful dish towels had been stuffed between and under the jars to keep them from breaking. It was beautiful—and almost more than Helen could manage. Ethan took it from her to keep her from straining her back.

"Oh, my God, that's gorgeous. We can't take all that!" What I didn't say was that Ida Mickens couldn't possibly have known we were coming back that afternoon. She must have forgotten it the day before.

"Please, she wanted you to have it," Helen insisted. "There's a note for you on the top there."

Ethan put the basket down and picked out the envelope. He put it in his pocket.

"I guess y'all won't be staying for the funeral."

"We have to go back to Nashville today. I have

patients to see tomorrow. I'll try to get back. When do you think? Tuesday?"

"Probably. I'll call. You know, it's funny how things work out, isn't it?" Helen's lip quivered. "Aunt Ida said last week you were just coming for the day and were going straight back home."

I had to admit the way my world had changed in the last twenty-four hours would not have been predictable using anybody's crystal ball. Meanwhile, Ethan was apparently still fishing around in a blank mind for an adequate explanation, so I spoke up.

"I have relatives over near Princeton, so we decided to spend some extra time."

"Oh, well, I'm so glad you did. If you hadn't, I wouldn't have had your help today, Dr.—Ethan, and I really needed it. Thank you so much."

Ethan's eyes went dark. "It was the least I could do. Your aunt meant the world to me. I'm going to miss her."

Helen reached up and wrapped him in a big hug. When she pulled back she was tearing up again. Before she had a chance to say anything, someone came into the kitchen looking for her.

"They want to know if you're ready to go to the funeral home, honey."

Helen nodded and dabbed at her reddened nose with the ever-present tissue. Then she turned to me and gave me a hug. "You take good care of our doctor now."

"I will." So many assumptions in that little exchange. He was theirs now. And mine. To take care of, as he had taken care of them. The thought settled on me like a warm blanket.

I started out through the living room, but Ethan grabbed my arm. "No. I've had enough." He turned me toward the back door. "This way."

We slipped out the door and threaded our way through the haphazardly parked pickups and Jeeps and old Chevys to the Beemer. The others had left the BMW surrounded at close quarters, and I wasn't sure I trusted myself to extricate it unscathed. But Ethan moved directly to the passenger side and got in without a word. I got behind the wheel and started her up, but I didn't put her in gear just yet.

Instead I turned to Ethan and waited until he looked up at me. "Are you gonna be okay?"

"Eventually." He reached in his pocket and took out the letter from Ida. He held it for a long, silent minute. "I'm afraid to open it."

I touched his face. "Ethan, baby, you know Ida. Whatever demons she had to live with, she'd lived with them a long time. She probably just forgot to give us the basket yesterday and meant to have it shipped."

He nodded, but he didn't look reassured. And to tell the truth, he'd spooked me now. My hands tightened on the steering wheel as I watched him open the envelope.

He scanned the first few lines and his hands began to shake. He glanced up at me with a gale of grief darkening his blue eyes. He read:

Dear Ethan and Asia,

Please forgive my messy writing, but I don't have much time.

A man came to the door after you left tonight. I don't much like strangers after dark, so I had the shotgun on him. Good thing, too, since it appeared like he meant me harm. Came at me on the porch waving some kind of pistol like they use to give polio shots with. Well, I set him down for a talk—he didn't say a whole lot!—but in the end I just had to use that "injector" to put him to sleep for a while so I could think. Good thing it wasn't poison in there, huh? Ha!

Now the good Lord and I had a little talk after that, and I believe He will forgive me for what I plan to do. I surely hope you will, too. You see, I figure this man was sent by the ones who took me so long ago. And I don't aim to go back there ever again. No, sir. I got lucky this time, but maybe I won't be lucky the next time they come for me. I'm 83 years old. Had plenty of time on this old Earth. Reckon it's time to go home to Jesus. I'd much rather be there than wherever this man wanted to take me.

There's a bunch of little bullets for this injector—surely enough to do the job I got planned. I aim to use them all so it'll look like I died in my sleep. I reckon the man will just skedaddle when he wakes up and sees me dead in the bed. No one else will know. It's not like Raylan Givens will be investigating my death!

I tried calling the number you gave me today, but it's storming up here on the mountain, and the call won't go through. So I'm writing it all down and leaving it for my niece to send to you. When you get this, I guess you'll understand, if anyone will.

And BE CAREFUL! If they came for me, they'll be

coming for Asia, too! She knows deep down in her heart, Ethan, like I always did: that place she sees in her dreams is REAL. And if she's half the woman I think she is, she'll fight the Devil himself rather than go back. I thank the good Lord that she has you now to help her.

Y'all take care of each other.

Love, Ida

I stared at Ethan's stricken face, my mouth suddenly spitless and sour, my lungs collapsed and constricted, unable to release the air in my chest or draw in a new breath. They had come for her. *They had come for her like they had come for me.* And she was dead because she wasn't going back to a place where the sun was white and the sky was green and children with bleeding hands worked in endless fields of cruel, cutting leaves.

"Do you think she could be right?"

I was only giving voice to my fear. I should have thought of how the man who'd been struggling to rid this woman of her "delusions" for years might have felt. Ethan looked like I'd ripped his heart out and left it bleeding on the front seat.

"I don't know," he said, admitting defeat. "The guy did leave—and he took the injector with him." He folded the letter carefully and put it back in his pocket. "Let's go."

Shaking, I backed and angled, tacked and rounded to get us out of the Rubik's cube of parked cars. As we bounced back down the dirt track, we passed a steady line of cars carrying mourners up to the Mickens place.

I didn't think to ask Ethan where we were headed. I just took a left at the end of the drive where it came out onto the road and turned back toward Clay Fork. I hadn't gone more than a hundred yards when he pointed at a wide spot on the shoulder of the road.

"Pull over."

"What?" There wasn't much time to make the cut. I looked at him to be sure that's what he wanted.

"Just do it."

I hit the brakes and eased the steering wheel over. The tires went off the road with a jolt and the car slid to a rough stop in the thin gravel of the turnout. Ethan flung open the door and staggered to the back of car. I turned off the engine and swung my head around to see him bent over, one hand on the fender to steady himself, retching his guts out.

My whole body clenched in sympathy. My poor, poor baby. He'd eaten almost nothing during the afternoon, though the ladies up at the house had pressed all manner of food and drink on him. Now what little he'd choked down was back up again and ending in dry heaves of bitter misery. I reached in the back for the water I'd bought earlier—it seemed like a lifetime ago now—and got out of the car to see if I could help.

Ethan straightened and walked a few steps away from the car. He didn't look back at me, and he didn't speak.

"Ethan?"

He stood for another second, then he crumpled to his knees, head bowed, shoulders slumped, arms slack. It was as if all the spine had gone out of him in an instant, as if all his bones had just turned to dust. I dropped the water and ran.

I could tell even before I got to him that he was crying. When I touched him, he wrapped both arms around my waist and buried his face in my chest and sobbed like a child.

"I'm so sorry, baby," I whispered, my own tears falling to join his. God knows I was scared and lost and desperately sad, too. But in that moment, the man who had held me so many times needed me. So I held him, cradling his head against my breaking heart, there on the side of the road. When he could find his feet again, we shuffled together back to the car.

We got in and sat staring at the empty road. "What now?" I asked him. We had to make some decisions, regardless of the emotional state we were in. Without knowing who was after us or why, it didn't seem sensible to go back to Nashville, where it would be easy for them to find us. We couldn't stay on the road forever, and any friends or family who took us in would be at risk.

"My family has a summer place on a lake in the Adirondacks." Ethan reached in the glove compartment, got out a map of the eastern U.S, and spread it out on the front seat between us. "It's usually empty this time of year." He studied the map.

I thought about my phone, with its GPS feature. But it didn't seem safe to use it with God-knows-who on our trail. I'd turned both our phones off in Bristol.

So I asked, "How long will it take us to get there?"

"A solid two, maybe two-and-a-half days of

driving. Especially if we stick to the back roads."

"Back roads. In these mountains?"

"They'll be looking for us on the interstate, Asia. It won't be easy to ditch this car and get a rental in the middle of nowhere."

He had a point. Baby would be easy to spot, even in all the traffic on I-81. I squinted at the alternatives.

"So what do you think? U.S. 19 to I-79?"

He shook his head. "U.S. 219, then 220 into Pennsylvania."

"Shit." I followed the thin red snake of a line on the map. "Then I'm driving, and if you need to puke again you'll just have to hang out the window."

As we turned back out onto the highway the ghost of a smile on Ethan's pale face made my heart ache.

That first leg of the trip was brutal, an hour backtracking to Bluefield to pick up U.S. 460, then more than three hours of weaving through the dark on the looping curves of two-lane U.S. 219. We had been battered both physically and emotionally before we even set out. By the time nine o'clock rolled around, I felt like I'd spent hours hauling in canvas on a ship in a storm-tossed sea. The grief we were both feeling had blown up a hurricane neither Ethan nor I felt like shouting over. We hadn't exchanged a word since Clay Fork except to verify directions.

I was so tired I could hardly speak when I called a halt to our flight. "Hey, there's a town called Marlinton coming up. I say we stop for the night."

Ethan sat up and looked at me. "Yeah."

We slowed as we came into the tiny town—one or two restaurants closing up at this hour, a darkened gas station, a convenience store blazing lights. We passed a bridge over the Greenbrier River and followed the river out of town again without seeing any place to sleep. I'd begun to think we were out of luck when I saw a massive sign for the Marlinton Motor Inn on the highway at the edge of town.

"Thank God." I turned into the parking lot. The place looked busy and well-maintained, though it wouldn't make anyone's Most Romantic list. The sign said "Vacancy," so as far as I was concerned, all systems were go.

I rolled to a stop in front of the office, and Ethan went in to take care of registration. I stretched some of the kinks out of my back and felt the fatigue sinking into my arms and legs. I'd be in bed soon, after a meal and a hot bath, with this day from hell behind me. I could wrap my arms around Ethan, and he could wrap his arms around me, and we could forget about our aching hearts for a few hours.

Things would look a lot brighter tomorrow after a good night's sleep.

I watched Ethan walk back to the car, and was reminded just how long a day it had been. He moved like an old man after hours of immobility in the car. He limped, and he held his left arm bent and close into his side, protecting the ribs that were undoubtedly cracked underneath the badly bruised muscles. God, I had forgotten—he hadn't complained, hadn't said a word about any of it since we rounded that bend in Ida's drive and saw there was trouble.

He climbed back in the car, the slightest grunt his only concession to the pain. "Two-twenty-seven. Around the side." He nodded to indicate the direction. He leaned back slowly in the seat and took a deep breath.

"You okay, babe?"

"Sore."

"I'll bet. We'll get you fixed up here in a minute."

I started up the car again and drove around the side of the building, looking for 227. It wasn't hard to find, toward the center of a second wing looking out onto a farm field. We'd have a walk to the restaurant, but the quiet would make up for it.

"Hey." Ethan caught me before I could exit the vehicle. "I registered using my license. Told the guy I'd pay with a check. We can't use our credit cards—they can track us that way. You understand?"

My heart sank. "Well, babe, I hope you have some cash in the bank. I think I have about a hundred bucks until my paycheck hits next week. And unless we get all this figured out before, say, Wednesday, I won't have a job to go back to, either."

It was true enough, but I meant it as a joke. Ethan didn't laugh, though. His jaw tightened until I could see a muscle jump near his temple, and he got out of the car without another word.

The room was big, with two double beds toward the front, a table and two chairs on the far side, even a little fridge and microwave. The wood paneling and mission-style furniture showed some age, but the bathroom and HVAC had been recently upgraded, so we'd found a retro paradise. I cranked up the heat and prepared to make myself at home.

Ethan lowered himself to the bed and struggled to kick off his boots.

"Here, let me help you." I hurried across the room to get to him.

"I think I should be able to get my fucking shoes off by myself."

"Shut up." I brushed his hands away, taking off the boots and setting them aside. He was cranky, that was understandable, but I wasn't going to let him get away with it.

I glanced up to see him studying me, his face somber.

"I'm sorry." There was such sadness in his voice, an emotion that was way out of proportion for the apology he was making.

I smiled to hide my concern. "We're both tired, Ethan." I stood up and tugged gently on the right sleeve of his jacket. "Easy does it, now." Once I got his right side free, I managed to slip the jacket off the injured left side. I knelt at the side of the bed. "Let me take a look."

He scowled, but he leaned back to give me access. I lifted up the tee-shirt and looked. His left side from the middle of his chest to his hip was a mass of black, blue and red. It was ugly and swollen, but there were no obvious knots or depressions in the ribs. I ran my fingers over the ribs as lightly as I could, trying to follow the outlines of the bones without causing him any more pain than necessary.

"Can you take a deep breath?"

He tried. He winced, but he didn't pass out. That was a plus.

"I don't know—cracked, but not broken? Hell, my medical knowledge comes straight from watching *ER* on TV, but that would be my guess."

"Mine, too," he said. "Golden Gloves, as a kid."

I grinned. "Really? You're full of surprises." My eyes dropped to his torso again—and lingered on the older crosshatching of deep scars across his right side. Unable to help it, my gaze flicked back to his face, and I saw him look away.

I dropped the shirt. "Okay. You get yourself into bed. I'll go get some food and some ice for those ribs. I'll be back in fifteen minutes." I stood up and lightly touched his uninjured cheek. "It's been a rough day, baby, but it'll be over soon. I'll be back as quick as I can."

CHAPTER FOURTEEN

"We're going to be fucking late again, Ethan." Elizabeth's anger was like an overheated radiator—scalding, too hot to touch. "Goddamn it! I've been waiting out here in the parking lot for twenty minutes. I told you five o'clock."

He threw his briefcase in the back of her Lexus and folded himself into the front seat, slamming the door on the driving rain outside the car. "What was I supposed to do, Elizabeth? The man's depressed, maybe suicidal. He was talking for the first time in weeks. Was I supposed to kick him out of my office just because you have to go to a cocktail party?"

"Uncle Arthur could have taken today's session, just for once. Jesus! You never think of these things." She jerked the car into gear and backed out of the parking space, narrowly missing the Toyota parked next to her.

"He doesn't know your uncle."

"What difference does it make? All of your talk won't do a damn bit of good if he's made up his mind to blow his brains out." Her beautiful face was contorted with rage.

"What do you mean, Liz?"

"Nothing. Shit!" She screeched to a halt at the end of the lot, waiting impatiently for the traffic to clear so she could pull out onto 21st Avenue. A long line of cars in the near lane gave little hope of a quick exit.

She exhaled a furious sigh and glared at his wrinkled corduroys and tweed jacket. "Oh, for chrissake, Ethan! Didn't I ask you to change for this?"

"Did you want to wait another ten minutes?"

"Well, you look like shit."

"Thanks."

Spotting a split-second's indecision on the part of another driver, Elizabeth shot into traffic, over-steering a foot into the far lane and causing a riot of blaring horns. "You knew this was important."

Ethan sighed and rubbed his forehead. The headache blooming there would most likely be with him until morning.

"They're all important, Liz. Every goddamn meeting, party, dinner and celebrity auction. We used to go places just for fun—do you remember? Just the two of us."

"Oh, please. Not again with the 'you don't send me flowers' routine." Her perfect lips crumpled into a sneer. "Your sense of romance would be a lot more appealing if it weren't so fucking useless. If it was up to you we wouldn't have any connections at all in this town. Who do you think pays for all the really crazy people you so love to take care of? Those celebrity clients I send your way, that's who. And this is the fucking thanks I get."

She swerved in front of a slow-moving panel truck to stop at a red light. The driver hit his brakes and slid to a stop behind them.

"Will you please slow down?" Ethan felt compelled to say it, though he knew it would only add fuel to the fire.

"Fuck you." Her hands tapped wildly on the steering wheel, waiting for the light to change. Up ahead the two lanes they sat in narrowed to one and merged with two others coming in from the left as they approached the Broad Street Bridge. Cars lined up with them at the light—waiting for the green. Elizabeth shifted from neutral to first gear and stared at him in defiance.

"Elizabeth." His heart suddenly started flailing against his ribs.

"You're such a pussy, Ethan." She looked back at the light. "I hate that about you."

On the other side of the bridge was another light, currently green, stopping traffic coming off I-40 and emptying the bridge of traffic backed up from the light they waited behind. Ethan saw her look down at that light and smile.

"Liz, you'll never make it." He used the calm, quiet voice he only used for his special clients, like the one he'd just left behind in his office.

"Wanna bet?"

The Lexus revved, the light above them turned green, the wheels spun on the wet pavement and they took off like a shell fired from a cannon. They sped past the first cars off the line, jockeying for position as the lanes funneled the traffic from three lanes into two again. They streaked across the bridge and she was fast, getting faster, but there was no time. He saw the light turn yellow. Then red. There was a blur on the left and a hard jolt, the car veered and something monstrous rushed in from the right to devour them . . .

"Ethan? Can you hear me, baby?"

He opened his eyes and saw a different world. Then he drew in a breath and the pain returned—real and as sharply defined as broken glass. A face swam into focus—eyes warm and golden-brown, full lips, high cheekbones framed with wavy hair.

"Asia?"

"Thank God! I was beginning to think you wouldn't wake up—not that you were sleeping very peacefully, either." She touched his face. "Bad dream?"

He turned his head and tried to get his bearings. A motel room. Dark. He struggled to sit up and was reminded of his wounded ribs. "What time is it?"

"Just coming up on five in the morning."

He fell back against the pillows. "Shit. Is that all?"

"Like I said, you haven't been sleeping well." She held some water to his lips. He sat up to drink it. "You were out when I got back last night. I kept some ice on your ribs, but you haven't had anything to eat and you're probably dehydrated."

His stomach roiled. The thought of eating wasn't a pleasant one.

She noted the look on his face. "Don't wrinkle your nose at me. You have to have something." She went to the fridge in one corner of the room and got out two small containers. "Applesauce or Jell-O?"

"Jell-O." The vote held little enthusiasm. He straightened up as quickly as he could, afraid she might try to feed him. His helplessness was already making him angry and taciturn. He just wanted to be left alone.

She handed him the opened container and a plastic spoon with a look that showed she recognized the signals he was sending, but would honor them only as long as it didn't interfere with her plans to take care of him.

"Thanks." He wouldn't look at her.

"Do you have any more of those pills?"

"What?"

"The pain pills you were taking. Do you have any more?"

He shook his head. "I took the last one in the car yesterday."

"What about your prescription pad? Do you have it with you?"

He thought about it. "Yeah, my briefcase is in the car. Why?"

"Because you need sleep, and you won't get it without pain meds." She seemed determined to ignore his attitude. "Write something up, and I'll go out and get it once the stores open later. We passed a

CVS in town last night."

His throat tightened. The throb of pain in his ribs intensified and the old, bone-deep ache in his thigh, familiar as the sound of his own name, spiked.

"I can't write myself a script, Asia."

"No, but you can write me one, Dr. Smartass." She arched an eyebrow at him in triumph. "And I should have enough money in my account to fill it."

Ethan shook his head, clenching his teeth. "We should just get on the road. I'll be fine."

"Uh-uh," she countered firmly. "We're going to hole up here for at least today. You're going to stretch out on that bed where you can be a little bit comfortable with a ton of Percoset onboard and heal up. No more arguments."

God, he wanted it so bad. Not the drugs so much, though the pain was like being slowly crushed in a giant red-hot vise. He just wanted to stop moving, to have one minute of peace to process all that had happened—Ida and Asia and death and hope and love and heartache and behind it all a mystery he couldn't fathom. He was so tired he couldn't think anymore. He could barely breathe.

With a sigh, he gave in. "Okay."

Asia smiled at him with an easy familiarity that made his heart leap in response. Her affection was a gift he couldn't accept. Not now. He looked away.

She considered him for a long moment. Then she left him and moved toward the door.

"I'll get your briefcase out of the car."

There was no use pretending he didn't hear the hurt in her voice. His fault, like all the rest. Shit, his patients were better off without his help. Ida Mickens might still have been alive if it hadn't been for him. And Asia? What an idiot he'd been to think he was going to protect her. She was in danger *because* of him.

Asia and Ida had been his patients, and his patient records were the key. The realization came to him with sickening certainty—he'd been unable to contact any of the other former patients he'd tried to reach because whoever had attacked Ida and Asia had already gotten to them. Someone had pulled their names from his records and taken them, one by one.

Who the hell were these guys? *And what the fuck did they want?*

His mind sheered away from the thought of what might have happened if Asia hadn't had that gun in her bag, if she hadn't had the bag in the bathroom with her, if—*damn it!* Ethan couldn't stand the thought of Asia being hurt. And yet he knew his own selfishness was hurting her. He'd allowed things to go too far between them because he'd needed it, he'd wanted it and, God help him, he still did.

He stood unsteadily and made his way to the bathroom. He noted clinically that his urine was dark and tainted with blood. Strange that he didn't remember the punch to his kidney, but the adrenaline had been pumping and there'd been the sedative right afterwards.

He stumbled to the sink to wash up, staring in mild shock at the face in the mirror. His left cheek was badly bruised; his lips cut and swollen. But it wasn't the bludgeoning that distorted his image and made his own face unrecognizable; it was the guilt. He'd once been able to trust the man who looked back at him. He'd been able to ask others to trust him. That was no longer possible.

Asia came back in with his briefcase. Refusing to meet her eyes, Ethan took out his prescription pad and leaned over the table to write the script he needed. The effort was enough to set his ribs on fire. He dropped the pen and grabbed the nearest chair, trying to breathe through it, but the dizziness grew into a swirling black fog boiling up in front of his eyes. He lurched back toward the bed and sat down.

"Lean back," Asia ordered, tucking a pillow behind his back. She lifted his feet onto the bed and covered him with the blanket.

He was shaking, and his head was pounding. "Dehydrated," he said thickly.

Asia nodded. "Told you." She pressed him to take a long drink of water. Then she sat with him, forcing him to eat the applesauce he'd refused before. After a while, he felt a little better, though the ribs were aching with a deep, grinding persistence. There was no position he could find to ease the pain.

She got up from the bed and grabbed the car keys. "I'm going for the meds. Do *not* move until I get back."

Ethan was in no mood to argue. He closed his eyes and, for an unknowable time, only opened them again when she was by his side with medicine or water or food.

The bedside clock read 12:30 the next time Ethan came close to full consciousness. He had to think hard to assign some significance to the numbers. The room was full of light despite the drawn curtains, so it was obviously past noon. What day it was completely escaped him. He turned his head—a fairly successful maneuver—and saw that Asia was not in the room with him.

There was a note on the bedside table. He rolled to one side and pushed himself up into a sitting position. The ribs protested, but did not scream. Progress had been made toward healing, though he recognized the dulling both of sensation and of thought meant he still had a full load of pain medication onboard.

He reached for the note and read: "Went to get the car fixed. May take some time. If you need anything, call this number. Front Desk is standing by, too, if you want some real food or anything else. Be back as soon as I can. Love, Asia. P.S. You had two tabs at 8:00 a.m. in case you don't remember!"

That explains it. His head felt like a balloon, and he could barely track the meaning of the note. What was wrong with the car? He couldn't remember her telling him anything about it. He lay back and tried to think about it, got nowhere and decided to call the number she had left him.

"Ray's Texaco."

"Hi, uh, I'm trying to reach Asia Burdette. She's having a car worked on?"

"Oh, yeah. Hold on, she's sitting right here. Ma'am, it's your husband."

Husband?

"Hi, honey!"

"Asia?"

"You feeling better?"

"A little. What's going on? What's wrong with the car?"

"You don't remember?"

"No."

"Water pump gave out. I had no choice."

Ethan's heart sank. "Are you sure?"

"The temperature gauge shot up like a freaking rocket. I was lucky to make it here before the damn engine exploded. The man ripped the old pump out and showed it to me." Her voice got very quiet. "And if you ask me do I know the difference between a water pump and a radiator I'm really going to get pissed off."

Even in his stupor, Ethan picked up her warning. "Okay. They can fix it?"

"Had to get the part from a junkyard in the next county, but they're putting it in now. Should be done in a couple of hours. Are you okay there alone?"

"Yeah, I'll be all right. I might even be a little hungry."

"Oh, that's good, babe. You sound a lot better."

"Yeah. See you later."

"Yeah. Hey."

"What?"

"Welcome back. I've missed you."

For a split-second, Ethan was ready to give her the answer any lover would have expected. He'd missed her, too. He missed her now, wished she were there so he could touch her face, kiss her lips, hold her. But he was no longer certain he could ask for those things, no longer sure she should give them to him if he did presume to ask.

"See you soon," was all he said. And hated himself for it.

I thought a lot about that telephone conversation with Ethan while I was sitting in Ray's Texaco waiting for the boys to finish up on the BMW. I had a lot of time to think about that and the way things had gone between us since we'd left Ida's place. Maybe I had too much time, because what I was thinking wasn't pretty.

I was telling myself that it's natural for a man to want to pull back a little when he's let his vulnerability show. A guy has his pride, after all, and any woman who doesn't recognize that risks a familiar label. The night we'd spent together would have been test enough for most men. What I'd felt from him had been more than just physical passion, and he had all but admitted it *was* more than that.

In the few hours after that night, I saw Ethan go through every emotion a human being can experience. Happiness, fear, anger, grief, sadness, regret—you name it, I saw it, raw and unfiltered. He'd been hurt, and drugged, and hurt again in a crueler way. He was still in pain, and the drugs he was taking now could only touch the physical part of that pain.

It should have been no surprise that he seemed a little unresponsive, even cold, on the phone. Or that he'd avoided looking me in the eye that first morning. *Give him time, he'll get over it,* I told myself. But I couldn't shake a sense of dread as I drove back to the motel in the newly restored Beemer. Maybe I'd already lost him. Maybe the night we'd shared had only been a glimpse of something I could never have.

I shoved those thoughts in the back of my mind and slapped a smile on my face as I went in the room. Ethan looked up at me from an armchair. He'd had a shower and a shave and almost seemed his old self.

"Hey. The car all good to go?"

"Good as new, according to Ray and the boys." I stripped off my jacket and threw it on the bed. I knelt by the chair, wanting to kiss him, but something held me back. I touched his arm instead. "You're looking a lot better. How do you feel?"

"Still a little sore, but I cut down on the meds." Again, he wouldn't meet my eyes.

C'mon, Ethan. Relax, honey. "Are you hungry? Do you feel like going over to the restaurant, or should I go pick something up for us to eat here?"

"I don't know. I just ate a little while ago."

"Oh, okay." I was starving. "I might go get myself something and bring it back then. Think I'll take a shower first, though." I stood up, trying not to show my disappointment. I kicked off my shoes and pulled my sweater over my head. "After four hours in that place, I smell like gasoline and cigarette smoke."

Ethan watched me with a strange look on his face. In that look was a desire so deep it took my breath away, but it was guarded with so much sadness, so much *regret*. My heart reacted with a heavy plodding thud against the walls of my chest. I went to him and knelt by the chair again.

"What's wrong?"

He shook his head. "Nothing."

"I can't help you if you won't talk to me." It was the wrong thing to say.

His face went hard. "I didn't ask you to help me."

"No, I guess you didn't." I was getting angry now, my own hurt coming to the surface. I stood up and walked away from him before I said too much.

"You should have waited to take the car." His voice held an edge sharp enough to draw blood. "We should have gone together. Those guys are still out there. You put yourself in danger, Asia."

I turned on him. "For chrissake, Ethan, I'm not made of glass. And I'm not stupid, either." I started to say he wasn't in much shape to play bodyguard, but I figured it wasn't quite right to kick a man in the nuts when he was down. "I had the gun with me, and I kept my eyes open. And, look, here I am, safe and sound. Now, if it's all right with you, I'm going to take that shower."

I took my things into the bathroom and shut the door. I might even have slammed the door. I think I heard him say my name before I turned on the shower, but I didn't answer him. *Fuck you, Ethan Roberts!* was what I was thinking. It wouldn't have taken much for me to say it out loud.

Two hours later I was nursing my hurt feelings and a dirty martini at the motel bar. I'd gone out intending just to get dinner, but the pine-paneled restaurant did double-duty after nine o'clock and the thought of going back to the room to face Ethan's cold, brooding ghost was breaking my heart. I didn't know what to do. Push him? Leave him alone? Talk to him? Don't talk to him?

I missed the man I had come to know over the weeks since we'd met. I missed his smile. I missed the comfort of his voice. And most of all, now that I'd had him, God, I wanted him again so badly. I wanted to feel his arms around me. I wanted to feel his naked skin on mine. I wanted his tongue in my mouth, his hard length inside me. Being near him without that was torture. It was as if he'd brought me out of a coma only to feel a lifetime of unbearable pain. I almost wished he'd left me unconscious and numb.

Tears began to blur my view of the 3-D waterfall advertisement behind the bar, making me feel ridiculous. I squirmed miserably on the barstool while the jukebox whined country-style.

"Set you up again, sweetie?" The bartender looked like she had hired on when the place was built and had lingered long past retirement age. The smile she bestowed on me was a sad little sympathetic one. "You know he ain't worth all that anyway."

I pushed the empty glass in her direction. "Yeah, give me another one"—I squinted at her nametag—"Dottie. I might as well get good and plastered. I sure as hell ain't gonna get lucky tonight."

Dottie served me up, then leaned across the bar. "Be careful what you ask for. There's plenty in here would be glad to oblige." She nodded at one of the local boys—broad shoulders, curly hair and a wide grin he'd been trying on every girl in the room. "Take him, for instance. He's married. Got three little kids at home."

"Of course. Don't they always? Jerk."

"Same thing wrong with yours?"

I laughed without humor and drank some more. "If only it were that simple."

"You don't have to talk about it if you don't want to, honey."

She wasn't getting an attitude. She was giving me a choice. I needed to talk, I just didn't know how.

"I don't mind."

"Okay, so what is it? Lemme guess. He's on drugs. He drinks. He can't keep a job."

"No. None of that."

"Another woman."

I shook my head.

Her eyebrows shot up and she leaned closer. "Not another man!"

I laughed out loud. I didn't know much about Ethan, but I was pretty sure I could be confident he wasn't a closet homosexual.

"No," I said firmly.

Dottie straightened back from the bar. "Honey, it don't sound like you have much of a problem at all. He ain't dying is he?"

"Jesus! No! Okay—he just won't talk to me. We were really close, something bad happened, and now he acts like he doesn't want to have anything to do with me. Except to order me around, of course."

"Does he blame you for what happened?"

"I don't think so." *How could he?*

"Then he probably blames himself."

"That's ridiculous."

"I didn't say it made sense."

"Hey, Dottie! Can we get a beer over here?"

She left to attend to a rapidly growing crowd of drinkers, and I felt my head beginning to spin. How could he possibly blame himself for anything that had happened? Ida Mickens and I shared something—an experience, an ability, a past life, God knows what—and someone wanted access to it. Whoever it was could have been watching us for years—in Ida's case, since she was a little girl. Ethan was only caught in the middle, trying to help us.

And if he did blame himself, why would that make him so unreachable? We were stuck with each other—we couldn't go home, we couldn't go back to our stupid, pitiful, lonely lives (and his looked to be just as bad as mine) even if we wanted to. We couldn't do anything until we figured out who was trying to get to us and why. He didn't think this was something we could talk about?

The damn, thick-headed, pea-brained, close-mouthed, stubborn son-of-a-bitch!

The more I thought about it, the angrier I got. The angrier I got, the faster I drank. Seemed like the liquor just wasn't hitting me like I wanted it to, though the glass in front of me was quickly just a damp memory of vodka and olive juice. Dottie filled it up again with a sideways glance, but she didn't have time to say anything. Things were getting busy.

I had worked myself into a proper funk, so I didn't

notice Ethan until he sat down on the barstool next to me. His eyes shifted from me to the empty glasses on the bar and back again and a frown took over his face.

"I got worried when you didn't come back after a while." His jaw clenched. "You didn't answer your cell."

"My cell?" It had never occurred to me that he would try to call. I'd bought two burner phones at the CVS when I'd gone for his meds. I'd set them up and forgotten them. I pulled the phone out and looked at it like it was some foreign object. Sure enough, the display indicated several missed calls. "Guess I didn't hear it. I had some thinking to do."

He made a point of looking around the noisy bar. "You used to do a lot of this kind of thinking, Asia. It wasn't particularly healthy."

An unreasoning rage rose in me. "Yeah, well, there for a while I had someone to talk to instead." I reached into my purse and threw a few bills on the bar. "Thanks, Dottie."

She inclined her head in Ethan's direction and mouthed, "You okay?" I lifted my chin and turned to go.

Ethan made the mistake of trying to take my arm. I shook him off. And that's when Curly from down at the end of the bar decided to intervene.

"Is there a problem here, ma'am?" He was maybe 6'3" and had thirty pounds of muscle on Ethan. Even if my boy had not been recovering from cracked ribs and God knows what else, a run-in with this guy would have been bad news. "Do you need some help?"

"I'm fine." I put a hand up to stop him, but no one was looking at me.

Ethan bristled. "I'm not sure this is any of your business."

"I could make it my business, buddy."

I stepped between the warring males. "This is not the time or place for a pissing contest. I'm perfectly capable of taking care of myself, thanks. Let's go home, Ethan." I took him by the arm and pulled. I thought for half a second that he might shake me off, but he just gave my would-be rescuer a final glare and came away with me.

We made it back to the room before we started in on each other, but as soon as the door slammed behind us, the battle was on.

"What the hell were you thinking?" Ethan paced like a panther in the cluttered confines of the hotel room.

"Me? You're the one who busted up in there and almost started a riot. I was just having a drink."

"A drink? Looked to me more like half a dozen."

"So what if it was? Maybe I deserved to cut loose a little bit. It's not like you've been a lot of fun lately."

"Oh, so you were just bored," Ethan shot back. "And this was your idea of fun—drinking alone in a bar?"

Hot tears sprang into my eyes; hot fury exploded in my gut. My voice shook when I spoke, betraying me. I clamped down on it hard.

"That's right. I was drinking all by myself for hours, thinking about how pissed I was at you tonight. I had nowhere else to go. Second, what business is it of yours how I choose to pass my time? You obviously weren't interested in spending any time with me. We're not married. You're no longer my doctor. My daddy's been dead a long time, and I'm not looking for a new one. So where do you get off telling me what to do?"

Ethan reddened. "Asia, those guys are following us. They could have been there. It's just common sense. And you want to tell me that guy wouldn't have been all over you in a heartbeat?"

"Oh, you wanna go there?" I countered. "As it happens, he hardly registered on my radar screen, but at least he seemed to be willing. He didn't appear to be afraid to touch me or to talk to me. He wasn't treating me like I didn't even exist." I stopped and ran a frustrated hand through my hair. "Shit, Ethan, you made me feel like I was back in high school. It was like I'd fucked the captain of the football team on Friday night and Monday morning he didn't even know my name."

Ethan's lips set in a thin line. "Asia, you know I never meant—"

It might have been the start of an apology, but I was on a roll now, and just drunk enough, too, and I was going to have my say. "You never meant to what? Ignore me? Shut me out? Leave me waiting for a word from you that showed you cared even a little bit? Goddamn it, Ethan, you can't tell me we didn't have something that night, something more than just a particularly good fuck."

Ethan stared at me for a long, wordless moment, then he turned away. My heart shattered into a thousand jagged pieces.

"Whatever we had that night was special." He didn't look at me, and his voice was like the fall of sharp rocks. "But a lot has happened since then—you may want to give that some thought."

I laughed bitterly. "I see. Very analytical. We're back to doctor and patient now, huh?"

He turned back to me. "I'm just trying to protect you, Asia."

"Protect me?" I was shouting at him now, tears streaming down my face. I had no pride; it hurt too much to hide what I was feeling. "From what? It's too damn late. The only thing that can hurt me now is you."

He stood, stricken, seemingly unable to move or speak or respond in any way to what I'd said. But deep in his eyes I saw a dark reflection of my pain, a shadowy counterpart to the anguish in my heart. I don't know if what I saw would have been enough to help us get through that awful moment to a place of understanding. We never got the chance. Motel management got the next move with a loud knock on the door.

After an eternity we spent staring at each other, Ethan answered it. He checked the peephole, glanced back at me, then yanked the door open and spoke with a barely controlled growl. "Yes?"

A very intimidated desk clerk stood outside with a fully confident security officer, one I might have seen keeping a lid on things in the bar. "Sir, I'm sorry, but there have been some complaints about the noise."

"Yes, I apologize. We had the TV on pretty loud.

We've turned it off."

"You're sure everything's all right in there?" The security guard was looking straight at me.

I stepped up. "Everything's fine. We're going to bed now. Sorry about the noise." Of course, my tear-stained face couldn't have helped, but I tried to make it seem like things had blown over.

Apparently they believed me, though the guard made a point of looming in the doorway a second longer than necessary. He backed off.

"Okay. Let us know if you need anything. Goodnight."

We closed the door on them and spared each other the slightest glance.

"Asia—" Ethan began.

I held up a hand. "No. It's late. I'm going to bed."

I got undressed without another word and crawled under the covers of the bed nearest the door. Ethan turned off the light, and I heard the mattress take his weight as he stretched out on the other bed. The minutes ticked by, and there we remained, each of us alone and miserable, until, despite everything, sleep claimed us at last.

CHAPTER FIFTEEN

"This job is almost finished, you know, Sphinx." The blazer handed her a fist-sized chunk of crumbly bread. "I took as long as I dared to place those laser markers in the far cavern walls. They won't need us for the rest of it."

Fourteen-oh-eight stared at the cavern that had been their sanctuary for nearly three months. "What does that mean? Will they let us work together again?"

The tiny woman met her gaze. "Maybe. Maybe not."

She stared at her boots in silence. There was suddenly a hollow pit in her belly that had nothing to do with hunger.

"What would you do, Sphinx, if you had a choice?" When 1408 didn't respond, Dozen pressed. "What would you do if somebody gave you a chance to leave this place?"

Something caused her heart to beat wildly in her chest. She stood up and started to pace.

"No one leaves this place unless they're dead."

Dozen grinned, her teeth flashing white against her dark skin. "Maybe. Maybe not."

Fourteen-oh-eight stared at her companion in exasperation. Every conversation she'd had with the woman since they'd met had been like this—infuriating, stretching her mind beyond its limits. And yet, 1408 couldn't envision a life in this hell without Dozen now. She wasn't the same person she'd been when Dozen had found her weeks ago. If her partner said there was a way to leave this place and go somewhere—anywhere—shouldn't she go?

The blazer got to her feet. "Come on. It's time to get back."

The two workers packed up their tools, hooked their harnesses to the permanent rigging lines on the cavern wall and, one after the other, hauled themselves up to the narrow passageway that led back to the main part of the mine. In the time since they had first broken through to the crystal cavern, they had enlarged the passage to the mine tunnel and now made their way quickly back to the entrance.

As they emerged they saw a light coming down the tracks toward them from the interior of the tunnel. "Just in time!" Dozen crowed.

"You always know. How do you always know?"

The woman shrugged as the handcart rumbled closer. "Intuition, my dear. That's why ya gotta love me."

The cart rolled to a stop in front of them, and the guard pushing it waved his stun gun at them. "Get on board and get moving! If we miss the last lift up, I swear I'll kill you both before I take my punishment."

They did as they were told, dropping their gear on the cart and taking up positions on either side of the push handles. They bent to their work, and the cart began to move back down the tunnel.

Soon the smaller passage opened out into a larger vein that led them into the heart of the mine. Workers in long trains streamed out of other passageways, their faces masked with dust and fatigue. At each junction, guards stood with stun guns and whip sticks. A smell of metal and grease and earth hung in the air. There was no sound but the shuffle of feet, the growl and thump of the machines and the drone of the lift announcements as the cages at each vertical shaft slammed shut and rose to the surface.

As their handcart neared the end of the line, 1408 and Dozen slowed their efforts and brought it to a controlled stop. The guard rose to his feet and pointed his stun gun at them. Then, unaccountably, he stumbled and nearly fell back to his seat. An immense, thunderous, bone-shattering concussion filled the space around them, shaking the floor and the walls, moving the handcart and the rails, their bodies, the people around them.

It went on for three seconds, ten seconds, a minute. It wasn't stopping, and the world was coming apart. Beams cracked and groaned, and pieces of rock fell from the ceiling and walls of the tunnels.

Lights flashed and popped and finally went out, leaving the mine in darkness. Dust billowed and choked the life from lungs and air filters. Supports collapsed and tons of mountain crushed screaming workers in pockets of tens or hundreds. Guards panicked and shot at dozens more trying to get at the lifts.

It was chaos. It was hell. Fourteen-oh-Eight cowered beside the handcart, unable to move or think at all. Until Dozen slapped her face.

"Sphinx! Look at me! At me!"

"I can't see you!"

"Open your eyes, dumbass!"

Dozen had a working headlight on and was strapping on her blazer's gear. She handed 1408 her rigger's harness.

"Get into this. We may need it."

Numbly, 1408 did as she was told, her fingers shaking. All around her, people were screaming, scrambling in the dark as the tunnels shook apart. There was no sign of their guard, and no one seemed to be paying any attention to them.

Dozen shouted above the chaos. "You remember what I asked you today? Now's the time, Sphinx. We have to take what the universe gives us. And you have to trust me. All the way. Do you understand?"

She barely understood anything at all, but she nodded anyway. What choice did she have?

Suddenly, the rumbling and the quaking stopped, and it was eerily quiet except for a sound that was like rain in the forest—loose dirt sifting from the ceiling and falling to the surface. Then the screaming began anew, and the moans and the calls for help from all around them. And from deep in the mine, the sound of the earth shifting, adjusting to its new conformation, regardless of what, or who, might be in the way.

Dozen gripped her shoulders and looked into her eyes. "Are you okay?"

"I-I think so."

"This ain't gonna be easy. We have to make it to a service shaft on Corridor Three."

Fourteen-oh-Eight suddenly felt sick. "Corridor Three is closed. We can't go there!"

"Who's gonna stop us?" Dozen grinned. "That service shaft is used in emergencies. I'd say this is an emergency. And I know some people who work that service shaft at times like these. They make a point of it."

"Why?"

A guard stumbled past, his arm hanging at an impossible angle. He stared at them from a face blanked by shock, but he did not stop.

"I'll explain later. Come on."

They stumbled, crawled and felt their way back down the tracks. The bigger passageways were largely intact, but many of the smaller feeder tunnels along the sides had collapsed or were partially blocked with debris. In isolated spots, workers were digging with their bare hands to get their companions out from under the crushing rock, even though in some of those spots, it was clear, no amount of digging would help. Captains and guards cursed and swung whip sticks freely in an effort to bring order to efforts to open essential routes—or maybe it was just to save their own lives.

Still, the lifts weren't running. No one was getting out.

They found a connecting passageway between Corridors One and Two that was relatively free of obstruction, and Dozen picked up the pace. But as they came around a bend in the tunnel they met a group of three workers, one of them bleeding badly from a leg wound and being carried between the other two.

One of the workers shook his head. "Can't go there. Tunnel entrance collapsed."

"Shit," Dozen spat. "Okay, thanks." She kept walking.

Fourteen-oh-Eight hesitated.

The worker turned to stare at Dozen. "Hey, stupid. I said it's blocked."

"I've got tools. You want to help, you're welcome to."

"Fuck you. You're crazy."

"Okay. Thanks."

The three staggered off toward Corridor One.

Fourteen-oh-Eight glanced after them.

"Thinking you made a mistake, Sphinx?"

"All we have is the spade. How are we going to get through anything with that?"

"I have a laser cutter." Dozen hefted it in one hand with a grin.

"How . . .?" Workers didn't have laser cutters. They used them under strict supervision, but they didn't keep them.

Dozen was already nearly at the obstruction. "Are you going to stand there asking questions, or are you going to help me?"

The blazer had her sensor pack out and was taking readings of the rockslide that blocked the passageway. Most of the debris appeared to be small gravel and earth, but the sensors picked out several large rock plates in the slag heap. Dozen used a stylus to mark a route around them on the screen. She showed the screen to 1408.

"We can get through here"—she pointed— "and here." She grinned at her companion. "Just goes to show—if you're going to be trapped underground, be sure you're with someone who makes a living finding her way through solid rock!"

Dozen used the cutter to make a few discrete cuts in the slide. Gravel and dirt parted and shifted at the site, leaving an opening high on one corner. They enlarged the hole with the spade and continued in that fashion, working through the obstruction until, after nearly an hour, they broke through to the other side.

"Oh, shit!" Dozen hissed from the top of the heap. "Stay down!" Lights blazed through the hole they had created. She peeked out from the side of the gap.

"They've got the emergency lights on, and the guards have crews formed up. They're already organized." Dozen watched for several minutes while 1408 held her breath. Then the blazer turned and looked at her companion. "Shit. Shit! Okay. There's only one way to do this. We have to have bigger balls than anybody else, that's all. You up for it?"

Fourteen-oh-Eight had had enough. She couldn't do this. She didn't even know what it was she was doing. All she knew was she was scared to death and she couldn't do it anymore.

"No. No! You're going to get us killed!"

Dozen grabbed her overalls and got right in her face. "Yes, I am, Sphinx. And so what? What the hell have you got to live for in this godforsaken place? Better to die trying to get out of here than to live forever as slaves. Now you can come with me, or you can stay here. I don't give a fuck."

Slaves. What did that word even mean? She remembered . . . something. But it was gone. And so was Dozen, scrambling out of the hole that led to Corridor Two.

Fourteen-Oh-Eight cursed and climbed out behind her. Shit, she was running toward a captain of the guard! What the hell was she doing?

"Yes, sir, that's what they told us, sir! We're here to open a passage to Corridor Three! There's supposed to be a secure emergency lift over there, sir. They want us to check it out."

"I don't know anything about an emergency lift on Corridor Three," the captain snapped. "Who gave you your orders?"

"Major Zandor. He told me to look for you specifically. Said if you got the job done there'd be something special in it for you, sir." Dozen was laying it on thick.

"Zandor, huh? I've heard of him." The captain thought it over. "How am I supposed to get that done with all this *shalsitt* going on? I don't have anybody to spare."

"Oh, don't worry, sir. We're specialized workers." She splayed her hands on her chest. "I'm a blazer; this is my rigger. We do stuff like this all the time. I have the tools with me. Just leave it to us. And you'll get all the credit!"

Several guards called for the captain's attention from other parts of the shattered corridor. He snorted with exasperation. "Get the fuck out of here. Get your asses smeared into jelly for all I care." He waved a hand at the guards watching that part of the corridor to let them through. Like a miracle, Dozen and 1408 were allowed to enter the passageway that led to Corridor Three.

Dozen cursed softly as she surveyed the route ahead. The cut-through was a jumble of broken beams and crumpled support structures, the twisted metal thrusting up through huge chunks of rock and reinforcing concrete like grasping arms. The tunnel had been lasered through solid igneous rock; the quake had loosened the supports where metal had been driven into the rock. There was little of the loose dirt and debris that had made passage so easy earlier.

Dozen studied the sensor screen. "We're going to have to cut through almost the whole passage. The only thing that's saving our shit here is that the passage is short."

She shook her head. "Okay. Let's try it here." She took out the cutter and made a wide swipe at a nearby pile of rock. A hole opened into the space beyond. She looked, crawled tentatively through and made a cut from the opening. Things shifted beyond 1408's field of vision. Dozen glanced back through the hole.

"Well, what are you waiting for, an invitation? There ain't but one way to do this."

"Shit," 1408 muttered, and dragged herself through the hole after her friend.

They worked their way along—Dozen cursing and sweating and cutting, 1408 following reluctantly behind—until at last they cut through into a larger space, dark as only the unlit underground can be, but cold with the movement of volumes of air.

"Is it Corridor Three?"

Dozen grinned. "Damn right! We're through!"

She squeezed through the hole into the space beyond and looked around, her headlight beam falling short in the looming dark. The space was immense, not a corridor at all, but a vast round dome from which the engineers had planned to start exploratory tunnels outward in an expanding array.

"Why did they close this?" Fourteen-oh-Eight stood close to the blazer, intimidated by the size of the space.

"I heard it was for lack of workers." Dozen gave her a wicked grin. "If that's so, then I say score one for the good guys. Come on, we don't have much time."

"Do you know where you're going?"

"Don't I always?"

"But you can't have been here before, Dozen," she insisted. "Closed means no access. There's nobody here!"

"No access except in emergencies. No one here except when the rest of the mine is fucked—like now! Weren't you listening?"

"When was the last emergency? I don't remember any!"

"The last one was before you got here, that's why."

Fourteen-oh-Eight stopped, her boots scraping on the rock of the tunnel floor. Dozen turned to look at her.

"What?"

"What do you mean, before I got here?"

"You don't remember." It wasn't a question.

"I've always been here." Her anger burned, her head pounded. She refused to hear these crazy things from Dozen anymore.

"No, you haven't. We've talked about this before, and it's always ended badly." Dozen snarled a warning. "I don't have time to explain it again. We're leaving this place, Sphinx. Now move your ass before I have to knock you out and carry you."

Fourteen-oh-Eight wanted to scream. Her head felt like it would split open with confusion and pain. She wanted to run back the way they had come. At least the mine, with its routines, was something familiar. She was lost here without any hope of direction. She couldn't go back, and she didn't know how to go forward. All she could do was follow the insane woman who stalked off ahead of her without another word.

They circled the rim of the central dome that was Corridor Three, finding little of the damage that affected Corridors One and Two. The shape of the space had protected its support structure from the collapse the more conventional tunnels had experienced. There were a few scattered debris piles, a few rockslides off the walls, but nothing to hinder their progress as they searched for the access passage to the emergency service lift that Dozen swore existed.

At last a dim glow on the wall indicated an emergency exit sign. They turned into the tunnel and immediately ran into trouble of the kind they had encountered on the other side, with one difference.

"Someone's already been here!"

"I told you, Sphinx." Dozen was triumphant. "Some people I know take advantage of this place at times like these. Come on."

They squeezed and pulled each other through the gaps in the rock, in a hurry to catch up with the ones who might have blazed the path. One hole nearly closed up on them as they stumbled through, and another was already collapsed and had to be re-cut before they could go on.

Dozen spat out a mouthful of dust. "Who was the fucking moron who cut these holes? He's gonna get us all killed." She stumbled across a bed of broken rock and climbed through the next cut. She was waiting on the other side when 1408 came through.

Across a small clear section of tunnel two workers lay beside a stuttering headlamp. Above them in the collapsed tangle of rock and metal was the start of a hole that looked like it had closed up again further in.

One of the two sat up to look at them. She might have been a young girl in her teens, though the dirt and the rags made it difficult to tell.

Dozen took a step toward the girl. "Where's your blazer?"

Shaking, the girl pointed to the rock heap.

"How long ago?"

The girl started crying, the tears running

through the dust on her face. "An hour or more. I think she's dead."

"I think you're right." Dozen didn't bother coating her words with any sympathy. "What about this one?"

"My sister. She'll be okay if we can get her to the other side, our blazer said." The girl's chin lifted. "I'm not leaving her."

Dozen looked at her with interest. "You and your sister have names?"

"I'm Lucy. That's Laura."

"Excellent! Well worth saving, then. I'm Dozen. That's—"

"Sphinx," 1408 blurted out.

Dozen looked at her with a slow smile. "Just as I was going to say." She took out the sensor pack and read the area around the failed cut. She glanced up at 1408, then took another reading at a different place on the obstructing pile and yet another reading further along. At each reading her frown grew deeper.

She blew out a breath. "Well, your blazer had the right idea, but made the wrong cut, I guess. This pile is a bitch, for sure. No matter which way we go, it's going to be unstable. The best bet is the same way she tried, which means we have to go right past her and hope that section holds this time."

Fourteen-oh-Eight—*no, Sphinx*—saw the look of horror on the girl's face and knew she must have worn the same one on her own. She tried to smile and put her arm around the girl's shoulders.

"Don't worry. Dozen is the best blazer there is. She'll get us through."

Dozen nodded a fraction, encouraging her to distract the girl while she made the cuts and went through to test the stability of the passage. The woman who made an effort to think of herself with a name now, instead of a number, knelt beside the small figure on the ground.

"What happened to Laura?"

"She broke her leg jumping off a transport car when the quake started. The guide gave her something for the pain to keep her quiet, and I carried her."

"Where were you working?"

"Corridor Two, Section 20. You?"

"New part of the mine. Blazing off the map."

"They say that's the best job in the mines." There was admiration in the girl's voice.

A new emotion—pride—rose to respond in Sphinx. "Yeah, it was."

Dozen made a number of cuts with the laser about shoulder height, surgically precise, carefully calculated to chip away at a point of weakness in the structure of the rockfall without destroying its overall integrity. But it took much longer than it should have to open a usable thirty-foot-long passage to the other side, and Dozen didn't seem to trust it even then. She checked and rechecked with the sensor pack for signs of instability in the pile, then insisted on crawling through the passage and back again before she let them try it.

"Okay," she pronounced. "We're good. Sphinx, you're going first, then Lucy. We'll strap the kid up so you two can pull her through, and I'll come behind her, okay?"

Sphinx nodded. Lucy looked scared, but she said nothing as they put the harnesses in place, the ropes leading behind to her younger sister.

Dozen grabbed Sphinx by the arm as she was about to hoist herself into the opening. "Watch yourself. I don't like the way this bastard is shifting. There'll be a little drop like this one at the other end, remember."

"Sure. I got this." She grinned to make the blazer believe it. Then she climbed up into the entry and led the way through the rough, narrow passage, slithering on her stomach, pulling herself along with elbows rubbed raw by the sharp rock. She could hear her breath catching raggedly in her throat as she worked her shoulders past the pinching turns in the tunnel, but she knew she would not give in to panic. She was not the same creature she had been so many weeks ago when Dozen had led her through the rock to the crystal cavern. She had a name now, and a purpose.

As she clawed across the rock, her hand touched something soft and pliable off to the left. She realized with a shock it was a bit of clothing, part of the blazer's body crushed by the failure of the previous hole.

She glanced back at Lucy. "Keep your eyes on

me. The turns are tricky here."

Sphinx reached the end of the cut and fell through to the tunnel floor on the other side. There were a few low red emergency lights gleaming in the darkness down a mostly clear corridor. She managed a sweaty grin. Maybe Dozen was right about the service lift after all. She stood up and helped Lucy out of the hole, and together they pulled on the ropes that were attached to the harness around Laura's shoulders.

"Hold up!" Dozen's voice wasn't coming from far inside the hole, but they couldn't see her or Laura. "The rope must be tangled on something. She's getting twisted in the passage."

Sphinx re-entered the hole without hesitation, crawling back up until she could see Laura's head and shoulders. She freed the constriction and tugged on the ropes, then backed out ahead of the child, while Lucy pulled. At last, they brought the unconscious girl completely out of the tunnel and stretched her out on the floor.

Sphinx heard a sound, just a whisper of sliding sand and shifting stone. She turned, expecting to see Dozen emerge from the tunnel, but no one was there.

"Dozen? You okay?"

"Sphinx! Give me a hand, will ya?"

She ran back to the hole, thinking maybe the gear was in the way, and ducked inside. It was dusty. It hadn't been dusty before.

"Dozen! Where are you?"

"Here! My damn leg is stuck!"

She reached out and found Dozen's hands, then her shoulders. "What happened?"

"Fucking hole shifted again. Now my leg is stuck. Damn it! I think it might be broken. Hurts like a sonofabitch! Come on. Pull! I don't think there's too much weight on it, but I can't move it myself."

Sphinx pulled as hard as she could. Dozen screamed, but she didn't move.

She couldn't see past the blazer's shoulders in the confined space. But the light from her headlamp showed her something she had never seen before—fear on her friend's face. Sphinx swallowed hard and took any sign of a tremor from her voice before she spoke.

"Can you get any leverage with your other foot?"

"I—wait, yeah, I think so. Okay, now try."

Sphinx braced herself against the sides of the passage and yanked—and felt something come loose as her partner yelled and lurched forward. She dragged and Dozen crawled the last few feet toward the corridor. Sphinx felt her feet dangle. She twisted and got her legs, body and head out of the hole, leaving her right hand still gripping Dozen's overalls where the blazer lay just inside the passage.

There was a sound—a deep, rumbling groan—then the mountain gave way and the hole snapped shut.

CHAPTER SIXTEEN

I woke up screaming into the pillow, my right shoulder an agony of shattering pain, my mind a deep morass of terrifying loss. I opened my eyes, but there was nothing but darkness. I tried to move, but the weight of a world held me down by one arm and my nerves shrieked with the torture of splintered bone and shredded muscle. I called out, but I knew the dead wouldn't answer.

From somewhere else, a light appeared. A voice I should have recognized spoke in my ear.

"Asia? Asia, wake up."

"Dozen! Where's Dozen?" I still couldn't move, couldn't see. Where the hell was I?

"She's not here, Asia. It's okay. It's me, Ethan. Where are you right now?"

"Corridor Three." My voice scraped against cold stone. "Dozen's dead, isn't she?"

I felt a warm hand on my forehead, my neck, then, very gently, my shoulder. "Jesus! It hurts!" If I had an arm, a hand, anything below that mangled shoulder, I couldn't feel it.

"I'm sorry, shhh, I'm sorry. Take a minute and rest. Breathe. We'll have you out of here soon. Do you remember what happened?"

The makeshift tunnel. Dozen was trapped inside. I opened my eyes, expecting to see a mine corridor, lit with emergency lights. Instead, I saw a hotel room, lit with a single lamp. Ethan knelt beside the bed, watching me intently. My heart was hammering, and my throbbing right arm dangled over the edge of the bed.

"Ethan?"

He smiled. "Welcome back."

I curled from my belly onto my left side and burst into tears. Ethan climbed onto the bed behind me and pulled me into his arms. He held me while I cried, and I cried for a long time, sobbing out all the pent-up grief from a trauma I'd long forgotten. Then he listened without judgment while I told him what I remembered of a place and time that couldn't possibly exist by anyone's rules of logic.

"This wasn't a dream, Ethan." He must have known that as well as I did. "That's why you brought me to see Ida. She and I . . . we actually experienced these things."

I felt him take a breath. "I don't know how, but there's no other explanation for it. You know you have a scar where that rock came down on your shoulder."

"What?" I sat up and stared at him. There was no scar that I knew of. And the pain of the injury had faded now to nothing again. As if it had never happened.

He wrinkled his brow. "On your shoulder blade."

When I just looked at him, he got off the bed and held out a hand to help me up. He led me to the mirror and turned me around. Then he lifted my tee-shirt over my head. I twisted and looked over my shoulder to see what he meant.

There, on my shoulder blade, was a long, ugly welt of scar tissue. I gasped. I'd never paid any attention to it before.

"What the hell? How could I have missed that?" It burned now where the memory of the injury remained.

Ethan shook his head, his fingertips tracing the line of the scar ever so softly. "The same way I suspect you ignored other changes in your body after months of hard labor: traumatic memory loss. Your mind simply refused to acknowledge it. The loss of your children compounded it. There's another scar, too." He raised a hand, hesitating.

"What is it? Show me."

"Some of my patients believe it's where the aliens insert a microchip to track them." He lifted the hair from my neck and rubbed a finger lightly across my hairline. "Right here, at the base of the skull."

My blood turned to ice, and I got so cold my nipples tightened. I clutched the tee-shirt to my chest in embarrassment.

I saw the hungry look in Ethan's eyes before he turned away to let me dress again. "I wouldn't blame you if you thought I'd switched places with one of my patients. I'm starting to sound a little crazy even to myself."

I shivered. "If you're asking me to be objective, I think you're asking the wrong person."

Ethan turned back to me and took me by the hand. He led me to the bed and sat down. "Asia, about last night . . ."

Oh, God! It felt like a lifetime ago, but not nearly long enough to live it down. I'd said a few things I'd give a lot to take back. *Shit!*

"I was drunk. I'm sorry—"

"No, you were right. You kicked my ass, and I deserved it."

"Ethan, I—"

He held up a hand to stop me, then spent a long moment staring at the space between us. The urge to fill that moment with words, to close that space with my body was overwhelming. I was so afraid of what he might say, so afraid that what I had said had presented him with some kind of stupid ultimatum, and now he was going to tell me we were destined to be "just friends." I was shaking so hard I gripped the bedspread to keep from flying apart.

Ethan didn't look up. He just started talking.

"I felt so guilty after we left Ida's place. It's all I thought about that long drive up here. Because of me, two people I love were put in danger and one was dead."

I looked at him in shock. Had he said the "L" word?

"What the hell are you talking about?"

His eyes, dark with self-blame, met mine. "My files, Asia. How else would they have known about you?"

"Oh, baby." I touched his hand. "Did it never occur to you that these people might have been watching us since we were taken? That they're connected to whatever took us? They've probably been watching Ida since she was ten." Of course, that didn't explain why they were so eager to get their hands on us now, but that was a mystery for another discussion.

He gave me a wry smile. "No, that never occurred to me."

"Well, it might have if you had talked to me."

"All I knew was that I hadn't protected Ida. I hadn't protected you."

My heart melted. He was an idiot. But what a sweet idiot.

"Jesus, Ethan. How could you possibly have known about those guys? And how the hell was shutting me out supposed to help?"

"The only thing I could think to do was distance myself from you." He moved, small tense motions of his shoulders revealing his frustration. "It was wrong. I knew it even as I was doing it, but I couldn't seem to stop myself. I couldn't bear to see you hurt because of me."

I blew out a breath, unable to hide my exasperation. "So you hurt me to keep from hurting me? That makes no sense."

He touched my face, tracing a line from my cheek to my chin with one tentative finger. "I'm so sorry, Asia. I wanted you so much, and I should have stopped, but I didn't and . . . we got so close so quickly . . . then when all that happened I thought it would be better if I ended things sooner rather than later, but—"

"But it was too late," I finished for him, my gaze locked with his. "After that night, it was way too late."

"For both of us. I know that now."

"And yet the man I spent that night with disappeared and was gone for days. What the hell were you hiding from, Ethan?"

A shadow fell across his face. "A ghost."

"Tell me about it."

He shook his head. "Another night."

"Hiding again?" I started to pull away.

"No. I will tell you. Just not tonight." He blocked my retreat with a hand at the back of my head. He drew my face close to his; I could feel his breath warm on my lips. "I'm tired of running; I'm tired of hiding. I'll stay as long as you want me."

My heart was thrashing wildly in my chest, anger morphing into something else entirely. I could barely find the breath to speak.

"And what if I said I want you forever?"

He pushed me down on the bed, his lips inches from mine. "Then I'll stay with you forever, Asia. Forever." He kissed me at last, his mouth hard against mine, his tongue, his taste, his heat, his desire opening me, pouring into me, creating a hunger in me only for him. I was instantly wet and throbbing, aching for the promise of satisfaction I felt pressing hard against my belly. He could have entered me then and there, and I would eagerly have come for him, but he had other plans.

He broke off his kiss, sucking at my lower lip as he withdrew, hard enough to leave it tingling. "I've missed touching you so much." His lips moved at my ear. "Do you know what it's been like watching you prancing around this hotel room the last few days—not being able to touch you?"

"Prancing?" I pretended to be outraged. "First of all, I haven't been prancing. Second, whose fault was it that you couldn't touch me? I was ready any time. And third, weren't you zoned out on pain pills most of the time?"

Ethan laughed, a sound that warmed me like a touch. "Well, yes, and thank God for that." He was still smiling as he brought me forward and lifted the tee-shirt over my head, then lowered me once more to the bed and pulled the panties off my hips. He stripped off his own clothes and straddled me, but before he could lower himself on top of me again, I put my hands on his chest to stop him.

"Not so fast."

He sat back on my hips and let me look, his eyes taking their own tour of my naked body. My hands wandered across the taut muscles of his chest, skimming the fan of fine hair in the center to tease his nipples on either side. He sucked in a breath and smiled as he jerked in response. I hovered across his ribs, my fingertips as light as butterfly wings, tracing the outlines of his injuries, old and new.

"Still sore?"

"Probably." His smile widened. "Not something I'm currently worried about."

"I'm so sorry, baby." I meant the older scars, too, and when I looked in his eyes, I could see he understood. I allowed my hands to drop, then, down over the hard lines of his obliques, to his belly and finally to the thick shaft that rose from between his thighs. I let one hand fall to cup his heavy balls and with the other I gripped that beautiful piece of his at the head and squeezed lightly. Ethan gripped the sheets and sucked in a breath.

I slid my hand down the shaft to the root and back up, loving the way the skin moved under my fingers, the way the hard flesh expanded beneath the skin. I did it again, noting the ridges and the veins, the warm pulsing in my hand when I closed my fist over the tip. I lifted my eyes to Ethan's face. He was in an agony of pleasure and so was I. It was as if I was touching myself when I touched him.

He moved down my body to face me, working himself between my legs so that every movement caressed me, tortured me. His hips rolled against mine, his mouth pressed at my temple, at my ear, at my throat. His heartbeat and mine slammed together until I pulsed and dripped with need.

"I've never wanted a woman the way I want you, Asia." His voice was a low rumble I could feel in my bones. "I'm hard for you every minute of every day. All I can think about is how you screamed when I was inside you. I'll do anything to make you scream like that again. I'll give you anything you want."

There was only one thing I wanted. I gripped the back of his thighs and ground my hips under him. "I want this."

He grinned. "When you're ready."

"Oh, God, I am so ready."

"Not as ready as you will be," he promised.

He drew back to kiss me, his tongue probing my mouth, his hand at my breast, rolling the nipple between his thumb and forefinger hard enough to hurt. Sensation flared between my legs so intense I groaned into his mouth, arching under him, forcing more contact with his rigid shaft. He shifted and his hand slipped between us to close around the head of his erection and guide it in maddening circles around my hungry core.

"Please, Ethan." God, I was desperate for him. "Please. Please." I grabbed his hips and pulled at him, broke off the kiss to bite at his neck and shoulder, raked my nails up his back and begged him, and at last he quit teasing me and gave me what I needed.

He plunged inside me—I was so wet I made it easy for him—and he made sure I felt him hard and deep and in all the right spots. He brought me up fast and wouldn't let me come down until I'd shuddered myself boneless and screamed myself hoarse for him. He came with me the last time and filled me with his sweet stuff, and, when it was over, he held me for what was left of that night. And if there is a finer way to apologize in this life, I'm sure I've never experienced it.

Ethan's face was the first thing I saw as I came to life the next morning. His eyes were the color of the October sky and his smile crinkled them at the corners when he saw I was awake.

"'Morning, beautiful."

If I hadn't been in love with him before, that

moment would certainly have clinched the deal. "Hey." I offered up my lips for a kiss.

He obliged with a tender, almost chaste, touch of his warm lips to mine. Then another. His lips wandered from my mouth to my throat, from my throat to my collarbone, from my collarbone to my breast. There he lingered, licking and nibbling at my nipple while my heart began to pound and my blood began to race to fill my willing flesh with heat again.

The mood was shattered with a loud knock on the door. We jumped apart; Ethan rolled off the bed and dove for my bag near the bathroom. He thrust his hand in the bag and came out with the pistol and was standing at the door before the second knock came.

Fortunately, the visitor announced herself before Ethan blew her poor innocent head off. "Housekeeping!"

"Jesus Christ!" I exhaled.

Ethan spoke to her through the locked door. "Uh, you need to come back later."

"Okay," came the reply. "Y'all take your time."

"Holy shit." Ethan sank down on the bed, his hand shaking as he put the safety back on the gun and lowered it to the floor. I crawled across the bed to put my arms around his shoulders. Then we both started laughing, howling hysterically with both relief and a sense of how ridiculous we looked, ready to fight the Men in Black in nothing but our birthday suits.

Ethan shook his head. "We need to get the hell out of here."

"I'm with you, *Kemosabe*. Whatever you had in mind for this morning can wait until we get to wherever we're going."

Busy throwing clothes in the direction of his overnight bag, he simply smiled, a smile that promised everything.

It didn't take us long to get organized, once we decided to go. At nine o'clock the housekeeper almost met Jesus. At ten o'clock we had packed the car, ready to head out.

Ethan backed the car out of the parking space and drove around to the office. "Hey, Baby's purring this morning. Guess those guys tuned her up, too?"

"Yeah, they had fun working on what they considered to be a classic. You're really lucky they could find the part."

"How did you pay for it?"

"Ethan, you were completely out of it, and I knew I didn't have the money to pay for it." My face grew red with embarrassment. "I didn't know what else to do."

He lifted an eyebrow. "What did you do? Rob a bank?"

"I used your credit card. Ray and the boys weren't too particular about who signed. I'm sorry—I couldn't exactly ask for permission."

The worry lines between his eyes softened into amusement, and he laughed. "Sure you could've. I might have said anything! But it's a good thing we're leaving here today. Our friends will trace that card in no time. Maybe I'll drop a few hints with the Front Desk as to where we'll be headed next; put them off the scent."

Since our pursuers would soon know about the Marlinton location, we made full use of it. Before we left town we went shopping for some groceries and for camping gear that Ethan said was essential. We got cash from more than one ATM—enough to tide us over for a while. We were feeling flush and almost giddy by the time we left, heading north on the same winding two-lane highway we'd come in on.

It was a crystal-clear fall day in the mountains. The sun was shining from a sky as blue as sapphires and the leaves were a patchwork of red and gold and stubborn green across the folded hills. We could almost believe we were a couple of tourists taking a drive over those torturous switchbacks for the pure pleasure of each other's company and the view from the next scenic outlook.

Yet if I stopped to assess my state of heart, below the tropical sea of emotions that washed around Ethan was a cold current of grief arising from my time in the mines of . . . *where?* I didn't even have a name for the place where I had lost a friend, but I missed her here and now.

I'd fallen silent as the late afternoon shadows lengthened. Ethan let me go for a while before he spoke.

"The memory that surfaced last night is on your mind a lot today, isn't it?"

I acknowledged the truth of his insight with a humorless smile. "Dozen is on my mind a lot today."

He nodded. "She would be."

"You can understand why people insist on having a body to bury. You know, widows of MIAs or kidnap victims' families." I stared out the window, seeing nothing. "They can't let go until they have those remains. I feel a little bit like that. It would be much easier to believe this whole thing never even happened—that it was all a dream or a vision. Except . . ." I looked at him. "Ethan, I know. I just *know* this place, these people, all of it was real. Dozen was real. Mose was real. And now they're dead. And, damn it, that hurts."

He took his eyes off the road to meet mine, lifted a hand to brush away the tear that had rolled down my cheek. "I know. I'm sorry, Asia."

It was quiet again for a long moment before Ethan took a different tack. "How's your shoulder?"

"Sore. Not like this morning, though. Weird, huh?"

He shrugged. "Not really. The physical body retains a lot of emotional memory. When a painful memory is released, the body will often release the pain physically, too. I have a few friends who do body and energy work around that kind of thing."

That was a new one on me, but I did remember a few massages that had come close to being spiritual experiences.

"Do you remember anything beyond the injury? I mean, do you remember what happened after the rock fell on you?"

I thought about it. Every detail up to that point was clear—the grit under my hands and knees, the smell of the earth in my nostrils, the sound of the mountain groaning all around me before a pain like a meat cleaver sliced into my shoulder blade. Afterwards there was nothing.

I explained this to Ethan. It didn't seem to surprise him. He was after something else anyway.

"Dozen was taking you somewhere to get out of the mine. This was an escape plan that had been set up ahead of time."

I nodded slowly, putting the pieces together. "She acted like she knew exactly where to go, what to do."

"She was working with others."

"Yes, but she never said anything about anyone else." I thought back over every conversation I could remember having with Dozen, even the most trivial. She had hinted at the truth, but never revealed anything of substance. She had been careful. She had had to be. Even 1408 might have betrayed her. "I guess she was never sure of me until the end."

Ethan shot a look at me, then looked back at the road, understanding. There was another pause while he moved on to the next question in his mind.

"The people she was trying to reach must have found you and got you out."

I smiled tightly. "Obviously, or I wouldn't be here. But there's a big piece of the puzzle still missing."

Ethan grinned. "Oh, you mean the whole time travel/space warp/little gray men connection?"

"I thought that was supposed to be your specialty."

"Um, no. My specialty is convincing people that there are no little gray men, no abductions, no time travel, no space warps. I'm in a little over my head here. For this we need Stephen Hawking. Or maybe Isaac Asimov."

"Well, I think it may be too late for Isaac. And Stephen's just going to tell us we're nuts. So we're back to you."

Ethan laughed. "The perfect circular argument."

"Then there's the question of who's after us. Are they government? Guns for hire? Aliens in disguise? Maybe we ought to let them catch up to us." I wasn't smiling when I said it. "Who knows? They might even be the good guys, trying to save Earth from the evil aliens."

Ethan looked like he might stop the car and shake me. "No. No, Asia. Good guys don't come at you with a strong sedative and no explanation. They don't make you disappear without a trace. They don't scare an old woman so damn bad she takes her own life." He turned back to the road, his expression set on grim. "I don't know who they are, but they aren't the good guys."

CHAPTER SEVENTEEN

By nightfall we had crossed into Pennsylvania, though the Appalachians stretched on in roll after unimpeded roll on either side. It was easy to see what a barrier they must have seemed to the restless farmers of the early days of the Republic, why the Conestogas made the long trek down the Wilderness Road to cross the Cumberland Gap into the Promised Land beyond those endless mountains. Even in this day of banked curves and smooth pavement, of internal combustion engines capable of carrying us at speeds unthinkable to our dogged ancestors, after five straight hours I was sick and tired of those damn mountains and ready to be done with driving in them.

So it was with some relief that we finally hit I-80 going east in Pennsylvania and took the Beemer up to speed for a brief final push before calling it a night. But the good feeling didn't last long.

When I called to check in with Rita, she sounded more than just worried. "Where the hell are you?"

"Long story. What's going on?"

"You tell me, 'cause it sure as hell looks like you

got yourself in a mess."

"Well, you may be right about that, but what makes you think so?" I kept my voice even, but my heart had kicked into overdrive and my mouth was suddenly dry.

"Those guys you were talking about Sunday? They paid us a visit at the office Monday afternoon." Fear was something I'd never heard in Rita's voice before. I cursed myself that I was responsible for putting it there. "They were rough characters, all right, but they seemed a little smarter than the usual credit bureau types to me. They asked a *lot* of questions, and they weren't happy when I kept saying it was none of their damn business, if you get my drift."

"Oh, Rita, I'm so sorry. What did you tell them?"

"I didn't tell them shit! What do you take me for?" She sounded really pissed now.

"I didn't mean—Rita, I shouldn't have put you in that position. I had no choice. I'm sorry."

There was a pause while my friend seemed to collect herself. When she spoke again, her voice was quiet, worried. "Just listen. They left that day, but they came back this afternoon, and they talked to JW. God knows what he told them. And when they left, JW came out and let me know in no uncertain terms that if you were to call or come in, I was to say you no longer have a job here."

The news shouldn't have surprised me. This was Wednesday, after all, and I hadn't showed up for work in three days—that was enough for JW even without the rest of it.

"Asia?"

"Yeah, I heard you. Figures. You're not in trouble over this are you?"

Rita exhaled loudly. "Oh, hell. You know that asshole can't do without me. He yelled most of the afternoon, but what could he do to me? I just said I didn't know a thing—which is the freaking truth, by the way. Girl, what the hell is going on?"

I glanced at Ethan, who met my gaze and slowly shook his head. I nodded to show him I understood.

"I can't tell you, sweetie. I wish I could."

"Are you okay? It's not something with that guy, is it?"

"No. I'm fine, thanks to him. I guess you could say we're in this together."

"Is that a good thing or a bad thing?"

"It's a hell of a lot better than being in it alone, that's all I know."

"But where are you? I went by the apartment, and the poor cat liked to knock me down for some attention. I took him home with me, since I didn't know when you'd be home."

"Good thinking, since I don't have a clue either."

"Those guys were scary, Asia. They meant business. You need to make sure you stay as far away from them as you can."

"I know. That's the plan. Thanks for everything, Rita."

"I was glad to do it, honey. Is there anything else I can do?"

"I'll be in touch when I can."

"Okay. I guess. You take care of yourself."

I closed the phone and looked at Ethan. I could

just see the planes of his face outlined in the dim light from the dashboard. The muscles of his jaw were clamped tight, and the tension I could read so plainly there was evident, too, in the hands that gripped the steering wheel and the forearms that served them.

"You heard?"

"Most of it." He glanced at me. "Is she all right?"

"Yeah, thank God. Guess they got what they needed from my boss and left."

His head whipped around. "What could your boss have told them?"

I shrugged. "Not a hell of a whole lot. My home address, I guess. I didn't put down any emergency contacts or family information on my application when I signed on. I was trying to make a clean break with Hazelett and all that had happened. Never got around to 'updating' my forms, either."

"Good. That's good." Ethan seemed to relax a little.

"Baby, you forget—I don't have any family to worry about." A minute passed in silence before I sat up and stared at him, newly terrified. "Maybe we should start worrying about yours."

Ethan shook his head. "My friends Dan and Lisa are visiting her mother in Florida. And my sister's okay—she's out of the country."

I tilted my head to look at him. "Don't you have a brother, too?"

He ran a hand through his hair and shifted in his seat, as if the mere mention of his sibling made him want to strangle something. "He's a broker in New York City. If anyone's in danger in this situation it would be the Men in Black."

"Wow. That bad, huh?"

Ethan blew out a weary breath. "We have history."

"Is there a chance he'd tell them where we are?"

He shook his head. "Brian thinks I'm a leftist hippie and my clients all lying social parasites, but he's reserved the pleasure of killing me for himself." Ethan didn't appear to be joking. "He won't tell them anything."

I exhaled and relaxed again. "Okay. So, Plan A is secure. Now, how soon can we stop for the night?"

Ethan looked uncomfortable. "Guess that depends on how you feel about driving. Because I have another kind of phone call to make."

The next exit coming up offered lots of choices for lodging. I decided to give the poor drivers of Pennsylvania's highways a break. "We're distracted enough. Let's get off the road before we kill somebody. Then you can call the President of the United States for all I care."

Ethan had been putting this conversation off for too long already, he knew, but still his fingers hovered over the numbers and wouldn't make the connection. It had never been easy to deceive Arthur Claussen. The man was good at what he did for a living, and he'd been doing it since Ethan was in kindergarten.

Ethan was going to find it difficult enough to lie about his reasons for being out of town and away from his practice for an unknown stretch of time. He seldom took time off for himself and never at short notice. Claussen would insist on an explanation.

But if Asia's name came up in the conversation, dissembling was going to take on a whole new dimension. Much as he admired him, even loved him, in a way, Ethan knew the blunt curmudgeon was uncompromising to the point of rigidity about some things. Especially the particular point of ethics that required a professional distance between doctor and patient.

Like most psychiatrists, Claussen saw that point as a law written in stone. Ethan had already taken a hammer and smashed it into bits—and would gladly do it again for Asia's sake. There was no going back for him, no matter what the cost. He simply didn't want to fight that noble battle tonight on a cell phone with low batteries from a hotel room in Middle of Nowhere, Pennsylvania, after a long day being chased by a Still Unknown Menace.

God, he was tired.

He took a deep breath and tried not to think of Asia enjoying a hot bath in the next room. Then he pressed the keypad for Claussen's number. After two rings, the old man picked up.

"Ethan, my boy, where have you been? I've been trying to reach you for days!"

"Really? I was afraid you might say that. I'm sorry, I've been out of town, and I've had a hell of a time getting cell service." It was his first lie. His expensive iPhone lay crushed and abandoned in a dumpster in Marlinton. "How are you?"

"Fine. Just fine. More to the point, how are you?"

"Well, actually, it's been a rough week. I got a

phone call over the weekend that a former patient of mine had died. Do you remember Ida Mickens?"

"Mickens. The woman from West Virginia? She lived at your friend's house for a while. You didn't have much success with her as I remember."

Yes, thank you, Arthur, for finding a way both to chastise me for getting too close and remind me that I failed to help in the same sentence. "Yes. She passed away this weekend."

"I'm sorry to hear that." Claussen's voice was not overly sympathetic. "You went to the funeral?"

"Yes. The family has asked me to stay on and help take care of a few of her affairs. She had some papers and so on, related to the delusions she suffered. I thought they might make an interesting case study. The family has given me time to go through everything before they get rid of her stuff."

"Ethan, you are always too quick to get involved with your patients, as I've told you more than once." There was a pause. "But in this instance, perhaps it will finally pay off. Let's hope it leads to something productive. How long will you be out of town?"

"I'm not sure. No more than a few days, I hope."

"Do you need help with your patient schedule?"

"No, thanks. I've already called everyone for the next few days and rescheduled."

"You could have called me. I would have had Marilyn call them for you, especially if you were having trouble with your cell."

Damn it! "I didn't think of that. I canceled the early part of the week before I left. Then tonight as soon as I could get reception, I called Cindy to take care of it. I had to take my new phone all the way up to the next ridge to get a signal." He laughed with what he hoped was convincing exasperation.

"Where exactly are you in West Virginia, Ethan?"

Asia chose that moment to emerge from the bathroom, her skin rosy and glistening with moisture, her breasts and the top of her thighs just covered by the towel she'd wrapped around her. She'd piled her hair on top of her head to keep it out of the bath—he'd never seen it like that before; it was sexy as hell—and her neck formed a long, smooth, curving line down to her bare shoulder that he longed to follow with his lips. She caught him staring at her and smiled.

"Ethan?"

"Oh, sorry. I—uh—I lost you for a moment there. What did you say?"

"Where are you again?"

"A place called Clay Fork, near Bluefield. But don't bother looking on a map. You won't find it."

"You have an uncommon taste for adventure." A taste it was clear Claussen did not share.

"They're good people here, Arthur. They needed my help. I was glad to provide it."

"Of course. Just don't forget there are those who need you here. By the way, are you making any progress with that girl I sent you?"

Any hope that he might escape the conversation unscathed slipped from his heart. "Which girl is that?"

"Come now, Ethan. Do I send you so many you can't keep track?"

"She has a name, then, Arthur. Let's use that." He couldn't keep a note of irritation from souring his voice. He turned formal. "You saw my last summary, I believe."

"That was, what? Three weeks ago? Nothing to report since then?"

Ethan took a breath. "In fact we've made the decision to terminate therapy. Asia no longer exhibits any of the symptoms that brought her to me. She's sleeping well, she no longer drinks to excess or uses drugs. She has accommodated her grief. She seems relatively happy and well-adjusted. Neither she nor I saw any reason to continue therapy." *Just don't ask me where she is right now.*

"Indeed." There was ice in Claussen's tone. "And you didn't see fit to consult me before you made this decision?"

He reacted before the warning buzz in the back of his head could stop him. "She was my patient, Arthur. The decision seemed unambiguous."

"It may have seemed so only because of your relative inexperience, Doctor. From my work with Asia Burdette, I find it very difficult to believe you've 'miraculously' cured her in so little time. What about the unusual nightmares you mentioned?"

Anger flared at the old man's insult. Ethan held on to it behind clenched teeth.

"She no longer has them." He refused to elaborate.

"Really." Claussen's voice dripped with sarcasm. "And you don't find that strange?"

"It is the point of the AL protocol, isn't it?"

"Of course. Yet your reports up to three weeks ago

made it seem that Asia was unusually resistant to the AL protocol. What do you suppose changed?"

Ethan felt his mind moving at the pace of a clumsy puppy trying to escape a pit bull's jaws. A step ahead he spied a tiny hole in the fence.

"I can only assume the course of therapy was different for this patient because of the trauma she suffered. After all, we both know Asia is not our typical AL patient. In the end, as you suggested, I believe she actually responded more to standard talk therapy."

There was a long moment of silence on the other end of the line. "A fascinating theory, Dr. Roberts. It's your contention, then, that this is a standard case of trauma-induced amnesia?"

"Yes." He hardly thought it would help him deflect Claussen if he said Asia had been abducted by aliens. He forced himself to use a more conciliatory tone. "And I apologize, Arthur. I know you have a special interest in this case. I just haven't had time to write up the results."

The old man seemed to accept the apology. "I'll be very interested to read your report. You will have it to me soon?"

"Of course. As soon as I get back."

"I look forward to it. Good night, Ethan."

Ethan snapped the phone shut, closed his eyes and leaned his head back against the headboard in relief. Asia, dressed for bed now, came across the mattress to his side, molded herself to him, drew a warm hand across his chest, pressed soft lips to his neck.

"The old man wasn't happy, huh?"

He exhaled. "I think he misses you in group."

She laughed, easing the tight grip of fear in his chest. "Maybe I'll go back for a visit. That'll learn him."

He captured her hand with his, turned his head to catch her lips with his kiss. He took his time with it, letting his tongue play lightly with hers for a long, sweet moment. He had no plans to take things further tonight, though his cock was ever ready to write checks his body could not pay. He was exhausted, an exhaustion he could read in Asia's body, too. It just felt so damn good to hold her. He took a deep breath.

"You smell good." That tang of far-off deserts over the sweetness of honey.

"Umm." Her eyes were already closing.

He brought the covers up around her and watched while she drifted off, knowing he wouldn't be far behind. His conversation with Claussen nagged at him. The old man was far too involved in this case; he'd been too damn pissed off to hear they'd terminated therapy.

A tiny shiver of apprehension snaked up his spine. Ethan shrugged at it, trying in vain to dislodge it. In the end, he was just too tired to think things through. He could analyze the problem tomorrow when his mind was fresh.

He turned out the light and slipped under the covers with Asia. Poised on the edge of sleep, he smiled with pleasure at the warmth of her body next to his, the warmth of his heart expanding in his chest, the warmth of his future with her in it.

But a lingering question blew an icy breath across his mind as he dropped off: Claussen had been expecting something out of Asia's sessions. What was it?

CHAPTER EIGHTEEN

Fall had only just begun to make an impact on the slopes of the lower Appalachians. When we'd started out in West Virginia, the leaves had only a blush of color. Here in the Adirondacks of New York, they were blazing. Everywhere I looked, the hillsides were splashed in maple leaf red and birch yellow and every shade of orange in between. Only the firs and the tall white pines remained unchanged to hold the promise of spring.

We had gotten a late start, and Ethan had chosen a two-lane route from Binghamton, north through Utica. So it was late afternoon when we passed the boundaries of New York's Adirondack Park. The autumn scenery grew even more awe-inspiring. The lakes of the Fulton Chain gleamed blue and untroubled through the trees to our right, reflecting the last of the afternoon's sunlight. In contrast, the tacky "housekeeping cottages" and motels along Route 28 could have been lifted off of a postcard from the 1950s and were full of leaf-peeping tourists.

We turned left just outside the town of Eagle Bay,

following the signs for Big Moose. But long before we reached another town, Ethan gave me a quick grin and took an unmarked road off to the right. "Almost there." His face was as lit with excitement as a kid's at the circus. He was coming home. My heart melted.

The road led us past several driveways cut into the thick forest. I looked hard, but I couldn't see the water, even though Ethan assured me the road was taking us around the lake's southern perimeter. Signs along the road announced private roads to camps with names like Richard's Retreat and Carter's Cove. Through the trees I could glimpse a few of them—massive log structures with the lake shining beyond or smaller cottages with a boathouse below. Unlike the highway we'd left behind, this quiet expanse breathed old money, and it was becoming more and more clear to me that Ethan had come from that world, whether he'd fully admit it or not.

He pointed to a driveway on the left. "We're here."

He pulled in and started down the steep gravel drive. On either side trees grew close to the gravel's edge, forcing Ethan to take the drive slowly. A couple of fallen evergreens nearly blocked the way. "I'll have to get the chain saw after those." Ethan wrestled Baby to maneuver around them. "Looks like we might have had a storm recently."

We emerged into a limited parking area in front of a large, dark-green clapboard house. Broad covered porches framed the house on two sides and overlooked the lake. A dappled patch of lawn dropped swiftly down a sharp slope to the lake, ending in a brief pebbly beach. A boathouse crowded the water to one side, painted to match the house. Tall trees leaned into the cleared space, the hundred-year-old oaks and the beeches in their fall finery interspersed with dark firs and cedars. The woods grew so thickly they blocked all sight of the neighbors on either side.

I parked the car, got out, and gazed at the place in open-mouthed awe. "Ethan, it's gorgeous."

He smiled and held out a hand. "Let me show you the lake before it gets dark."

He led me down to the water's edge as the sun was going down behind the trees, thin shafts of light finding their way like fingers out over the water. It was still, and quiet except for the steady trill of crickets and far out across the lake the weird warbling call of—

"What the hell is that?"

Ethan laughed. "A loon. Never heard one?"

"Television doesn't do it justice." The air coming in off the lake was beyond chilly; even in my sweater and jacket I shivered.

Ethan put an arm around my shoulders and pulled me in close. "Better?"

I snaked one arm around his back and snuggled closer. "Oh, yeah."

We watched as the shadows lengthened and the mist settled across the water. On the other shore, the barely rippling surface reflected back the brilliant colors of the hardwoods and evergreens around the lake and on the slope of the mountain behind it. Here and there along the shore a boathouse or a stretch of beach leading down to the water betrayed the presence of a camp. At this hour, or at this time of year, maybe, there were no boats—and no other humans—to spoil the serenity of the lake.

"You know, this lake is famous," Ethan said. "Sort of."

I searched my memory banks. "Okay, I give up. Why's that?"

"A woman named Grace Brown was murdered up here in the early 1900s. Theodore Dreiser wrote a novel based on the story."

"*An American Tragedy.*"

He looked at me in astonishment.

I shrugged. "I minored in English while I was in college. Saw the movie, too."

"Movie?"

"*A Place in the Sun*, with Montgomery Clift and Elizabeth Taylor? I think Shelly Winters got the old heave-ho." I looked out at the smooth, cold water and shivered. "This is the place, huh? It's actually a little creepy, now that I think about it."

He held me tighter, and I was suddenly grateful for his warmth, his nearness, his protection.

After a minute, I spoke again. "You spent summers up here?"

"No, usually we just got a couple of weeks. The rest of the summer I was stuck in Syracuse doing day camp at the YMCA. Some years I got lucky, and I stayed on with my cousins."

"You must have loved it."

"I thought it was heaven." He smiled as he looked across the water. Then he looked back at me and turned so we were face to face. "Now I'm sure."

He drew my lips toward his, and I smiled beneath his kiss, meeting his tongue with mine as he slipped inside my mouth. I teased and toyed with him for a long moment before he withdrew.

He stroked my cheek. "Come on, we'd better unload the car and get settled while we still have some daylight."

I didn't want to, but I let him go. For once I felt like there would be time to finish what we'd started. I took a deep breath of pine-scented air and followed him back to the house.

Inside the huge, rambling lake house Ethan euphemistically referred to as the "camp," my sense of having been caught in some kind of time warp intensified. The high-ceilinged central room was wrapped in deep-silled windows looking out on the lake and paneled everywhere else in thick pine. The air inside was as frigid as that outside—Ethan explained that the house wasn't winterized—but the place was warm with family memory. Photos on the walls and every surface, some of them nearly as old as the camp itself, showed smiling faces in groups of four or ten or twenty. The rest of the décor looked like an L.L. Bean catalog. I was in love.

I volunteered to set up the kitchen and make dinner while Ethan unloaded the gear and brought in wood for the fireplace and wood stove that served the center of the house. He sweated and hauled while I banged pots and pans. Before long the fires were bringing the temperature up from bone-chilling to cozy and the smell of the Burdette family recipe for pasta sauce was mixing enticingly with the tang of wood smoke.

Ethan brought in the last of our things from the car and dropped them behind the sofa that faced the fireplace. Then he pulled out the sofa bed and threw the new sleeping bags we'd bought in Marlinton over the thin mattress, added a couple of pillows and stood back to admire his work.

I cocked my head at him. "I take it this is also the master bedroom?"

He grinned at me. "There are lots of real bedrooms off of this one, but no heat. We'll be warmer in here. And the bathroom around that corner has an electric heater, so you should be nice and toasty all night long, even if you have to visit the facilities in the middle of the night."

"That's very thoughtful, hon." I was teasing, but I appreciated it all the same.

He came behind the breakfast counter to the kitchen sink to wash up. After he dried his hands he caught me from behind as I stirred the sauce on the stove and nuzzled my neck.

"I'm starving. When's dinner?"

"Now soon enough for you?"

"Perfect."

"Open that bottle of wine, then, and I'll dish this up."

We ate side by side at the counter, so close our knees were nearly touching, taking the time to ask each other the things we hadn't had time for until now—the silly little things, the important things.

We were lingering over our wine when Ethan got up to throw an extra log on the fire. "The fireplace was built when the camp was built in the '20s." He stirred the embers into flame. "Doesn't give off much heat except up close. The wood stove is the real heat source." He grinned up at me. "In case you were wondering."

"In fact, I was just going to ask." *Must be a guy thing.* "Yesterday you said your sister was out of the country. Where is she?"

"Italy." He sat back down and refilled our wine glasses. "She's a buyer for Saks in the city."

"Saks." I was seriously impressed. "You mean, Saks Fifth Avenue. In New York City."

He smiled. "Yeah. That's the one."

A tiny piece of observational data slid into place in my brain. "Ah, that explains that gorgeous leather jacket I saw hanging on a peg in your hallway back home. Well worn, but *very* expensive. A gift from Sis?"

"Okay, just how long have you been stalking me?" The smile turned to laughter. "Did you go through my bedroom closet, too?"

I blushed and scrambled for a comeback. "I may not be able to afford them, but I can appreciate nice clothes. Sis and I are going to be very, very good friends."

"You'd like Sarah." His eyes suddenly caught mine, and his voice went soft. "She'd like you, too."

"I'd like to meet her. Are you two close?"

He shrugged minutely. "We were growing up. We don't see each other much now, but we talk. She's the big sister, you know. She worries."

"So, okay, let's see if I have this straight," I said.

"You all grew up in Syracuse, where Dad and Mom were . . ."

"A college professor and"—he hesitated—"a patron of the arts."

I gave him a double-take.

His mouth twisted in a wry smile. "Mom's family has money." He gestured at the room around us. "This is the Hamilton family camp, not the Roberts's."

More pieces fell into place. I began again. "Okay. A college professor and a patron of the arts, and as soon as they graduated from high school, Baby Bro and Big Sis skedaddled for the bright lights of the Big City while little Ethan followed his dream to become a country music star in Nashville, right? Where'd you go wrong, bubba?"

Ethan had just taken a drink of wine and barely managed to choke it down around his laughter. "Guess my radical upside down banjer-pickin' style jest didn't ketch on."

"Sad, really. So many stories like yours in Music City." I looked at him. "So, what's the real story? How did you end up in Nashville?"

His smile faded, and he studied his wine glass. I could see he was weighing how much to tell, how much to leave for another time, how much to forget had ever been part of the story at all. I waited, knowing he needed to tell at least some of the story. After a while, he took another drink and began.

"I was in my final year of residency at Johns Hopkins in Baltimore, doing pretty well. I liked them, they liked me. I was on track to be offered a staff position in the hospital there, and I was happy about it. It was interesting work, a really diverse patient population, and I was learning a lot. I had some good friends in town, too."

I guess my puzzlement showed, because he stopped talking. "So why did you leave?"

The corners of his mouth quirked upwards. "The usual reason. I met someone."

"Ah." I forced myself to keep breathing.

"Her name was Elizabeth," he continued, his eyes on his wine glass again. "She was studying at the School of International Studies at Hopkins. When she graduated, she was offered a position at a firm back home in Nashville. She asked me to go with her."

My heart was trying to break free of my ribcage, and I had to fight to keep my voice steady. "You gave up everything for her."

His eyes met mine. "It's not quite as romantic as it sounds. Yes, I loved her, but I was young, and she was manipulative. She gave me an ultimatum, but she sweetened the deal. Her uncle offered me a fellowship at the Psychogenesis Institute."

I took in breath in a little gasp. "You were married to Claussen's *niece*?"

He nodded, his expression guarded. There was obviously a lot more to this story. I wondered how much I should push to find out. I nibbled around the edges.

"But you no longer work for him. Was it because of the accident?"

He shook his head. "The work was interesting, but after a few years, I got tired of research, so I opened my own practice. That was before the accident."

"Psychogenesis is a research institute?" My confusion no doubt showed in my face. "I thought Claussen was just a psychiatrist, like you."

"He still does clinical work, like the therapy group you left. But most of his time is spent on small-scale research projects. Lots of government grants, that kind of thing. He has a special interest in people who construct elaborate paranoid fantasies, but can still hold down a job and maintain relationships. People who believe they've been abducted by aliens, for example."

I gave him a sly smile. "People like me, you mean."

"Six months ago I would have said so, yes." He had the grace to blush.

"You said he invented the AL machine to help them?"

"That was the idea. And it works most of the time."

"Except when it doesn't."

He nodded. "Except when it doesn't."

I thought about what he'd told me while I sipped at my wine, but there was something I still didn't quite understand.

"So you don't work for Arthur Claussen, but he still sends you patients?"

"It's not that uncommon. Docs do it all the time when they get busy or the case is a little out of their field." The explanation seemed reasonable enough, but the expression on Ethan's face didn't match his words. He frowned, distracted.

I should have heeded the warning signs, but I pressed on. "Okay, I guess I get it. Still, it must have been hard at first, striking out on your own. How did your"—I stumbled over the word—"wife feel about it?"

Ethan sat back and took a drink of his wine. "Elizabeth was opposed to my leaving Arthur." His tone had suddenly become detached and formal.

"She didn't want you to have your own practice?"

He was tired of sharing, I could see it in his eyes. "She would have been fine with it, as long as all my patients had been rich, famous and merely neurotic." His lips compressed into a line. "Poor and crazy she couldn't handle."

I slipped an arm around his neck and pulled him close. "Well, baby, poor and crazy is sure what you have now."

I touched my lips to his, opened my mouth to receive him when his tongue slipped eagerly inside, enjoyed the wine-flavored swirl of his kiss for the space of several heartbeats. Then I left my counter stool to stand between his thighs, my arms around his waist, my head on his chest, just wanting to hold him and have him hold me for a moment. I could hear his heart beating beneath my ear, strong, a little fast, with the same excitement I felt.

I felt him exhale with satisfaction as his arms tightened around me. "You're just the kind of crazy I need, Asia Burdette."

Ethan emerged from the steamy bathroom with only a towel standing between him and the chillier air of the hallway. But the wood stove was doing its job, and he thought he might actually get away with making love to Asia in front of the fire without freezing his ass off. He grinned as he approached the great room.

Asia was wrapped in a blanket and sitting in the bentwood rocker by the fire. She offered him a slow, sultry smile and opened the blanket to welcome him. She was naked underneath, her skin pink and glowing with an inner warmth he could almost feel from where he stood. He pulled in a breath, the blood rushing to his groin so quickly it left him light-headed. He was so hard so fast he groaned, and his hand involuntarily gripped himself as the towel dropped to the floor.

Her smile widened in appreciation, and he heard her breath leave her in a sigh. He dropped to his knees between her thighs, gathered her in against him, her arms around his neck, her breasts pressing against his chest, her belly warm against his cock.

"Oh, yeah, that's what I've been waiting for." Her soft murmur drizzled like warm honey over his skin.

He turned his lips to her ear. "I'm going to open you like a beautiful, mysterious puzzle box. I'm going to find all your loveliest, most secret places, and I'm going to set them on fire, one by one. I'm going to discover whatever it is that makes you shiver and moan and beg, and I'm going to use it to make you come for me."

She was already trembling under the effect of his words, her breath warm and ragged against his cheek, her hands sliding across the skin of his back. She liked to hear him talk. He moved his lips to the sensitive places at her throat and under her jawline and kept talking.

"I want to hear you come for me, Asia. Not just once or twice, but over and over again. I love it when you say my name. I love it when you tell me what you need. I love it when all those little muscles inside you just go wild."

She moaned and found his mouth with hers, parting her full lips to take him in. His tongue plunged deep, a prelude to the more intimate penetration to come. She welcomed him with a gentle suction, and he felt her breasts rising against his chest as he lingered over the hot, sweet taste of her mouth, the delicious velvety slide of her tongue on his. His heart hammered, pumping the fevered blood into his straining cock, setting up an ache that engulfed his whole body.

Then she reached for him, took his drum-tight head and the top third of his shaft in her warm hand and squeezed hard. He groaned into her mouth, grateful for the rough touch that diffused some of his immediate need. At the same time he knew only a stroke or two along his throbbing length would be enough to send him over the edge. He placed his hand over hers, a signal she understood to release him.

He broke off the kiss and made himself slow down, trailing his lips from her warmly pulsing throat to the satiny skin of her breasts. He cupped both round, firm globes in his palms, teasing the taut nipples with his thumbs until Asia's head fell back against the chair and her eyes closed in pleasure. He lowered his head to one perfect breast and took the tight pink tip in his mouth, licking and suckling and circling it with his tongue as her fingers curled in his hair and soft little moans escaped her with every breath. He moved to the other breast and gave it the same devoted treatment, refusing to be hurried.

His deliberate pace was torture for Asia, who was writhing under him now, wanting more. He sat back on his heels and let his fingertips caress the inside of her thighs, the silken creases where her legs joined her hips.

"Oh, God, I want you so bad and you haven't even touched me." The breathy rasp of her voice made him ache to possess her. "How do you do that?" She pushed back in the rocker so that she was open to him, her hands skimming his forearms to encourage the play of his fingers.

"You can feel how much I want you. Your body can't resist that." He used his thumbs to spread the slick, tender folds of skin, revealing the swollen clit at the heart of her desire. He bent to put his mouth to the sensitive nub and breathed her in, reveling in that exotic desert honey smell and the taste that was hers alone. She arched under him as he lapped and suckled, working the buttery flesh under his tongue until she was desperate and moaning with need. He slipped two fingers inside her and stroked just as the throb of her arousal became the rolling contractions of orgasm and she flooded his mouth with her juices, calling his name and nearly sliding out of the chair.

As soon as he could, he moved to change places with her, enjoying the look of eager agreement that came over her face when she saw what he planned next.

She straddled him and slowly lowered herself onto him. As she settled onto his hips, he gasped at the full sensual impact of their connection. Fully sheathed in her creamy heat, it was all he could do to hold back the climax his body demanded. The least movement of the rocker took him deeper into her welcoming flesh, or pulled him back against the tight grip of her intimate embrace.

"God, that feels so good. I can feel every inch of you, you're in so deep." Her voice trailed off into a broken moan as he rocked slowly forward and back again.

She sat back so he could see her and, shameless, he watched as he pushed into her, took a voyeur's pleasure in the watching as he took a lover's pleasure in every stroke. He thrilled to see her breasts jounce as he moved with her, her belly flutter with every quick indrawn breath of intense desire. He lost himself in watching her, though his blood was on fire and his climax was becoming more inevitable with every thrust. Her head was back, her eyes closed, her skin lit with a sheen of fine sweat. She was the most magnificent creature he had ever seen, and his heart swelled with love and pride as he realized: *she belongs to me.*

He brought his hands down to her hips and began to lift her as they rocked, extending each stroke. He felt his own need spike as she groaned and the heat flared inside her, the fire intensifying toward a conflagration that would consume them both. He kneaded her swollen nub with his thumb, wanting to see her find that ultimate pleasure while he filled her, wanting to feel her explode into climax around his cock, wanting to feel it take her, body and soul, as he held her. At last she screamed and collapsed forward onto him as he speared up into her, the ripples of her orgasm squeezing him from tip to root in continuous waves. "Oh, God, Ethan!" Her moan, his name, was like a mantra, repeated with every shudder of breath, with every lift of her hips, until at last he could feel the desperate pulsing of her inner muscles begin to slow.

He had the strength for one more move and he made it now, standing with Asia in his arms to take two steps to the bed. He laid her down and reseated himself inside her, smiling as she wrapped her long legs around his waist and pulled him in deeper. They moaned together as he filled her and her silky grip claimed him. He drove up into her, experiencing a fierce joy as she opened ahead of him, pushed back against him, swallowed him to the hilt. He pulled back almost all the way so he could have the pleasure of plunging in deep again and again, and each time he felt her give him more of herself. He was close, so close, but he held back, just a few moments longer.

Then she looked up into his eyes, and he saw something he'd been waiting all his life to see. The truth of it stunned him, stole his breath and stilled his beating heart, resonating deep within him. He slowed his movements, wanting to savor what he was feeling.

"Asia," he whispered. "My Asia."

"Yours and no one else's." She still held him with those golden-brown eyes. "Tonight and for the rest of my life, Ethan."

"God, I love you. I'm burning up with it."

"Show me."

He started to move again in long, slow strokes and God! if he thought he'd been ready before he'd had no idea, because soon she was sobbing his name over and over and urging him deeper and harder until he couldn't remember who or where he was. The universe contracted until there was nothing but her body and his, nothing but her sweet welcoming heat and his scorching need, nothing but the pulsing waves of her orgasm contracting along his shaft as she came yet again and the pounding response of his own release beginning deep in his belly.

At last his climax erupted out of him, propelling him forward and deep inside her. He came like a dam bursting, flooding her willing body with his come, flooding his open heart with emotion. And when it was done, he lay gasping for breath, caught by surprise, as if by some kind of sexual—*no, some kind of emotional*—tsunami.

"Jesus, Asia."

"I know, baby." She clung to him. "I know."

He lay inside her for a long time after it ended, waiting for his heartbeat to return to normal, pressing his lips against her neck and her shoulder, too used up to move. She seemed in no hurry for him to go. She held him close, her hands moving up and down his back, her kisses brushing his cheek.

After a while he raised himself to his elbows and

looked down at her. He smiled and bent to touch her lips with his. "That came close to a religious experience."

Asia laughed softly, warming his heart. "Well, I didn't see God, but I'm pretty sure I called His name a few times. And yours—a lot. Damn, but you do things to me no one has ever done before."

Ethan grinned and nipped at her neck, proud of himself. "Good. Just the way I planned it."

"But there's something else you need to know." She waited to say more until he'd raised his head again to look at her. "What I feel for you has to do with so much more than the sex. The sex is only as good as it is because I love you, Ethan. Deep down where it counts. Where things take root and start to grow and can't be gotten rid of easily. Do you know what I'm talking about?"

Suddenly he was shaking, his breath caught in his tightening throat. Her eyes were locked on his, and he couldn't look away. Did he know what she was talking about? Just a few days ago he'd been wondering if maybe she had a key to unlock the prison he'd built around his emotions. Turns out she hadn't had a key, she'd had a fucking sledgehammer. And he wasn't sure she was through smashing walls yet.

"People will say a lot of things when they're making love, Asia, but I meant what I said." He reached out to touch her face. "I love you. I'm still on fire for you. And I believe that fire will be burning inside me for the rest of my life. For you, Asia. Only for you."

CHAPTER NINETEEN

Cold. Cold metal beneath my naked skin. Cold air in the vast room surrounding me, with not even a sheet to drape over my body. Bright. The lights arranged in vast banks high above and positioned close around the table so the Grays could do their work. Screams, some close, some further away. Some my own. And pain. Ripping, searing, mind-breaking pain that would not end.

I felt the touch on the back of my neck and shivered. Though I must have known it was Ethan's fingertips that swept the hair aside and gently traced the line of the scar that lay hidden there, my body reacted as if Death himself had run a skeletal finger over my skin. Before I could stop myself I hissed, "Don't," and flinched away from his hand.

My eyes flew open, my heart thrashing against my ribcage. It was early; the sun had just lifted above the lake to fill the great room with golden, dust-sprinkled light. The dream—*no, the memory*—dissolved into a bitter aftertaste. And it came to me that I had just cruelly rejected the man who had given me the most incredible night of my life. Feeling awful, I rolled over to look at him.

His eyes were dark with shadow. "I didn't mean to wake you."

His face was closed, hard, as if he'd only expected my reaction. There was a lifetime of hurt behind that expression, and something inside me wanted to crush the ones responsible for it. I cursed myself for reminding him of it, no matter what my reasons had been.

"I'm sorry, baby." I reached out to draw him closer. "I was half asleep. Something about that spot on my neck—it just scared me, that's all. I didn't mean to snap at you."

His hand smoothed my hair, traced a line down my cheek. "My fault. I should've guessed you'd be sensitive there." He brushed my lips with his and smiled. "How'd you sleep?"

"Like a baby." It was a lie. The truth was I needed a distraction from the memory that had just surfaced like so much black oil on the still water of my consciousness.

I wanted a reminder of why I should be in no rush to leave our warm bed. I wanted to feel my body, my heart, still humming with the afterglow of the night we had just spent in that bed—the love we had shared, the things we had said. I didn't want that to end. In fact, I was greedy for more.

I moved closer to Ethan, threw my leg over his hip so I could feel him between my thighs, slid my hand under his arm to his back so I could feel his muscles under my fingertips.

"We don't have to get up yet, do we?"

He pressed into me so I was certain to know that he was growing harder by the second. "It's still early."

Desire flared deep in my belly in response. I rolled him over onto his back and molded my body to his, my breasts to his chest, my belly to his. I cradled his shaft along the crease of my hip and massaged it with a slow grind until he groaned, a sound that rumbled deep in his chest and vibrated in my own. I smiled and bent to tease him with a flick of my tongue across his lips.

"Good. Because it's my turn to drive you crazy." I nibbled at his chin. "And that might take some time."

His eyes lit with anticipation, a smile played at the corners of his mouth. "I seem to have all morning."

In fact, the morning was mostly gone before I let him go at last. Apologies were such pleasurable things between us.

At last, sated and connected once again, I lifted my head to kiss him and found him smiling at me. "'Morning, beautiful."

"'Morning," I returned, my lips brushing his.

"That certainly was a damn fine way to start the day."

"I wasn't in the mood for oatmeal."

"Lucky for me."

I started to move, thinking to head for the bathroom, but he held me back. "I had an idea of something to do today."

"Oh, yeah?" I settled back down against his chest, my upper body lifted just enough that I could look into his face. He was wearing a serious expression again, one that might have worried me if his arms weren't still warm around me.

"That scar on your neck. I thought we might get it checked out."

Despite everything, a shiver ran up my spine. Of all the things he might have said, this was the least expected.

"What do you mean, get it checked out?"

"I have a friend, a doctor at a clinic in Rome. He could take an X-ray for us. If there's something there, he could remove it so we could take a look."

I slid off his body and sat up in the bed, pulling the sleeping bag up around my chin. It was as if all the blood in my veins had suddenly been replaced with water the temperature of the lake outside.

Ethan's hand stroked my back. "It might provide another piece to the puzzle, Asia. But if you're not ready, we don't have to do it."

"Another piece to the puzzle," I repeated. "Proof, you mean. Proof that all these things I've been telling you are real."

Ethan sat up and turned me to face him. "Asia, I don't need proof. I have pages and pages of notes from the sessions we had with AL. I have pages of notes from Ida's sessions. I've seen the scar from the tunnel collapse—something you didn't even remember until three days ago. I believe you because I believe in you."

I smiled at him and reached up to touch his face. Thank God I had found him.

"If there is something under that scar, though," he went on, "others might find it a little easier to believe.

And we might be able to convince someone to help us. We can't keep running forever."

A lump formed in my throat that made it hard to say anything. No, we couldn't run forever. And we couldn't hide up here in the boonies, either, as pleasant as it might be. Eventually we had to go back to our lives. Or, at least, Ethan had to go back to his. I'd never had much of one to start with. When we met, I'd asked him for my three hours back. It was beginning to look like he'd done that. Beyond that, I hadn't thought—until this very moment.

My heart developed a tiny, very painful crack.

"You're right." Before I could chicken out, I committed myself. "Why don't you call and set something up? Let's go see your friend."

The ride to the little city of Rome was relatively short—just over an hour by the scenic route Ethan chose—and quiet. I hadn't felt much like talking since we'd decided on this course of action, and Ethan, sensing my mood, had let me be. I didn't want him to know how much the idea of holding an alien probe in my hands that had been removed from my body scared the hell out of me, so I kept it to myself.

There was a sense of *ending* in the air that morning, a feeling that something was close to being over. For the first time since the goon squad attacked us, I took the time to sort through the pieces of what I knew and realized what questions remained hardly mattered anymore. Whether I wanted to believe it or not, I had been stolen from my life and press-ganged into another one, a life of emptiness and slavery and deprivation in another time and place, for how long I don't know. Through the bravery of Dozen and unknown others, I was rescued from that life and returned to my own, with the loss of three precious hours and at an unbearable cost. Did it really matter now who took me, or why? Did it matter precisely who was interested enough in my story that they wanted to kidnap me and keep me as a guinea pig in a lab somewhere? I wasn't sure anymore. What really mattered was whether we had the power to stop them.

I glanced at Ethan and felt that teeny crack in my heart grow a little wider. He would do anything to protect me, even at the cost of his career, or his life. He'd said so, he'd done so, but even more, I'd seen it in his eyes, in the way he touched me, held me, made love to me. What he didn't know was that I would do the same for him, given the chance. Despite the things we had said to each other last night, perhaps *because* of what we had said, that chance was bound to come. Sacrifices would be made.

I was so lost in my thoughts I hadn't noticed that the woods had thinned and yielded to suburban office parks and housing developments and strip malls until Ethan hit the first red stoplight and turned to look at me.

"Are you all right? You can still change your mind if you want to."

I met his gaze. "No. I need to do this. Are we almost there?"

He nodded. "Just ahead." He scooted forward

when the light turned green, then took the next right into an artificial "town square" of dark brick and glass office buildings. He pulled into a parking space near one of them, and we went inside. The lobby was full of sun and tall plants and moderately expensive furniture; the receptionist was pleasant and efficient; the registration procedures were dull and routine. I had no job; I had no insurance. This was going to be a cash-only transaction. I was hoping Ethan could strike a deal. Ethan's friend came out himself to meet us. He burst through the waiting room door—tall, African-American, with light skin and dark eyes and a huge grin for a friend he hadn't seen in what Ethan told me had been six years.

"Ethan! Man, I couldn't believe it was you on the phone this morning!"

Ethan's grin was just as big as they exchanged a back-slapping hug. "It's good to see you, Dom." He turned to me. "This is Asia Burdette. Asia, Dominick Carter."

The doctor smiled and offered me a hand in greeting. "Ethan and I used to get in a lot of trouble together in high school."

"Really?" I lifted an eyebrow. "You'll have to tell me all about it."

Dr. Carter opened the door that led to the interior of the clinic and ushered us in. "Nothing would give me more pleasure." He merely smiled when Ethan groaned theatrically. "How long are you folks in the area? Maybe we could do dinner or something?"

Ethan gave the appropriate social responses, feeding Carter a tolerable line about how and why we were in the area, asking about the wife and kids and so on, smoothly keeping his friend's attention while I struggled to control the rising panic that threatened to send me screaming back into the parking lot. My pulse was roaring in my ears and my palms were clammy by the time we reached the doctor's office. I was grateful we hadn't gone directly to the nurses' station to check my vitals, or they might have called a code on me right then and there.

Once we settled into our chairs in front of the doctor's desk I knew I'd run out of time. Carter looked at me with bright professionalism.

"So, what can I help you with today, Asia? Would you prefer to speak to me alone, or do you want Ethan to stay for this part of things?"

I glanced at Ethan, a smile twitching at the corners of my lips despite everything. "Actually, I'd prefer to have him with me for as much of this as possible. I'm a little nervous about medical procedures."

Carter returned my smile. "That's not unusual. I don't make a terrific patient myself. Ethan said something about an old neck injury?"

"Yeah, well, it's the damndest thing." I spun the lie we'd concocted to cover the truth. "I cut the back of my neck on a metal window frame when I was a kid— you know, just one of those stupid accidents. I'm leaning out the window, I pull back and scrape my neck and end up in the emergency room with stitches. Anyway, just lately the thing has started aching like a sonofagun. The last couple of nights I could hardly sleep. Ethan thinks maybe there's a splinter or something in there trying to work its way out. Do you think that's even possible? I mean, after all this time?"

Carter's brows had come together in puzzlement as I told the story, but a smile replaced the frown as I finished up. "Tell you the truth, Asia, I'm not sure. It's not unheard of for that kind of thing to happen." He got up and moved to the back of my chair. My heart started beating a little faster. "Do you mind if I take a look?"

I shook my head. "No, of course not."

He brought an examination lamp over to put some light on my neck. I felt the warmth—and renewed panic—as he switched it on. My fingers gripped the arms of my chair, and I tried to breathe. He moved my hair aside to take a look.

"Now if you'd asked me last week, your story wouldn't have been very high on the weird scale. I had a guy in here who'd swallowed a hearing aid battery instead of his heart pill and wanted to know if it was going to kill him."

I felt his fingers probing the scar, and my eyes opened wide in fear. Ethan gazed back at me, letting me know nothing was ever going to hurt me again the way I'd been hurt when that scar was left on my neck. And because I believed him, I could stand Carter's hands on me, I could survive the last few seconds of the exam.

Carter straightened at last and turned the light off. "Well, it's a little red and raised there. It's certainly an unusual scar. I've never seen stitching like that before."

I gave him a shaky smile. "Yeah, my mom said I

made quite a mess of my neck."

He pinned me with a hawk-like stare. "You look pale. Is it that painful?"

"Well, it's nothing like having a baby, if that's what you mean." I tried to give my best impression of nonchalance. "When you touch it, it feels like a needle working its way into my brain stem." I was lying, of course. What I felt wasn't pain at all, really, just the *memory* of pain. But the memory was just as I described it.

The doctor massaged the back of his own neck in unconscious empathy. "I don't know, I guess they could have left a little splinter in there. The only way to tell is with a scan. A CAT or MRI would be best, but we can't risk it if that frame might have been steel. We'll just have to run an X-ray and hope it'll show us something. Wait here a minute, and I'll have one of the nurses set it up, okay?"

I nodded, too drained to speak. It was up to Ethan to answer, "Thanks, Dom," before Carter swept from the room.

Ethan leaned forward and took both my hands in his. He searched my face. "This is more difficult than you expected, isn't it?"

I couldn't answer him. My eyes dropped to his hands, so warm and strong and steady, a lifeline I suddenly found I desperately needed.

"I won't leave you, Asia. You're safe here with me and Dom. This is an X-ray, just a brief, noninvasive procedure that you've given the doctor your permission to perform. Now I know you understand all that intellectually, but you have to know it emotionally, too. Repeat it to yourself until it makes sense in here." He touched me very gently in the center of my chest.

I glanced up at him and managed the tiniest of smiles. "Thanks, Doc." The words came out in a frightened whisper. I took a deep breath and tried to follow his advice.

He grinned at me. "I think you'll find my fees have gone up since the last time you were in my office."

"And I think I might have paid in advance this morning." I released a nervous laugh.

The office door swung open and Carter stood in the doorway with a nurse right behind him. "The nurse will take you down the hall to X-ray. I'll see you folks in a few minutes when the films come back, okay?"

I took a deep breath and got to my feet. Fortunately the office space was tight; no one noticed Ethan as he put a hand under my elbow to steady me. I was grateful for it as we made our way down the corridor. Everything had taken on the skewed aspect of a drug-induced haze, the result of hyperventilation and too much adrenaline. My heart was battering the inside of my chest and my lips were stuck together over my dry mouth.

Ethan left me outside the X-ray room with a final squeeze of my fingertips, and it took every bit of courage I possessed to walk the few steps to the machine. Thank God I was allowed to sit for the films, or I would have passed out for sure. Once again, Dr. Carter's people did their jobs well. The big machine buzzed benignly, I was asked to change positions a few times, and I was sent back into the hallway and Ethan's arms within minutes.

Ethan leaned in close as he walked me back up the corridor. "You okay?"

I nodded, beginning to find my breath again.

We waited outside Carter's office for a while before he called us in to view the films. My nerves spiked again as we sat down across the desk from him, but my fear was quickly replaced with surprise.

"Well, there's nothing here that I can see." The doctor turned his chair to point at the films in the backlit viewer behind him. We sat forward in our chairs to peer at them. The scar, which had been circled, showed up as a slightly lighter mass, but nothing hard-edged stood out. "You would hardly know there was anything there if we hadn't marked the scar for you."

Ethan and I looked at each other. His face was unreadable.

Carter shrugged. "Sometimes you get a little phantom pain in the area of an old injury like this. No one knows why." He pulled out a prescription pad. "I can give you some lidocaine cream to put on it and some Tylenol-3 so you can sleep at night. That should calm things down. If you're still having pain by the time the prescription runs out, see your regular doctor and talk to him or her about the possibility of a cortisone shot, okay?"

"Okay." I tried not to seem like a complete idiot, though I couldn't think of a single intelligent thing to say. Was I disappointed that he hadn't found an alien probe in my neck? Relieved? Or just confused?

"Thanks, Doc."

Again, it was left to Ethan to say all the right things, which he managed as adroitly as ever. Carter walked us to the lobby, where we said our goodbyes amid promises to get together before we left New York, and we finished up the paperwork. Ethan and I made it all the way out to the car before I collapsed and started shaking like a Chihuahua in a snowstorm.

He pulled me close and held me until I could breathe. "It's okay, Asia." He smiled at me and brushed the hair out of my face. "Let's get you home."

The afternoon had turned gray and cold by the time we pulled up in front of the lake house, and a gusty wind was blowing off the water. I shivered in the kitchen, putting on water for tea while Ethan got a fire going in the fireplace and threw another couple of logs into the woodstove. Soon enough, though, the fire was snapping bravely against the draft and things were starting to warm up. Outside, the wind had blown up a rattle of raindrops against the windows. I was glad to curl up with my mug and microfleece on the bed and watch the flames dance in the fireplace.

Ethan stretched out on the bed beside me, propping himself up on one elbow and balancing his own mug of brew in front of him. He wasn't watching the fire, though. He was watching me.

I turned to look at him and smiled. "Okay. I guess I'm ready to talk about it."

"Only if you want to."

"I don't think this bed is big enough for the two of

us plus the great big elephant we brought with us back from the doctor's office."

Ethan smiled. "You have a point."

"So. No alien probe. No proof."

"Right. But that's not the only problem."

"No." My stomach was suddenly churning. "Because if the probe is no longer there, where is it? I mean, was it removed? And if so, who removed it?"

"Exactly." Ethan took a thoughtful pull on his tea. "Asia, what if your loss of memory about the time you spent in captivity wasn't the result of trauma? What if it was the result of a deliberate effort to make you forget?"

I sat up and stared at him. "What do you mean? Brainwashing?"

"Well, yes, in a word. Drugs, electroshock, psychomanipulative techniques. There are any number of means to the end. No doubt a more advanced culture would have a few I'm not aware of." His jaw tightened as his gaze fixed on the fire.

I started to shake again, though the room was thoroughly warm now. "My memories of the time I spent there . . . I was empty, blank, unable to feel anything until Dozen . . . I thought it was drugs. Are you saying they did something to my mind?"

Ethan sat up, set down his mug and grasped my trembling hands in his. "Whatever it was had no lasting effect, Asia. Your mind is whole and strong and fully intact now."

I searched his eyes. "How do I know that? Just this morning something else came back—a memory of being examined when I was first taken. That's why I jumped when you touched me. How do I know there's not more—worse—still in there?"

"There may be pockets of memory still protected by your healthy mind, Asia. That does happen." Ethan had slipped into professional mode. I should have been annoyed, but I found myself clinging to that reassurance instead. "Once you feel completely safe, you'll release them, and I'll be here to help you through it. I have a feeling you've already acknowledged the worst of it. The narrative stream is complete. The only gaps are the actual abduction and return and your recovery from the shoulder injury, perhaps because you were unconscious during those times."

I wanted to believe him, God knows I did. But the sense of violation that had begun with the knowledge that I had been taken was now complete with the knowledge that they had rearranged my mind. To make me forget. As if that was even possible.

The tears pooled in my eyes and began to roll down my face. "Why would they do that to me? Who were they that they could do that?" Even as I spoke I knew: I hadn't been the only one. I'd simply been one of an uncounted number of those taken and somehow returned.

Ethan gathered me in and wrapped his arms around me. I pressed my face to his warm chest and gave in to what was left of my grief for the life I had lost, for all the lives lost.

"They can't have been human to hurt you like they did." His hand stroked my hair. "My Asia, my sweet, beautiful Asia." His voice became a magical murmur, a soft, warm salve for my aching heart.

And I know, if I were taken again today, I would cling to that one moment so strongly they could never take it from my mind—that memory of Ethan holding me in the firelight as afternoon turned to darkest night and whispering my name so it sounded like love.

CHAPTER TWENTY

The next day dawned freshly scrubbed from the overnight rainstorm, the sun and a brisk morning breeze drying up the droplets shaking loose from the trees and the eaves. The high-ceilinged great room, with its many windows, was cold and drafty when Ethan woke up and rolled awkwardly out of bed. Squinting against the diamond-hard light, he stumbled toward the bathroom. Along the way he offered up a curse for the pain in his leg that had kept him up half the night and another for the lingering soreness along his ribs that hit him when he lurched and caught himself against the doorjamb.

After he'd finished at the toilet and the sink, he studied his haggard reflection in the mirror for a long minute. The Vicodin he'd prescribed for himself back in Marlinton sat on the bathroom counter, the bottle still fat with pills. He'd been sparing with them, doling them out only when he *really* needed them. He licked his lips. His leg throbbed. He turned and went back to the living room.

Ethan built up the fires in the fireplace and the woodstove before he slipped back under the covers with Asia. It was already past nine, but given the night he'd had, it seemed like a good morning to lie in.

Asia gathered him in against her warm body and rubbed her hands along his arms. "You've got goose bumps."

"Cold out there," he confirmed, pulling her close, loving the way she felt against him.

"You had a rough night last night. Your leg or your ribs?"

"Both."

She ran a soft hand down the side of his face. "I'm sorry, baby. Did you take a pill?"

"Should have. Too late now."

She put an elbow under her head to consider him. "Do something for me, Ethan."

He looked at her and smiled, curious. "Anything."

"Tell me about the accident."

He went cold and boneless inside. "Why the hell would you want to hear about that?"

"You know all my secrets." There was no trace of resentment in her tone. It was just a statement of fact. "Don't you think it's about time I knew a few of yours?"

He reached out, touched her cheek, tried hard to find his voice around the lump that had formed in his throat. "I wasn't trying to keep things from you."

"I know. Still."

"You're right. It's just . . ." His heart began a slow, reluctant thudding in his chest. He didn't want to do this.

"Ethan." She stroked his arm. "You've helped me

so much. Let me help you just a little. Please."

She deserved this promised honesty from him. It wasn't so much about allowing her to help him, though God knows he could use the help. It was that she'd had enough people in her life hiding things from her. He was tired of being one of them.

Ethan took a deep breath, rolled to his back, stared at the ceiling. "We'd been arguing in the car. I was working, we had a fundraising event to go to, and Elizabeth was mad because we were going to be late."

When he paused, she prompted him. "Who was driving?"

"She was." He paused again, ordering his thoughts. "It had been raining. The streets were wet." *But that wasn't important, was it? Only one thing was really important.* "She was going way too fast when we came up on the light. I watched it turn yellow, then red. She didn't try to stop, didn't even hit the brakes. She deliberately ran the light." He heard Asia gasp, but he kept his eyes focused on the ceiling overhead, seeing that red light through the rain-spattered windshield.

"When I realized we were going to run the light I looked to my right. I saw"—*Death*—"a truck bearing down on us. It hit us broadside. The car rolled twice and landed on the driver's side. Liz died at the scene. They had to cut me out of the car. It took them over two hours."

"Oh, Ethan." Her eyes fixed on him, wide with sympathy and shared pain. "You were conscious the whole time?"

He tried to breathe against the memory of

constricting, excruciating pain, the cold rain dripping from the twisted metal, mixing with the blood and the tears on his face, the smell of gasoline and fear and death.

"Yes."

Her hand was on his chest now, soothing him. "God, it must have been awful."

"I had nightmares for a while," he admitted. "Went through therapy. The whole deal."

She smiled a little. "Seems we have a lot in common."

"More than you know." He turned his head to look at her. "This isn't easy for me to talk about. Hell, I try not to even think about it. It wasn't a burden I wanted you to have to carry, too."

Asia rose up on her elbow to stare down into his eyes. "Ethan, if you give me your heart, you give me everything in it. If it's heavy, I'll carry it gladly. Haven't you already shown me you'd do the same for me?"

His hand shook as he reached up to touch her hair.

She leaned down and kissed him, long and slow and deep. When she ended it, she snuggled in close to him, laid her head in the crook of his shoulder and wrapped an arm across his chest.

"You must have been so unhappy. For so long."

"What?"

"You and Elizabeth. I can't imagine what it must have been like for you."

Ethan sighed. He really didn't want to talk about this, but he knew he had to. It was the last of the poison in the wound. If he didn't drain it, the wound would never heal properly. He'd given that same advice to his patients a hundred times. Time he followed a little of it himself.

"We never had a mature relationship, a full relationship, in the first place." He'd only recently begun to understand that. "We didn't value the same things, we didn't want the same things. And it got worse once I left the Institute. I'm not sure . . ." The words that came to mind were ugly, hurtful, but he knew the truth of them. "I don't know how much longer our marriage would have lasted anyway. But then Liz started having trouble sleeping. She had nightmares, bad ones. She started seeing a therapist from Arthur's office, but it didn't help. She tried meds. Things got worse. She wouldn't let me help."

"It must have hurt that she shut you out."

The memory of that hurt still burned in his chest. He'd tried so hard to reach her, right up until the moment when it might have made a difference.

"She said something that afternoon in the car— something about how all our talk would never stop someone who was determined to—" He hesitated, fearing this last confession. "It triggered all my alarms, but I didn't act on it. It was almost like I was daring her to do something. How screwed up was that?"

"You couldn't know she would try to commit suicide and take you with her, no matter what she said." Asia would stand for no argument. "Had she ever tried anything before?"

"No, but she was volatile, she was upset, and I just made it worse. I'm supposed to defuse those kinds of situations, not set them off."

"Ethan, you weren't her therapist in that car, you were her husband. You were tired and angry; she was selfish and impulsive. Things were said. Actions followed that had tragic consequences. It's not like she planned it ahead of time. You don't really think that, do you?"

He thought about it. Dan Parker had asked him the same question any number of times. Ethan had denied believing that Elizabeth had planned to kill herself that day, but he'd always carried a tattered scrap of nagging doubt. Today he searched for that doubt and found it missing.

Something eased around his heart. "No. If Liz had actually planned suicide, she would have chosen another method, I'm sure. She was vain enough that a car accident wouldn't have been her first choice." He'd been fighting his own battle for life in a hospital room when Elizabeth's funeral was held, but he was told the casket was kept closed. "She was just so damn angry."

"That wasn't your fault, Ethan." Asia turned his face to hers. "You know that, right?"

He rolled to his side and pulled her close to him. Her face, across from his on the pillow, was so full of love and concern that it left his prison walls in ruins. He took a deep, free breath.

"I'm beginning to. You know, you make a pretty good therapist, Dr. Burdette."

She smiled, and his heart warmed. "Thank you, Dr. Roberts. Now, let's see how good I am at massage therapy, shall we?" She gave him a quick kiss, then moved so she could lay her warm hands on his aching leg.

Ethan looked up at her, the dark curls framing her beautiful face, the graceful lines of her shoulders and arms leading down to her strong hands on his body, and his heart was instantly full. There was no hope of expressing any of it in any way that made sense. So he simply closed his eyes and gave himself up to her sweet ministrations.

It had been nearly noon before they'd left their warm bed in front of the fire. And although Asia had been quite happy with the three orgasms he'd given her in thanks for the massage she'd given him, Ethan had thought she still deserved something special. He'd proposed a trip up to Seventh Lake for lunch.

They were lingering over coffee in front of one of the restaurant's two fireplaces when Ethan pulled out his cell phone. "Are you okay here for a minute? I need to check in at the office."

"Oh, you mean there's a world out there somewhere beyond those trees? I'd forgotten." Asia smiled at him over her cup. "Sure, go ahead. I'll just be napping here in front of the fire."

He couldn't resist running his fingers through her hair, kissing her upturned lips before he rose to go. His life was completely turned upside down, and he'd never been happier.

Ethan crossed the restaurant, the cell phone a warm weight in his hand. He'd just powered it up and stepped outside when the damn thing rang, startling him so that he almost dropped it. He pushed "talk" and answered, his heart hammering.

"Jesus Christ, Ethan, where the hell have you been?"

"Dan? I've been out of cell range for a few days in . . . uh . . . in West Virginia." The lie scratched his throat. "How'd you get this number?"

"Cindy gave it to me." Dan's voice was strained, angry. "What the fuck are you doing in West Virginia?"

"I had a funeral to go to." He worked to keep his voice matter-of-fact, though a growing sense of dread was stealing his breath. "Calm down and tell me what's wrong."

"A funeral? Oh, Jesus. Not Mrs. Mickens?"

At the mention of her name Ethan found his grief was still fresh. "Yeah. The family asked me to stay on and help out for a few days."

"Oh." Dan fell quiet for a long moment. "I guess that explains some things. I'm sorry, E. I'll miss her."

"Thanks, man. Me, too. Now will you tell me what's wrong?"

"Well, I don't know. I get back from Florida and my voicemail is full of messages—people calling about you, wondering where you are. I couldn't get hold of you. I got worried."

"People?" Ethan's heart sped up. "Like who?"

"Claussen, for one. He practically accused you of running off with a patient, of all things. I assured him that wasn't remotely in the range of possibility. I was right, of course, wasn't I?"

"With a patient? You know me better than that."

"I know what you've told me about a certain *former* patient. And I don't trust Arthur Claussen any further than I can throw him, you get me?"

Dan was angling for the details, but Ethan held back. "Okay, message received. So who else is looking for me?"

"One of the girls from Arthur's office called. She sounded frantic. I guess he fired her ass for some reason and now she needs to talk to you. Please tell me you weren't boinking the hired help."

"Jesus, Dan, you really have a low opinion of me lately. You remember the conversation we had about my former patients who didn't respond to AL treatment? I asked Amanda to track down a few of them. Now you're telling me she's been fired?"

"You think there's a connection?"

From the ice that was sliding down his spine at the moment, Ethan would have said yes. "I don't know," he said instead. When all of this was over, he would tell Dan the truth. Right now he couldn't afford to lose another friend.

Dan refused to let him off. "You need to let me help you, E. All this sounds like it's adding up to trouble."

"I can't, Dan. Not right now."

His friend sighed. "I thought that's what you would say. By the way, Claussen and the girl weren't the only ones calling. Just yesterday afternoon I had a visit from two guys that looked like they wanted to make me an offer I couldn't refuse."

Ethan's lungs constricted around his breath. "What did they want?"

"They were looking for one of your patients—Asia Burdette." Dan said it like they'd been discussing the weather. "Had some wild story about how she'd last been seen with you. In West Virginia."

"And you believed that shit?"

Dan dropped all pretense of calm. "I believe they'll put a hurtin' on you and her both when they find you, Ethan. Whatever it is you've got yourself into, these guys mean business."

"Yeah. What did you tell them?"

"I told them to go fuck themselves, what else?"

Ethan smiled, in spite of himself. "Thanks, Dan. For everything."

There was a pause on the other end of the line. "Ethan, are you sure about this?"

"I've never been surer about anything in my life." He felt the certainty of it settle into his heart.

"Ah, fuck. Got it that bad, huh?" Dan released a tiny sigh. "And the girl?"

"Says it's the real deal."

"Damn. Well, there's no accounting for tastes." Dan's voice lifted with humor now—and affection. "Any other time I'd say I'm happy for you, man. Instead I think I should just say be careful. You're not going to tell me what's going on, are you."

"No. I wish I could."

"Damn it." There was a pause. "Finish this, Ethan, whatever it is, and get your ass home." Then the connection went silent.

Ethan pulled up his contacts for Amanda's home number. He waited while the phone rang, watching the cars roll by on the highway, wondering if even now the same highway was bringing a faceless enemy closer.

At last a high-pitched feminine voice answered with a tentative "Hello?"

"Amanda?"

"Dr. Roberts! Thank God, it's you! I've been trying to reach you at all your numbers, but all I've gotten is voicemail."

"I know, I'm sorry. I've been out of cell range for a week or so. What's going on?"

"I got fired from the Institute." Her voice sounded reedy and thin. "Last week. Dr. Claussen didn't give me any notice or anything, just said to pack up my stuff and leave. He was so mean about it."

"I'm sorry, Amanda." Ethan genuinely regretted his part in it. "Did he say why?"

"Well, I had been late a few times. And my supervisor really didn't like me, but I didn't think I was doing *that* badly. And then he comes out of his office and tells me himself that I'm fired. Just like that. It was like the office supe didn't even know about it. Then he says he's gonna be out of the office all this week and *poof*, he's gone."

His chest tight, Ethan probed deeper. "I hope our little project didn't have anything to do with it."

"Oh, I don't think so. I don't think anyone knew about that. I was pretty careful. I figured you wouldn't want anyone to know about your research."

"Yes, well, thanks for that." He wasn't convinced she'd been as discreet as she thought. "Did you find any of those people I asked you about?"

"No, you know it's the strangest thing." Her voice

dropped. "It was like they had all disappeared off the face of the earth. One was actually dead. I found a death certificate—a car accident, I think. The others, I couldn't find anything—no work history, no medical records, no debt records, no SSN's, nothing. They'd been, like, erased, or something. Weird, huh?"

"Yeah, weird. Who was the one with the death certificate?"

"Uh . . . I think, yeah, it was the Air Force guy. Lieutenant Colonel Bradley Conners, 46 years old."

Conners. Damn it. Handsome, strong, haunted green eyes, two little kids. "That's too bad. When did he die?"

"Uh, let's see. January of this year. Car went off a bridge into the Potomac near D.C."

Ethan felt the added weight as Conners' body was added to the pile of guilt he carried. Ethan prayed he'd been alone in the car when he died.

"Thanks, Amanda. I appreciate all your hard work. How about I send you a check for your time?"

"Oh, no, Doc, you don't need to do that. Now, if you had a line on a job, that's something I could use."

"Tell you what. Talk to Jessica Peterson at ACP Counseling on West End. They were looking for office staff a couple of weeks ago. Tell her I said for you to call, okay?"

"Sure, yeah, thanks, Doc! I appreciate it."

"If I get the chance, I'll give her a call when I get back."

"That's really great. Thanks."

"'Bye, Amanda."

He snapped the phone closed and stood for a

moment, one arm braced against the post supporting the porch roof. The sun threw a hard-edged light across the deep green and vibrant colors of the tall trees lining the road, but it gave off little warmth. The brisk wind was sharp with the edge of coming winter. Ethan scanned the trees, the impossibly blue sky, the dark ribbon of road. He thought through the information he had been given, considering his options. Then, chilled to the heart, he turned and went back to Asia.

In this world there was no light, no shadow, no color, no shape. There was only the sound—constant, unchanging, bone-deep—filling her ears, her lungs, her body with a never-ending hum. Around her she was dimly aware of movement, of air brushing past her face, as if someone had walked nearby. She tried to respond, struggling to lift her eyelids, or a finger. They were as heavy and inert as mud.

She slept.

And woke again. The sound was still there, making her bones vibrate. Other noises swirled in the air around her—snatches of conversation in a language she could not understand, the clink of glass and metal, the crackle of plastic, the whisper of fabric. Someone touched her, moved her. Still she could not force her eyes to open, could not force her lips to move or her throat to utter a sound. She was suspended, caught like a fly in amber. Abstractly, she thought she should feel panic, rage, *something.*

All she felt was a mild, disconnected curiosity. And tired. So very tired.

She drifted back into sleep.

A hand touched her face, brushed the hair from her forehead. Rough fingers, warm. A voice. A man. Very close.

"Hey. You've had a tough time, sweetheart, but you're almost home. We'll have you back to your family soon, and you won't even know you've been gone."

"Three minutes to jump, Cap."

"Thanks, crewman. I'll be right there."

"You know she can't hear you, Sam. And I've never seen you take this kind of interest in the cargo before. What's the story?"

"First of all, they aren't cargo. You of all people should know that, Doc. Besides, this one is special. Rayna gave up a lot to get this one out. I'm gonna make sure she gets back home if I have to set her down in her living room myself."

Another touch. "Just a few minutes more, Sphinx. I'll get you there, I promise."

"Captain Murphy?"

"Coming. Time?"

"Jay minus sixty."

The voices grew fainter, then disappeared altogether. There was nothing but the hum for an unknown time. She drifted again, until she was suddenly aware of movement, lots of it, jostling and shaking and turning her body against the pull of gravity until she wasn't certain just where that pull was coming from. She floated, weightless. Then she slammed heavily against the restraints that held her. There was no pain—*there should be pain,* she thought disjointedly—just that odd sensation of being jerked around by an unseen force.

She heard the shriek of alarms. A call, brassy and loud, booming from every direction: "Battle stations! This is not a drill! All hands to battle stations!"

Then voices, shouting, shrill. "What the hell is going on?"

"Gray destroyer was waiting for us when we came out of the jump." More jostling, throwing her abruptly against the restraints. "Shit! We're taking a beating."

"Get this sickbay ready for casualties, *stat*! What are you standing around for—you act like this is your first time in a fight, Korda!"

Closer, almost in her ear. "Sorry, hon. You'll have to wait a little longer to get home."

"Shit, if we don't beat these assholes off in record time, she's liable to get home with a lot of explaining to do. We're already running late."

"Damn it. Time's almost up on her meds, too."

"What are you doing?"

"Giving her a little more joy juice. Can't take a chance on her waking up in the middle of all of this. Sleep well, sweetie. See you on the other side. If any of us make it."

I sat up with a jerk, my heart crashing against my ribs, my breath rasping in and out of my throat. It was a moment before I realized my eyes were open and I could, in fact, see. The big, open room. The fire, dying down to ruddy embers. Ethan, awake now and up on one elbow, staring at me in concern.

"What's wrong?" His voice was still thick with sleep.

"A ship. I . . . I think I was on a ship. And I was coming home."

"What kind of ship?"

I shook my head. "I couldn't see anything. I could only hear them talking. And I could hear . . . the engines, I guess." I looked down at him. "Now you *will* think I'm nuts. The dialogue was like something out of *Battlestar Galactica*."

Ethan reached out to take my hand. "Tell me what you remember."

When I had finished, my gaze met his. "That's the last piece, isn't it? It even explains the three hours."

He nodded. "They were trying to bring you back to the same moment you were taken, but got caught in some kind of battle." He smiled. "You're right, though. It does sound a little far-fetched. Travel across space and time. Beings from advanced civilizations fighting it out on our doorstep."

"Beings," I repeated. "Advanced civilizations. You know, it's funny, but these people sounded just like you and me. Dozen was human, just like we are. They aren't the ones that took me. I still don't really remember the ones that took me."

Ethan reached up and drew me down into his arms. "Advanced or not, the universe still seems to be broken down into good guys and bad guys. Thank God the good guys found you. And brought you back home to me."

Three hours too late. I started to shake in Ethan's arms. Those hours had cost me so much.

"What is it?" He refused to relinquish his hold on me.

"I wanted someone else to blame." The misery that had remained buried deep in my heart was suddenly rising through my chest to choke me. "Now I don't even have that."

Ethan pulled back and tipped my face up to his. "So, now what? You want to blame yourself for what happened to your children? After everything you've learned?"

"I wasn't there, Ethan. I should have been there."

"Asia, you had no control over what happened to you or your children." His eyes were bright with righteous anger. "You were abducted, and despite the best efforts of your rescuers, you weren't returned in time to save the ones you loved. I hate to say this, but it is possible you might not have saved them even if you'd been in the house."

He paused to let his meaning sink in. When he continued, his voice was softer, his expression warm with compassion.

"We can't control everything that happens to us, Asia. Even blaming the ones that took you would be a useless exercise."

That much I could understand. The ones who had

taken me remained faceless, untouchable.

"Maybe you're right." I sank back into his arms, tired of a search for answers that only seemed to bring me pain. Maybe it was easier to try to believe it was all meant to happen the way it did, as horribly, wretchedly painful as that was.

Yeah, and maybe it was better not to think about what might or might not be part of the Big Plan, for fear of tempting Fate to make some modifications.

CHAPTER TWENTY-ONE

The next morning I cooked up the last of our eggs and bread for breakfast and took stock of what was left in the pantry for the rest of the day.

"We're good on peanut butter, babe, but we'll have to eat it out of the jar," I reported. "There is a can of tuna fish, though, and a box of noodles. Oh, and a bottle of wine. So dinner's a go."

Ethan smiled. "Are you telling me we need to make a grocery run?"

"That depends." I turned serious. "Just how long were we planning to stay?"

He avoided my gaze and got up to get himself another cup of coffee. "Long enough to be sure you're safe."

"Ethan, you have patients who need you back home. My job may be history, but yours doesn't have to be."

"It's only been a few days." He took up a post leaning against a counter, rather than coming to sit down at the table with me again. "Cindy will handle things until I get back. I could even give Arthur another call if that'll make you feel better." The look on his face made it obvious that was about the last thing in the world he wanted to do.

"Didn't Amanda say Arthur's planning to be out of the office himself for a few days?"

When Ethan still wouldn't look at me, I got up and stood in front of him, knee to knee, hip to hip. I put my hands on his waist and smiled up at him, enjoying the feel of him molded to my body in all the right places, warm and so enticingly male.

"Hey. I'm in no hurry to lose this." I pressed closer to let him know what I meant. "But you know as well as I do we can't stay here forever. We're out of cash; I'll have to use the credit card today. If those guys are still looking for us, they'll find us eventually. Might as well fight them on our home turf, what d'you say? Maybe call the FBI or somebody."

"And what if these guys *are* the FBI? Or they just think we're crazy?"

"We've already determined they're not." I grinned up at him. "The second part is your department."

He shook his head. "I wouldn't be the first psychiatrist to exhibit symptoms."

"Okay," I said with a sigh. "But we've got to do *something*. They've already looked for us in Nashville. Maybe there's some advantage to hiding in plain sight while we get some help on this."

He slid his hands around my back and pulled me closer. "How did you get so damn smart?" He bent his head to kiss me, his tongue slipping past my parted lips to carry a taste of coffee and his own special sweetness into my mouth. He stopped after a while to wrap me in his arms and hold me for a long, silent moment. Then he pulled back to look at me.

"It should take them at least two or three days to find us once we use the credit card. Another couple of days in paradise. Is that too much to ask?"

"Sounds like heaven to me, baby."

For the first time since our arrival at the camp, we decided to divide up the work that morning. I went into town to do the shopping while he stayed behind to take advantage of the clear weather to tackle the fallen trees that were crowding the driveway. I kissed him goodbye and left him swearing at a cranky old chainsaw while I hit town to run the errands we had neglected for the week we'd been at the lake—food, gas, cash.

It took me longer than I expected. By the time I made it back, the afternoon shadows were beginning to edge out over the road as I turned down the drive toward the house. The downed trees were gone, and, as I pulled into the yard, I saw Ethan dumping a wheelbarrow-load of freshly cut logs next to a woodpile in the back of the clearing.

Before I began to unload the groceries, I went to admire my sweaty workman. "Damn, boy. You sure do know how to work a chainsaw."

He turned from the respectable pile of wood to grin at me, and I must admit my heart tripped. This was a whole new look for the man I'd come to know. His oldest, most comfortable jeans hugged his hips and long legs, showing fades and creases and wear in all the right places. An ancient thermal shirt stretched across his broad shoulders and chest, just barely tucking into a heavy work belt slung below his waist, making me want to pull it out to reach the skin underneath. Very woodsy and, uh, primal.

He arched an eyebrow at me. "What? You thought I was the kind of guy who never got his hands dirty?"

"If I'd known you were so good at manual labor I would have thought up some stuff for you to do long before now." I laughed, unable to resist teasing him. "You want some lunch?"

"In a little while maybe. I'm going to take care of a couple of old snags threatening the boathouse while the weather holds." He squinted up at the sky, which had begun to show a few streaming clouds. "Should be done in less than an hour."

Good thing, too, because *he* just might be on the menu when I got ready for lunch. "Okay. I'm going to put the groceries away. See you later, Paul Bunyan."

I got the groceries into the kitchen and went to work putting them away. I'm not sure when I became aware that a car was coming down the driveway. My mind was on other things—lunch; what might come after; even, in the back of my consciousness, the need to plan for the trip back to Nashville. I wasn't expecting a visitor. So when I looked up from stashing the plastic bags under the sink, it was as if the car, a nondescript gray rental sedan, had just appeared in the yard.

I pulled in a breath so sharp it was nearly a scream.

I backed up to the kitchen counter, my eyes on the car, my hands feeling behind me for the knife I knew was in the dish rack. My hand closed on the handle, and I made myself breathe.

There was no back door in the house. To get to Ethan, I'd have to go out a window from a back bedroom. He couldn't have seen the car from the boathouse, and I was sure he couldn't have heard it; the chainsaw was going again.

I started to turn for the back hallway when I saw the car door open. Only one man emerged, and my jaw dropped when I saw who it was. Dr. Arthur Claussen heaved his bulk out of the driver's seat and stood for a moment gazing at the house.

What the hell?

Despite the fact that it must have been obvious Ethan was the one running the noisy chainsaw in back, Claussen walked deliberately up the path and clumped up the stairs to the porch. Frozen in place in the kitchen, I watched him do it. And even though I knew it was the inevitable consequence of his actions, I flinched when I heard the knock on the door that meant he wanted to come in.

It was only when I heard him speak my name that I moved to answer the door.

"Asia? It's Arthur Claussen. I'd like to speak with you. Please."

With me? He wants to speak with me?

Feeling like I was swimming to the door through a sea of cold molasses, I forced myself to put the knife down and leave the sanctuary of the kitchen. My body wasn't responding to the commands of my brain in the usual way, or maybe it was that my brain wasn't giving any commands at all. All I could think was that this was the end of everything. I couldn't fight Claussen with the knife like I could have fought the Men in Black. He was a threat on an entirely different scale.

My hand reached out and turned the knob, and the door swung open. The old man stood on the other side of the screen door, an unlikely smile on his face. The chainsaw still buzzed in the background, making it necessary for Claussen to raise his voice.

"Asia. I'm so glad to see you. You look well. May I come in?"

By some miracle I found a reply. "Dr. Claussen. Ethan's around back, if you'd like to see him."

"Actually, I'd like to speak to you in private, Asia, if you don't mind. Before I see Ethan."

My heart turned to stone and dropped like a dead weight into the black pit of my stomach, leaving nothing but a bleeding hole in my chest. I knew with blinding certainty what he would say to me, what he would demand of me. Worse, I knew what my answer had to be. I stood aside to let him in.

Claussen's critical gaze swept the room before returning to my face. "You realize what you and Ethan are doing is quite inappropriate."

"What we're doing?" Though I knew what he was talking about, I couldn't seem to keep from baiting him.

"Don't play coy with me, Asia." He waved at the bed. The kitchen. All of it. "You are Ethan's patient. Even if you are not familiar with the rules, he is. I could have him before a review board based on no more than what I see right now, and he would never practice psychiatry again. Is that what you want for him?"

What I wanted was going to mean nothing to Claussen, that much was certain. How I played this was going to mean everything.

When I didn't reply, he went on. "I can tell you it would be a great loss to his other patients, who depend on him. It would be a huge disappointment for me personally, since I consider him a protégé, someone I had hoped would someday take over my practice and further my research." He paused, watching me. "Do you have nothing at all to say?"

I glared at him, defiance warring with crippling pain in what was left of my heart. "I suppose the fact that we love each other would have no bearing on the matter?"

Claussen smirked. "Love is a very subjective term, open to interpretation in any number of ways. Lust, however, is quantifiable and has a measurable impact on judgment. Given your physical attributes, Asia, and Ethan's long, self-imposed isolation from the fairer sex, I'm not surprised he lost his head. The only question now is how much do you intend to have him suffer for it?"

"Me?" Anger won out. "You're the one imposing the sanctions."

"Yes, and make no mistake, Asia, those sanctions will be severe. Ethan *will* lose his license. Permanently. I'll make certain of it. You know as well as I do what it would mean to him to be unable to use his God-given gift to help people. After a while I suspect he'd even begin to resent you for taking that from him."

The room was abruptly quiet, the only sound the monstrous booming of my stone heart from the pit of my belly. The chainsaw had quit. I prayed Ethan would burst into the room and save me; I prayed he would stay outside and save himself.

When I said nothing more, Claussen pressed his point. "Once the process gets rolling, Ethan will quickly be crushed under the wheels of a very heavy bureaucracy. Still, I may yet be in a position to divert all of this, depending on what you decide to do."

I stared at the man who was taking my life apart with no more compassion than a plumber for a stopped-up sink. "You fucking bastard. You're supposed to be his friend. You would do this to him?"

"I am his friend. And I'm doing it *for* him. If you truly love him you'll do what is necessary also."

Damn it to hell. Something in my hardscrabble Tennessee soul had always known it would come to this. Ethan and I came from vastly different worlds. And though we shared a love forged out of a similar kind of pain, who knew how long that love would survive once I'd cost him everything that meant anything to him? We'd been fooling ourselves to think we could live this dream in the real world.

Fists clenched, I looked up at Claussen. "What would you want me to do?"

Claussen smiled. "You always were a smart girl, Asia. Smart. And a survivor, from the beginning. We'll leave this afternoon. I'll take you to the airport in Syracuse, buy you a ticket to anywhere you like and give you enough money to make a new start. The only thing I ask of you is that you never contact Ethan again. Your relationship with him ends today."

A hot knife went through the place in my chest where my heart used to be. Tears stung my eyes. I blinked them back and tried to be practical, though everything in me was screaming "Run!"

"Why would you do that? You're holding all the cards. Why sweeten the pot?"

"Because, my dear, I know Ethan Roberts." The old man shook his head. "He won't give you up without a fight. You and I both know this is for the best, but if he thinks he has a chance of holding on to you he'll risk his career to do it. I'm not a monster, Asia. I care for Ethan. And I know you have few resources of your own. I don't expect you to start over without help."

I wanted to come up with some argument to change what had to be, but there was no need to think it through. What he was saying made perfect sense. I wanted to pretend there was some hope, but there was no need to hold back my tears. What I was feeling was perfect desolation. I should have known this hurricane was coming. The only reason I hadn't seen the clouds gathering overhead was because I'd forgotten to look up. And now all I could do was hang on as the wind howled and the water rolled.

"We're going to hell, Claussen. Both of us. My only consolation is that I'll get to watch you burn." Then, red-faced and choking on my pain, I turned my back on him and ran down the hall.

My hands shook as I took my toilet articles from the shelves in the bathroom and stuffed them in my bag. I kept my eyes carefully averted from Ethan's things, my gaze sliding off his razor and his toothbrush and the tee-shirt hanging behind the door. Numb, I went back out to the great room and rummaged through the corners for my clothes, folding them as quickly as I could with shock-clumsy fingers.

I was almost done when I heard the screen door bang and turned to see Ethan standing in the entryway. He barely glanced at Claussen. He just pinned me with those eyes the color of the Arctic Sea.

"What are you doing?"

Claussen stood and faced him. "She's doing the sensible thing, Ethan, what she should have done several weeks ago. She's leaving. With me. Now."

I couldn't look away from Ethan's face, the evidence of devastation written there, the loss and hurt so clear in his eyes, the betrayal etched like a flaming scar along his clenched jaw. He never took his eyes off me as he spoke to Claussen.

"I can't imagine why she would do that, Arthur. She's not your patient. Actually, she's no longer my patient, either. This is hardly a situation that requires a therapeutic intervention. And I don't think you could convince me that she called you for help."

God, no! He didn't think I . . .! Jesus, I was so fucking miserable.

Claussen wheezed out a laugh. "I'm not here to help the young lady, much as she would seem to need it. On the other hand, you, Ethan, are a stubborn, willful and often blindly idealistic man. I'm here to help you. To save you from yourself, really."

"Then you could have saved yourself the trip." Ethan stood as if he were carved out of stone. "Which brings me to my next question. How did you know we were here?"

"Oh, that was almost too easy." The old man lifted a shoulder. "I had some questions after we talked the other night. When I couldn't reach you on your cell phone, I called the Mickens family. Friendly folks. Of course they told me you hadn't even stayed for the old lady's funeral. And that Asia was with you. Then it was just a matter of guessing where you might choose to hide out for a few days. Where else but the family vacation cabin you'd told me so much about? Although . . ." Claussen chuckled, and it made me shudder. The fucker was enjoying this. "This must have been quite a trip for that old jalopy of yours, Ethan. I'm amazed you made it all the way up here without a major breakdown."

"It was quite a trip for you, too, Arthur. An unnecessary one. You could have said whatever you needed to say to me at my office in Nashville in a few days."

"I'm not certain you would have been listening." Claussen waved his hand. "You seem to be doing all of your thinking with the wrong part of your anatomy these days."

Ethan lunged forward, taking more than one step before he stopped himself, his muscles quivering in an effort to keep his anger in check. Then he smiled, a feral baring of the teeth that was more warning than retreat.

"You know, you're right, in a way. I've been

listening a lot more to my *heart* lately. At last, after all these years, I've discovered the ability to feel something more than just pain. I love Asia. She loves me. You won't talk me out of that."

Claussen snorted. "Ethan, please. Do I have to point out how fortunate it is that I was the one that found you here shacked up with your patient in your little hideaway, and not a member of the Professional Ethics Committee?"

"You *are* a member of the Professional Ethics Committee."

"Actually, I'm the Chair of the Committee, but I am also your friend and mentor, *Dr.* Roberts. And I'm offering you—and Asia—a way out of this mess."

"Fuck you. This isn't a mess, and I don't need a way out of it."

Oh, God. He was going to talk his way right out of this deal if I didn't do something. I took a step in his direction.

"Ethan, don't."

"You're very much mistaken if you think I'm bluffing," Claussen warned. "I have what it takes to ruin you. Your girl knows enough to do the right thing. Why don't you listen to her?"

Ethan's voice got menacingly quiet. "What the hell are you talking about?"

I put myself between the two men. If they kept arguing, either Ethan would end up strangling the old man, or I would lose my nerve. "Go on out to the car, Doctor." I struggled to sound like I meant it. "I'll be there in a minute."

"I'm not through with him." Ethan started

forward.

I put a hand on his chest and held his angry gaze. "Yes, you are. I'll explain the rest."

I sensed rather than saw the frown on Claussen's face as he turned to leave the room. He paused to lay a hand on Ethan's shoulder. "It really is for the best, my friend."

Ethan pivoted and flung off the offending touch like so much garbage. Then he curled up a fist and went after the old man, and if I hadn't been close enough to grab him, he might have ended any chance at all of saving his future. As it was, Claussen stood backed up against the counter for an endless moment, looking as if his obedient Labrador retriever had suddenly ripped off his arm. Ethan returned his stare with an icy blue hatred until the man who had once been his friend found his feet and scrambled out the door to his car.

I was trembling all over now, and my legs turned to water as Ethan turned back to look at me. I dropped to the edge of the bed, my arms wrapped around my body in a futile attempt to hold myself together. He came no closer, but stood watching me from a few steps away, hurt and accusation burning so intensely in his eyes that I wanted to shrivel up in the heat of it.

"Asia, what's going on?"

"Baby, we knew this day was coming." From the first day I walked into his office and couldn't stop my heart from leaping against my ribs. From the minute our lips touched and our bodies melted in that hotel room in Bristol. I had no regrets. But we had both known there'd be a price. It was time to pay up.

Ethan shook his head in dismissal. "You think his threats mean anything? I'll have friends on any review board he puts together. You're no longer a patient. I'll probably get off with a warning and a fine. We've got bigger problems to worry about."

"No." My fear and my anger put an edge on the word that was only sharpened by the frustration that he wouldn't take the danger seriously. "You shouldn't fight this. He's determined to bring you down if you oppose him. That's what he says, and I believe him."

Ethan knelt in front of me and took my hands in his. "Asia, did you think I would let you go without a fight?" His eyes searched my face for the answer. "You are the best thing that has ever happened to me. I won't live my life without you. I'll take whatever the review board has to dish out, even if it means I never practice again."

Shit. I can't do this. I'm not strong enough. God, please help me.

"No. You have to listen. Your work is too important to just throw it away. And you know if you go up against that review board, even if you win, your career is shot. How many of your clients come from Claussen? He's offering you a way out that won't leave any marks on your reputation."

Ethan blew out a breath in exasperation. "What the hell are you talking about? Damn it, Asia, what did that bastard say to you that he wouldn't say in front of me?"

"He said that he would put me on a plane this afternoon and pay for me to disappear. Set me up in a new place." Despite the tears that stung my eyes, I tried for a lighter tone. "I'm thinking maybe Santa Fe."

Shock constricted his voice and left him grasping for words. "Asia, you can't."

I pushed on. "In return, he won't haul your ass in front of a review board."

"You know we can't trust him."

"I *don't* trust him."

"Then for God's sake, Asia! Why would you do this?"

I didn't want to answer him, because I knew this was the clincher, the final blow in a fight I didn't want to win, but needed to. In the depths of hell, the Devil was laughing.

"Because someone out there is looking for me, Ethan. One day soon they're going to find me. They're going to use me like a monkey in a lab, and there's not a fucking thing we can do about it. Unless I disappear. For good."

Ethan shook his head. "Asia, you know I would die before I let them take you."

I put a finger to his lips. "Yes, but I can't let you do that. I *won't* let you." I stroked his cheek with a shaking hand and tried hard not to cry at the desolate capitulation I saw in his eyes. "Claussen may not have the right reasons, baby, but he just may have the right idea. A new place. A new identity. What better way to shake those guys? If I have to go, at least I'll know that you're okay."

"Don't do this. We'll find another way."

He gathered me up and held me, his embrace

fierce and desperate and full of everything that could never be again for us. God, I wanted to stay there, wrapped in the love we had for each other. It took all the courage I had in the broken chip of rock that was my heart to pull out of his arms, to look at his face for the last time, to say the words that I knew would break his heart.

"I have to go."

"Promise me you'll let me know where you are."

I stood up, gripped my bag and headed for the door.

He grabbed my arm. "Promise me, Asia."

I wouldn't lie to him, so I waited until he let go. "I'll never stop loving you, Ethan. No matter where I am."

Then I walked out, and I shut the door behind me.

CHAPTER TWENTY-TWO

Ethan watched Asia cross the yard to Claussen's car, no more able to stop her than if she were fully alive in a newly created world and he nothing but a ghost caught in the disintegration of the old one. Everything he'd begun to live for was passing with her into that new reality. His life, his dreams, were dying along with all that had once been. The din of destruction roared in his ears.

He stumbled out onto the porch and threw out a hand to support himself on the railing. Claussen slammed the sedan in gear and scratched out of the yard, spitting gravel into the sparse grass as the wheels spun. Ethan saw Asia's tear-streaked face at the side window, and her gaze, full of love and regret, caught his. As the car snaked up the drive and out of sight, his broken heart twisted in his chest.

"No," he whispered. Then louder, "No, damn it!" How could it end like this? After all they had been through together. After all the pain they had suffered before they had found each other. Anger rose in him that was beyond words, beyond thought, almost beyond control. He knew it wasn't like him. He knew it was dangerous and nonproductive and unhelpful and all those other things psychiatry was established to take care of. But he was like a bear in a pit-trap, maddened and in pain, with no way out. He only wanted to lash out at whatever came near, to use his body to smash things and his strength to wreak havoc.

The big, log-splitting ax was resting against the woodpile at the other end of the yard. A jumble of oak logs waited to dry before they could be split easily into fireplace-size pieces. They were still a little green, but Ethan was hardly in the mood to be reasonable. He jumped off the porch, strode across the yard, grabbed the ax and the nearest round and went at it like the madman he was.

He didn't think about the pain still lingering in his side from his cracked ribs. He didn't think about Claussen. He didn't think about aliens or Men in Black. He didn't even think—much—about Asia. He just swung the ax. Over and over. Angrily. Hating the wood. Murdering it. Making it suffer like he was suffering. Splitting the wood to its heart like he had been split to his heart.

Until he swung the ax, and it hit with a *thunk* and stuck deep in the unyielding center of a green oak round a foot across. Cursing, Ethan pulled and rocked and tried to wedge the ax out of the wood with no luck. The blade was buried deep and was not coming out without major intervention, meaning most likely the chainsaw.

Defeated, the sweat rolling off him in the thin late-autumn sun as if it were midsummer, Ethan kicked a piece of wood toward the woodpile and turned back toward the house. The thought of going inside the empty place to face the reality of Asia gone tightened his chest with despair. God, how was he going to get through this? She had only been gone half an hour. How would he survive the afternoon? Tonight? The rest of his life?

He blundered into the kitchen and opened the cabinet next to the sink. He pulled out a bottle of bourbon and took a long swig without bothering to get a glass. The liquid seared his throat and burned a fiery pathway to his unquiet stomach. Tears started in his eyes that thankfully had nothing to do with Asia. He took another drink and carried the bottle with him to the bathroom. He flipped on the shower and began to strip out of his clothes. He saluted himself in the mirror.

"Maybe you and me will just get drunk tonight, old buddy," he told himself. "Won't be the first fucking time."

But then he lifted the top of the clothes hamper and saw just a single item in the bottom—a tee-shirt. Asia's tee-shirt, a little blue one with long sleeves and a scoop neck that had always made him want to kiss her at the place where her pulse throbbed in her throat. He pulled it out of the hamper and held it to his face, inhaling her smell off the soft fabric, a smell like desert wind and honey, and the tears did threaten then. He couldn't help it. He wanted to sob like a child because that smell brought back what he could never have again and *damn it* he wanted her so bad that he was aching and hard and *shit!*

It was all he could do not to sink to the floor and give in to the misery, recognizing with the tiny part of his brain that was still functional that this was a necessary part of the grieving process. A last scrap of pride kept him on his feet, pacing and miserable and unaware of the passage of time. He had no idea how long it had been before he stumbled into the lukewarm shower, but at least he was able to breathe by the time he got out again. And he was clean.

He pulled on fresh clothes, upended the bottle of bourbon once more—he wasn't feeling any effects yet, that was a bad sign, he knew from past experience—and padded through the hallway into the great room. *Fuck!* It was freezing cold in there. He'd neglected to start a fire, and the afternoon had long since begun to slide into evening.

Adding another long stream of curses to his opening salvo, Ethan piled wood into the woodstove and got the blaze going. He had enjoyed the task when Asia had been there. He'd loved hearing her puttering around in the kitchen while he worked, loved knowing she'd be curling up in front of the fire as soon as it started to roar, loved just having her someplace nearby. Now he resented every second of the work. He cursed the darkness, cursed the cold, cursed the emptiness in the house and in his heart. The tears stung his eyes again, and he cursed himself. He slammed the door shut on the woodstove and didn't bother with the fireplace. *Come on, man, get a grip.* He straightened from the fireplace and reached for the bourbon once again. He started to pace and found himself in the kitchen, staring out the window at the failing light. Mist was gathering over the lake, softening the edges where the trees stood like sentinels against the purple twilight sky. In the yard by the house he spotted the ax stuck in the green oak round still where he'd hurled it in frustrated rage, the split wood scattered like dead bodies around the woodpile.

And his faithful old BMW with the sun-bleached yellow paint and numerous rust spots, with the leather interior that was worn like a pair of faded jeans and fit his body like a broken-in baseball glove, with an engine that sounded like a tank and drank oil like a Russian drank vodka. He lifted the bottle of bourbon in the direction of his car.

"To you, my friend." He took a hefty swig of bourbon. "Fuck Claussen if he can't appreciate you!"

He took another drink, realizing with something between giddiness and relief that he was starting to feel some effect from the liquor. "Fuck Claussen anyway! Fucking asshole!" The man had been his friend, his mentor, a part of his family. And he had just snatched Ethan's heart out of his chest without a single regret. For what? To protect him? "Well, fuck you, old man, I don't want your protection!"

Satisfaction crossed his face in the wake of his declaration, and he started to take another drink, just to see if he could recreate the brief feeling of defiant devil-may-care he'd just experienced, when the bottle paused halfway to his mouth. *The car.* What was it Claussen had said about the car? The buzz in his head was a hindrance now as he struggled to get the words back. *I'm amazed you made it up here without a breakdown.* An offhand comment? God knows the old man had given him enough shit about that car over the years.

But his smile. He was taunting him. *Like he knew.* There was only one way he could have known about the breakdown and repair of the water pump in Marlinton. *If he'd been tracing the credit card.*

"Man, you are really drunk." The words fell like stones in the silence of the kitchen. But suddenly there was a noise in his head that was not the buzz of drunkenness. It was the scrape and *thunk* of chess pieces moving across a board dark with the color of blood and fire and metal. Pieces that connected Asia Burdette and Arthur Claussen and the Men in Black. Pieces that included a naïve young psych resident at Johns Hopkins as a pawn in a game that involved alien abduction and lost time and the death of innocents.

And when the pieces stopped moving, Ethan saw it all clearly: Claussen's sudden appearance on their doorstep had had nothing to do with any doctor-patient ethical bullshit. It had everything to do with Asia's case. *Claussen* had been the only one with access to his patient files. *Claussen* stood to gain from the research if his former patients had been dragged off to some laboratory. *Claussen* was the connection. *Claussen* was to blame for Ida Mickens's death and Brad Conners's and—

"Oh, my God. Asia!" He dropped the bottle of bourbon in the sink, ignoring the clatter and the gurgle as the rest of the liquor went down the drain. He dove for the phone and prayed Asia's cell phone was charged after so much time of disuse in the dead zone of Adirondack Park. His call went directly to voice mail. "Damn it!"

There was a stack of phone directories, all of them long outdated, in one of the kitchen drawers. He clawed at the books, praying for one with a Syracuse cover. *There!* He ripped through the pages until he found what he was looking for, then punched in the number for Syracuse Hancock International Airport. He prowled the kitchen floor, alternately cursing and punching more numbers, his heart hammering, as the automated system sent him through an endless list of options before he reached a human who could answer his question.

"Flights to Santa Fe? No, sir. There would be no direct departures for Santa Fe. The closest flights would be Albuquerque via Chicago or Cincinnati. What airline, sir?"

What? He couldn't think. "Any airline. All airlines!"

"There's no need to shout, sir. I can hear you just fine."

"Sorry. It's kind of an emergency. Uh, a death in the family."

"Oh, I am sorry for your loss, sir. I'll see what I can find out for you."

The line clicked and began playing an elevator version of "Leaving on a Jet Plane." Ethan regretted having dropped the bourbon in the sink. Instead, he used the time to start a pot of coffee. He was going to need the caffeine to counteract some of that whiskey in his system because he intended to burn up the highway with Baby once he got the flight information. If he wasn't already too late. *God, please don't let me be too late.*

"Sir, are you there?"

"Yes, yes, I'm here."

"I have a 6:15 p.m. departure for Cincinnati on US Airways. That's boarding now, sir. Then I have nothing until 9:30 p.m. this evening on Delta Airlines. That has a one-hour layover in Chicago, with a connecting flight to Albuquerque. Would you like me to connect you with a Delta ticketing agent?"

Six-fifteen. Too early even for Claussen to have made the two-and-a-half hour trip to Syracuse. *Thank you, God!*

"No, thank you. I'll do it online. Thanks for your help."

"You're welcome, sir."

Every second counted now and Ethan was acutely aware of his alcohol-retarded reflexes and spinning head. He tried hard to focus—keys, wallet, cell phone, charger (*where the hell was the fucking phone charger?*). He poured himself a go-cup of coffee and congratulated himself on remembering to switch off the machine. Then he shoved his feet into boots, his arms into his jacket and ran for his car.

He stopped dead with his hand on the door handle. *Sweet Jesus, what if Claussen never took her to the airport at all?* He thought about it, his head still light as a balloon. What were the chances the old man had driven all the way up here from Nashville? Not likely.

Ethan shook his head and went with Plan A. If he

was wrong, he'd have to give up hope. And that he refused to do.

The Beemer gave him no trouble when he turned the key in the ignition. It was as if Baby knew this was important. And bless his sweet girl. Asia had filled up the tank in town that morning. He pointed the headlights down the drive and stepped on the gas, nearly jerking the steering wheel out of his hands as the wheels straightened to align with the ruts in the road.

Ethan was grateful now for the work he'd done earlier to clear the drive. He made it to the road quickly, turned out onto the pavement, and pushed the engine up to speed. He took the curves much too fast, slopping coffee onto his jeans, but he ignored the sudden heat on his thigh. He just prayed the deer stayed out of the road tonight. He had to make it to the airport before that flight took off.

There was no way to avoid the villages along Route 28 or the sheriffs patrolling them, who tended to frown on speeders with out-of-town license plates blowing through their towns. Ethan cursed and sweated his way through every one of them, until he made it to the Thruway interchange just north of Utica.

Once he hit the interstate, though, he floored it. The traffic was relatively light—thank God it was Saturday—and the cops evidently had other things to do. He began to make some progress. And at last his mind began to clear.

Ethan realized with a nauseating heaviness in his stomach that Claussen was perfectly positioned to help anyone—government agents, private labs, even the aliens themselves—with an interest in extraterrestrial contact. The doctor had been working for years with patients who *believed* they had been abducted by aliens. He would be the ideal person to identify anyone who actually *had* been abducted—the ones, like Asia, who responded differently to AL therapy.

And I played right into his hands. All these years. How many have I helped Claussen find for them? Bile rose in his throat, hot and bitter, threatening to choke him.

A car horn blared on his right, and he swerved back into his lane, hands shaking on the wheel. *Shit!* He sat up in his seat and put his mind back on the road. Asia was not going to be a victim of his stupidity. He was going to get to the airport in time. He was going to find Asia before Claussen got her on that plane to wherever he meant to take her.

And they were going to beat this trap that Claussen had set for them, if he had to kill the old man to do it.

CHAPTER TWENTY-THREE

"Go ahead, my dear, check the account. I assure you it's legitimate."

I stood at a BankAmerica ATM machine in the Syracuse Hancock International Airport terminal and eyed with some skepticism the debit card Claussen had just handed me. My daddy had always told me there was no such thing as a free lunch, and I wasn't about to believe that had suddenly changed. Still, I didn't have much choice. If Claussen had decided to back out on his agreement now, I was up shit creek.

I slid the card into the slot and keyed in the password he'd given me. I hit "Check Balance." Then I began to wish I had a paper bag, because I was hyperventilating.

Claussen smiled that oily smile of his. "Do you believe me now?"

I could only nod.

"Why don't you take out enough cash to do some shopping? We have some time to kill, and I'm sure you could use a few new things for the trip."

Which I suppose was his tactful way of saying the two pairs of jeans and a sweater that I'd been living in for—*how long has it been anyway?*—were no longer adequate.

We had plenty of time, since we'd already taken care of buying my ticket on a 9:30 p.m. flight to Chicago, with a connection to Albuquerque. I figured that was close enough to Santa Fe for now. With what was in that account he'd just showed me, I had enough to buy a car, put a deposit down on an apartment, and take my time getting a job. Money wasn't going to be the problem. I refused to let myself think of what the real problem was going to be. I refused to let myself think at all.

I put my enemy through the wringer, making him wait while I tried on leather jackets and sleek pants and swirling skirts and sheer blouses and even a couple of pairs of shoes. Then I made him carry the bags while I sorted through a few scarves and belts and such. Too bad there were only one or two nice women's boutiques in the airport. I could have done a lot more damage in a real mall.

At close to 8:00 p.m. I bought a new suitcase and repacked everything but the outfit I'd chosen to wear on the plane. Then I parked Claussen across from the women's restroom nearest the security entrance to North Terminal B. My flight was due to take off from Gate 25 down at the end of that terminal.

"I'm going to change before I get on the plane," I told the old man. "Would you mind watching my stuff? I'll just be a minute."

Claussen frowned, as if he was reluctant to let me out of his sight, but what could he say? "Certainly. But don't be long. You don't want to be late."

I didn't bother to answer him. What did he think I was, fifteen? I took my shopping bag into the restroom and, since the facility was empty, went into the handicapped stall where I'd have some room to maneuver. I stripped off my old things and folded them. Then I slipped into the silky white blouse, the pencil-thin black pants that hugged my ass just right and the great little leather jacket that had cost way too much, but looked too good to pass up. I exchanged my trail runners for some dressy, but comfy, flats, and I was good to go.

I left the stall and paused to check my look in the mirror. And that was my undoing. The woman who stared back at me was lost and empty, dressed for a future that meant nothing to her. Just that quickly the breath left my lungs, the strength left my legs and I gripped the nearest wall to keep myself from falling to the floor.

What the hell are you doing? I asked the miserable creature looking back at me.

Goddamn her, she squared her shoulders, blinked back tears and answered, *I'm saving Ethan's life.*

I fled the restroom and scuttled back to where Claussen was waiting, any lightness of mood I might have jinned up with my spending excesses gone like the money itself. I refused to acknowledge his presence, even when he complimented me on my new look. Only when I had thrown my old jeans and sweater in the suitcase with the rest of my things and zipped it up did I spare him a glance.

"I think I'll go wait for my flight by the gate." Generations of my polite Southern ancestors were urging me to thank him for what he'd given me, but all I could think of was what he'd taken from me. My mouth stayed obstinately closed.

Claussen rose to his feet. He seemed to consider offering his hand, but read the look in my eyes and held back.

"Thank you for making this easy for Ethan."

A lump formed in my throat. I swallowed hard. "There was no way to make this easy for Ethan. But if you still think of yourself as his friend, I'd appreciate it if you'd watch out for him." I couldn't, I wouldn't say any more. I turned with as much dignity as I could muster and walked toward the security gate.

"Damn it, where are all you people going? There's got to be a parking spot around here somewhere."

Ethan circled the short-term section of the parking garage with increasing impatience, tires squealing as he rounded each tight corner to the next level up. Time and his temper were growing shorter with each level he passed without a place to stash the Beemer so he could dash into the airport terminal.

At last, he spotted a van with its taillights glowing red, preparing to back out of a spot. He waited, hands drumming on his steering wheel, while the van's driver adjusted dozens of unknown details before actually driving the vehicle. The van pulled out at last, and Ethan came within inches of clipping the slowly departing behemoth as he pulled into the just-vacated space. Then he was running for the terminal entrance, making for the information kiosk as soon as he got inside.

It was 8:45 p.m. Asia would already be waiting at the gate to board the plane. Without a ticket he wasn't getting beyond the security checkpoint. He flashed a smile at the bright young thing working the information desk.

"Ms. Rogers," he read off her name tag, "I wonder if you could help me?"

She blinked at him. "Well, I'll try, sir."

"I have to get a very important message to my girlfriend. She's already at the gate. She doesn't have a cell phone. I don't have a ticket. Can we call her at the gate? I really have to speak with her directly before she gets on that plane."

"Well, the phones at the gate are really for airline use. We could page her."

If Claussen was still with her, that wouldn't do. "I really wouldn't want her to miss that plane, though. And she shouldn't be running all over the airport." He tried looking embarrassed. "We're, uh, we're expecting."

"Oh!" The girl beamed at him. "Let me try calling the gate, sir. What flight is it?"

He gave her the information and held his breath while she called the gate. He imagined Asia's voice on the other end of the phone as he spoke to her, allowing himself to believe for one second that it might just be this easy.

But he saw the frown developing on Ms. Rogers' face as she listened and eventually hung up the phone, and his hope turned to something approaching panic.

"I'm sorry, sir, I'm just getting a busy signal at the gate. Let me check and see if they've started boarding." She tapped at the keyboard on her desk while Ethan's heart thumped wildly in his chest. It was 8:48 p.m.

"I don't see that they've started the boarding process. We'll have to page her to the security gate, but she should have time to meet you there. Are you sure you're all right?"

Ethan forced himself to take a deep breath. "I'm fine. I had a long drive to get here is all." He smiled again, aware of the impact it seemed to have on the girl. This wasn't usually his style, but he *had* to get to Asia in time, and he wasn't above using whatever assets he had to do it.

"Okay, I'll call ahead to the security gate and tell them you're meeting someone there. Then I'll start the page. It'll be the North Terminal B checkpoint. Got it?"

He nodded. "North Terminal B."

"What's her name?"

"Asia. Asia Burdette."

"I'll take care of it, Mister . . .?"

"Doctor. Dr. Carter. Thanks for your help, Ms. Rogers."

She smiled. "You're welcome, Dr. Carter. Good luck."

Ethan took the escalator to the second level two steps at a time, ignoring the pain that ripped through his thigh with every other step. At the top he peeled off to the left for the North Terminal B security gate. Overhead he could hear Ms. Rogers' clear voice calling for Asia Burdette to meet her husband at the appointed place. He could only hope Asia would both hear and understand the message—and be free to act on it.

Ethan approached the security checkpoint, skirting the lines of shuffling travelers with their carry-on bags filing through the scanners, to speak with the officer who had the look of The One in Charge off to one side.

"My girlfriend was at one of the departure gates," he explained. "They've been paging her to meet me here. Asia Burdette?"

The massively muscled guard turned to peer down at him, not bothering to uncross his arms from over his burly chest. "If you are not a ticketed passenger, you are not allowed on the other side of the security barrier, sir."

"I understand that, officer. She's supposed to come out to meet me on this side."

The officer looked at him with no expression. "Okay."

"They were supposed to call you from the Information Desk to let you know I was coming."

The man nodded.

Ethan tried very hard not to show his exasperation. "All right if I wait here for her?"

The officer appeared to assess his threat potential. He indicated a spot slightly to the right of where Ethan was standing.

"You can wait there, sir."

Ethan shifted to the designated spot and craned his neck to watch for Asia in the concourse behind the checkpoint. He checked his watch—9:10 p.m.—and he heard the call for boarding Delta Flight 1754 for Chicago at Gate 25. *Shit!* He started to pace. The guard turned to glare at him, but he couldn't stop. He just tightened his circle, a tiger in a very small cage.

Then he saw her—and, God, she was gorgeous! She'd bought new clothes, expensive ones—his sister would approve—and she looked sleek, sophisticated, and, oh, hell, yes, sexy. She was looking for him with an expression of intensity and single-minded focus on her face that he'd never seen before. He suddenly realized it wasn't the clothes or the expression, but the woman that had changed in the few weeks he had known her. This was the true Asia Burdette that was coming to him, the full and complete version. God, how he wanted her to stay.

He called her name. Her head turned, and her shocked expression nearly stole his nerve. Then things began to unfold with frightening speed.

As Asia neared the security gate from the other side, two men closed on her from behind. They moved in tandem, with military precision, and they looked . . . *familiar. Shit.* Ethan shouted a warning, just as a heavy hand landed on his own shoulder. He spun, saw Claussen's face, and took a swing. The old man went down easily, but they had drawn the attention of the security guard. The guard took a step, grabbed for Ethan and missed. He heard the man curse and call for backup as Ethan vaulted the simple metal barrier that stood between him and the North Terminal concourse.

By now, the security checkpoint was in an uproar.

Weapons sprang from their holsters, citizens dove for cover, whistles blew, alarms blared. Ethan searched the scattering crowd for Asia and the two goons, who hadn't made it far. She fought and screamed as the two caught her from either side. She slipped her arm out of one attacker's ham-fisted grip and used her elbow to strike the man's chest, her fist to hammer at the man's groin. Her delaying tactics gave at least one security guard time to close in on the group. Ethan reached them at the same time and hooked an elbow around the neck of one of the men to pry him away from Asia's side. The man countered with an elbow to his ribs—*damn it, the same fucking ribs he broke before*—and the two of them crashed painfully to the floor.

"All right, hold it right there! Don't move!"

Ethan looked up and saw only the blue steel barrel of a police-issue Smith and Wesson. He didn't move, even though the guy he'd pulled off Asia was tangled uncomfortably beneath him and growling in his ear.

"Get up. Slowly." The command came from the uniform holding the gun. "Keep your hands where I can see them." This guard wasn't the same one Ethan had spoken to earlier. There seemed to be an unlimited number of uniforms of all types surrounding them now.

He rolled to his feet and stood, pressing a hand to his side, where a sharp pain bloomed over his battered ribs. Asia took a step in his direction, but another guard had her in handcuffs and yanked her back. He felt hands jerking his arms behind his back, placing cuffs on his own wrists, but all his attention was on Asia.

"Are you okay?"

She smiled tensely. "I'm fine. Think I'm going to miss my flight, though."

He grinned. "That was the plan."

The humorless Transportation Security Administration officer on duty when all hell broke out at the North Terminal B security checkpoint strode up to take charge of the situation. From the shade of red on his face, the big man hadn't appreciated being given the slip so easily. He glared at Ethan as if he would gladly kill him, but he spoke to his staff instead.

"Take these individuals to the Security Section and sit their butts in isolation until the Chief gets someone from the VIPR team in here."

"But, sir, that's my girlfriend," Ethan protested. "I was only trying to protect her. Those guys were attacking her. I saw them from where I was waiting for her."

The guard turned to him. "Shut the fuck up. Those security gates are there for a reason. For all I know you're a fucking terrorist. You're all fucking terrorists, as far as I'm concerned. Anyway, you're in custody now, and we'll just let the big boys sort your asses out."

The Security Section at the Syracuse airport was a cramped and cluttered open space, so the "isolation" that had been ordered consisted of seating each of the combatants at a separate desk with a different sour-faced guard and making sure none of us talked to any of the others. While we waited for Security Chief Al Varinski to call in the TSA/Visual Intermodal Protection and Response team from wherever, the staff members who worked at the desks started with the paperwork and a rash of stupid questions.

The questions were the basic ones—name, address, origin, destination. And although I was already scared shitless, I realized this was the easy part. The more difficult interrogation would come later. Ethan's outburst had already given me a clue to the story he'd be telling. I planned to back it up as best I could, just adding some bullshit about a trip to Santa Fe. Hearing the page. Going to meet him. Being attacked by two unknown assailants. I wasn't planning on telling anyone anything about our history with the two thugs—like they would believe me if I did.

The real question was what had happened to Claussen. I hadn't seen him since Ethan had punched him in the mouth, just before the two guys had grabbed me. How had he managed to escape being scooped up with the rest of us?

When my clerk was done with me I turned to glance at Ethan. He was watching me from where he sat two desks over, one booted ankle resting across his knee. His lips curved upward in a tight smile, and I tried to smile back at him.

"I'm sorry," I mouthed silently.

He shook his head. "I love you," he mouthed back.

I couldn't imagine going through this without him, but just looking at him wasn't nearly enough. I needed to touch him, to feel the warmth of his hand in mine or his arm around my shoulders. I needed to hear him say it was going to be okay, even if I knew it wasn't. If they separated us for good before I got any of that, I wasn't sure I could handle it.

But, of course, that's just the kind of test fate had in mind for me, and sooner, rather than later. The outer door to the Security Section banged open, and Security Chief Varinski swept in with two other officers—and Arthur Claussen. They came to a halt in front of me, and my heart suddenly started misfiring in my chest.

Varinski, a balding pipsqueak of a man who was all uniform and no balls, spoke to the clerk processing my paperwork. "The woman is being released into this gentleman's custody. He has all the requisite paperwork."

"I don't think—" I began.

"What? No!" Ethan shouted from across the room.

"Restrain him." Varinski waved a hand in Ethan's direction. "I've had just about enough of this bullshit."

As guards rushed to hold Ethan in his seat, Claussen just smiled and spread his hands. "You see, Chief? This is what I've been dealing with. Between her delusional behavior and his violent tendencies I've had my hands full!"

Varinski nodded. "I can see that. Good thing you finally caught up with those two."

"Excuse me, just what does that paperwork say?" I craned my neck to see.

The clerk looked up at me with a strange mixture

of surprise and sympathy. Then she smiled.

"Now don't you worry about that, honey. They're going to take good care of you."

Cold fear coiled like a snake in my belly, and one look at Claussen's face confirmed what I suspected. I reached across the desk and snatched the papers from under the clerk's pen. I had time to read the words "Orders to Commit . . ." and ". . . mental incompetence . . ." before the papers were snatched back and a guard had his heavy hands on my shoulders, pressing me into the chair.

"You fucking bastard," I spat at Claussen.

"Now, Asia, that is hardly a reasonable tone of voice."

"I'd say it's an entirely reasonable reaction to being kidnapped." My voice had gone deadly quiet. "I'm no more insane than you are, but of course you're the one with the credentials." I turned my head to Varinski. "He's not my doctor. You can look up the records. Up until a month ago I was seeing Dr. Ethan Roberts in Nashville, Tennessee—the man you happen to have in custody."

Varinski actually looked confused for a moment.

Claussen laughed. "Oh, yes, that's part of her delusion. Roberts was under treatment himself in my clinic for a time. That's where they met. A sad case."

"Check the records!" I sat forward in my seat.

"Quiet!" Varinski looked at Claussen. "Doctor?"

"I have the files right here, Chief, if you'd like to look at them." He shrugged. "It might take some time."

"That won't be necessary. Roberts says himself

he's her boyfriend." The little man had made up his mind, but he asked for confirmation anyway. "And you really think he's a threat to security here at the airport, Doctor?"

"Oh, yes. He is positively a risk. He'll have to be processed through the legal system before I can continue his therapy. Regrettably."

My fear had hardened and compressed into a diamond of sharp-edged fury now. "The only one at risk from Ethan is you, Claussen. He was here to save me from you. He didn't trust you, and now I see why. You were working with those thugs all along, weren't you?" I had hurt Ethan for nothing. My heart twisted in my chest. "God, I was such an idiot."

Claussen's eyes narrowed. "Now you really are babbling, my dear. Are you sure you're feeling all right?" He turned to the clerk. "All done with that paperwork?"

The woman pulled out a stamp and hit a few pages with it. Then she handed the sheets to Claussen. "There you go, sir."

Guards took up position on either side of me, and I was forced to stand. My heart was keeping up a pounding protest in my chest, as if my blood had thickened past the point of movement in my veins. Ethan struggled in his seat against the hold of his guards, called my name even as I reached out a hand to him. Then I screamed "No!" and tried to run. Trapped like a fly in a web, I felt my feet leave the floor as multiple pairs of hands grabbed me and held me still. There was a sting at my neck. Then everything went black.

"Asia!"

Ethan fought his way out of the chair, elbows pivoting to bash the ribs of the guards holding him at either side. The grip released on his left, and he wrenched his arm free. He twisted and brought his fist up to strike under the man's chin on his right and managed three steps before he was tackled and slammed to the carpet-covered concrete floor. The wrists that had been handcuffed in front of him were repositioned behind him, the cuffs were tightened to grind into his bones, and his shoulders were torqued nearly out of their sockets as he was jerked roughly to his feet and pushed back into his chair.

The guard he'd eluded before loomed over him. "If the VIPR guys weren't due here in five minutes, I'd kick your fucking ass but good. Sit there and don't move or I'll do it anyway."

Ethan could taste blood and one cheek burned where his face had met the carpet, but all he could think about was the terror in Asia's eyes as the man he'd once called friend took her away. His chest tightened, and he had to force himself to breathe. Claussen had Asia now with all the weight of legality behind him. He no longer had to go through the elaborate pretense of spiriting her away to some location where no one knew her before grabbing her and throwing her in the back of a van. What would happen to Asia once Claussen had her was a question Ethan hadn't allowed himself to ask before. Now the question filled his mind.

That day at the clinic, a simple medical procedure had triggered memories of abuse and humiliation, leaving her emotionally exhausted and vulnerable. She'd survived it because he'd been there. How long could she survive being probed and prodded at some isolated lab, alone? Asia was strong, she'd been through much worse, but . . .

Ethan saw her face that night after they'd left the clinic, wet with her tears; he felt her hair, so soft in his hands as he cradled her head to his chest, and he ached for her. He would never forgive himself for letting her be hurt this way. Every muscle in his body clenched in frustration. He *had* to find a way to get to her.

The door to the outer office swung open again, and hope flared briefly in Ethan's heart. But it wasn't Claussen returning with Asia. From Varinski's reaction, the mismatched pair in bureaucratic-standard black suits was the help he'd been waiting for from the Transportation Security Administration's special investigation team.

Ethan thought the male partner of the team certainly looked the part—close-cropped black hair, tall and muscular and with the kind of easy grace in his movement that meant athletic training, or street-fighting experience, or both. His dark-skinned female partner, on the other hand, was as tiny as he was tall, coming only to his shoulder and weighing maybe just over a hundred pounds. She did look as wired as a Jack Russell terrier, though.

The woman stopped in front of the Security Chief and gave him the once-over. "Chief Varinski? I'm

Cheryl Kopic, from the Syracuse FBI office. This is my partner, Frank Martin." She offered credentials for inspection.

Varinski studied the badges and frowned. "We were expecting Tom Carver from VIPR."

"Yeah, Carver called us and asked us to pick this guy up," Martin said. "We have an interstate warrant out on him. That okay with you?"

The TSA chief shrugged. "I don't give a shit who takes him as long as you got the paperwork straight. That's him over in the corner. He don't like to play nice."

Varinski pointed in his direction and the three of them frowned. Ethan stared back evenly. He didn't know how he was going to do it, but he had to convince these people to help him.

It took a few minutes for the required paperwork to be signed. Then the Security Chief nodded at Ethan's guards and they got him to his feet.

Agent Kopic stepped closer and nodded. "Okay, Chief, we'll take it from here. Thanks for holding onto him for us."

Varinski scowled at what was soon to be his ex-prisoner. "No problem. You're sure you can handle him with just the two of you?"

Martin grinned. "Oh, yeah. She's tougher than she looks, you know."

"Oh, a real ball-buster, huh?" Varinski barked out a laugh.

Kopic glanced at him, and the corners of her mouth lifted. "You wouldn't want to find out, Chief." She took Ethan's arm and steered him toward the door. Ethan wasn't inclined to argue with her—he could feel the energy coming off her—and, besides, he wanted the agent on his side.

Her partner nodded at Varinski on his way out. "We'll send you a copy of the full report in a couple of weeks."

The three of them moved silently and quickly through a series of little-used service corridors that led them out into the employee section of the garage. Ethan gave a thought to his Baby, abandoned in a short-term parking slot and no doubt slated for towing in a few hours. Then he was hustled into the backseat of a black Ford Explorer with tinted windows and the time for thinking of anything but what was going to happen next was over.

The man slid in behind the driver's seat and started up the engine. His partner got in beside Ethan and winked at him.

"Just give us a minute to get out of this garage and away from any security cams and then we'll get those handcuffs off you, sweets."

CHAPTER TWENTY-FOUR

I woke up with my head on fire and my mouth full of sawdust. When I opened my eyes, I panicked, believing I was blind, but it was only that the darkness was complete, smothering any hope of sight. The least movement brought on a wave of dizzy nausea, so I stopped moving, waiting until the cot I was lying on decided to obey the laws of gravity.

I dozed off and woke again, I don't know how much later. By then the dizziness was tolerable, and I could sit up, though my head still pounded and every muscle was stiff and sore. I must have been on that cot for hours, trying to sleep off the effect of the drug Claussen had given me. My stomach was empty, and I needed a bathroom—badly. Jesus, just how long had I been here? And where, exactly, was here?

Somewhere, a control switch was thrown, and light panels in the ceiling began to glow dimly, illuminating my eight-by-twelve cell—plain, gray cement walls; smooth, gray cement floor. The cell was equipped with a stainless steel sink and toilet, a television screen recessed into the wall behind a heavy plastic protective cover, a few magazines and a remote on a shelf cut into the wall below the TV. It had a door with a wired-glass window slot like an old school room but no windows.

My heart began to beat with slow-metered dread. I clamped down on my reaction. It was too soon to panic. *Wait and see what Claussen wants.*

I focused on simple things. I stood up, fought the dizziness and the lingering nausea, made my way to the toilet and used it. I splashed tepid tap water over my face and felt a little better. I ran both hands through my hair, fingers combing through the tangles and fluffing up the flattened, shapeless mess it had become. Then a control was touched again somewhere, and the lights grew brighter. I peered at my reflection in a doll-sized mirror above the sink, and it showed me the truth. My eyes were still shadowed with fear, my skin the same gray as the walls of my cell.

I went to the TV and the shelf underneath. The magazines were ancient and of no interest—*People, Ladies Home Journal, Good Housekeeping.* I tried the remote. The TV came on readily enough, but this wasn't your everyday cable. No news channels, no local channels. No channels at all. Some old movies, some cartoons, reruns of *I Love Lucy.* It was like I'd landed in the *Twilight Zone* version of an old folks' home. Despite the frothy nature of the selections, the offerings did nothing to ease my fear about this place. I released a soulless laugh and turned off the set.

The lights brightened yet another notch, leaving no shadows in my cell. Full daylight now, I supposed. My stomach growled, hoping for breakfast. To pass the time, I stretched my aching muscles, loosened my joints, did push-ups and sit-ups and lunges and squats until I'd shaken off the chill of the cell and rid my mind of the fog from the drugs. And at last I heard noise in the corridor outside my door.

The door swung open, and a guard stepped inside my room. He was massive—six-five, 270 pounds at least—and he carried a Taser. I backed against the far wall, heart hammering. Behind him, a woman dressed in blue hospital scrubs carried a tray. Despite everything, my mouth watered.

The woman actually smiled at me. "Hungry, hon? Eat up, then we'll take you down for a shower before you have a visit with Dr. Claussen, okay?"

I said nothing, just stared at the tray. She took that as a "yes" and left the tray on a table that pulled out from the foot of my bed. As soon as she and the Hulk left me alone, I fell on it like a vulture on roadkill. As long as I had one bite of egg or toast or peach yogurt to mop up, I refused to think about what the rest of the morning might bring.

Ethan stared at the woman in the seat beside him, unable to formulate a response, while the skin around her dark brown eyes crinkled with amusement. She offered no further explanation, merely laughed as her partner took the sharp turns in the parking garage at breakneck speed and shot through the exit onto the service road leading away from the airport. As soon as he was well away from any airport buildings, he pulled to the side of the road and turned around to face the backseat with an engaging grin lighting up his face.

Ethan looked from the man in the front seat to the woman in the back seat. "You guys are not really FBI agents, are you?"

"Well, we do work in law enforcement." The man who'd introduced himself as Frank Martin gave up a dry laugh. "The scope's a little bigger, though. You want to take those things off him, babe?"

The woman turned him in the seat, used a key to open the cuffs on his wrists and released his arms. Ethan rotated his aching shoulders and rubbed at the raw chafe marks on his wrists. The movement activated the injury to his ribs, and he winced.

"Thanks."

"My pleasure, sweets." The woman cocked an eye at his face, a curious finch examining a new feeder. "How'd you get the bruise on your cheek? One of that asshole Varinski's lugs?" She dug around in a bag on the floor while she waited for the answer.

"I made a move for Asia when Claussen took her. The guards face-planted me."

The woman produced a chemical icepack from the bag and broke the seal on it with a quick punch. She held it to Ethan's face until he put a hand up to take over. "I'm sorry." She looked at him and gave him a tight little smile. "We'll get her back, don't you worry. I'm Rayna Murphy. Asia knows me as Dozen. We were together on Gallodon IV."

Ethan gaped, the icepack and the hand holding it dropping into his lap. "She thought you were dead."

Rayna's abundant energy faltered for a second. "I

came pretty close. Lucky for both Asia and me the rescue team was practically sitting on us when that tunnel collapsed. Took us both home."

His mind was suddenly spinning. Gallodon IV—*another planet*. The tunnel collapse. And Dozen, alive, sitting next to him. Here. And now. Everything Asia had told him was real. He'd believed it. Now he *knew* it.

"She told me what you did for her," Ethan said. "She wouldn't be here—"

"Asia was special—I knew it as soon as I saw her." Rayna gave his hand a quick squeeze before placing the icepack back on his face. "Within weeks, her eyes were as bright as starshine. She was resistant to the Minertsan mindwipe program. I got to her as soon as I could to try and get her out."

"Resistant?"

"Uh, yeah, well, lots to talk about, but this isn't the best place for it." The man in front stuck out a hand. "I'm Sam, by the way—Solomon Armstrong Murphy, but just Sam works for most people."

Ethan shook the man's hand and settled back in his seat as Sam turned out onto the road again. Something clicked in his head, and he glanced between his two companions.

"Murphy? The two of you . . .?"

Rayna's lips twitched, and she made a show of looking out the window. "Yeah. We tied the knot six months ago."

Ethan couldn't help but smile. "Congratulations."

Sam grinned. "Thanks!"

Questions swirled in Ethan's mind, so many

questions leading in so many different directions that he hesitated, not knowing where to start. But it was the questions he doubted even Sam and Rayna could answer that weighed most on him. He started with those.

"Where is she, Rayna? Do you know where Claussen's taken her?"

To his surprise, she nodded. "We have an idea. We know Claussen's been working with an extra-governmental research group for the past two years—something called Daystrom Futurgenics. They have a small facility in Hunt Valley, Maryland. We're hoping he took her there."

Ethan vaguely remembered Claussen mentioning a business trip to Maryland once or twice. "That's where we're going?"

"You got a better idea?"

"No, I'm all for it. I'm just hoping you've got some extraterrestrial backup waiting when we get there."

Sam glanced at him in the rearview mirror. "I wouldn't expect a lot of boots on the ground. By our standards, this is a full-scale landing team. But don't worry. We can handle it."

There was something evasive about Sam's answer. "You know it's not just the old man you're dealing with here, right? He hired those two you saw in the Security office to try and kidnap us both once before and nearly succeeded. And he hired others to attack Ida Mickens." He looked at Rayna. "Do you know who she was?"

Rayna met his gaze and didn't look away, though he could see she knew what was behind his question.

"Yes. I'm sorry about Ida, Ethan. We got here too late to help her."

Ethan felt anger stirring deep inside him like a bear awakening in a dark winter cave. "So you've been watching Claussen."

"Yes."

"For how long?" The bear growled low in his throat.

Rayna stared him down. "Does it matter, Ethan? We're going to take care of—"

"How long?"

"From the beginning." Rayna sighed. "Claussen works for us."

Ethan fell back in his seat, his lungs collapsing, straining to take in another breath. His eyes darted to the front seat, where Sam was dividing his attention between the back seat and the road.

"We were trying to solve this little mystery quietly." Rayna went on without emotion. "We usually don't like to take a direct approach. But when you and Asia turned up missing, we had to send in the troops."

"This little mystery," Ethan repeated, biting off the words. A mystery that had led an old woman who should have died peacefully in her sleep to kill herself instead. A mystery that now had a woman who'd overcome a soul-killing tragedy facing yet another round of torture. A mystery that he was beginning to suspect involved him much more deeply than he knew. And for what? That was what he had yet to understand and the rage was threatening to overwhelm him.

His voice shook as he spoke once more. "Maybe you'd better start at the beginning. Tell me what the hell is going on. And don't leave anything out."

The nurse who'd brought me my breakfast returned a while later, alone this time, to take me down the hall to the shower. Smiling brightly, she gave me some toilet articles and a towel and stood just outside the stall while I "freshened up." My own clothes were gone when I got out of the shower. I realized with a flare of angry humiliation that I wouldn't get them back when the nurse handed me a pair of scrubs to put on and some slippers for my feet.

Once she had me "dressed" for the day, the nurse steered me past my cell and into another corridor. This one led to something that looked like a classroom, with several desks and a monitoring station. She sat me at one of the desks and left me alone. I heard the lock slide solidly into the doorjamb as she left.

Fear began to seep out of my bones and into my stomach, making it churn. My heart started to beat at the speed of a lab rat's. This was a fear I thought I'd left behind, but now I saw it had only hidden deep in my body, waiting for the right circumstances to re-emerge.

A desk. A test.

This will be the easy part.

Later there would be the lab and the wires. The cold steel. And the probes.

I began to shake.

Then the screaming will start.

Jesus, I couldn't stop shaking.

The door to the corridor opened and I jumped, my hands fluttering in my lap. Claussen swept into the room and the door locked behind him. I stood, swallowing the bitter taste of terror in my throat. I backed up to give myself the space I needed to maintain some semblance of control.

Claussen simply smiled at me and took a seat at the monitor's desk.

"Good morning, Asia. How are you feeling this morning?"

"How am I feeling?" My hands clenched into fists. "Angry, resentful, betrayed, trapped. I feel like kicking you in the balls and blowing your pretty facility to hell. Anything else you'd like to know?"

Claussen looked bored. "It was just meant to be a pleasantry. I wasn't truly asking for a report on your emotional state. We'll determine that as we go along."

"That should be easy enough to determine." I lifted my chin. "You kidnapped me. You're holding me against my will. You've threatened to ruin the life of someone I care about. The emotional state of any rational person under those circumstances would be highly fucking agitated, wouldn't you say?"

"Why don't you have a seat, Asia?" Claussen waved mildly at a desk. "We're going to start with some easy questions today, just to get a baseline."

"Fuck you. Oh, and fuck your baseline."

Claussen's eyes narrowed. "We can do this here, with an oral test. Or we can do it under restraint in the lab, with a brain scan. Your choice. I actually prefer the oral test. Believe it or not, it's more accurate for my purposes. But if you'd rather have the equipment and the drugs . . ."

He knew what my reaction would be. My body was screaming at me. Heart, lungs, stomach, muscles—*NO! NO! NO! NO!*

I sat down.

"Good." He smiled, the smug bastard. "Now. Tell me your full name."

"Asia Lynne Burdette."

"How old are you?"

"Thirty-one."

"And what did you have for breakfast this morning?"

What?

When I didn't answer, he repeated the question. "What did you have for breakfast this morning?"

I glared at him. "Eggs, toast, peach yogurt."

Sam and Rayna exchanged a tight glance as if they knew it might come to this. Rayna shook her head.

"There are rules, Ethan. We couldn't tell you everything, even if we wanted to."

Ethan grabbed her forearm. "You're giving me some kind of fucking no-interference bullshit after all you people have done to screw things up here? Asia deserves an explanation for what happened to her. I worked with Arthur Claussen for years. Goddamn it, I need to know what's going on."

He was shouting now, and Rayna had to fight to

loosen his grip on her arm. Sam cursed and pulled the Explorer off the road in a squeal of rubber. He turned and had a hand on Ethan's throat before the SUV had fully come to a stop.

"Hey, I sympathize, buddy, but I will put you in a fucking coma if you lay a hand on my wife again." His hand tightened. "You get me?"

"Sam!" Rayna touched his shoulder where it hung over the front seat. "I got this. He wasn't hurting me."

The big man released his grip and shook his head. "Look, neither one of us is what you might call a stickler for the rules. But in this business we have to be careful. You know, some of that science fiction *baraz* wasn't too far from wrong—at least the part where some asshole goes to a less advanced planet and fucks everything up. We've seen it happen. So we *will* keep a low profile, understand?"

"It's not like I have CNN on speed dial." Ethan coughed, turning his head to ease the throb in his neck.

Sam snorted. "Wouldn't matter a whole lot if you did."

Ethan knew with professional certainty how quickly one man with a wild story of alien abduction would be dismissed. "Just tell me who you are."

"We work for an organization called the Interstellar Council for Abolition and Rescue." Sam broke it down. "It's Rescue's goal to put an end to the kind of thing that happened to Asia. Some of our people work on the legal end—passing laws and so forth. Others work in enforcement in those parts of the galaxy where governments have abolished trafficking and slave labor."

Ethan's mind balked at the scope. "You're talking about governments *all over the galaxy . . .?*"

"I know it's a lot to take in," Rayna said. "But, yes, it's a busy little galaxy out there. Sometimes a nasty one. Slave trafficking is a profitable business, and not everyone agrees that it should be abolished. Unfortunately, there's not just one big happy Galactic Senate to regulate things, so we have to fight our battles in every solar system and region of space that has a governing body to negotiate with. Thank God that's not my job."

"Yeah, Rayna preferred the easy work—organizing underground resistance and escape networks in the labor camps." Sam smiled fondly at his wife. "At least until that mountain fell on top of her."

Rayna made a face at him. "Like your job was a piece of cake—chasing slave ships in a tin can held together with spit and thermoglue."

Stunned, Ethan followed the banter with only half a mind. The fact that these two obviously sane human beings were confirming a theory he would have said only weeks ago was insane had fully hit him. All the disparate pieces he'd collected since Asia had challenged his view of the universe had at last coalesced into a frightening new model.

"So you're saying there are other . . . species . . . out there that use humans as slaves?"

Sam and Rayna nodded.

"Their technology is advanced enough that it is economically feasible for them to forcibly remove people from Earth and take them to wherever they need them as labor."

Sam and Rayna nodded again.

"Humans in particular? Seems like a long way to come for workers."

"Not really, when you figure that your solar system sits smack on the central jump node—uh, sort of a space/time shortcut—for this quadrant of space," Sam replied. "And, by some asshole trick of the gods, humans have nearly the same environmental requirements as the biggest slave-trading species out there, a species we've nicknamed the Grays. With one big advantage. We're not susceptible to the mind-altering effects of certain crystal-borne fungi. Add to it that humans are adaptable, smart, and strong, and you're just asking to be whisked away to the labor camps."

Ethan shook his head. "They've been doing this right under our noses without anyone knowing it?"

"Well, not exactly." Sam pointed at the sky. "People see UFOs. For years people have been claiming they've been kidnapped by aliens, but no one's believed them. You should know that better than anyone."

Shame flushed hot through Ethan's chest. "Most of the people I worked with were—" He was going to say "delusional," but he stopped, then shook his head. "No. Some of them—from what you say, they must have been telling the truth." His voice fell to a whisper. "I should have believed them."

Rayna put a hand on his arm. "You believed Asia. You believed Ida. And from what I know of you, you treated all your patients with respect, whether you believed them or not."

Ethan sensed something left unsaid, a truth this explanation concealed rather than revealed. He probed for it.

"You said Claussen worked for you. Doing what?"

"You know, rescuing people from labor camps or slave ships isn't just a matter of picking them up and dropping them back on their home planets. Early on, Rescue couldn't return people at all. They started colonies on planets like Terrene, where Rayna comes from." Sam was avoiding the direct question. "Then we found a way to send them back and, guess what? The people we returned were much happier if they didn't remember what had happened to them."

Ethan's breath tightened, anger beginning a slow burn in his belly again. "You brainwash them."

Sam corrected him. "The Minertsans—the Grays—brainwash them. To make them more docile. We restore what we can, then we take them home, based on what we find in the implants."

"The implants," Ethan repeated, thinking of the scar on Asia's neck. "But those memories are not complete. You purposely wipe their memories of their time in captivity."

Rayna returned his challenge with one of her own. "Think about it, Ethan. If you had a choice, would you want to be returned to your old life with your memories of being abducted and living as a slave intact? Or would you rather wake up in the morning just like every other morning, remembering only a good night's sleep?"

He shook as he answered her. "Asia didn't just

wake up the next morning like every other morning. Somebody fucked up—there was a battle, the ship was late, and she lost everything. Then she started remembering what you had programmed her to forget. That wasn't in the plan, was it?"

Sam stared at him. "You know about the firefight?"

"Asia remembered it."

"Jesus." Sam's face was ashen.

"I said it before." Tears welled in Rayna's eyes. "Asia is special."

After a moment Sam turned to explain, his voice subdued, almost apologetic. "We have the technology to eliminate short-term memory patterns associated with specific experiences, and it works with all but a few individuals." He paused, struggling for the right words. "For most people, returning is painless. They have no memory of being gone at all. No nightmares. No scars. And because we can manipulate space-time with the jump, no lost time. The transition is smooth. If people start getting nightmares or flashbacks, it's an indication the original treatment is breaking down and a brief booster program helps to get them back on track. That's where Dr. Claussen—and others like him—come in."

"A booster? Jesus Christ, that's what AL is." Ethan's jaw clenched. *And me. I'm in this, too. Up to my fucking neck.*

"Yes," Sam replied. "Rescue developed the alpha wave synchronizer to help returnees reintegrate into their lives. It works very well, usually. But once in a while, someone like Ida—or Asia—comes along. They're resistant to programming."

"That was a good thing for her in the camp, sweets, you can believe that, no matter how much pain it's caused her since then." Rayna's gaze locked on his. "It helped her survive."

"You have to understand, Ethan," Sam pleaded. "What people like Claussen do for us is essential to our mission. The people we return would be lost without someone to help them adjust."

"I might be more sympathetic if I'd had a choice about my role in all this." Ethan's guts twisted with the knowledge. "Claussen told me nothing about what we were really doing."

"He wasn't free to tell you anything," Rayna said.

Ethan pinned her with a dark stare full of the guilt he carried for Ida and Asia and all the others. "And maybe it was just easier not to mention that we were 'reprogramming' these poor people to forget the very real trauma that had affected them. I might not have been so cooperative if he'd told me the truth."

Rayna met his stare with clear-eyed calm. "Their trauma is real all right—and more horrible than you can imagine. Would you have them relive it every minute of every day? Look deep in your soul, Ethan, and tell me: if you knew a way to spare Asia the pain of her memories—if there had been no battle when her ship came out of jump to delay her return, and you truly *could* make her forget her time on Gallodon—would you still insist on your principles? Or would you let her forget and live her life as she was meant to?"

Ethan felt his heart sink into his belly as he realized he didn't have an answer to that question.

Or, no, he did have an answer, but it wouldn't be the one a young, idealistic psych intern might have given. It probably wasn't the one he would have given six months ago, before Asia Burdette changed his life forever. He knew now that he would do anything to spare her the pain he'd seen her endure.

"Arthur Claussen wasn't always motivated by greed or arrogance." Rayna's soft voice was full of emotion now. And what she said was hard to hear. "In the beginning, he was more like you than you know."

The knowledge came to him at last, the fog lifting to reveal a hidden landscape. "Elizabeth had been taken, too." Her nightmares. The drinking to avoid them. Her withdrawal. The fear masquerading as hostility. It had all been there, if only he'd had the eyes to see it. His muscles, bunched tight with awful memory, began to tremble.

"She was one of Psychogenesis's first cases, the reason we contacted Claussen." Rayna confirmed everything with a slow nod. "We needed a test case for the AL protocol. He worked through another of his associates to try and help her, but failed."

Ethan remembered the young female therapist who'd been no more than Claussen's puppet, but he had no idea the extent of what went on in the sessions. "Liz never told me." His voice was a ragged whisper.

"I'm sorry." Rayna laid a warm hand on his arm. "She'd been taken so young . . ."

Ethan swallowed the tears that would have choked him, called up the anger that still roiled in his chest.

"Did you know what Arthur was doing? Kidnapping people who didn't respond to the AL protocol? Was that part of your plan, too?"

"No," Rayna said. "Sam and I were sent in to investigate when you and Asia took off. We asked for the assignment. Asia is sort of a special project for me." She smiled, then went on. "We found out about Ida and Conners and the others the same way you did. Claussen has a contract with a black ops agency of the U.S. government to 'debrief' his subjects."

The memory of the anticipatory gleam in Claussen's eyes when he introduced his new research partners, the glib Colonel Gordon and the unsmiling Dr. Park, flashed through his mind. Would they have told him the truth if he had agreed to join the team?

Ethan seethed with thick outrage. "What happens to the patients when he's finished?"

Rayna shook her head, her jaw tight. "We don't know yet."

"There are so many out there—so many who've been Taken." Sam's face was lined with a weariness Ethan hadn't noticed before. "Your world isn't ready to join the galaxy. Can you imagine the panic if it became widely known that the people of Earth are being stolen into slavery and their governments are powerless to stop it? We do our best—and I know it sounds cold—but even Rescue has to pick its battles. I'm sorry, Ethan. We can't save them all."

Despite their warmth, Ethan turned from them both, his face a mask pointed at the darkness outside the vehicle. He curled in on himself, struggling to keep his fracturing heart in one piece, to keep his soul from drowning in the rising black tide of his guilt, to keep his thoughts focused on the task before him despite the anger that threatened to erupt into mindless rage.

Asia was all that mattered now. It might not be possible to save everyone, but this one would not be lost. They had to find *her*. They had to save *her*. Asia was everything.

CHAPTER TWENTY-FIVE

So many questions. A morning full of them. Names. Places. Years. The random bits of data that make up a life. In this case, my life.

Where were you born, Asia?

What was your mother's maiden name?

Where did you go to high school?

What was your first job, Asia?

What is your favorite color?

And the one Claussen repeated like a mantra, a nonsensical "control question" thrown in at set intervals to see if I was still paying attention:

"What did you have for breakfast, Asia?"

For two hours, the answer had been the same: "Eggs, toast, peach yogurt."

"Good." Claussen closed the laptop. "We'll let you take a little break now."

The doctor heaved himself to his feet and lumbered out the door. I stood up and stretched, glad to be rid of him, but my nerves twitched with apprehension. He wasn't done with me, and the bone-deep memories of my torture at the hands of the aliens told me the next phase of his experimentation was likely to be much less benign.

The door opened again and the nurse poked her head in. "Need a break, hon?" She waved me in the direction of the door. "C'mon down the hall with me a sec."

I followed her down the hallway to the restroom, grateful for the chance to leave the room, grateful for the chance to move, to expand my vision beyond four walls. I used the facilities and washed up and would have lingered in the Spartan space if the nurse had let me, but she seemed well aware of the schedule.

"Let's go, hon." She planted her feet and nodded. "Wouldn't want to keep the doctor waiting."

She led me down the hallway, but she didn't stop at the room we'd been in all morning. She kept walking, looking back at me when I hesitated. "C'mon, Asia. We're in a different room for the next part of the test." She spoke calmly, like there was nothing to be worried about.

I knew better. *This is where it starts.* My heart thundered in my hollow chest. My mouth went dry. My eyes searched the empty halls for a place to run, even though I knew there was no place to go. I was trapped as surely as any lab monkey—every contingency planned for, the cage secure, the doors locked, the escape routes blocked. Still, everything in me screamed, *GET OUT NOW!*

A door opened along the hall ahead. Claussen and two hefty orderlies stepped into the corridor.

"There you are, Asia." He gave me a condescending smirk. "I thought you'd gotten lost."

The orderlies came up to flank me, and, despite

what I knew, my feet started moving. Traitors, they took me against my will to the doorway where Claussen waited, still smiling. He stepped aside, and the two orderlies behind me crowded me into the room. I wanted to stop, I would have stopped, but the big men each grabbed an elbow and kept me moving, propelling me toward an examination table in the center of the room.

I tried not to panic. I fought to hold on to a life raft of rational thought in a raging sea of primitive, fear-driven physical reaction. The place itself telegraphed *PAIN! VIOLATION! HUMILIATION! DEATH!* though there was nothing in sight to trigger those thoughts. There was the examination table, covered in a cheerful pink sheet, with a pillow at one end. There was a desk, with a device I recognized from Ethan's office—the alpha wave synchronizer. *Not so neutral in effect after all, then. Or does it depend on who is wielding the tool?* There was a cabinet, latched, its contents not visible from the outside. There was some equipment off to one side, covered and ignored as if it would not be needed.

Yet my body was trembling, my heart flailing, my mind shrieking, *Get out!*

My nostrils flared at the smell of alcohol and the hot-dusty scent of electronics. My pupils shrank against the bright lights. I looked at this room, and I remembered agony. I feared for my life. Worse, I feared for my sanity.

Claussen was watching my reaction closely. "Asia, there's nothing to be afraid of. We're not going to hurt you."

"You've already hurt me." I took refuge in anger. "What you are doing to me is wrong by every standard of your profession. That doesn't bother you?"

"You really are rather good at manipulation, Asia." Claussen didn't look at me as he said this. He was busy writing something down. "I applaud your spirit. However, the truth is that I am not harming you but helping you in the long run. And helping others, too, by the way. If we can discover how you manage to resist programming so effectively, we can improve our techniques. Then you, and others like you, will never suffer from the memory of your . . . time away . . . again."

I stared at him. "My 'time away'? You make it sound like a fucking vacation. And you want to know something? The only thing worse than remembering that something horrible happened to me, is knowing something horrible happened, but not being able to remember what. No one asked me if I wanted a mindfuck. Your techniques amount to rape, Claussen."

"An interesting perspective." He gestured to the exam table. "If you please . . .?"

The two orderlies scowled at me. The nurse smiled. My knees nearly buckled under me, but I took the last few steps to the table and sat up on the pink surface.

"Lie down, please."

Hating myself for my compliance, I did as he said. The nurse began dabbing cold gel on my temples and forehead. Then she placed several small, round disks over the gel, connecting the wires both to AL and to a souped-up EEG readout machine she'd rolled up to the table from a corner. For record-keeping, I suppose.

"Tell me, Asia," Claussen said as the nurse went about her business. "If you had been given a choice when they rescued you from the labor camp, would you have chosen to remember your experiences?"

The idea of forgetfulness was so seductive. How could I truly say I would have chosen to remember? I couldn't have known the programming wouldn't work for me. They could even have told me there was a chance it might not work, and I might have tried it anyway. To forget all the pain and the awful darkness of that time, the things they had done to me. Would I have wanted to remember?

"No." The admission scalded me. "I would have wanted to forget. But I can't. I'm not sure anyone really can."

Claussen smiled down at me. "Ah, but that's where you're wrong. Most people can. We just have to find a way to make you forget, too."

He started to turn away, but I stopped him with a challenge. "And who chooses what I forget and what I remember, Doc? You?"

He turned back to me. "Well, yes, in this case, I am in control of the process. Obviously."

I wasn't sure where I was going with this. I only knew I wanted to postpone the next step as long as possible. Every muscle trembled as I struggled to keep my voice even and my arguments reasonable, to keep him talking at all costs.

"And I don't suppose you're tempted to expand the scope of your little procedure to include subjects beyond my time in the labor camp?"

His eyes narrowed. "Why would I do that, Asia? What other subjects would be of interest to me?"

"My feelings for Ethan present a problem for you, Claussen." God knows why I kicked him in the teeth with that. No good could come of it, I knew it as soon as the words came out of my mouth. But it was too late now. I blundered on. "It would be pretty convenient for you if I forgot all about him, wouldn't it?"

Claussen's expression grew furious. "Well, you have me there. It would have been a great deal better for everyone if you and Ethan hadn't decided to play house. It took me longer than it should have to see what was happening. I trusted him. I waited for him to do the right thing. I told others he had things under control, that *I* had things under control. I *hesitated*. Now we'll be lucky to have any say at all in what happens next."

He seemed to lose focus for a moment, lost in thought. Then his steel-gray gaze found me again. "Your emotional connection with Ethan is not my first priority. It's considerably more difficult to eliminate positive associations in the brain than negative ones—ask any drug addict. I may need a lot more time to accomplish that goal." He brightened. "But, we'll see! First things first!"

He turned and switched on the alpha wave synchronizer. "Now, tell me your full name."

I shivered and shook, unable to stay still on the

table. Claussen nodded at the orderlies, who stepped up to fasten the restraints that had remained hidden beneath the demure drape of the pink sheets. Oddly, I felt more secure bound at the wrists and ankles, and the shaking began to subside. Only the roar of blood in my ears and the slam of my heartbeat betrayed my fear.

"Your full name, my dear?" Claussen repeated.

From a long way off, I heard my voice answer him. "Asia Lynne Burdette."

"How old are you?"

"Thirty-one."

"And what did you have for breakfast, Asia?"

"Eggs, toast, peach yogurt."

"What the hell is this stuff?" Sam held up a small plastic container, his nose wrinkled in disgust.

"Peach yogurt," Ethan informed him from the back seat, a spoonful halfway to his own mouth.

Rayna pointed a spoon at him. "It's healthy. Eat up."

"Why couldn't we stop at that other place—what is it, Macdougal's?"

"McDonald's," Ethan supplied.

"Yeah." Sam's face lit up. "They have those meat slabs on bread—uh, hamburgers. I like those."

"You like those a little too much." Rayna frowned at him. "I can't be waiting around for your flabby ass to catch up with me all the time."

"Ooh, I love it when you talk dirty, baby." Sam, who was well over six feet of solid muscle, looked as if he'd settle for having her for breakfast. "But really, a man needs some sustenance. This ain't getting it."

Rayna tossed a bagel at him. "Try one of these and shut up. I didn't have time to get you a steak dinner."

Ethan smiled. "It's not bad with coffee."

"That why you're so skinny, stick boy?"

He shrugged. "Sometimes I forget to eat."

Sam gaped at him in the rear view mirror. "That's impossible."

Ethan nodded out the window at the glass and brick building that housed Daystrom Futurgenics. "How long will we have to wait?"

"The nanoprobes I planted take about an hour to disperse." Rayna waved a hand at a computer screen that was currently blank. "They should start feeding data back soon. Then we'll have the information on which to build some kind of plan."

Frustration ran like a buzzing current along Ethan's nerves. "I still don't understand why we can't just break in there and take her." The building was isolated, far from any others at the end of an access road in a maze-like business park. "And we *drove* all the way here in a *car*, for God's sake. You came halfway across the galaxy to rescue Asia—you can't use your technology now, when it counts?"

"Look. Ethan." Sam spoke slowly, as if explaining something to a two-year-old. "Do you remember what I said about keeping a low profile? We can't exactly go zipping around the atmosphere in a nil-gravity vehicle without attracting attention. De-materialization beams require energy use that can be detected and are generally imprecise without sensory data—which we lack in this case. We have to go slow or risk failure *and* exposure. Do you get it?"

"But she's in there." He stared back at the building. "God knows what Claussen's doing to her."

"We only think she's there." Rayna touched his arm. "We have to be sure before we bust up into the annual meeting of the National Society of Toy Manufacturers. Try to be patient. She's stronger than you think, Ethan. She can hold out until we get there."

He nodded, but his heart was breaking. He didn't know how much longer he'd be able to sit here helplessly while Asia endured whatever torment Claussen had devised for her only a few hundred meters away. Time was running out. He would have to act soon, with or without the help of extraterrestrials seeking to keep a low profile.

Firelight flickered as a wet, windy afternoon turned to a night as cold and sparkling as diamonds. Wrapped in warmth, I lay and listened to Ethan's steady heartbeat beneath my ear, his silky murmur repeating my name like a caress.

"They can't have been human to have hurt you like they did," he said. "My Asia, my sweet, beautiful Asia."

"Asia. Pay attention now, Asia."

No. Firelight. And Ethan. I won't forget.

"Asia?"

I groaned and opened my eyes. "Yes."

"Are you ready?"

It hurt to speak. But if I didn't—"Yes."

"Tell me your full name."

"Asia Lynne Burdette."

"How old are you?"

"Um." I thought. The knowledge was slow in coming. "Thirty. No. Thirty-one."

"And what did you have for breakfast today, Asia?"

I opened my mouth, but nothing came out. It had seemed like such an easy question earlier. In fact, I'd been answering the same damn question all fucking day. And now . . .

"Asia?"

My head rolled on the pillow, causing an explosion of pain. "What?"

"Answer the question, please."

Confused, so fucking confused. Like I'd just woke up after a hundred years.

"What was the question again?"

"What did you have for breakfast this morning?"

I searched for the missing data in my mind like a six-year-old looking for an "A" in her alphabet soup. Only this can of Campbell's had apparently been cooked up without that all-important first letter. The information just wasn't there anymore. Did I have breakfast? Had there even been a morning to this day? The first thing I remembered was being in the classroom with Claussen. Telling him to fuck himself. Being threatened with what he eventually used on me anyway—the drugs, the machines. And now . . .

"What did you have for breakfast, Asia?"

I began to sweat. I pulled against the restraints—useless, I knew. I'd fought hard against them when he'd come at me with the needle a while ago. Had we only been at this a day? It was all so fuzzy now.

But damn it, I should be able to remember breakfast, shouldn't I? Eggs, or pancakes, or bagels and cream cheese? Orange juice or coffee? Nothing seemed to make a connection. They were words, pictures in a magazine or a Denny's menu. They weren't *memories,* the taste and the smell and the texture adding up to a piece of something in my mind that made sense.

Tears burned in my eyes—*damn it, I won't cry! I won't!* But I did. Teardrops rolled down my face and pooled on the pink sheet of the examination table.

"Asia, what did you have for breakfast this morning?"

My voice was little more than a sob. "I don't remember."

Claussen smiled, triumphant. "Good. I think we're done for today."

I raised my head, though it felt like a sack full of glass shards. "Fuck you, Claussen. At least I remember I'm a human being."

But he'd already turned away, drawn by a commotion at the door of the lab. We had visitors.

"Colonel Gordon. Dr. Park." Was that fear in Claussen's voice? "I didn't expect you until tomorrow"

A short, muscular Asian man approached the examination table and frowned down at me. His eyes were cold, clinical.

"Is this the subject?"

Claussen and an older, taller man in uniform

joined us. "Yes, that's her. We've made some progress today."

"We're not pleased with the way you've handled this, Arthur." The colonel stood off to the side, too occupied with upbraiding his subordinate to observe the "subject." "The delays. And that business at the airport? Messy. We've had a lot of work to do cleaning up after you."

"I apologize for that." Claussen glared at me. "But I think Asia will be worth the trouble."

"Yes. The preliminary information seems quite promising." Dr. Park considered me like a specimen on a slide. "I have some ideas about how to proceed with the research."

Terror squeezed my heart. Claussen had been bad enough. This bastard was clearly cold enough to slice open my brain while I was still breathing.

I made an effort to speak, and my voice emerged in a breathy rasp. "Fuck your research, Doc. I won't cooperate."

His gaze flicked briefly in my direction, dismissing me. "Your cooperation won't be necessary."

"We're transferring her to the Greenbelt facility," the colonel said. "We'll let Park have a try."

Claussen protested, his hands spread wide. "But, Colonel Gordon, I haven't finished my testing."

"Park will continue with the testing as he sees fit." Gordon was a man who gave orders and expected them to be obeyed. "Why would this subject be any different from the others? You've gone outside our usual protocols and risked exposing this project over her and now you want to keep her to yourself? I suspected there was something special about her from the first report, and your behavior confirms it. Our agreement specifies full disclosure and cooperation, Doctor. She's going with us."

My gaze met Claussen's. Jesus, he was looking at me with something like pity. My heart started a rapid-fire stutter. There was a scream deep in my chest—of horror, of rage, of frustration and helplessness—but I couldn't find the breath to let it out. I could only watch as the end of my life unfolded in front of me.

The doctor turned to the others in the room. "I want her ready to move in fifteen minutes. Where are her records?"

The colonel placed his hand on Claussen's shoulder and brought him closer. "You realize I had to call in some favors to pull your fat out of the fire this time, Arthur."

The old man nodded feebly. "Yes, yes, I understand. And I appreciate that."

You ass-kissing bastard.

"I wasn't so inclined to help your friend."

Oh, God. Ethan!

"He embarrassed my organization. And he knows too much. As soon as I get back to Greenbelt I'm issuing new orders for his termination."

My blood turned to ice. All this was going to be for nothing. All the torment I'd put Ethan through. All the heartache and doubt I'd been through myself. All the torture. All the mind-ripping fear. All for nothing. I clenched my teeth and held back a howl.

Claussen spared me a glance, looked back at

Gordon and nodded. "I understand."

I shook as they unfastened the restraints and lifted me to my feet, but I refused to look at Claussen. I bit my tongue until I tasted blood, but I would not speak. I had made up my mind. They wouldn't take me out of here without a fight. I would watch for the right time and try to make a move. For Ethan, if not for myself.

CHAPTER TWENTY-SIX

Hunched together in the back seat of the Explorer, Sam and Rayna stared at the screen on what looked like an ordinary laptop. Ethan watched them with growing impatience.

"Well?"

"She's definitely there," Rayna confirmed. "Her EM signature is clearly visible in one of the interior rooms."

"Her what?"

"We all have a unique electromagnetic signature, sort of like a frequency at which we all vibrate. Some psychics believe they can detect it as an aura." Rayna gave her lecture absently, distracted by what she was seeing on the screen.

Ethan shook his head. "Next you'll be telling me ghosts are real, too."

"Not really." Rayna still didn't look up from the screen. "Just leftover EM traces."

Sam made some adjustments to the equipment and frowned at the screen. "We have Asia's specific EM markers so we know what to look for. Good news is, she's there, and she seems unharmed. Bad news is, there's about a dozen other EM sigs in there, and we have no way of knowing whether those belong to your two-meter-tall muscle-men or curvaceous, blonde nurse-types."

Ethan was no longer listening. He was on the far side of the seat and had a hand on the door handle before his companions noticed he'd moved. He hit the door lock and bolted from the vehicle toward the sidewalk in front of the Daystrom building.

He could hear their protests behind him, but he ignored them. His thought, his body, were directed like a missile launch at the man he'd seen exiting the building from a side door—Arthur Claussen.

The old man was busy entering text into a cell phone, his head bent over the device as he moved slowly along the sidewalk. Ethan ran silently toward him. At the last instant Claussen's head snapped up, and he gaped at his former protégé in wide-eyed astonishment. Ethan swung a fist into his jaw, knocking him backward. The old man tripped and landed heavily on the pavement, the phone flying out of his hand.

Ethan dropped on his chest, his hands clamped around his throat. "Where is she, you son of a bitch! If you've hurt her, I'll fucking kill you!"

"Ethan, get off him! *Now!*" Strong hands grabbed him from behind and pulled him off Claussen's still form. He struggled, but Sam held him firm.

"Buddy, believe me, I'm feeling you, but you can't kill the fucker in broad daylight. Besides, we need him. Calm down before I have to hurt you."

Ethan shook off Sam's hold and dragged in a few

breaths. He glared at Claussen.

"Asia. Where is she?"

Rayna knelt and put some sort of small pistol to Claussen's temple. She spoke to him quietly.

"Get up. You're taking us back inside."

Claussen struggled to his feet, his eyes wild. "Ethan, who are these people?"

"Shut the hell up and walk." Rayna moved the gun to his kidney.

"No." He shook his head. "She's not there."

Ethan grabbed him with a growl, his rage hot and close to the surface. "What the hell are you talking about?"

The old man's eyes darted from face to face. "They're taking her to another facility. It's out of my hands!"

"But they were just here." Ethan snatched at Claussen's throat. "Where? Where are they?"

"M-maybe they haven't left yet." The old man lifted a shaking hand to point. "The southwest wing of the building. There's a loading dock."

"Come on." Sam was already dragging Claussen toward the Explorer. "We'll take the vehicle. Ray will take the inside."

Rayna pelted for the building while the three of them loaded up the SUV and peeled out of the front parking lot, racing for the southwest wing. They careened around the corner of the building, and Sam gunned it down a stretch of access road toward the far end of a second lot. To Ethan it seemed miles away, too great a distance to make up in too little time. They would be too late. And the most precious thing in the world to him would be gone.

"There!" he shouted. At the end of the building, a van sat in front of the loading dock.

Sam shot full-speed through the empty parking lot toward it. Grinning, he tossed a small pistol into Ethan's lap. "It's set for wide-beam stun. Just point and shoot."

"What about Asia?" He couldn't see her.

"She'll wake up with a headache, just like the rest of them. Shoot!"

The men around the van were shouting and waving them off. But at least one of them had a gun. He raised it to fire.

Ethan leaned out the window as Sam swerved violently left to give him a target. Something ripped into his right shoulder, laying it open with blazing agony. He fought to hold on to the weapon as his hand went nerveless and slick with blood.

Sam was shouting his name, but Ethan could barely hear him. Gunfire erupted from several weapons near the van now. The Explorer spun and evaded. Bullets sprayed across the bumper and hood.

Sam brought the SUV around again, desperate to give Ethan a shot. His vision blurring, Ethan brought his good hand up to steady the pistol. He aimed in the direction of the van and did his best to squeeze the trigger. Then the Explorer lurched, and the pistol slipped from his numb grasp.

"Some idiot's making a move to grab the woman." The guard crouched at the door, looking for an opening. "Get her in the van—*now!*"

I could hear gunfire on the other side of the door and my heart kicked in my chest. *Ethan! And the police?* The two burly orderlies on either side of me tightened their grip and hustled me outside.

I stepped out the door and lightning hit the ground at my feet. A brilliant white flash lit the space around me, searing my vision, and for a moment it was as if the oxygen had been stolen out of the atmosphere. I gasped and fell to my knees, sucking in air.

One of the orderlies with me had fallen away. I couldn't feel him. The one on my right had gone to the ground with me, but he seemed as disoriented as I was. I found my feet first, clapped my hands together, and took a swing in the direction of his jaw. I connected with a satisfying *whump* and heard the man curse. I sidestepped as he lunged for me and threw out a kick that caught him in the head. This time he went down for good.

My field of vision was still like bright sun reflecting off the ocean and there was a maddening buzz in my ears. But I knew this would be my only chance. I ran, stumbling over the asphalt, just trying to put distance between me and that horrible place.

Suddenly someone blocked my path—a uniform, a lab coat, several others. Hands grabbed me, held me, lifting me off my feet though I fought them with everything I had.

"Get off me!"

"Hold her while I get my bag." Park. God, I hated him.

"No!" My elbow connected with a man's face. He

cursed and fell back, but another took his place.

Someone laughed—Gordon. "Damn! She's a little spitfire, isn't she?"

They wrestled me to the ground. Desperation had me scratching and kicking like a wildcat.

"Jesus Christ! Look out!"

The high-pitched whine of an engine on overdrive swept rapidly closer until it was nearly at my head. Tires squealed. Gravel crunched. The men holding me down scattered, shouting. I rolled to my knees and looked up.

And there, weighing into the crowd of guards, fists swinging, was Ethan. Another man fought beside him, bigger, a born brawler, and thank God for him, because Ethan was hurt. His right arm was torn open at the shoulder, streaming blood and nearly useless. Ethan flattened one guard with a brutal left, but two others plowed into him from behind and drove him to the ground. They pinned him there, fists slamming into his face, and his friend couldn't get to him.

"No." I tried to move. "Ethan."

I felt cold steel at my neck, a hand like a vise on my biceps. "Get up."

I stood, though my legs had no strength. I struggled to breathe, though my lungs had no air and my heart had stopped beating. Ethan was on the ground, motionless, and I stared at him, willing him to move.

Colonel Gordon snapped an order to his men. "That's enough. Get them on their feet." He kept his hold on me as he looked my two would-be rescuers over. "Ethan Roberts, I presume. Who's your friend?"

Ethan said nothing. He hung in the grip of two guards, barely able to stand. He met my eyes, and my heart clenched in my chest. His despair, his longing were written so clearly in his battered face. I lifted my chin and tried to smile for him. He had nothing to be ashamed of.

The man who had fought with him turned his head and spat blood at the feet of one of the guards holding him. He shrugged when the guard glared at him.

The colonel laughed. "Well, you people are nothing if not amusing. Your girlfriend here is quite the little scrapper, too. And for a bunch of amateurs you've sure given us a run for our money for the last few weeks. That's all over now. Asia's going to use her abilities to serve her country, like she should have been doing all along. And you boys. Well."

He turned and shoved me toward the van. "Let's go."

"No!" I twisted to look back at Ethan.

His brave, bloodied face and the love in his eyes were the last things I saw before the world went ice-white and I fell into a deep hole of unconsciousness.

The face that hovered over mine was familiar. Dark skin. Ebony eyes, now shadowed with worry. Short, tight curls framing a face that radiated humor and determination and uncompromising courage. This was someone I knew. But she couldn't possibly be here.

"Dozen?"

The face broke into a huge grin. "You remember me?" She turned to gesture at the man next to her, the one who had been fighting at Ethan's side. "Sam, she remembers me!"

She squeezed my shoulder. "Damn, Sphinx, they said you were one of the most resistant cases they'd ever seen, but I had no idea you were that good!"

Confusion, disbelief, joy, delight, astonishment—all of these emotions and probably a few more I couldn't name kept sweeping through me like a program in random access mode. I didn't know what to feel, much less what to say, so I just grabbed Dozen and held on, tears streaming down my face.

"I thought you were dead."

She pulled back and smiled at me, her own eyes wet. "I damn near was. But," she took a deep breath, "six months in a rehab hospital and I was almost good as new! New femurs, new vertebrae, new pelvis—did you notice I'm almost two inches taller? Oh, and new name, too. Real name's Rayna. Tacked Murphy on the end when I signed the contract with this guy. But enough about me—we're here to take care of you, sweets."

I sat up, the world spinning crazily around my aching head. "Where's Ethan?"

"Here."

I turned, and in a heartbeat I was in his arms. Ethan was there, whispering my name with a breath as warm and real as my own. He was holding me at last, when all I'd had to cling to under hours of assault was a fading dream. This was more than rescue; it was salvation.

"My beautiful Asia." His arms tightened around me. "I'm so sorry. I'll never forgive myself for letting Claussen take you."

I buried my face in his chest and shook. It had been my fault—all of it. Ethan had nothing to be sorry for.

"Did they hurt you?" He growled out the words. "If they hurt you I'll kill them myself."

I pulled back to look at him, and it hit me that I knew something he didn't yet know. I had learned something strapped to an exam table in a cold lab in the building behind me.

"No, Ethan. They didn't hurt me. Claussen didn't hurt me. I knew you'd come for me. And it didn't matter what he did." I stretched out a hand to touch his face. "I would have forgotten everything but you."

"God, you break my heart, Asia. I'm so proud of you." He gathered me in again, as if he couldn't hold me close enough.

I just wanted to stay wrapped in his protective warmth, in his familiar comfort. But the man Rayna had introduced as her husband was standing by, shifting from foot to foot.

"I'm sorry. We've got business to take care of."

That voice. I'd heard it somewhere before.

Ethan stood and pulled me gently to my feet. "Are you okay?"

"I'm fine." I nodded toward his shoulder, which had been wrapped in cotton gauze. "How about you?"

He shrugged his good shoulder. "The bullet went straight through. And these guys put some amazing stuff on it. Hardly hurts at all."

My eyes narrowed. "Uh, okay. So, are you going to tell me how you got here?"

The big man got tired of waiting and took a step closer. "Hi, I'm Sam, and that's a long story. I think we might need to save it for later."

"Sam. Have we met before?"

He turned the most amazing green eyes on me. "Like I said. A long story for later. But I do begin to see what all the fuss has been about."

Was that a blush on Ethan's face? He turned to Sam.

"Did you find the stun gun?"

Sam held up a weapon, then tucked it in his waistband. "Wouldn't want to leave that lying around."

"Stun gun," I repeated. "Is that what did all this damage?"

"Yeah. Lucky I had your six, huh, Sphinx?" Rayna grinned and turned to Sam. "I've called for a pickup. Locals are two minutes out."

I looked around and saw at least a dozen men in paramilitary jumpsuits restrained and lying unconscious side by side near the van and the loading dock. Dr. Park and Colonel Gordon were among them. They'd all been stripped of their weapons, which were in a neat pile beside them.

Sam nodded. "I've still got a bit of a mess to clean up. If you'll excuse me." He moved off to oversee the final mopping up.

"The doctor and the colonel were working with Claussen," I said to Rayna. "He can explain what they're doing here. Are you going to explain what *you're* doing here?"

The woman I'd relied on through all those horrible months in the mines of an unknown world, the one who had saved my life more than once, held my gaze. "We're here to put things right, Asia. As much as we can."

I blinked, and it suddenly made sense—her role in the labor camp, her appearance here and now. Even the familiar voice belonged to Captain Sam Murphy, whose ship had once been delayed three hours on the way to Earth. I looked at Ethan, wondering if he knew. He nodded confirmation.

The last reason for holding on to my hatred and fear fell away. How could I blame these people for what they had done? I knew what they had sacrificed to bring me home.

Rayna walked around to the rear of a shot-up Explorer and opened the back door. "Sit up."

I peered into the back and saw Arthur Claussen lever himself upright from the floor of the vehicle. With a hiss of anger Ethan left my side and headed for the back of the car. I scrambled to follow him.

Claussen looked shriveled and weak in the back of the SUV. Rayna glowered down at him.

"How many 'patients' in this facility, Doc?"

The old man shook his head. "Asia is the only one currently."

"That makes it simple, then." She nodded in the direction of the building. "Everybody on staff gets a pink slip this afternoon. This branch of Daystrom Futurgenics is closing up shop effective immediately. Where were they taking Asia?"

"There's another facility in Greenbelt." Claussen looked at me, then looked away. "Park runs it, but they've never let me visit there."

"But your patients ended up there, didn't they, Arthur?" Anger rolled off of Ethan in heated waves. I'd never felt that in him before, didn't know he was even capable of it. It was as if he'd been holding it back for years. "Your patients—and mine. After you were done with them here, Park got them. And what happened to them after he was finished?"

Claussen tried to hold Ethan's gaze, but failed. "I don't know that either. I'd always hoped they were . . . rehabilitated."

"You hoped?" The words came out in a shout. "I tried to find them, Arthur. They'd disappeared. All traces gone, as if they never existed. Except for Conners, who's dead. And Ida, of course. She wouldn't let you take her. You son of a bitch." He started forward, but Rayna caught him.

"Don't worry, sweets." Fearless as always, she looked up into his face. "We've got this."

I put a hand on Ethan's back, felt the muscles roped with tension. He took a breath, but the anger remained in his body, unrelenting as stone.

Rayna turned back to Claussen. "The Greenbelt lab is closing down, too. We'll send in another team to see to it. And you, Dr. Claussen, are retiring from psychiatric practice due to health concerns."

"The people who run Daystrom have a lot of connections," Claussen protested. "How are you going to explain all this? And I don't have any health concerns!"

Rayna lifted her shoulders. "Oh, I'm sure it won't be hard to find a few irregularities in the company accounts, irregularities for which Park and the colonel will be found responsible. That will supply a good reason for their disappearance. And I regret to tell you that you do have health concerns. You're losing your memory."

Claussen shrank back, horror draining the blood from his face. "No! You can't!"

"Yes. We can. And we will. But don't worry. We won't take any more than is necessary to protect Rescue. And Asia and Ethan, of course. You made this very easy for us, Doc. No family to relocate. No friends to provide explanations to. Your colleagues will cluck their tongues over the fact that your stroke left you unable to continue your work, but they won't really miss you."

I watched Claussen's face as Rayna laid it out, and I almost felt sorry for him. I could tell by the way Ethan listened with his head down and his jaw clenched that he felt it, too. Of course, the old man wasn't beyond using that remnant of feeling to his advantage.

"Ethan!" He stretched out a hand. "You aren't going to let these insane people do this to me—please! I was only trying to help Asia. You know that!"

"Do I?" Ethan looked at him, the expression in his eyes deep and cold and unyielding. "It seems that all you've done for all these years is to use me to hurt the ones I love. First Elizabeth. Then Ida and Asia. As cruel as it is, I'm glad these people are going to erase your mind. I can't seem to help myself."

"Ethan, you can't mean that. You know I loved Elizabeth."

"Maybe you did, but trying to repress her memories killed her. You did that to her, Arthur. And if there is one argument against taking your memory, that would be it. You'll be able to forget what you did. I never will."

Ethan had started to tremble, the emotion he couldn't express in action leaching out of him in rolling tremors. I reached for his hand, squeezing him back when he latched on with surprising need.

Another surprise: Claussen sighed. "She wasn't stable, Ethan. She never had been. I should have known better than to try and save her. I should have warned you when she first brought you home to me. But she seemed better at first. I thought . . ." He slumped to one side in the back of the SUV. He looked aged beyond his years, defeated, used up. "Never mind. The past is the past. Perhaps it's time we both let it go."

Ethan considered him. Then he looked at me and took a deep breath. "I might actually agree with you there, Arthur. The future seems much more interesting." Something about the way he said it, his voice warm and intimate, melted my heart right down into a puddle in my chest.

Sirens began to wail in the distance. Rayna grasped Claussen by the elbow and stood by as the old man clambered out of the vehicle. She walked him over to a spot near the unconscious bodies of Gordon and Park.

Then she spoke to Sam. "Are we ready for pickup?"

He nodded. "Ready."

Sam and Rayna backed up a few steps in our direction. The air began to crackle and pop as if we were inside the speaker of a badly tuned radio. The noise grew unbearable, until I was forced to cover my ears and squint to protect my eyes. Then, suddenly, there was nothing but silence, and the smell of ozone. And when I looked up, Gordon and Park, Claussen, the guards and all their weapons were gone.

The sirens were coming closer.

"We have to move before the locals get here. Just one last thing to take care of." My friend stepped closer, her expression uncommonly serious. She glanced at Sam, who simply nodded. "We'll need someone to replace Dr. Claussen in Nashville. We'd prefer it be you, Ethan. People with your kind of skill and heart are hard to find. And you're already familiar with the protocol. But if you don't want the job, we'll understand."

"If I refuse, do I get to experience the protocol myself?"

Rayna grinned. "What good would it do? You'll be living with the woman who could beat the system with half a brain. She'd remember everything."

Ethan smiled, but I could tell he wasn't ready to give Rayna the answer she wanted. Too many doubts still haunted him—or maybe the past still had a hold on him despite his interest in the future.

Rayna could see it, too. "Think about it. Talk it out between the two of you. That's the way things'll work from now on, trust me."

"Oh, yeah." Sam shook his head. "*Lots* of talking."

I suddenly found myself staring at my feet, embarrassed by their assumptions about Ethan and me. Now that the adrenaline of the rescue had worn off, I was shaking with doubt. The last time we'd spoken, I'd walked out on him. Before that, the only promises we'd made had been whispered in the throes of passion—hardly the basis of a long-term relationship. Maybe once he'd seen I was safe, he'd be ready to move on. He ought to at least have that chance.

I felt his hand beneath my chin, lifting my face to his. His blue gaze had warmed to the color of a tropical sky.

"Whatever we decide, we'll decide together." He smiled at me. "And we'll let you know."

EPILOGUE

I crossed the room to Ethan's desk and set the cup of fresh coffee next to his elbow. Absorbed in the journal article he was writing, he looked up from his computer with an absent smile.

"Thanks."

I wasn't about to let him get away with that. I went behind him, wrapped both arms around his neck, and began to nibble at one earlobe. His hands went slack at the keyboard, and he closed his eyes.

"Mmm."

"Um-hmm." My hands slid down his chest and over his belly, stopping just short of his belt and the growing bulge in his jeans below that. He shifted in the chair, and his hands caressed my arms. I kissed his neck and backed off to grin at him.

He looked up with a smile, capturing one of my hands in one of his. "Extended coffee break?"

"No, just making sure you're paying attention. Don't want to get to be an old married couple just yet."

He pulled me into his lap—a lap pleasantly accentuated by the thick ridge of his erection—and kissed me thoroughly. "Just because we've had an anniversary doesn't mean we're an old married couple." He trailed his lips along the underside of my jaw and down my throat. "And don't ever think I'm not paying attention."

"Too bad you've got an appointment in five minutes or I'd take you up on that coffee break."

"Damn. Can't be a regular—Barry's not due until 1:00. Must be someone new."

I grinned. "Yep. New and very special, remember? Ray's bringing him herself."

"Oh, yeah!" Ethan's eyes sparked with anticipation. "Is Sam coming, too?"

"Ray didn't say. I don't think this is a social visit, though. Definitely a new client from Rescue, but she was very mysterious in her email."

Ethan frowned. "Mysterious how?"

"I don't know." I shook my head. "Lacking the usual details, for one thing. And why the special delivery?"

"Now you've got me curious."

I moved from his lap to a spot in the chair next to his desk. I had a thrill of déjà vu as I sat there, the smell of the coffee and the old leather of the chair mingling with Ethan's own scent to take me back to the beginning of our adventure together.

It had been spring when we'd started, an April day a lot like today, the leaves tiny and bright green on the trees outside his window, the rain running gently down the glass. Not much had changed in the big living room he used as his office in the house we now shared. The floor had been freshly waxed and new rugs scattered over it. My degree as a Licensed Clinical Social Worker had been tacked up on the wall alongside Ethan's medical diplomas. The rest of the house actually looked like someone lived in it. Otherwise it was much as Ethan had kept it the day I met him and he changed my life. And I his.

I must have been drifting along with those thoughts, because I didn't see Rayna and our new client come up the walkway to the front door. Ethan had gone back to work on his article. We both jumped when we heard the doorbell.

We grinned at each other—part embarrassment, part anticipation—and went together to answer the bell.

We opened the door and stood gaping at what was on the other side for a long moment. My heart started a slow thud in my chest, and I reached for Ethan's hand before I could say a word. His hand gripped mine like he felt we both would be swept away if he let go.

"Ethan, Asia." Rayna's energy was as effervescent as always. "This is Jack."

With Rayna on the front porch was a boy of about four or five, his hair dark and shaggy, his large blue eyes solemn and unnaturally old. He looked at us, but said nothing.

"Hi, Jack," Ethan and I said together. Smiling, I stepped back a little. "Want to come in?"

Jack looked up at Rayna. She nodded.

"Don't mind if we do."

The two of them came into the front hall and Rayna shook off the rain, shrugging out of her coat before helping Jack out of his. She handed both dripping garments to me and led the boy to the battered, comfortable couch in front of the bay window in Ethan's office. Ethan claimed the chair he always used with his clients. I hovered near the doorway, uncertain.

"Coffee, Ray? I just made some fresh." I was desperate to break the ice. "I've got milk and cookies, too, if you'd like some, Jack."

Jack lifted one eyebrow. I took that as a "yes." Rayna winked at me. I scurried off to the kitchen, wondering whether I was trying to be helpful, or just trying to escape. I fumbled with the coffee, nearly dropped the container of milk, ripped open a new package of Pepperidge Farm with enough force to break into the National Treasury and stood shaking in the center of my kitchen for a full minute before I was ready to join the group again.

What was Rayna up to this time? She'd brought us all kinds of returnees in the months since we'd taken on this job for Rescue—men and women of all ages, people who'd been gone for years of "outside time" or mere days, people rescued from outbound slave ships or from labor camps as I had been, from markets or brothels or private estates. But a child? Rayna had never brought us a child before—and something deep inside me said this was no ordinary case.

I took a steadying breath, picked up the tray I'd filled with the coffee, milk, and cookies, and walked back out to the main room. I put the tray down on the desk and handed Jack the milk and a chocolate chip disk as big as his hand. He accepted them silently, catching my eyes for a swift second.

"You're welcome," I whispered.

I gave Rayna her coffee and perched beside Ethan on the arm of his chair. He captured my hand again in that grip that told me he was as nervous about this as I was. We both knew something was up. We looked to Rayna to explain.

She set down her coffee cup. "Okay, I'll get straight to it, since I can see you two are on the edge of that chair. We found Jack in a processing center on Del Origa." We must have looked blank, because she elaborated in the next breath. "The Grays have a few of them around their sector of the galaxy—central hubs where lots of people are brought in, examined, assessed, then shipped out to the actual worksites. We were damned lucky to find the place—been looking for it for months.

"Anyway, the capture was real ugly," she went on. "The facility was well fortified and the Grays didn't give it up without a fight. Lots of innocent people got caught in the crossfire. By the time our guys made it inside, there were only a few hundred people left alive, and there was precious little data available to reintegrate them back on their home planets."

Rayna paused and watched Jack, who munched his cookie, his eyes roving around the room. "There were a couple dozen kids in a special compound, separated from their parents. No records on them. We were able to reunite a few with their families. Most we couldn't. We've had to improvise."

"How do you mean?" Ethan sat forward to get the details.

Rayna was never one to mince words. "We're looking for placements for them."

"Placements?" I repeated, though I knew what she meant.

Ethan made it clear. "You mean homes."

"Yep."

"Foster homes or permanent ones?" I asked.

"The chances we'll find their parents or anything that will link them to their homes is virtually nil."

I studied the boy who sat motionless on the couch next to her, his hands gripping the half-empty glass of milk, the eyes that had seemed too damn old for his innocent face now cast downward toward the floor.

"There's something special about this particular little guy, isn't there." I made sure she knew I was on to her. "A reason you brought him to us besides your thought that we might need some company."

Rayna's mouth ticked upwards at one corner. "You always were quick on the uptake, Sphinx. Yeah. Jack is resistant to programming, like you. He remembers everything. Including, it turns out, his parents' names. They were taken along with him, but killed in the raid. No other identifying info."

Jesus God. My heart broke for the boy, who sat regarding me now with that ancient blue gaze. What must it be like for him, carrying the weight of all that memory on those child's shoulders? I could hardly bear the weight of it, and I had had years to build up the strength to do it. And Ethan to help me.

But that was what Rayna was asking us to do, wasn't it? Help this child find the strength he needed to live under the burden he had to bear. I'd certainly never planned to be a mother again. Physically, I was capable of it, but I hadn't been sure that emotionally I could handle the task. Yet who was better suited to help *this* child? Not too many adoptive parents would be in a position to understand a child who believed he'd been kidnapped by aliens—and could recount the story in detail. And I wouldn't be doing this alone.

I looked at Ethan and saw the same fear in his expression that I knew he could see in mine—a fear that we could never be adequate to this task. I saw something else, too. Wonder. And joy. And excitement. He smiled at me and squeezed the hand he still held tightly in his own.

I sucked in a breath and turned to Jack. "Are you finished with that milk, buddy?"

He nodded and gave me the glass.

I set it aside and held out my free hand to him. "You want to come with me and Uncle Ethan and take a look around the house? You know, we have two cats hiding around here somewhere—one named Jesse James and the other named Pippin. Do you like cats?"

He hesitated only briefly, glancing at Rayna to make sure it was okay. Then he stood, and the three of us set off to explore our home together.

There was something about the way the stars wheeled in the sky overhead that sent a shiver down my back as I nosed the old Ford out of the parking lot and turned away from the lights of town. Something in the way they seemed to follow me down the empty road toward home, though that was a crazy thought, and I knew it. On a stretch of Deerhorn Road just after Dry Run Bridge I began to shake, a sense of dread taking hold of me so strong it squeezed the breath out of my lungs. I punched the accelerator, pushing the truck up to its rattling limit on the twisting curves. I needed to get home, before . . . before . . .

I rounded the last bend, my throat raw, my heart pounding, the engine whining in protest. But whatever I thought I would see was not there. All was quiet along the road where I lived—starlit sky arching over the harvested fields, houses scattered loosely along the country mile, dark and sleeping at this late hour. The lone lights along the road were shining over the garage and porch of my old farmhouse.

I pulled up in my yard and cut the engine, sat listening to the motor ticking as it cooled and the crickets trilling in the hayfield near the house. Nothing disturbed the rural peace except my ragged breath, puffing out against the rapidly fogging side window of the truck. I opened the door, got out, and closed it as quietly as I could, given the rusting hinges and the slightly bent frame.

I went inside my house. Exhaled. Glanced in to see the babysitter asleep on the couch, the TV droning on. Then I padded up the stairs to where my children were sleeping, peaceful and safe.

Micah had slipped into bed with Samantha. They were curled up like kittens under her Lion King comforter, with a menagerie of stuffed animals and half a box of Crayola crayons. I kissed them both on the warm, impossibly soft skin of their cheeks and left them to their dreams.

Down the hall on the right, Ben had his own room. He opened his eyes when I went in to check on him. I sat on the edge of his bed, smoothed the dark hair back from his forehead and smiled at him.

"Hey, bud, what are you doing awake?"

"I waited up."

"Really? Kinda late."

"I wanted to tell you something."

"Oh, yeah? What?"

"You remember that night you didn't make it home?"

I jerked like he had slapped me. The room, the scene suddenly took on the surreal quality of a dream. I tried to wake up. I tried hard. Nothing happened. My dead son continued to look at me, waiting for me to answer.

"Yes," I whispered.

"It wasn't your fault."

"I—I should never have left you."

"It's okay, Mom. You weren't meant to come with us."

"To come with you where?"

He shrugged, grinned a huge grin. "Here."

I didn't want to, God knows I didn't, but I had to ask him. "Ben, that night. Do you remember—"

"Yeah, Mom." He touched my hand. "It didn't hurt. We weren't scared. We just went to sleep. The smoke came, and we woke up Here."

Oh, God! I had so many questions, so much I wanted to say to him. But time was short; I could feel it. I gathered him up and held him close.

"I love you, Benjamin. And your brother and sister, too. I miss you all so much."

"Love you, too, Mom. I just wanted to say goodbye."

My eyes snapped open, and I shot upright in bed, my heart booming inside my ribs. Grateful tears slid down my face and began to soak the neck of my tee-shirt while my only breaths came in great gulps of air taken between sobs.

Ethan sat up beside me, shocked out of his own deep sleep. "Jesus, Asia, what's wrong?" He pulled me into his arms and held me tight. "What is it?"

I almost laughed. "Nothing. It's good. Oh, God, Ethan. It's so good." And then I told him.

I don't know what I expected. An analysis, maybe. A gentle dismissal. But his hand shook as he brushed a stray curl from my forehead. And as he bent to touch his lips to mine I could taste the salt of his own tears on his face.

"My sweet Asia. No one deserved that more than you."

Warmth bloomed in my chest as I sank into his embrace. "You think it was real?"

"I'm not sure it matters." His lips brushed my forehead.

Then there was a sound, so small I almost missed it, near the door. A shuffle. A sniffle.

Ethan pulled away and looked toward the foot of the bed. "Hello."

In the light from the street, a shadow was revealed, about four feet tall, boy-shaped. The shadow stood silently watching us, waiting for a reaction, or an invitation.

"Hi, Jack," I said. "Did you have a bad dream?"

The shadow nodded.

"Want to sleep in our bed?" Ethan made the offer though it broke the rules we'd only just agreed upon that afternoon.

The shadow moved, ran to my side, scrambled up and under the covers. Jack snuggled close to me as I lay down and hooked an arm around him. Then Ethan pressed his chest to my back, molded his hips to mine, and wrapped his arms around us both.

His lips at my ear carried a whisper: "I love you."

And in that warmth we slept, unbound by the past, tethered only to the future.

THE END

ACKNOWLEDGMENTS

Unchained Memory would not have seen the light of day if not for the unflagging support and just plain hard work of a host of people. I can't begin to say how thrilled I am to be able to thank them by name:

-My tough and discerning critique partner Linda Thomas, who always made me laugh even as she turned the screws.

-My fellow science fiction romance writers and critique partners Laurie A. Green and Sharon Lynn Fisher, who have shared this road with me from the beginning, come hell and high water.

-My lifelong friend Joyce Dame, R.N., the mental health professional who helped make sure Dr. Ethan Roberts was within bounds, though walking a thin line. Any misinterpretations of medical ethics are my own.

-My gang of beta readers, including my daughter Jessie Wenger, my husband, Graeme Frelick, Nikki Miller, Petra and Ray Blazer, Daryl Durham, Peggy Robinson and the members of the Cultural Expressions Book Club of Richmond, Virginia, all of whom provided valuable insights.

-My editor Deborah Kreiser, who polished this rough stone into a shiny gem. I've always said every writer needs a good editor; now I really believe it.

-And, finally, my incomparable agent and publisher Michelle Johnson, who has worked *tirelessly* to make this book happen. She believed in me and in *Unchained Memory*, and because she believed, reality was forced to conform. Thank you, Michelle, for all your faith and energy.